Lifelong romance addi[...]
New Zealand. Writing [...]
with happy endings an[...]
create. You can follow [...]
facebook.com/jcharrov[...]
and twitter.com/jcharro[...]

Ever since **Lisa Childs** read her first romance novel
at the age of eleven (a Mills & Boon story, of course),
all she wanted was to be a romance writer. With
over forty novels published with Mills & Boon,
Lisa is living her dream. She is an award-winning,
bestselling romance author. Lisa loves to hear from
readers, who can contact her on Facebook, through
her website, lisachilds.com, or at her snail-mail
address, PO Box 139, Marne, MI 49435.

If you liked *A Week to be Wild* and *Legal Seduction*, why not try

Off Limits by Clare Connelly
Ruled by Anne Marsh

Discover more at millsandboon.co.uk

A WEEK TO BE WILD

JC HARROWAY

LEGAL SEDUCTION

LISA CHILDS

MILLS & BOON

First Published in Great Britain 2018
by Mills & Boon, an imprint of HarperCollins*Publishers*
1 London Bridge Street, London, SE1 9GF

A Week to be Wild © 2018 JC Harroway

Legal Seduction © 2018 Lisa Childs

ISBN: 978-0-263-26637-5

MIX
Paper from
responsible sources
FSC® C007454

A WEEK TO BE WILD

JC HARROWAY

MILLS & BOON

For D, who loved a good romance.

CHAPTER ONE

OLIVIA NOBLE WALKED behind the elderly professor,
passing through the chrome-and-glass doors etched
with the name of the swanky restaurant on the thirty-
first floor of The Shard, London's tallest building.
Her belly, jittery enough from the long, hair-raising
elevator ride, flipped at the panoramic views dotted
with the city's iconic landmarks. As a native New
Yorker she accepted gravity-defying skyscrapers as
part of life, but she avoided ones of this magnitude
wherever possible.

'Ah, the others are still at the bar.'

Professor McBride gestured Libby ahead of him,
towards the party of suits. Libby's legs wobbled on
her four-inch heels as she crossed the plush carpet,
trying to master the hold adrenaline had on her body.
Her poor adrenal glands were wrung dry. This sophisticated, elegant restaurant might as well have
been a roadside diner for all she noticed.

Head of her own marketing business in New
York, she was used to public speaking. That didn't
mean she enjoyed it, or that nerves hadn't gripped

her for the whole forty-minute presentation she'd given this morning at the London Business School. In fact, she'd been blown away when invited to speak at such a prestigious seminar, unaware that anyone across the pond had even heard of her small up-and-coming company.

The rest of the speakers were clustered at the bar, forming small huddles, deep in conversation. Several glanced up as Libby and Professor McBride approached—faces she recognised from the seminar, and one face in particular that demanded more than a fair share of her attention. A face that was hard to ignore.

Alex Lancaster.

His stare lifted from the conversation taking place before him, settling on her over the tops of the heads separating them and practically stripping her bare. A shiver originated in her ovaries and snaked south to join the wobble in her legs. Those eyes… The intensity with which they pierced the recipient of his undivided attention…

Wow. Close up he was… *Wow*. A movie-star bad boy, a gentleman rogue and a geeky surfer dude all rolled into one mouthwatering package. Not that he had much of the surfer dude on display at the moment, attired as he was in a tailored three-piece suit that had probably cost more than the annual mortgage payment on her modest six-hundred-square-foot apartment. The only nod to his wilder side was the slightly dishevelled flop of dark hair, which looked as if it refused to be tamed, no matter what he did.

Libby clenched her thighs together, her twitchy fingers gripping her bag.

'Glass of wine, my dear?' Professor McBride asked.

Libby nodded, her eyes hot as she stared back at Alex Lancaster for longer than was polite or wise. Likely she was not the only woman in the room who found that staring at this disarmingly attractive specimen of manhood pushed semipornographic visions into her head.

She rolled her shoulders and looked away, blinking the burn from her eyes. A snort gusted over her top lip. Who was she kidding? Her thoughts veered firmly towards the absolutely pornographic where he was concerned. She tugged at the hem of her tailored jacket. Time to get her head back in the game.

She was a professional, a well-respected member of the business community who owned her own successful marketing business—credentials that had prompted her invitation to London to speak at the 'Inspiring Business Leaders of the Future' seminar.

She darted her attention back to Professor McBride and his lengthy introductions to those closest, all the while willing her greedy eyes to stay away from the lure of Mr Lancaster, the only other person close to her age in the group.

Libby zoned out of the tedious conversation, discreetly blowing through pursed lips and lifting wisps of escaped hair from her too-warm face. How could that man have such a profound effect on her? Perhaps her PA was right, and she did need a 'good seeing to'. She'd have to give the perceptive Scotsman a raise, or finally sign up to that dating app he kept shoving in front of her.

Mmm…maybe not.

Fickle thoughts drifted back to the smokin' billionaire across the restaurant. Forget swiping left or right. She could just swipe him out of that suit, tangle her fingers in that too-long hair while she directed his smart, arrogant head south… The dark scruff covering his angular face scraping across her sensitive inner thighs…

Whew! Potent stuff. There must be something in the English water—it was the only explanation for her train of thought.

She cleared her perilously tight throat, yanking her mind out of the gutter, her gaze from the toes of her favourite shoes and her attention back to the drone of Professor McBride's voice.

'…and this is Alex Lancaster, one of our former golden boys, university benefactor and the major sponsor of today's seminar—although I'm sure he needs no introduction.'

Professor McBride's ass-kissing drawled to a close as his attention was requested by a university faculty member with a penchant for purple highlights and matching purple accessories.

Before she could mentally prepare herself for the

close-up impact of his dazzling good looks, Alex had enclosed Libby's hand in his larger one, setting off a cascade of tingles; little flicks of flame dancing along her wrist and raising the hairs on her arm.

Damn...

Smokin' was an insult. Brains, business acumen and indecent levels of sex appeal—Alex Lancaster had certainly won the genetic lottery.

And of *course* she knew of him. *Everyone* knew of him. Besides, she'd done her research prior to flying in yesterday. One of Britain's youngest billionaires, he wasn't the richest, but his reputation for intuitive, if not somewhat reckless, business decisions was surpassed only by his brooding charisma and the dazzling smile that somehow managed to appeal to women of all ages.

Perhaps it was the single dimple in his cheek—simultaneously boyish and wicked. Or the incredible expressive eyes the colour of burnt sugar that regularly stared out from the glossy magazine covers he graced. Either way, he was utterly disarming. So much so that her voice completely deserted her—no doubt it was attending the 'Get Alex Lancaster Naked' rally being hosted by her libido and sponsored by her erogenous zones.

'Ms Noble. Great talk.'

His mouth kicked up, unleashing the full force of that dimple. Damn, that smile could melt the underwear clean off her body. And his voice: smoky…rich bourbon in a cut-glass tumbler.

Her sharp, tight-fitting suit—her signature out-fit—transformed into a straitjacket. It was the only explanation for the hot flush misting her skin and the prickle of every tiny hair covering her body.

'Nice to meet you, Mr Lancaster.'

Libby pulled her hand from his. Not that the move offered relief from the inferno engulfing her. He was too close. Too virile. Too everything.

Get a grip, Libby. He's just another suit.

Right—if by 'suit' she meant a walking advertise-ment for 'Hot Boardroom Dudes'. Perhaps he could start an internet craze. She'd be the first to sign up.

'You deserve every scrap of your reputation.' He rubbed his knuckles over one lightly stubbled cheek, his dark gaze sparkling.

Libby's missing-in-action tongue returned to her mouth. 'Well, that's a rare talent, Mr Lancaster—one that the gossip rags and business pages fail to credit *you* with.'

Libby wiped her palm along the length of her skirt, her body half turned away from him so he wouldn't see the gesture that gave away the effect he had on her. The thought of this man's focus honed on her, even simply her online business profile, shunted heat to the most inconvenient places.

At his small frown, she continued. 'Perfectly dis-guising an insult within a compliment.'

She glanced over his shoulder, raising her eye-brows in acknowledgement of someone she recog-nised as she made to bypass him.

'Excuse me.'

Arrogant, sexy...

He laughed. A head-thrown-back bellow that forced more gold flecks into the burnt caramel of his irises.

A waiter blocked Libby's escape route with the delivery of her Pinot Gris, the elegant wine glass glistening with condensation. She bestowed her politest smile on the handsome waiter, still preparing to walk away from the charismatic jerk before her. Even if he *was* pleasing on the eye and the six-foot-three embodiment of most women's filthiest fantasies. Fantasies she'd never imagined until she'd slid her eyes over Mr Testosterone there.

'Forgive me…' His hand on her arm stilled her. 'What I should have said is that yours was by far the most entertaining of the lectures given this morning. I've heard of your work. I'm a businessman and I keep abreast of international business news.'

His mouth caressed the lip of his own wine glass, and he held her gaze over the rim, a mix of devilment and challenge warring for control in his slightly narrowed, sinfully provocative stare.

His hand, still on her arm, burned a hole through the fine wool of her favourite jacket. Large, tanned, with a sprinkling of dark hair smattering the wrist that poked from the cuff of his expensive linen shirt. Slight calluses marred the perfection of his long, elegant fingers, and she glimpsed clean square nails before he withdrew.

She had the absurd urge to ask him if he had a daily manicure. Was that how pampered British billionaires filled their days? Of course it was dwarfed by other urges that involved those large callused hands and her nipples.

It really had been too long…

Free from his touch, she regained her composure, her intellect wrestling it free from the clutches of her hormone-riddled body.

'I see. I'm sorry I can't return the compliment. I missed your talk.'

And she'd never worked for any IT giant. Why would she have crossed *his* radar?

Still looking at her as if his X-ray vision had burned holes through her clothing down to her lacy underwear, he shrugged one large shoulder.

His charcoal-grey suit encased his frame like a glove. She'd bet her beloved cat, Dumbledore, that it was cashmere—probably bespoke Savile Row. A copper-coloured tie brought out those ridiculous sparks of fire in his eyes and highlighted his decadent, cry-worthy black lashes.

Libby curled her fingers into her palms to stop herself fanning her flushed face.

Back to her escape plan.

As if anticipating her, he stepped sideways, facing her full-on, his broad chest eclipsing her vision. 'I'm glad I met you today. I'd like your professional advice, actually.'

He took another sip of wine, his bold stare raking

her face and dipping to her throat. If he'd gone any lower this conversation would be over, regardless of his pretty face and intriguing request.

'Perhaps we could sit together…discuss it over lunch?' Then came the eyebrow lift. Perfectly executed, devastatingly tempting.

Had her body not reacted so overwhelmingly towards him, she might have agreed. The company he'd founded in his late teens, Lancaster IT, had gone global in recent years, with sales of its software to the Asian healthcare market shunting its drool-worthy founder and CEO from wealthy to obscene. Any business association her marketing company might have with the new IT giant making international waves would surely provide her with the kudos she needed to take her *own* business to the next level.

But she abhorred arrogance. Alex Lancaster was not only renowned for fly-by-the-seat-of-his-pants business decisions that left wiser, more experienced competitors shaking in their hand-stitched Oxfords, but his personal life was equally reckless. Just thinking about this daredevil playboy's antics brought her out in an icy chill.

She demurred—after all, he *was* incredibly influential. 'I'm flattered. If you ask your assistant to call mine, I'm sure we can set something up.'

She took an embossed business card from her purse and passed it to him, careful to keep her fingertips away from the thrill of his.

'Although my personal client workload at present has me a little over-committed.'

What was she *saying*? This was a dream scenario for her small but growing business. Was she palming off an account of this magnitude on to one of her juniors? Seriously? All because he was twice as hot in person, made her thighs tremble and soaked her expensive lingerie—her one indulgence.

He flipped the card between his fingers in a continuous hypnotic loop of digital gymnastics. Mesmerising. What *else* could he do with those talented fingers?

Libby dragged her gaze away. His sexy stare was back. Pinning her heels to the carpet. Normally she tolerated awkward silences, especially in business settings. But he rocked her cool composure.

'It—It's all there…on my website.' *Babbling.* A successful twenty-eight-year-old businesswoman with a master's degree in marketing was babbling.

He didn't once glance at the card, which still tumbled lazily between his long, tanned fingers. 'I'd really like your personal input. You've done wonders for Kids Count.'

Why would her work for a small US charity interest him? Although it *had* landed her a prestigious industry award.

His lips caressed his wine glass, his eyes watching her over the rim. 'I'm involved with a charity too.'

He tucked the card into the inside pocket of his jacket, close to his chest.

The gesture, strangely intimate, made heat pool low in her belly. She definitely needed to get laid.

Tonight.

'I'm willing to pay.'

His talk of payment sealed the deal. 'I'm sorry.'

Heralding from one of the UK's most affluent families, and growing up in the family business, he had founded his first company on a ten thousand pound loan from his businessman father.

Well, some things weren't for sale.

No doubt he was used to getting everything he wanted. Calling the shots. Bossing people around. Well, not this chick.

Liar. He could boss her around in the bedroom any time.

'I'd be happy to connect you with Sonya, my top marketing executive and business partner—although she's soon to go on maternity leave so I suggest you get in quick.'

No way could she work personally with this man. Not after a simple glance across a room and a professional, perfectly polite handshake had triggered a full-blown hormone implosion. Images of them tangled in the crisp white sheets of her king-sized hotel bed rocked her back on her heels. Would he be as demanding in the bedroom? And would she concede, give him what he wanted? She could make a few sexual demands of her own…

The tip of his tongue traced along his lower lip—a snake-charming manoeuvre that held her gaze captive for long, silent seconds. She shook her head, dragging her eyes away.

Her libidinous thoughts stunned her. Perhaps he'd doused himself in genetically modified pheromones?

Time to get away from him and his unsettling magnetism.

'Nice to meet you.' Libby abandoned polite convention and kept her hand by her side. Best not to touch him again in case she needed to rush to the bathroom and put herself out of her own misery.

As if he knew her thoughts, he let a half grin dance on his twisted mouth. His chin lifted, lazy eyes raking her. 'The pleasure was all mine, Olivia.'

He delivered her name with a cut-crystal English accent and a side helping of gravel that spoke directly to all her wide-awake lady parts.

Libby winced, wishing her laptop's webcam would explode.

'You said *what*? Are you crazy?' Sonya rubbed her rounded belly, twisting on the sofa and putting her feet up on the low coffee table in Libby's New York office.

This video call and the five-hour time difference between New York and London meant her right-hand woman was taking her lunch break, relaxing on Libby's sofa. Apparently it was more comfortable than the sofa in Sonya's office—although Libby suspected her friend just missed having her to bounce ideas off. They were a great team. More than that.

Sonya's face filled the screen as she leaned forward, peering through cyberspace. 'I can't possibly do that account justice in the time I have left.' She flopped back on the cushions, as if the act of merely speaking exhausted her. 'Why would you even suggest me? He clearly wants *you*. And you're there, on the ground.'

Sonya took a bite from her sandwich and shoved another cushion into the small of her back.

They usually ate lunch together on days when they were both in the office, discussing accounts and synching their diaries. Today, for some inexplicable reason—she blamed jet lag—Libby had shared the details of her meeting with Alex Lancaster and now had to pay the price.

'He's arrogant—and surprisingly rude for an Englishman.'

And sexy as fuck, with dreamy eyes, and an edge that made her want to defy him to see what happened…

'Throwing his money around.'

And looking at her as if she was a medium rare steak and he'd been living off beans for months.

Right, and she hadn't objectified *him* at all? His tight ass in his perfectly tailored trousers? No? Her gaze hadn't once dipped to the bulge at his crotch, wondering what lay beneath the fine fabric?

Of course she couldn't tell Sonya about her body's insane, treacherous reaction to him. Sonya had known Callum. She'd read something into her meeting with Alex Lancaster that simply hadn't been there. And she definitely couldn't confide her surprising fantasies to her bestie. She barely knew where they'd come from herself. No. It was just unfortunate timing.

Three years without sex really was too long. She hated to concede it, but her assistant, Vinnie, was right.

'So?' Her friend waggled a finger at the camera. 'It's business. This account and his contacts could help us expand into Europe, Asia—the world.'

Sonya's 'duh' look of incredulity soured Libby's tea—a less than satisfactory brew made from the meagre selection in her hotel room. She pushed it away, sipping water from a bottle instead, stalling for time.

Refusing to hear his proposal didn't make sense. *Business* sense. But instinct had brought her this far in her success story, and the same instinct told her to stay away from Alex Lancaster. He was just too charismatic, charming, virile. Nope. Her reaction to him this afternoon confirmed it; he was dangerous.

She didn't do danger. And despite his enormous accomplishments, she couldn't abide his reputation for recklessness.

'Well, if *you* take the account the effects for the company will be the same.' She plastered on her best convincing smile. 'There's a hefty bonus in it. Think of all the baby stuff you could buy.'

Wow, low blow, Libby. Cheap shot.

Sonya huffed. Probably she was too uncomfortable to appreciate the merits of Libby's inducements.

'No way. I won't have time. I'll end up handing it over to you anyway, when I go on maternity leave. And, to be honest, I should have quit by now. I don't want to have this baby in the elevator with only Vinnie for assistance. You know how he fusses. I'd end up killing him and *then* where would you be?'

A queasy roll of the stomach put an end to Libby's thoughts of popping out for dinner. She'd yet to find a temporary stand-in for Sonya—the would-be candidates they'd interviewed so far had been woefully inadequate to fill such capable shoes.

The pair were cut from the same cloth. Had studied at the same college. The same business school. When Libby had started out, Sonya had come on board and they'd created Noble and Pullman, investing in the joint venture, teaching each other as much as they'd learned from each other.

Any day now, there was going to be a substantial Sonya-shaped hole left in their small but precious company.

As if he'd heard his name mentioned, Vinnie, Libby's outspoken and at times frankly inappropriate PA, entered her office, poking his head over Sonya's shoulder so his face filled the screen. She waved, relieved to have a reprieve from justifying her inexplicable reluctance to work with Lancaster IT—or rather its sexy founder.

'How are things going, Vinnie? Any more responses?' She'd approached a few medium-sized firms here in London, hoping to drum up a little new business before she returned home in a few days.

'"No" really.'

Vinnie spoke with a thick Scottish brogue she failed to understand most days.

'Do you want me to make some follow-up calls?'

Libby sighed. She was good at her job. Could sell anything. But still she sometimes struggled to sell herself. Never quite outgrowing her humble, wrong-side-of-the-tracks beginnings.

'No. I'll take care of it—and if I can't see anyone I'll just be a tourist for a few days. Perhaps I'll meet the Queen.'

She couldn't remember the last time she'd taken any holiday, and the two worried faces peering back at her from her laptop screen confirmed that her suggestion wasn't just alien to *her*.

She needed a change of subject, before Vinnie pulled up a list of London's singles clubs and Sonya told her—again—that it was 'time to move on'.

'Are you taking care of Sonya?'

Her friend's eyes rolled.

Vinnie smiled. 'Well, you know what she's like… Let's just say I'm trying. If I end up delivering this wee one…' he stroked Sonya's belly and she batted him away '…I want a bonus.'

They all chuckled, but the sound held a nervous undertone. Libby shouldn't have left the helm at such a crucial time. She'd been lured by the all-expenses-paid trip to a city she'd always dreamed of visiting and had been flattered that they'd asked for her personally to speak at the conference.

'I came in to tell you I've had Alex Lancaster on the phone this morning. He called asking for your personal number,' said Vinnie.

Libby straightened in her chair, her heart thumping double time.

'Don't worry, hen. I didn't give it to him—although he's a determined young fella.'

Libby pressed her lips together. Vinnie needed no encouragement for the ridiculous things he said. 'Young fella' hardly did Alex Lancaster justice.

'He seemed to know where you're staying, so he may call. Said he had a "business proposition".' Vinnie made air quotes, a small smirk on his face. 'And wanted to discuss it before you left the UK.'

The one mouthful of tepid tea she'd managed sloshed inside Libby's hollow insides.

Sonya's eyes rounded to the size of her pregnant belly. She lumbered into a sitting position, glaring into the webcam. 'He *really* wants you.' Her shrewd eyes narrowed.

Libby chewed her lip, evading comment. The last thing she needed was this unlikely pair of would-be matchmakers getting the wrong idea about Alex Lancaster's intentions and her own position. She'd already said too much.

Flutters invaded her chest at the thought of speaking to him, of seeing him again. *Stop.* She didn't have to take his call. She'd already heard his proposition. Her answer would be the same.

With that, the hotel phone rang on the desk next to her, making all three of them jump. She stared at the device for two or three rings, frozen. It had to be him. No one else knew where she was, with the exception of the two people staring at her with excitement and intrigue shining in their eyes.

'Answer it,' Sonya said, gesturing wildly at Libby to accept the call.

They waited. Expectant. Sometimes it sucked that these two knew her so well.

Rolling her shoulders back, she chided herself. Act professional. He was just a businessman. Just another potential client. Libby covered her mouth with her index finger, shushing them. Then turned the laptop away so it faced the wall. Sonya and Vinnie would hear her side of the conversation, but they wouldn't see her face while she answered the call.

'Libby Noble.' *Shit*, her voice was all breathy—as if she'd run a marathon.

She relaxed her clenched fingers, slipping her feet from her shoes under the desk and flexing her toes into the plush pile of the carpet. Libby's neck burned, just knowing that Sonya and Vinnie were listening from the laptop beside her. They'd worked and played alongside her for the last four years, seeing her at her best and at her worst. Although the 'play' had been virtually non-existent since Callum's death.

'Olivia—Alex Lancaster here.'

His voice rasped down the line, scraping at her earlobe. She rolled her eyes. Why couldn't he have a normal voice? A boring monotone that left her cold?

Libby cleared her tight throat. 'Mr Lancaster.' That was better. Clipped, curt, taking no shit. 'How can I help you?'

He chuckled. The bastard actually *chuckled*. 'You *can* call me Alex, you know.'

His voice was huskier over the phone, his dashing accent stronger—or perhaps without the visual distraction, her senses were more acutely attuned to every nuance of him.

Fantastic.

'I hoped to persuade you to reconsider my offer.'

Just listening to him speak made her think of sex. His voice, deep and authoritative, screamed control. It should be a real turn-off. She hated being told what to do. Perhaps it was the change in time zones, messing with her biorhythms. She smoothed a crease from her skirt, her restless fingers needing something to do. Something other than itching to twist through his decadent flop of hair.

'I thought we'd concluded things this morning.'

'Had we?'

All she'd really concluded was that she was ridiculously attracted to him, and that her hormones were securely at the helm, sailing the Libby ship into uncharted waters. Waters fraught with wild fantasies. Just a hint of danger. Enough to thrill.

'I wanted to tell you a bit more about the project.

I think I mentioned I'm chief executive of a charity based here in London.'

Had he? She'd been too focussed on the rasp of his hand and the head-rush caused by his spicy scent.

'It's called Able-Active. Have you heard of it?'

Libby spun a pen on the desk, its hypnotic circling matching the frequency and rhythm of Alex's rumbling speech. Autocratic, imposing, seductive... She could listen to him for hours...especially if he talked dirty.

'No, I'm sorry. I haven't.'

Her own voice was relatively low and husky for a woman. But his curled itself around her like a comfort blanket—warm, sensual and with just enough scrape to bring to life every nerve ending in her body. Particularly those tightly clustered between her legs.

'Yes. And there's my problem. At the moment the charity can only accept participants from the South East. I want to extend it throughout the UK's other major cities. There are a lot of kids with different needs out there, Olivia—kids who deserve the experiences Able-Active provides.'

He'd pricked her interest. 'What kind of charity?'

She quickly typed Able-Active into the search engine on her mobile phone and brought up the website.

'It's for kids with all kinds of different abilities. A recreational adventure centre, outward bound type of thing.'

'I see. Well, I wish you luck with that venture, Mr Lancaster. It sounds very worthwhile.'

Damn him—couldn't he have a few obvious flaws? Bad breath, poor taste, a warped sense of humour…?

'It *is* worthwhile and…'

He paused, as if he sought the right word. Perhaps Mr Ruthless McReckless had a soft centre…

'It's important to me. That's why I want the best people working on it.'

Ooh, flattery.

'I've done my research. The best people is *you*. I read about your award. And the CEO of Kids Count wrote a very flattering piece about you in *Charity Times*.'

Silence settled, thick and cloying, pushing Libby back into the chair. Of *course* he'd researched her. He'd hinted as much this morning with his comment about her reputation. He was an astute businessman, intuitive, quick witted, driven. Any self-respecting would-be employer would do his homework.

She'd done the same; spent most of the afternoon scouring the internet and his website. Of course she'd missed any mention of his charity work. Too busy drooling over pictures of him shirtless on some exotic island. Too focussed on replaying his TED talks over and over just to hear the scrape of his voice. And too absorbed in imagining what he looked like under his urbane business suits.

This smacked of a personal crusade. No. He probably applied the same drive and determination to any enterprise he was involved with.

She remained silent. Why this reluctance to work with him? He brought something out in her—some perverse streak of her personality that revelled in denying his wishes. A battle of wills? Not very mature of her and bad for business.

'Any number of firms could handle that kind of strategy.'

Yes, she'd worked on a campaign for the American charity, but surely he could find what he needed here in the UK.

He gave a small sigh. 'Look, I get what I want, Olivia. You've proved yourself to have a clear and savvy understanding of the current social media climate. You have a flair for clever and innovative imagery and Kids Count are benefitting markedly. I want the same for my charity.'

His charity?

'That's why I put your name forward to the London Business School when they approached me to speak at today's seminar.'

She stifled a gasp. *He'd* personally recommended her? And, as he sponsored the conference, *he'd* flown her here all expenses paid—including this hotel room. Her gaze skittered to the bed. The image of him naked and sprawled there, telling her what he wanted with that upper crust voice of his made her heart hammer. Not that she'd give it to him.

I get what I want. His arrogance…

Again, her mind veered. *Did* he want her? Fantasise about them together as she'd done since the moment she'd met him? Well, as much as it would cost her, both professionally and personally, she'd have to show him he didn't always get what he wanted.

She cleared her throat. 'Well, I hope you have yourself the best accountant over there at Able-Active. Not many start-up charities have such a large marketing budget.'

Her personal services didn't come cheap, no matter how attractive the man paying the check.

'You let me worry about that. Can you start tomorrow?'

Arrogant, presumptive asshole.

'Mr Lancaster. Throwing money at me won't change my mind.'

If anything, it made her inclined to hang up. Unlike Mr Sexy Billionaire, *she* hadn't lived a privileged childhood full of skiing holidays and the right private schools. Her daddy didn't own a super-yacht—in fact, she didn't *have* a daddy. Like her single parent mother, she'd worked hard every day for everything she had, and she appreciated every cent she spent—despite the designer clothes she wore and her top-of-the-range car. *Frivolous* was not a word in Libby's vocabulary.

'Well, what *will* change your mind?'

His voice dropped to a sultry drawl. The one she imagined was his bedroom voice.

Imagined or hoped?

Had he asked her to work for his IT company she'd have already ended this conversation. Her eyes drifted over the images on the Able-Active website. Smiling faces…kids joyously experiencing the thrill and accomplishment of some outdoor adventure.

'It's very important to me, Olivia.'

The way he spoke her name—her full name—as if it was their little secret.

'Why?' She whispered the request, as if the intimacy of his answer warranted such secrecy. Alex Lancaster—full of intriguing contradictions?

'Personal reasons.' The pitch of his voice lifted a fraction. 'I had a sister.'

Had?

'Let me offer a sweetener.'

He didn't want to talk about his sister. This she understood. She had no-go areas in her past too.

'Lancaster IT's marketing contract is up for renewal in two months. If you help me out with Able-Active the contract is yours.'

She gasped. 'Regardless of how good my work is? That's ridiculous.'

Was he mad? How had he become so successful so young? Rash decisions and financial extravagance wouldn't have cut it. She'd been right about him. Reckless.

'Just do what you did for Kids Count and I'll be happy.'

Mmm… What would a happy Alex look like? Libby vacillated. Sonya was right. A high-profile account like his would shunt their company into the big league. Finally reward them for years of hard work. Surely she could control her startling attraction to him for long enough to get the job done and get out? And hadn't she been hoping to attract new business while here in the UK? This was a dream scenario landing in her lap.

Still she wavered.

A compromise?

'Perhaps Sonya could mock up some drafts and I'll step in once she goes on maternity leave.'

That made no sense. What was *wrong* with her? She flushed, knowing Sonya could hear the gibberish coming out of her mouth. Libby was here. Sonya was in New York and about to deliver her baby any day.

'I want *you*.'

Not fair.

She closed her eyes as her overactive libido spun off into fantasyland, taking her pounding heart along for the ride. How would it feel to be the recipient of that bare statement in another time, another context? Would he give what her body clearly craved? A couple of mind-blowing orgasms? Nothing more. Would she concede to his control, loosen the tight command she subjected every aspect of her own life to just for one blissful minute? Give him everything?

She slowed her rapid breaths and mentally slapped herself. She was a hard-assed career woman. She employed twenty people, won lucrative contracts and industry awards. She didn't crumble when faced with an attractive employer. No matter how intense his golden eyes or how sin-dipped his gravelly voice. And, these days, she never conceded control. It wasn't worth the risk.

But this made good business sense. A connection of this visibility would allow her to pick and choose Sonya's stand-in. And by the time her friend returned from maternity leave they'd be ready to take on the world.

She'd have to be careful. Despite her daydreams, a man like Alex would quickly take anything she gave.

She sucked in a breath, confident in her abilities to handle him. Decided, she was all business.

'I'll have my assistant contact yours to make the arrangements.' Libby lifted her chin, although she knew he couldn't see the gesture.

'I'll have the contracts drawn up.'

She could almost hear his victory grin slither down the phone line.

'Pleasure doing business with you, Mr Lancaster.'

She hung up, all the air leaving her in rush, one word lingering in her dry mouth. *Pleasure.* Would it be?

When her face felt cooler to the touch, she turned back to her laptop screen and her colleagues.

Their grins said it all.

Damn. What had she done?

CHAPTER TWO

ALEX LANCASTER STOPPED the treadmill and reached for the towel he'd thrown over the handrail, using it to the wipe the sting of sweat from his eyes. He preferred to run in the Oxfordshire countryside, or along the banks of the River Thames. But on the nights when he stayed in the city his office treadmill just had to suffice. And today he needed to push himself twice as hard to outrun the restlessness.

Despite his forty-minute workout, thoughts of the enigma that was Olivia Noble had dogged his every step.

Briefly checking his phone for urgent messages, he clicked off the TV that dominated one wall of his spacious office, silencing the business news, and headed for the en-suite shower.

Alex ducked his head under the pounding spray, ignoring the flicker of interest from his cock—a renewed flicker brought on by the curvy, sophisticated brunette. He'd admired her enough from afar, but in person she'd blown him away. Sassy, shrewd, cutting through his bullshit, as she'd no doubt call it.

He closed his eyes, recalling the sexy timbre of her husky voice. She spoke as if she had a bad case of laryngitis or a lifelong smoking habit. She didn't have either. He'd scoured every detail he could find about her on the internet, filling in the blanks with his vivid, slightly perverted imagination.

An imagination inspired by the thick, glossy dark hair she wore fastened at her nape in an elegant ponytail, by the provocative curve of her rounded hips concealed by the figure-hugging pencil skirts she wore and the tiny glimpse of pale, creamy cleavage he'd seen that morning when she'd moved away from him, her blouse tugging across her breasts and revealing just enough to make him hard for the rest of the day.

Of course their verbal spat on the phone hadn't helped either.

He scrubbed shampoo into his scalp, his fingertips punishing. He'd never had to work so hard to entice someone to work with him. His employees loved him. He gave them stellar health insurance cover, more holidays than were legally required and fat bonuses for a job well done. He even offered his top software designers and their families a week's stay a year at his boutique winery in Oxfordshire as a loyalty inducement. Consequently, he retained his best staff in what was a highly competitive global industry.

Olivia Noble had almost sounded *insulted* when he'd discussed her fee. Surely she wasn't that naive?

Like it or not, money made the world go round—any good businessperson knew that. And, from his research, Olivia certainly deserved the title—something that doubled her allure in his mind.

She had graduated first in her year with a Bachelor of Commerce degree, had a master's degree in marketing, and in four years had taken her company from a start-up to one of the top ten marketing firms in New York. Her work on the high-profile Kids Count charity had dragged her from obscurity to his attention.

Did her reluctance have anything to do with the sparks of chemistry that seemed to arc between them? Did she feel it too? That almost frenzied pull?

He soaped himself more vigorously, turning the dial on the shower down to tepid, to cool the blaze she'd evoked.

She'd wanted nothing to do with him earlier today. He'd planned to woo her to work with him over the lunch put on by the Business School. But she'd acted as if she couldn't get away quickly enough. Straight talking, no simpering or inane flattery.

And hadn't that been a big fucking turn-on? Another point in Ms Noble's favour.

Most women he met struggled to conceal the spark of excitement in their eyes, as if in meeting him they'd been handed a winning lottery ticket. Sadly, regardless of how attractive they were or how much they shared in common, he could never quite be sure their interest was in him the person or him the young entrepreneur listed on *Forbes*.

Not that Olivia had been able to fully conceal the flush of her chest or the rapid flutter of the pulse in her neck. He'd felt it too. The immediate slug of fascination that had had his head swivelling in a double-take the minute she'd stepped onto the stage to deliver her speech to the packed auditorium of keen undergraduates.

And close up… He'd had to discreetly adjust his cock in his slim-fit trousers as she'd walked away from their frustratingly brief interaction, trailing a light floral scent in her wake. He'd wanted to follow her, his nose to the ground like a bloodhound, sniffing at her sexy four-inch stilettos.

Roughly towelling himself dry, he analysed their arduous phone conversation. *Why* was the delectable Ms Noble so reluctant to take the account? He'd seen her body of work. She was amply capable of running both the Able-Active marketing strategy *and* that of Lancaster IT. The majority of her current client base was situated in the States. Surely she saw the benefits of expanding globally? And why had her initial refusal stung his modest ego? Lancaster IT ranked in the *Financial Times* 'Global 500', so it couldn't be his professional credentials.

He slipped into jeans and a clean shirt, selecting a blazer from the supply he kept at work. He grabbed his phone, frustration mounting. He'd grown accustomed to getting what he wanted, and if things went against him, he made them work. Refused to give up.

Perhaps Olivia's aversion was to him personally.

No, that didn't make sense. She hadn't been able to hide her body's unconscious reaction any more than he'd been able to hide his. She *must* share his personal interest—her reluctance was for mixing the two. But they were similar in many ways. Driven. Career-focussed.

He'd just have to convince her they could have the best of both worlds. That they needed to scratch this itch and then put it aside and focus on the important work ahead. Rewarding work. Work that would make a real difference and allow him to put some of his wealth into creating change. Or at least help him atone for Jenny…

He swallowed, forcing his mind away from a well-worn, unwanted path. He had to move forward. Use past mistakes to make good future decisions.

He blew out a slow, controlled sigh, his mind returning to Olivia. She'd eventually relented, her manner turning brisk, putting him in his place.

His cock twitched again, and impatience urged him to fire a brief text to his driver.

By the time he was seated in the back of his car, speeding through the streets of London, now devoid of rush-hour traffic, he'd formulated a charm offensive.

If a lucrative business deal couldn't tempt out her reluctant smile, he'd have to find other inducements.

* * *

Libby sighed. Her fingers absently swirled the stirrer in her martini and the general hubbub of the hotel bar behind her faded to background noise.

She'd longed to sleep, to enjoy the luxurious tub in her deluxe room and put today behind her. But, jet-lagged, fractious and horny from her encounters with Alex, sleep had drifted further out of reach with each passing minute. The alcohol wouldn't help— not with the sleeplessness *or* the horniness—but sitting in the impersonal confines of her beige room, thinking about Alex and his offer, wasn't an option.

It was a good offer. Before meeting him she'd have jumped at it. But now…?

The more time she spent with the captivating businessman, the greater the risk of her succumbing to her attraction to him. An attraction as alarming as it was alluring. Alex Lancaster wasn't the type of man to take no for an answer, and her yes wasn't given lightly these days.

Someone invaded her personal space.

'Why don't you drink that so I can buy you another one?' the man in the suit said, leaning too close and wafting her with beer-fume breath.

Great, this was the last thing she needed. She looked up, unsmiling. Why did guys assume a woman alone in bar must clearly be waiting for them? He was cute enough, if you ignored the leer and the breath, but her body couldn't muster one drop of enthusiasm for the predictable stranger.

The same body that had spent the entire day lusting after Alex Lancaster. The same body that still reminded her with soaked panties and chafed nipples that it had been three long years since she'd sought pleasure with another. Perhaps that was the reason Alex had got to her with little more than a raised eyebrow or the twist of his kissable lips.

Impervious to her go-away stare, Beer Breath slid one hand to the centre of her back and leaned over to reach for her phone, which was on the bar beside her untouched martini. Her hand beat his there. *Just.*

He pouted, swaying closer to bump shoulders with her. 'I was only going to give you my number, so you can call me when you've finished stirring that one to death and I can buy you another.'

He raised bushy eyebrows, the leer widening.

'Right...' Libby shrugged, shaking his hand from between her shoulder blades. 'But I'm fine.'

He grinned, signalling the barman.

Damn. He wasn't going to give up without a fight. That bath and the beige walls of her room looked increasingly appealing now. She should at least try to sleep. She'd need all her wits tomorrow—dealing with Alex would sap every scrap of resolve she possessed.

'I'm so sorry I'm late.'

The man occupying her thoughts swept up beside her on a cloud of freshly showered deliciousness, his hand taking a proprietorial hold of the back of her barstool and his smoky, heavy-lidded smile stripping her naked.

Alex.

'Hi.' Libby closed her slack-jawed mouth and swivelled to face him, turning her back on the stranger, never one to pass up a golden opportunity. She hated rudeness, but if Beer Breath was too stubborn or thick-skulled to take the hint…

Alex kept his stare on her, his smile genuine and warm enough to melt her underwear clean off, and then signalled the waiter with a flick of his wrist.

Libby sensed the moment when Beer Breath slinked away, and the hairs on the back of her neck settled—but only temporarily, because Alex hadn't taken his eyes off her. In fact, he was looking at her as if he was seconds from devouring her whole.

She shivered, delicious tendrils snaking to all her erogenous zones. 'What are you doing here?' Libby took a slug of her previously untouched drink, the burn calming her enough to meet his bold stare with one of her own.

'I came to invite you out for a late supper. I was on my way to Reception and then I spotted you here.' His hand slid from the back of her stool, and he settled into the one next to her, passing his order to the waiter before returning his disconcerting focus to her.

She stared back, lost for words and missing the proximity of his hand on her chair. He was close enough that his warmth traversed the space between them, but far enough away that she battled her body's urge to sway closer. And keep on swaying.

'What?' One corner of his mouth kicked up. 'What kind of host would I be if I left you to fend for yourself on your first night in a strange city?'

She couldn't help the snort that left her. 'The non-stalker kind...?'

He took the jibe with a cocksure arch of one brow, sipping wine while his poised stare flicked over her face from feature to feature.

Libby flushed hot all over. The 'stalker' comment had been beneath her. He hadn't once touched her, hadn't bought her drink, hadn't tried to grab her phone, hadn't even chased away her unwanted admirer—he had simply given her the out she'd wanted. The rest was all *her*.

What was *wrong* with her? Rudeness to a generous host and influential employer? All because he'd awoken needs within her? Needs too long dormant. Needs she'd never had before. Needs threatening to overwhelm her in their intensity.

Hardly his fault.

He dropped the bland smile, and a small frown crinkled the skin between his brows. 'It's a public bar, Olivia. I'm being a gentleman. But if you don't want company, just say so and I'll leave.'

He shrugged.

Simple.

Of course he would. Alex Lancaster didn't need

to stalk women. They probably lined up, forming a polite, orderly, English queue.

She swallowed, her throat tight. 'Thank you.' She tilted her head in the direction of Beer Breath's exit path. 'He was about to become a persistent pain in my ass.'

He barely acknowledged the man in the suit, and his continued casual perusal made her limbs jittery and lodged a ball of restless energy low in her belly.

'So, have you eaten? Dinner?' One eyebrow lifted and he licked red wine from his plush lower lip.

A simple invitation. One she'd offer herself to a visiting business colleague new in town. Why, then, did it feel like more than an offer of a shared meal? Or was that simply her overactive libido filling in the blanks?

'I'm not hungry.' Her voice emerged as barely a croak.

No argument, no persuasion.

'Tell me…' He leaned a little closer, his stare a little more penetrating, searching hers. 'Why the reluctance to work for Able-Active?'

Alex cut straight to the heart of an issue. She admired that. But no way could she explain her reticence without giving away a whole heap of personal stuff. Stuff she did her best never to think about.

She ducked her head away from his intensity, her sleeveless, lightweight blouse as cloying as a thick, woolly sweater.

He ploughed on. 'You think I'm arrogant.'

A statement.

She shot him a glance, surprised to see amusement lingering on his face.

He gave another shrug, as if he had her all worked out. 'I see it in your eyes.' He rested his elbows on the bar, leaning closer. 'I'd like you to extend your stay. All expenses covered, of course.'

'Why?' Her head spun, reeling from the arrogant request.

Hadn't they already established that she wouldn't roll over and do whatever he asked? If he didn't seem to have a hotline to her long-dormant libido she'd laugh in his sinfully handsome face.

'Able-Active doesn't happen inside an office. I want you to experience it, to really understand my vision. I'd like you to stay a fortnight.'

He took another sip of wine, giving her time to respond.

Her jaw fell, her fidgety hand stilling around the stem of her martini glass. 'Are you *nuts*?'

Clearly Libby was nuts, too, because for a fleeting moment she considered it. Then she sobered. Even if she wanted to jump when he clicked his fingers, she couldn't. She had Sonya, her heavily pregnant partner, to consider. Yes, she could work from anywhere in the world with a Wi-Fi connection for short periods and, yes, she'd cleared her desk before flying to the UK, but a fortnight away from the office…

He laughed—a deep rumble that curled her toes and transformed him from sexy, assured businessman to sexy boy-next-door, all grown up. He turned his stool to face her, leaning back in a relaxed slouch, his thighs spread.

In invitation?

Libby's eyes burned with the effort of maintaining eye contact and not succumbing to a visual tour of his denim-clad crotch. Time to be clear. If this working relationship was to be successful, he needed to understand a few things.

'You know, I'm sure you're used to it, but you can't always have your own way.'

She plucked the olive from her drink, holding it between her teeth while she stared him down. Two could play Mr Lancaster's game. If he thought she'd simper at his flattery, drop to her knees no questions asked, he wasn't as smart as she knew him to be.

She bit into the salty olive, allowing her tongue to linger on her lips.

His pupils dilated—a subconscious tell over which he had no control. Then he shrugged, as if he didn't care either way. But she knew that wasn't true. Like her, he'd likely achieved his success by expanding control over all areas of his life. Personal and professional. But did he *need* that control, like her? Did he feel as if he was spinning off into the inky blackness of space without it, like her?

He tilted his head, his astute gaze leaving her mouth at last. This time when he met her eyes she wanted to curl up and hide.

'I'll make you a proposition.' He lifted the glass to his lips, taking a sip while his words sank in.

Libby shook her head, determined to wrestle back the upper hand. 'I've conceded enough to you in our short acquaintance.'

Alex bit his lip, hiding a smile.

Bastard.

He flared his nostrils, sucking in a breath and tilting his head back to consider the ceiling. *Good.* She posed a challenge—no doubt a novelty to someone in his position. She could almost hear the cogs working in his head.

'Fair point.' He rubbed his index and middle finger along his lower lip. 'How about for every concession you make, I'll make one too?'

He shifted, his thighs parting a fraction more, as if he were growing uncomfortable. Was she having a similar effect on him as he had on her?

His voice dropped. Slow. Deep. Intimate.

'Equal. Mutually satisfying.'

He took another sip of wine. Waiting. Watching her over the rim.

Libby recrossed her legs, her thighs clammy. 'A negotiation? I warn you, I'm good.'

Not that she had any experience with *this* kind of deal. How to be a high school sweetheart, how to be a girlfriend, how to be a fiancée—yes. But how to handle this searing sexual chemistry and keep enough distance to emerge unscathed? Could he tell she was making this up as she went along?

He grinned.

Thought he had this in the bag, did he?

He gave a slow nod. 'I know that. Research, re-member? The best.' He leaned forward, closing the distance between them, his voice a low whisper, eyes aglow. 'What do you say? Up for a little…adven-ture?'

Her mind raced, her heart beating its way into her throat.

Yes.

No.

'It depends…'

Were they even still talking about work? Did it matter? Perhaps Sonya, Vinnie and her hormones were right. A no-strings dalliance was exactly what she needed—slake this intense thirst she'd thought long extinguished, then finish a rewarding and lu-crative job and move on.

As if he'd read her mind, he said, 'Come on.'

Libby leaned closer. His low voice called to her, zinging straight between her legs. From this distance, she could see his pulse flicking in the notch at the base of his throat, the dark hairs peeking over the open neck of his shirt, could smell the detergent he used on his laundry.

His voice continued—persuasive, tempting. 'You're a perceptive, intelligent woman…'

She braced one foot on the floor, her body sway-ing towards his as if she was hard of hearing and needed to lean closer to his tantalising mouth. Her hand landed on his thigh, steadying her balance, but the denim was a poor barrier to the heat and bulk of his taut muscles.

'You feel this insane chemistry too.' His stare smouldered, his breath tickling her neck.

She practically sagged into him. She wasn't alone. Wasn't imagining this. But should she act on it? Did she dare?

'I want you.' He held eye contact, his stark statement hanging in the crackling air between them. 'Physically, professionally.'

He spoke as if he was negotiating a business deal. Calm, collected, poker-faced.

A tiny shrug of one shoulder. 'Stay.'

He made it sound so easy—a foregone conclusion. And she was sorely tempted.

All the time they'd talked, he hadn't touched her. His hands were still relaxed on the arms of the barstool when all she wanted to do was slide her fingers through his silky dishevelled hair and angle his head until he kissed her. Kissed away the doubt. Kissed away the memories. Kissed away the loneliness.

She sat back, her hand slipping from the rock-hard muscles of his thigh. Time to wrestle this back under her command. Get a grip of herself and this situation. Give him a taste of his own medicine.

The trouble was, lust had robbed her brain of its usual quick wit and all the negotiating skills she'd bragged about. Every single comeback or demand had fled her mind like sand falling through the holes of a sieve.

Perhaps she'd transmitted her thoughts telepathically to him, because he said, 'You need control?'

Could he see her that clearly? Were her fears, her hang-ups, so clearly displayed on her face?

He'd dropped the smile, his expression now serious, as if he understood the momentous battle raging inside her. She wanted him too—had spent the day thinking about him, about what it would be like to feel his touch, feel his mouth, feel him move inside her…

The urge to give in to that curiosity, that need, was overwhelming.

He dipped his chin, ensuring that she saw him—saw both the sincerity in his stare and the flare of the same battle inside him.

'I'm man enough to concede it. What can I do to give you what you need so we can both win?'

A silent groan had Libby's eyes drooping as she took in a long, ragged breath. What an intoxicating offer. Could she *do* this? Separate business from pleasure? Keep things casual between them? On *her* terms? Give him a concession or two and take what he was willing to concede?

She opened her eyes to his continued stare. The slight flare of his nostrils was the only sign that he too experienced the anticipation that fluttered in Libby's belly, bringing her to life.

Until she spoke, she was clueless as to how she'd respond. 'I'll give you a week.'

A week?

He nodded. So accommodating. So skilled at negotiating this fragile truce.

But she, too, could strike a pretty deal. Time to see how much he was willing to relinquish. Could he be a man of his word? Was he really interested in a deal? Did he want her enough to agree to her terms?

There was only one way to find out.

She leaned closer, her lips parting on a barely there gasp as their knees made contact. She dropped her voice, as he'd done. 'If we're working together…' her eyes flicked to his crotch, still displayed before her '…and fucking, I won't be bossed around.'

Another nod. Another delicious concession.

Her mind raced, searching for a compromise that, as he'd put it, would allow them both to get what they wanted. She'd never fought so hard. Her self-preservation demanded every inch of ground acquired.

The ultimate test of his mettle would come. Could he withstand what she had planned for him? Would her nerve hold?

Libby's temperature reached boiling point, seconds away from spontaneous combustion. She shook her head slowly, commanding his full attention. 'You won't get your own way all the time.'

He shrugged again, the small half-smile returning. 'If I had my way…' he lifted his wine glass, taking a sip, his eyes slowly raking over her mouth '…I'd have fucked you at the top of The Shard this morning. Had you screaming my name with that sexy voice of yours.'

Her gasp sounded so loud she expected the whole population of the bar to turn in their direction.

He quirked a scornful brow. 'Seems to me, *you* are the one getting her way, Olivia.'

Danger. He reeked of it. Not that her personal safety was in question. But she should run all the same.

Still he stared, his eyes flicking between hers. Still her breaths gusted in and out through parted lips. She held his searing eye contact. A challenge. Battle lines being drawn.

Finishing her martini in one swallow, she slid from the stool, coming to stand between his still spread thighs. She leaned close, her heavy ponytail falling forward, a few strands of hair getting caught in the stubble covering his strong jaw.

With her lips mere millimetres from his ear, she whispered, a thrill tingling up her spine.

'*Quid*….'

Closer.

'*Pro*…'

She could almost feel the fine hairs on his earlobe tickle her lips.

'*Quo*…'

Leaning back, she took the key card from her purse and pressed it into his palm, turned on her heel and left the bar on shaky legs.

CHAPTER THREE

HE'D NEVER KNOW how he managed the walk from the bar and across the hotel foyer with his steely hard-on, but he caught up with Libby in two strides. He deliberately didn't touch her. Hadn't touched her all evening, although it had almost killed him. But she'd touched him.

Her handprint still burned his thigh, scorched clean though the denim and spoke directly to his cock. The brush of her bare knees, the scent wafting up from her thick, luxuriant hair… He groaned, digging into deep reserves for discipline over his body.

She walked close. Her arm brushed his and the sway of that long, lustrous ponytail tapped his shoulder in time with the clack of her heels across the marble tiles.

They reached the lifts. He pressed the call button, dragging her light floral scent into his lungs until the head rush made him close his eyes for a split second. *Fuck*. He needed to pull himself together, to grapple back some semblance of mastery. At least over his libido.

He mimicked her, staring straight ahead, his eyes trained on the digital display as the numbers fell, heralding the lift's arrival.

His mouth burned to kiss her. To see if her plump, pouty lips tasted as good as they'd looked when she whispered the word *fucking*. On the surface she oozed cool, untouchable sophistication. Not a glorious hair out of place or a wrinkle in sight. But the deal she'd brokered—bold, assertive, knowing what she wanted—what a turn-on. Perhaps it was an American thing. Perhaps it was pure Olivia.

Quid pro quo.

That should have raised his hackles, but he was keen to discover her brand of give and take.

Perhaps he was losing his mind. But, oh, how he'd love to mess her up—to tug out that hair tie and slide his hands through those long, silky tresses, to feel them slither over his face, his chest, his abdomen while she kissed him… How would that austere exterior crack at the height of passion? With her full lips swollen by his kisses, her luminous eyes glazed and punch-drunk? Her smoky voice calling his name with that native New York accent of hers?

At this rate, he'd need a cold shower just to remain in her company. What did she have planned for him? Would he be able to keep it together?

The lift arrived. As the doors opened he saw the car was empty. He cast a glance sideways. He waited, hand out, inviting her to step inside first, all the while battling the urge to push her up against the wall and fuck her right there in the elegant foyer of the Windsor Hotel, Park Lane.

You won't get your own way all the time.

Right now, he'd gladly take ten per cent. Used to controlling every aspect of his life, especially his sex life, he knew this game he'd agreed to would test every ounce of his willpower.

As if she knew the direction of his thoughts, she poked her tongue out, sliding it along her lower lip, flooding his groin with fresh heat. She stepped inside and he followed, his hands forming fists by his sides to stop himself from touching her.

Doomed. He was *so* doomed.

If she looked down she'd see the effect this negotiation had had on him. The effect *she* had on him. He longed to readjust himself in his jeans, but he couldn't break the spell she'd wound around him as surely as if he was already tangled up in a cloud of that glorious hair. What would she look like naked? With that silky, decadent ponytail liberated until it covered her bare shoulders, the tips brushing her breasts?

She stepped in front of him, leaning over to press the button for her floor. The arch of her long, graceful neck called to him. The phantom taste of her skin lingered on his lips as if he'd already indulged.

He sucked in a breath through flared nostrils, turning to stare at her. *Fuck*, she was irresistible. Sassy, smart, sexy as hell and completely unimpressed by him. Most women he dated suffocated him with their cloying need to please. To be exactly what they thought he wanted. Olivia Noble didn't care *what* he wanted, and good for her. She called the shots. She spoke plainly. He'd never met a woman like her.

She stared back with a momentary flash of hesitancy and a series of blinks of those long lashes over rounded eyes. His chest pinched at this tiny hint of her vulnerability. But he wouldn't let her off the hook. She'd started this, raised the stakes. And he'd agreed to play give and take—not his usual style—instinct telling him she needed to stay in control at all times.

Why? He'd have to flex his patience if he wanted the answer to that secret.

His body strained, every muscle primed to close the deal. To put them both out of their misery and taste her. But he knew the prize on her terms would be worth the wait, the sacrifice.

She heard his prayer.

Stepping up to him, her bottom lip trapped beneath her teeth, she slowly tunnelled her fingers into his hair. The bite of pain tingled over his scalp as she twisted the strands and angled his head. Her dark stare bewitched him. She reached up on tiptoes and slid her mouth over his, eyes open. Bold, demanding—and so fucking arousing he almost embarrassed himself, almost sagged to his knees.

And then he kissed her back, maintaining eye contact, his fists tightly clenched at his sides to stop himself from taking what he wanted more than his next breath. The kick of satisfaction he got from torturing them both and withholding his touch tightened his balls, ramping up his need until he feared he'd have to break his word and gorge on her like a greedy, selfish addict. Here. *Now.*

When she pushed her tongue into his mouth, whimpering her frustration and pressing her body against the length of his, he gave up the fight with a groan of both frustration and surrender. His fingers gripped the soft cheeks of her arse, lifting her and pressing her where he needed to feel friction. So close, but not close enough.

He spun her around, pressing her into the mirrored wall of the lift and crushing his steel-hard erection into the flat of her belly.

She deepened the kiss, her mouth voracious, as if she hadn't been kissed in a very long time. A travesty, if it were true. She deserved to be kissed every second of every day.

He snaked one hand towards the hem of her skirt, now regretting that it hugged her curves so tightly. He'd have to work to peel it up her legs, raise it high enough to part her thighs, hoist her above the gleaming chrome handrail that ran around the lift at waist height. Need raged through him, weakening his knees and making his hands rough, impatient. He tempered the roar of hormones spiking his blood with deep breaths.

Slow. Savour.

The lift pinged, announcing their arrival. Neither of them seemed in any hurry to break the searing kiss that had left their chests rising and falling in unison. Alex used every ounce of strength he possessed to pull back, pushing her skirt down just before the door slid open.

The corridor was deserted.

Without a backward glance, although looking a little flustered, Libby led the way to her room. Alex swiped the card she'd given him in the bar. Her eyes—huge dark pools in the dim lighting of the corridor—beguiled him. His blind confidence wavered. He was used to commanding every aspect of his life, and this power exchange, while exciting, left him adrift. Would he be able to concede to her wishes, whatever they were? For more of her, he'd certainly die trying.

But curiosity won.

'What do you want?'

He'd promised her a compromise, give and take, control. He'd do everything in his power to give her what she needed.

She pushed inside the room, flipping on lights and kicking of her heels, revealing toes painted with deep red nail polish.

As the door snicked closed behind him she turned.

He'd been right. Their kisses had left her mouth gloriously swollen, and the slight flush of beard burn marked her chin and cheeks. She was more beautiful than ever, and his fingers itched to complete the transformation—to undo her hair, currently featuring in all his filthy fantasies, and strip her of her prim clothes, expose the soft, feminine curves he guessed lurked beneath.

When she finally found her voice, it was so smoky he expected it to trigger the fire alarms.

'What do *you* want?'

That was easy to answer. A dream come true. 'I want to touch you. All of you.' He curled his fingers into his palms, his breath trapped behind his tight throat.

She nodded, eyes heavy, the tip of her tongue touching her top lip. '*I* want you to sit there.' She indicated an armchair in the corner by the windows.

He nodded, but his feet seemed cemented to the carpet while his mind played catch-up. He'd showed his hand too eagerly. She planned to deny him. Could he handle this? He burned for her, and the chair she'd indicated might as well be some sort of medieval torture device or wired to the mains.

She swallowed, her colour high. But it was not the flush of embarrassment, rather the glow of arousal.

'I want you to watch me.'

Fuck. She was trying to kill him. He was about to become a statistic. His throat closed tighter, his heart beating itself an escape path between his ribs.

'I want that too.' His voice was seriously strangled.

Get a grip, man.

He shrugged off his blazer and tossed it on the

desk. His jeans were too tight, constricting his manhood, but he'd do what she asked, what he'd agreed to, in order to earn her trust. Olivia—enchanting, provocative, intriguing—was the ultimate reward and certainly worth the discomfort.

He settled, sinking back into the upholstery, thighs spread as wide as the chair would allow. His hard-on was a stiff rod, pressing at the fly of his jeans. He forced his fingers to uncurl, resting them on the arms of the chair as he tried to slow his excited breaths. Whatever she was about to do would slay him. But he'd die trying to maintain the boundaries she'd demanded.

His compliance was quickly rewarded. She undid the top few buttons of her silky blouse, revealing the spill of perfect breasts over the top of a lacy, pale peach bra. His eyes fought not to roll back in his head. He wouldn't miss one second of the vision before him.

Her chest rose and fell in cadence with his own. At least they were in this together. Suffering together.

Staring him down, she hoisted up her skirt, bunching the fabric around her waist until her matching panties came into view at the juncture of her long, shapely legs. Her hands trembled slightly. If he hadn't been watching her every move with almost frantic eyes, desperate to see everything, he might have missed that revelation.

Was she nervous? Excited? Having second thoughts? Pain lanced his chest.

Please don't regret this. Please don't stop.

Fuck, she was a wet dream come true. Somehow this tease was twice as hot as if she'd stripped naked.

But he didn't have to wait long to see more of her. With a small sigh, she hooked her thumbs into the waistband of those panties and peeled them down her legs, dropping them without ceremony and settling on the edge of the bed.

She faced him, vulnerable but still in control. Breathtaking, but still composed. Time slowed, stretching to infinity while he watched and waited and breathed.

'Don't move or I'll stop,' she whispered.

A nod. He was incapable of speech.

Just when he thought he'd shatter if he didn't kiss her, touch her soon, she slid her thighs open. He tried to keep his stare fixed on hers, but he wasn't the man he prided himself on being, because with a hissed *'Fuck...'* he capitulated to his body's needs, his eyes zeroing in on the patch of dark curls and her glistening sex.

She was wet. Soaked.

Two or three feet. That was all that separated them. In one stride he'd be there, touching her slick heat, kissing her gasps away, feeling the scrape of her nails as he worked her to orgasm.

His own nails, blunt and useless, dug into the chair's fabric, his knuckles tight with the force of staying put. His breath see-sawed through flared nostrils, and his mouth pressed into a grim line as he lifted desperate eyes to hers once more.

She'd clearly decided he would comply, because with an aching slowness that tested every scrap of his substantial self-control she moved her hand between her legs, her fingers sliding into place over her clit.

A slug of lust punched him in the chest.

She gasped, her head falling back as if she was as close as him to slamming over the edge. She licked her lower lip, sultry eyes on him, and shifted, bent one leg up on the bed and braced the other on the floor, opening up the view to him.

His cock strained, begging for release. He gripped the armrests tighter, clinging to prevent himself from ripping open his fly and joining her in self-pleasure. But she'd told him to sit, to watch, and this was the most erotic thing he'd ever witnessed.

His breathing, now perilously fast, echoed around the room.

She moved her hand slowly at first, tentatively, as if she'd forgotten the rhythm of pleasuring herself. Or perhaps she'd never done this before. Perhaps she was as blown away by her bold, uninhibited display as he was. *Fuck.* The thought of some other lucky bastard being treated to this show forced icy shards through his chest and he bit his tongue, the pain reminding him to stay seated when every nerve in his body relayed messages to his brain to move. To go to her.

As her fingers picked up speed he lost his grip on sanity, his stare darting wildly between her pleasure-drunk face and her frantically circling fingers. She dropped back on her elbow, the edges of her blouse slipping open, revealing more of the lacy concoction concealing her breasts.

He gritted his teeth. He resented her clothing now. It blocked what he instinctively knew would be a sublime body from his view. He made fists, the urge to tear the fabric from her curves so overwhelming his legs shifted, restless with inactivity.

Her whimpers drew his gaze to her face, but his eyes flew back between her legs in time to see her slide a finger inside herself before returning to her clit. He'd been right. She was soaked. The quiet noise of slippery skin on slippery skin echoed inside his skull and her scent, rich and erotic, reached his nostrils across the small space separating them.

He was losing it. His brain was shutting down. Not enough oxygen. Too much stimulation. Testosterone overload.

She stared at him, her moans growing increasingly erratic. Breath catching. Lips parting. Thighs jerking.

She was close.

He was done.

With a powerful lurch he flew from the chair, his whole body rejoicing, joining his addled mind until his head filled with triumphant screams. He fell to his knees between her thighs, his focus zeroed in on her sex.

He'd assumed she'd stop. That was her rule. But

clearly she was as gone as him—well past the point of no return. Well past reason.

He looked up…a moment's hesitation.

She whimpered. Gave a single nod. Desperation in her eyes.

Batting her still moving hand aside, he slammed his mouth over her slick folds with a grunt, glorying in the euphoria of touching her at last.

She yelled—a cry of ecstasy—twisting her fingers in his hair.

He groaned out his pent-up frustration. Her taste coated his lips, his tongue, the back of his throat. He located the hard, swollen nub of nerves, flicking wildly with the tip of his tongue before sucking down on her—hard.

He stared up from between her legs. Her head thrashed from side to side as she watched him, her cries growing louder, more primitive. He managed to push a single finger inside her tight warmth just before she exploded, her internal muscles a contracting wave around his finger and her thighs trembling against the sides of his face. He kept his mouth glued in place, wringing the last spasms from her, while the uneasy swirl of triumph and failure stole his high.

With a final gasp she twisted away, pushing at his head when only seconds ago she'd been pulling.

He released her, wiping his mouth on the back of his hand and staggering to his feet. His cock was harder than ever. She lay on the bed, boneless, her beautiful face flushed with the aftermath of intense pleasure, but her eyes were wide and wary, as if she was uncertain what he'd do next.

Fuck. He'd failed. She'd set him a test and he'd bombed spectacularly. Now he wished she'd tied him to that chair—although he couldn't be sure he wouldn't have torn the building down, trying to get to her. The sight of her had been too much for the mere mortal he'd proved to be.

He held out his hands, their fine tremors matching the adrenaline jitters pounding the rest of his body. For a second he thought she'd refuse. Tell him to get out. But she struggled into a sitting position, put her hands in his, allowing him to pull her up so that he stood between her knees where she sat on the edge of the bed, dishevelled and breathtaking.

Slowly, as though coaxing a frightened animal, he cupped her face. Her hair, still in its ponytail, was less than immaculate, with freed wisps clinging to her forehead and cheeks. Her eyes had lost their unfocussed haze, and pleasure was draining away to be replaced by a wariness that shrank his balls.

This hadn't been part of the game—wasn't in the rulebook. He'd messed up.

He released a sigh—slow, controlled, careful not to expel all his frustration in one explosive blast. He bent over her, eyes fixed on hers, and placed a single, firm, closed-mouth kiss on her lips. The effort of withdrawing almost buckled his knees, but he dropped her face and stepped back.

She'd been perfect. Given him everything she'd

said she would. Given him an experience that he'd remember on his deathbed. And he'd failed her. At the first hurdle.

Without a word he turned away, his back on fire, urging him to look at her again. But as the heavy hotel door closed behind him and he made his way to the lift on legs with the potential to let him down at any second, he congratulated himself. He might have fallen short, let her down. But he was damn proud of the hidden strength that allowed him to walk away.

CHAPTER FOUR

LIBBY'S SCALP REBELLED. She'd pulled her hair into a
severe braid this morning, as if an austere hairstyle
might protect her from the reckless impulses of last
night. Impulses that had not only had her agreeing
to work with Alex Lancaster, but to stay in London
for a week when she'd planned to be back in New
York in two days.

Not to mention the crazy tit-for-tat deal they'd
brokered—the one in which she'd pleasured herself
in front of him, forced him to watch, and come so
hard she was certain her heart had stopped for a beat.

She stepped from the elevator, the chafe of her
stocking tops grazing her thighs, which were already
embarrassingly slick.

She'd almost cancelled. Called his PA. Booked
an earlier flight home. She wasn't a coward, but the
thought of what she'd done, of seeing Alex again in
the cold light of day…

Whilst last night's antics had blown her away with
the best orgasm of her life, she'd be lying if she said
she and Alex had concluded their business—either

with Able-Active or in the personal game they'd begun.

His face flashed before her. He'd kept his word. Conceded control. Hadn't once balked at her demands. She'd never have guessed a man as powerful and influential as him would be able to shelve his arrogance and give her what she needed. And now what had started as a battle of wills, a way to deal with her lust for him, had become the most daring and exhilarating game ever.

Not that she'd expected him to follow her instructions to the letter. She had almost sobbed with relief when he'd prowled from the chair and finished her off with his mouth. She closed her eyes, remembering the sight of him looking up at her from between her thighs.

How had he managed to walk away unfulfilled? She'd been on the verge of running after him, dragging him back to her room and riding his magnificent-looking cock. Not that she'd had a chance to get her hands on him. He'd barely broken a sweat. The man had some frustratingly impressive willpower. She'd just have to try harder.

But business first.

Libby pushed through etched glass doors emblazoned with the company logo and approached a sleek, minimalist reception desk.

'Libby Noble for Alex Lancaster.'

Late last night, after showering, she'd checked her e-mails, spying one from his PA, Molly—the young woman now sitting in front of her, according to a name plaque on the desk—advising her of today's itinerary.

'Ah, yes, Ms Noble. He's expecting you. I'll show you in.' Molly stood, her outstretched arm directing Libby towards another set of etched glass doors and an office beyond.

Her legs threatened to give out. She swallowed, plastered her most convincing, polite smile on her face and steeled herself against the impact of seeing Alex again—steeled herself like a butterfly about to enter a hurricane.

He stood at his desk, shoulder to shoulder with a shorter man in his forties. Their focus was directed to the screen of the tablet the other man carried, but as she hovered in the doorway Alex lifted his head, harpooning Libby with a dark, inscrutable stare across the space that divided them.

A flush of heat slammed through her, and the hurricane morphed into a tropical cyclone on the surface of the sun. She'd been right to fear the impact. It hadn't lessened.

Even though she'd broken her dry spell, achieved some measure of relief from the sexual haze she'd been in since meeting him, the blow was twice as potent as the first time their eyes had met across a room.

She saw him now. The true him. Her eyes had been cleared of the self-imposed veil of abstinence. His raw sexuality simmered beneath his cultured, polite exterior. He stripped her with his stare, leaving her aching and needy and desperate to sample more of him than his spectacular mouth.

Libby swayed on her heels—a minute wobble in his direction that told her everything she needed to know about her chances of her steering her mind out of the bedroom and into the boardroom. No amount of prim business suits or severe hairstyles could protect her from Alex's potent sex appeal and her body's awakened cravings.

From behind her, Molly cleared her throat. 'Ms Noble.'

Of course—they weren't alone.

Alex gave a single nod to his assistant. 'Thanks, Molly.'

The older man moved into Libby's peripheral vision.

Alex kept his eyes on her. 'Olivia, this is Jeremy Wells, my financial director.'

Jeremy tucked the tablet under his arm and moved in her direction.

Dragging her thoughts and her eyes from Alex, Libby smiled, heat warming her cheeks from her transparent leering at Jeremy's boss.

Get a grip.

Alex sat on the edge of his desk, observing their interaction with an indifference that sent an army of ants marching beneath her skin.

'Olivia will be in charge of marketing for Able-Active.'

His voice held none of the sexy drawl of last night, but the way his mouth caressed her name reverberated through her body until she felt the memory of that mouth's intimate caress between her legs. A memory constantly at the forefront of her mind.

Jeremy offered a surprisingly limp handshake and a tepid smile. 'I'll leave you to your business.'

Alex nodded again, his stare back on Libby, flooding her body with wave after wave of turbulent heat. But she'd yet to see what she wanted to see—the same aching discord currently pounding *her* equilibrium.

Hormones. It was just hormones.

'Molly, could you please bring coffee downstairs?' He quirked an eyebrow at Libby in question.

She nodded to the younger woman, confirming that he'd guessed her beverage of choice.

'I'm taking Ms Noble on a tour of the Able-Active office.'

Molly nodded and retreated, seemingly completely unaffected by the decadent rumble of her boss's voice, whereas Libby felt it wash over her, lifting every hair and tingling every nerve ending.

She wanted more of it. More of the sexy grunts and groans he'd uttered last night from between her thighs. More of him asking her what she wanted, handing her control on a silver platter. More of his buttoned-up English accent cursing as he finally reached his limit of self-denial and lunged for her.

Who knew this part of her lurked inside? What had he unleashed?

They faced off, alone at last. He gave nothing away. She prayed her own transparency matched his. Would he renege on their deal? Send her home? Perhaps he'd simply pretend last night hadn't happened and get straight down to business?

Not that he was dressed for business. She indulged herself, eyeing him from head to toe. She'd expected another of his expensive suits, to see his magnificent body encased in fine tailoring and crisp linen, but he wore jeans and a graphic T-shirt—an outfit that did nothing to diminish his attractiveness. If anything, it heightened it, and the T-shirt was a playful touch of whimsy that almost curled her lip in a smile. Alex Lancaster a gamer? She'd been right about the geeky surfer dude.

She lifted her stare from the casual, low-slung fit of his jeans, which showcased the bulge of his crotch. A bulge considerably smaller than the one he'd walked away with last night, when he'd left her hotel room unsatisfied. Fresh heat climbed her neck. She should have stopped him. Given him some relief. Finished him the way he'd finished her.

Her knees wobbled at the memory of his mouth on her, those dark eyes piercing, watching while she exploded on his tongue…

Damn. Must she eye-fuck him at every opportunity?

Her face burned. But the intensity of the look he

gave her provided little respite from the boil of her blood.

The speech she'd prepared fled. She scanned the room rather that look at him, while her brain scrambled for suitable morning-after conversation—the spectacular view of the London skyline, the tasteful, minimalist art on the walls and the rich aroma of leather from the expensive furniture.

When her gaze ended its tour back on him, he continued to watch her with slightly narrowed eyes.

'I wasn't sure you'd turn up this morning.'

That was the last thing she'd expected him to say. *Fancy a repeat performance? Want to lean over my desk while I fuck you from behind? You're a selfish lover and the deal is off.* All those were closer to her imaginings.

'Why? I agreed. I'm a professional.'

Sometimes. When she wasn't drooling over him.

She was a big girl—one who could separate personal from business. Not that she'd ever been tested before now. Oh, how she hoped her faith in her own abilities was justified.

Liar.

Right now, all she wanted to do was strip him from his dressed-down street clothes and see if she could make him hard with just her mouth.

His expression inscrutable, his eyes flicked over her face and he stood. 'Shall we?'

He moved to the door, holding it open and ges-

turing her to re-enter the real world. So calm. So
indifferent.

Clearly they weren't going to discuss last night.
Discuss the inferno of chemistry they'd fanned to
life. Only her mind was stuck there. Stuck on vivid
images of him splaying her over his desk, his sofa,
the floor, and continuing where they left off in her
hotel room.

But Mr Lancaster was all business this morning.
And that was where her head belonged. In the game.
The game of marketing for Able-Active and the game
of bedroom *quid pro quo*. She wouldn't become professionally distracted from the first and she *couldn't*
become personally distracted by the second.

She crossed his office, her eyes flicking up to his
as she passed him in the doorway, and headed back
the way she'd come to the elevators. He walked beside her, his arm so close she could reach out and
touch him. Perhaps she should. Apologise for last
night. For leaving him…hanging. Suggest they rectify the imbalance of the situation later tonight.

He pressed the call button and they both gazed
up. The feeling of *déjà vu* was strong enough to send
licks of flame trickling down Libby's spine. Just like
last night, the elevator was empty. Alex pressed the
button for a few floors down and the doors closed.

The crackle of tension ricocheted around inside
Libby's head. She craved more of those searing, all-
consuming kisses. *Damn*, the man could kiss, and
she'd already experienced his phenomenal oral skills.

But instead of dispelling her torrid urges it had only intensified them. She wanted to stop the elevator and beg him to fuck her right here, right now.

Her eyes scanned the interior of the car, searching for security cameras.

And then the doors slid open, and his upper-class voice dragged her from her fantasies.

'After you.'

Seriously? She could barely walk. Her nipples ached, her panties were ruined and her fingers twitched to get hold of him. She should have asked him to spend the night—that way she could have quenched her thirst with the perfect wake-up call this morning.

Alex, by comparison, seemed calm, efficient and businesslike. The ultimate professional. While she longed to play hooky with him, forget marketing budgets and brand awareness strategies and spend the week holed up in her hotel room, living out every dirty fantasy he'd inspired.

No. He'd definitely changed his mind. A cold, hard rock settled in her stomach.

He led her down a corridor that was a carbon copy of the one housing his office, again holding open the door for her to enter ahead of him when they reached their destination.

Libby stalled. 'Office' was a fairly grand term for what was essentially a small room with two desks, a single computer and a phone.

A woman in her early twenties looked up from the screen and stood on their arrival. 'Hi, Alex.'

First-name terms? Of course.

He smiled, and Libby glanced away.

'Hailey, this is Olivia Noble. She's agreed to help with our marketing campaign. Put us on the map.'

He turned to Libby, the smile for his pretty young employee sliding from his face.

'Hailey is the charity's only full-time employee. The rest of the staff are volunteers.'

Libby shook hands with the woman, noting the way her eyes lingered on Alex. She didn't blame her. 'Magnetic' didn't really cover his appeal. And her resentment of Hailey, a woman she'd just met, originated in disappointment. He hadn't brought her to this quiet part of the building for a repeat performance of last night. He wouldn't be laying her over this desk and redressing the orgasm imbalance.

Damn.

If they'd been alone she might have broken her number one rule. Might have dropped to her knees in front of him, taken him in her mouth, given him something other than work to think about.

'Any progress on the mountain biking trip?'

Alex took a folder from Hailey's desk, his eyes scanning the contents.

Libby shook the tantalising images from her head. She could do indifference too.

Hailey nodded. 'Some luck with the accommodation, thanks to the Welsh Tourism Board, but staffing is still an issue.'

Alex traced his bottom lip with his finger and thumb, his attention held by the paperwork in his hands.

Olivia cast her observant eye around the sparsely furnished and featureless room. One employee, an uninspiring space and staffing issues—hardly the picture of a successful Alex Lancaster venture. Why devote so much of his time to a fledgling charity? Time he could spend in more lucrative ways, building his empire. Surely Lancaster IT kept him busy?

With conversation clearly over, Libby followed Alex to the room's spare desk, where he pulled out a chair for her before taking the second and moving it so they sat at right angles, rather than facing each other. *Damn.* She'd hoped a block of wood between them would coax her hormones into submission, or at least remind her to stay professional.

She busied herself with her tablet and her phone and then slid off her jacket, draping it over her bag at her feet.

Cool, calm, professional.

Right.

Her thighs still felt the imprint of that stubble he wore on his chin.

His low voice penetrated the lust filling her head as they faced off.

'Are you okay? You seem…uncomfortable.'

Damn him—how dare he be so…unaffected? Her

gaze flicked down. At least her hands weren't trembling.

'Not at all. I…'

She couldn't confess the real direction of her lewd thoughts. Him. This desk. More orgasms good enough to make her forget her own name. Time for Plan B. Her trusty go-to—honesty.

'I'm a little surprised, that's all.'

He leaned back in his chair as he had last night in that armchair. A lazy slouch, thighs spread, one eyebrow cocked…waiting.

How was she going to get through today?

She squirmed, swallowing hard, then pointed around the room. 'I guess I expected something… *more*. Something flashier.' She clasped her hands on the desk in front of her.

He was silent for so long, she felt beads of moisture dotting her top lip. Silent and watchful.

'I see.'

He hardened his stare and Libby fought the urge to hide in the restroom. *Fuck*, was it possible that work Alex was even hotter than play Alex? He certainly carried an intense air of authority she hadn't witnessed before. One that should leave her cold, and angling for a heated debate, but it only heightened the ache between her legs.

'You've made assumptions about me…developed preconceived ideas.' He held up his hand, silencing the denial on the tip of her tongue. 'The scruffy jeans and T-shirt have thrown you, and now this slightly shabby low-tech office has compounded those impressions.'

Haughty. The word perfectly described his cold voice. *Had* she made assumptions? She tried to remain open-minded, unbiased—especially where business was concerned. But with her humble past and his reckless reputation… An oil-and-water combination. Perhaps she'd subconsciously doomed this opportunity to failure. And if that were true there'd be no more…recreation.

She fought the weight on her shoulders.

He leaned closer, capturing her rapt stare and holding her breath to ransom. 'I told you on the phone yesterday—Able-Active doesn't happen in an office.'

Her eyes landed on his mouth. The hypnotic movement and the sound of his passionate voice were entrancing, luring her back into sensual waters. Waters that lapped at her, bringing every nerve ending screaming back to life.

'It's about adventure.' His gaze dipped to her mouth. 'Thrill. Adrenaline.'

His lips caressed every word as they'd caressed her clit, and the phantom tingles there reminded her how good it had been.

Were they still talking about the charity?

If the hot billionaire and his business proposal had had her panting, this passionate philanthropist with his sleeves rolled up would suffocate her. How would it feel to be the focus of all that…*passion*?

He continued while her brain reeled, trying to untangle his words from her overactive imagination.

'Just because our clients are intellectually-disabled teens and young adults, it doesn't mean they don't want the same things from life that any other teen wants.' A shrug. 'That any of us wants.'

He leaned back in his seat and Libby's heart stuttered back to life.

His finger and thumb traced his bottom lip in that way of his—a sign of deep contemplation. 'Everyone deserves to experience that kind of...*rush*.'

She shivered, convinced he was referring to last night and her display. But he'd said nothing, done nothing even remotely inappropriate. It was *her* mind stuck in the gutter. *Her* mind choreographing a repeat performance of that rush he'd described so eloquently.

Alex steered her wayward thoughts back to business. 'Have you visited the UK before?'

Libby cleared her throat, pressing her thighs together. 'No. This is my first visit.' What was *wrong* with her? Last night should have cured her of this fervid need crawling beneath her skin.

He nodded. Stared. 'Let me show you what we have so far and where I'd like us to be in six months.'

His voice had snapped out of that low, confessional tone, was brisk and businesslike again. He flipped open the folder, forcing her attention away from him.

By the end of the morning he'd outlined his vision for the charity and, despite her best attempts at professionalism, Libby was as sexually frustrated as ever.

'Up?' Libby quizzed Alex.

His brief, decisive nod gave little away. When he'd suggested lunch she'd refused, preferring to work through and grab something later—alone—allowing herself some distance from his perplexing proximity. But he'd made a persuasive argument, stating that he'd missed breakfast, and her loud, rumbling stomach had chosen that precise moment to announce that she had too.

He nodded, those dark eyes cryptic, penetrating. All morning, he'd kept his hands to himself, never once touching her, as if he was maintaining a professional line and refusing to cross it. While *she'd* lusted and leered, ashamed of the lewd direction of her thoughts. Clearly he was more adept at separating business from pleasure. Or maybe, as far as he was concerned, they were through.

The slow simmer that gripped her every time she looked at him or thought about him drained away, leaving chills in its place.

After a beat, he said, 'Pinot Gris or Sauvignon Blanc?'

The elevator arrived, interrupting her answer, which was still forming from the scramble of her thoughts. He ushered her inside, his hand finally finding the small of her back—the first time he'd touched her since his mouth had left her last night. The zing of electricity was so strong she expected to find her panties singed.

All morning she'd battled to stay professional while craving his touch. As he'd waxed lyrical about the Able-Active team, their inspirational clients and the multitude of ideas he had to expand their scope nationally, she'd fought to drag her eyes away from his animated features, lit up with an enthusiasm that had left her envious. Envious of his colleagues, who probably saw this side of him daily. Envious of his beloved clients, who inspired such heartfelt passion. And envious of the women who'd experienced that intensity transformed into a different kind of focus— one she craved like the next lungful of oxygen.

What had he asked her? Wine...

She lifted her chin, determined to appear as unaffected as him. 'I prefer Pinot Gris, but I don't mind. I'll probably pass.'

The last thing she needed was to add alcohol to the heady mix of hormones and endorphins bubbling through her blood. Any further lowering of her inhibitions in Alex's presence and she'd start clawing at his clothes in public. How could he be so unruffled?

But was she imagining the tension that built inside the elevator? He stood so close she could almost feel the tickle of the dark hairs on his arm, and the clean, soapy scent of him wafted over her on a cloud of warmth.

The air thickened as the car ascended. Libby

locked her knees; scared she might sway towards him, throw herself into his arms or just simply press the emergency stop button and strip.

'I thought you said lunch? Is there a restaurant in this building?'

It looked just like a typical office block. Still, this was his city. She merely hoped they'd arrive at their floor soon, so she could put some more space between them. Or persuade him to fuck her in the restroom…

'I'm taking you to a restaurant I own. The Pinot Gris there is world-class.' His gaze dipped to her mouth, his tongue swiping his bottom lip.

Was he thinking about wine, or tasting her?

'You can allow yourself one glass, surely?'

His mouth curled. Was he daring her? He'd lost some of that morning's surliness, and his eyes danced with gold flecks. To say she'd missed relaxed, playful Alex would be an understatement. But she admired his ability to compartmentalise—a skill she normally shared.

The car juddered to a halt, its doors opening to another bland, deserted corridor.

Where was he taking her? Was she about to become a murder statistic?

Hysterical laughter threatened—a side effect of too much adrenaline.

At the end of the corridor Alex swiped a card through a lock and held the door open for Libby. The narrow concrete stairs were draughty, and the height from the windows spun her head and flipped her stomach into her throat, pushing the thought of wine and even lunch far from her mind.

Alex took her hand and pushed open a fire door, escorting her onto the roof.

Her feet stalled.

No rooftop restaurant with views of the Thames.

No murderer's lair.

Just a helicopter.

Gripping her waist, he ushered her frozen with shock form towards the sleek white death trap.

She dug her heels into the concrete, skidding them to a standstill. 'I'm not going in that.'

His brow dipped, puzzlement cloaking his amused eyes. 'Of course you are. It's only a thirty-minute ride.' He cocked a brow, his mouth twisted in challenge. 'You'll love it.'

In two strides he'd opened the door, was holding out his arm, enticing her inside a form of transportation she'd never experienced and never wanted to.

The wind whipped loosened strands of hair across her face, blinding her. Her stomach fell, settling somewhere behind her wobbling knees. The height of this building alone was enough to drain her adrenal glands. Just like at The Shard yesterday, being inside this skyscraper was enough of a trial for her, let alone standing on top of it with the elements determined to send her plummeting to the ground.

He strode back to her side, face contrite and eyes soft. 'Olivia. I'm sorry.'

He reached for her cold hand, his warm fingers clasping. She clung to the lifeline, some of her fear dissipating at his touch.

'I should have warned you instead of trying to surprise you.' His thumb rubbed the back of her hand.

Her fickle mind switched. Now she prayed for the release of a ground-swallowing demise. She hated anyone seeing this weak side of her, but especially Alex. Fearless, sophisticated Alex, who thought nothing of jumping into a helicopter for lunch at his favourite restaurant.

He was still talking, still cajoling. She forced herself to hear him over the ringing in her ears.

'It's very safe. Weather conditions are perfect. I have thousands of hours in the air and that Pinot really is worth it, I promise.'

Her belly flopped again. She glanced down at her stiletto-clad toes, almost expecting to see it there on the concrete. Decision time. Ride in a helicopter or get blown from the roof? Accept his challenge or admit defeat and concede the bargaining chip? It was a close one.

She willed her breathing into submission as her mind dithered. At least he'd dropped the cocky smirks of moments ago and the hard, inscrutable stares present all morning and seemed genuinely concerned.

As if he'd made the decision for her, he turned back towards the door to the stairway. 'Okay. I'm sorry. I was wrong. We'll go somewhere else for lunch.'

He slid his arm around her shoulders, as if guiding a child or an old lady safely across the road.

'No.' Her declaration surprised both of them. 'I'll go.'

What was she saying? She didn't need to impress him. She could admit she'd prefer not to put her life in the hands of a man she barely knew inside a chunk of flying metal. There'd be no shame in that. He didn't need to know why she had an aversion to death traps, or to anything she considered risky. It was an aversion founded in past experience—one that had changed her life for ever.

No. That labyrinth of sickening memories wasn't going to help her get off this roof with her dignity intact.

'You sure? There's no pressure.'

He pushed a stray wisp of hair behind her ear, his eyes tracing her features but his fingertips failing to make contact.

'We'll do whatever you want.' His voice was low, sincere, calming.

The echo of those words from last night reminded her of the power she held. It surged through her veins, dispelling fear, forcing steel into her skeleton and re-directing her thoughts from all things death-related.

Latching on to her attraction for him, she blurted out the thought that had occupied most of her mind since the minute she'd walked into his office that morning.

'I want you to kiss me.'

In an instant his face hardened, as if she'd slapped him. She swallowed, her cheeks hot. *Why* had she said that? If the deal was off, their sexual exploration over, she'd just set herself up for rejection.

Rejection and humiliation all in one morning— way to go, Libby.

Her gaze fell to his crotch, saw the bulge there expanding before her eyes.

No. He was still in this with her. The chemistry was still alive. She straightened her spine, the surge of power, of control, imbuing her limbs with courage.

'Kiss me and I'll go.'

Wow—pushy, much? But she was already so far out of her comfort zone she'd need a map to locate it again. She might as well get what she wanted from this situation.

He dropped his hands to his sides and made fists, his fingers flexing. Still trying to keep things professional? Acting the gentleman? Having second thoughts?

She took a half-step closer until his clean, soapy scent reached her, giving her a head rush that had nothing to with dizzying heights or stomach-dropping rides.

'Kiss me like you're telling me that you wanted to fuck me last night instead of leaving.'

Please—before she came to her senses and fled, or passed out.

His nostrils flared as he sucked in a harsh breath, focussed his intense stare on hers.

'I did.'

His voice, full of gravel, scraped her raw—as raw as the hunger she saw flare in his eyes.

'I did want to fuck you last night. You told me to watch.'

Yes. She'd got what she wanted—but the hollow victory had left her cold.

He closed the gap between them by another half step. 'I can't get the taste of you out of my mouth.' His gaze flicked down, scorching her from head to toe. 'The image of you lying there, your hand working between your legs…'

He dropped his head back, closing his eyes for a second before he pinned her with his penetrating stare once more.

'Believe me, I've wanted to kiss you all fucking morning.'

His admission knocked the air from her lungs, and a surge of triumph banished the last of her doubts.

'Why don't you then?' Barely a whisper.

His lips thinned, air gusting out of flared nostrils. 'Fucked if I know.'

They reached for each other, closing the distance with a lurch. He slammed his mouth over hers and she practically jumped up to meet him. His arms locked around her waist to catch her in mid-air. Her fingers delved into his hair as he pressed her close, their mouths opening and tongues sliding with ravenous need. The icy fear of moments ago trickled away, replaced by the sluggish thrill of euphoria. Her limbs liquefied, and the thud of her heart was loud enough to block out all her reservations.

Yes. This was what she'd craved since last night. The knowledge that she wasn't alone in her furious attraction to this man. He felt it too. Their searing connection. The all-consuming rush. The need to feed the fire with any available fuel.

They pulled back, breath gusting.

Alex gripped her face, his eyes darting between hers. 'You sure?'

She couldn't speak. His concern, his consideration in the wake of that kiss was too much.

She nodded. Another stomach flip—although she couldn't tell if it was fear this time or the heady knowledge that there'd be more of those kisses if she wanted them. More of *him*.

He slid his hands from her face, one capturing her hand. Warm, confident, his grip was firm and comforting. With a single resolute nod that filled her with belief in his piloting skills he turned them back towards the helicopter.

But for all her bravado and bravery, the clack of her heels on the concrete roof echoed.

A death march or the soundtrack to an adventure?

CHAPTER FIVE

'TOLD YOU IT was worth it.'

Alex eyed her over the rim of his wine glass. The early-evening sun glinted off her dark hair, revealing glowing streaks of gold. The same gold streaks that flashed in her eyes when she challenged him, berated him or when she was turned on.

How quickly he'd grown to crave those flashes—a sure sign that he'd got to her, whether to rile up her keen mind and razor-sharp wit or to witness the unapologetic hunger that mirrored his own. Despite the professional business attire and the way she tamed her hair, Olivia claimed her sexuality as she owned her forthright manner and articulate negotiation skills.

She put her glass to her lips and his eyes were mesmerised by their plump curves and the tiny flash of pink tongue.

She swallowed, shrugging one elegant shoulder. 'It's okay. I've had better. Californian wines are the best in the world.'

At least her acidic sense of humour had returned,

along with the colour in her cheeks. *Fuck*, what an idiot he'd been. He should have *asked* her, rather than assumed she'd be happy to fly. His bird was his favourite mode of transportation. And some primitive part of his brain had wanted to impress her with a flashy stunt. A dick move.

But he'd made good on his promise. The flight to his Oxfordshire boutique winery and restaurant had lasted only thirty minutes. She'd even managed to open her eyes for long enough to enjoy the views, and a begrudging, tight smile had hovered on her beautiful mouth.

As soon as they'd landed he'd ushered her to the Thames-side restaurant on his estate, where the glass of wine had been chilled and waiting for her on the best table in the house.

She placed her glass back on the table, her eyes scanning the three-Michelin-starred restaurant. Two or three other parties occupied tables in the conservatory, which was decorated with a sea of twinkling fairy lights that bounced shards of light off the silver dinnerware and the crisp snow-white table linen.

'So *this* is how you impress women?'

He laughed. She slayed him. The twitch of her mouth and the haughty tilt of her chin let him know that she was far from affected by him *or* his lifestyle. Her poise, her cutting wit, her acerbic tongue, her uncompromising cut-to-the-chase attitude—all of it made him want to put on airs and graces just to rile her up and see that flash in her eyes and the dismissive shake of her head. Why was sparring with her such a turn-on?

'I don't usually have to work so hard. And now I'm curious as to why you're so impervious.'

What would it take to impress her? A prize certainly worth having.

Her eyes hardened and he discreetly adjusted his ever-present erection.

'Is that what this is about? You show me your chopper and I fall at your grape-crushing feet? You'll have to pay better attention if you're expecting me to gush over your clever piloting skills.'

She opened the heavy embossed menu, lifting her nose and focussing her attention on the contents.

The flutter of her pulse at the base of her elegant neck gave her away and he shifted in his seat. *Fuck.* She turned him to steel—a pretty constant state and a bloody uncomfortable way to walk around. But he wasn't complaining. The throb reminded him of the deal they'd brokered, adding a fresh slug of adrenaline to course through his bloodstream.

Two of his favourite things. The heady thrill of a business negotiation and the buzz of exhilaration just before you jumped from the cliff's edge.

And the prize? Not only had this feisty, independent brunette agreed to lend her experience to his fledgling charity, she'd also instigated a game of control tag. A game that, as he saw it, he couldn't lose. A game that was still on, even though he'd disregarded her rules and gorged himself on her last night.

Not that he regretted that for one second. The memory of her taste was still potent enough to fog his mind.

His stomach growled. He was hungry for food, but even hungrier for her. That brief taste of her mouth on the roof of Lancaster Tower earlier had done little to quench his craving. He'd been hard since leaving her hotel room last night, his balls a heavy ache that he'd carried all day while she sat mere inches away, her scent tantalising, her luminous eyes seeing through him and her voice scraping over his nerve endings until he'd contemplated banging one out in his private bathroom like a randy teenager.

He'd forced himself not to touch her—determined to fight his attraction to her in case she called off the deal. He'd half expected her to bail, simply not to show up for their meeting. When she'd asked him to kiss her he'd thought he'd hallucinated. The urge to drag her into the helicopter, splay her over the leather seats and taste her again had been so powerful he'd had to bite the inside of his cheek until he'd tasted blood.

Watching her now, all elegant and poised, ignoring his attempts to wine and dine her and feigning absorption in the first-class menu, he wanted to scrap dinner and follow the commands from that dirty mouth of hers.

'I can recommend the filet mignon.' His lips twitched. 'The chef is a genius.'

He lounged back in his seat, enjoying the view of

the slight flush at the base of her throat. What would that skin taste like? Better than any filet mignon—he'd bet his beloved helicopter on that.

She sniffed, her eyes trained on the menu. 'I'm a vegetarian.'

Damn. It irked him that he knew so little about her, an inconvenience he planned to rectify as soon as possible.

Why wait?

'Tell me something about yourself. Something I couldn't know from reading your business profile.' He stretched his legs out under the table, searching for hers.

She stared. 'Why?'

Her fingers clenched around the base of her wine glass. His probing had clearly raised her hackles.

He sipped his wine, enjoying her rising colour. 'Because we're not animals, Olivia. Our sexual chemistry is intense, but that doesn't mean we can't talk in between fucking. *Your* word, by the way.'

She shrugged, the pulse at her neck fluttering again, her smile sweet. 'I just did. I don't eat meat.'

Touché. Bewitching. He pressed his lips together.

'Tell me something about *you*,' she said. 'Something none of the women you've impressed has ever asked you.'

That, right there, was what intrigued him so much. She was so unexpected, unpredictable. She didn't give a damn about impressing him in return. She wasn't interested in learning his preferences so she could mould herself into what she thought would be his perfect woman.

Fine. He could be blunt too.

'No one's ever asked me to watch them pleasure themselves before.'

A hint of pink touched her cheekbones, but her stare remained bold, direct, captivating.

'Poor you.' She glanced back at menu, as if they'd discussed the weather.

Alex bit back his delight as the waiter arrived to take their order.

When they were alone again, she said, 'Why am I here? I appreciate the world-class dining experience, but you asked me to do a job—not to drink wine and eat truffle-infused mushrooms.'

He fought a smile. She cut straight to the chase, and her caustic turn of phrase... Did she *know* how much she turned him on?

'I did. A job you accepted with one mutually satisfying condition.'

The colour in her cheeks heightened. 'A job I could do perfectly adequately from my hotel room or even from New York.' Her eyes hardened.

He ran his index and middle fingers along his lower lip, studying her until she shifted in her seat, revealing an alluring glimpse of pert breasts in the V of her blouse.

Last night he'd seen dark nipples through the lace of her bra. He wanted her naked, to taste those nipples, to nibble, scrape and suck until she squirmed and writhed and perhaps even came. Would she be that responsive? Instinct told him *yes*.

He hardened his own stare. 'I thought we'd established the parameters of our working relationship?'

A little reminder of their deal. After all, if she intended to torture him as she had last night he'd push her boundaries in return. *Quid pro quo.*

At her silent scrutiny, he continued. 'I want you to fully experience what I have in mind for Able-Active. As I said this morning, you can't do that in an office.'

She wasn't buying it—was still looking at him as if he'd sprouted a second head.

'You need to experience the thrill. If the kids can do it, *we* can, right? You said yourself that the Able-Active headquarters is completely uninspiring.'

And he wanted to get her out of those elegant suits in more ways than one.

'What exactly will it involve?'

Wary eyes, darker than midnight.

He shrugged. 'Mountain biking, boating, kayaking, abseiling. You name it.'

Her brow pinched. 'Why? I don't need to hurl myself from a climbing wall to understand the concept.'

He clenched his jaw, pinning her with his stare. 'You agreed to stay a week. I agreed to your terms. Are you backing out of our deal?'

Fuck, had he pushed too hard? Was this over before it had begun?

She flushed, her eyes dipping to the crystal glassware. 'No. But I won't be blindsided either. If you expect me to participate I'll need advance warning.'

'Why? Spontaneity is more rewarding.'

As last night had proved. He hadn't intended to declare his hand. But the results…

A head-shake. Decisive and unyielding. 'Maybe for you.' Her chin lifted as she glared him down. '*I* like to plan.'

'Control?' His cock stirred again, remembering the last time she'd taken the lead.

A staring contest ensued, and the space between them sparked with tension. He was half tempted to cancel the food they'd ordered, clear the restaurant and hope her next demand would be that he fuck her on this very table, with the one-thousand-thread-count tablecloth clutched in her elegant hands as she came around him.

As if she knew his filthy thoughts she traced said tablecloth with her index finger. 'Let's say I *do* don a cycle helmet or a lifejacket. Couldn't we do all that in London? Why here?'

He sobered, his lips turning in while he chose his next words. 'I live here.' He flicked his head in the direction of the main house he'd pointed out from the helicopter. 'When I'm not in the city.'

He glanced down to where he rubbed the edge of his thick linen napkin between his thumb and fore-finger, the hair rising at his nape as it always did when he was this close to his biggest vulnerability.

Well, she'd wanted to know something about him no one else did.

'I wanted you to see this place.' When he looked up, he had her full attention. 'I have bigger plans for the charity. Bigger than I outlined to you today.'

A small nod, encouraging him to continue.

'Eventually I'd like Able-Active to have an employment arm. The statistics on unemployment in the disabled population are depressing.'

He shifted in his chair, forcing his voice to remain even, although this topic of conversation usually led to gut-wrenching impotence.

'I'd like the winery here, the hotel, perhaps even Lancaster IT, to broaden its sphere. Improve on its equal opportunities policies, perhaps even become a world leader in reducing those unemployment statistics.'

It would be a start, at least.

Serious, with a small frown scrunching her forehead and her eyes thoughtful, she said, 'Why?'

Her neck flushed, as if her own candour had shocked her.

'Why what?'

She took another sip of wine, gave a small shrug. 'I get it. You want your company to have a social conscience.'

His jaw tensed. 'My company *does* have a social conscience.'

'Sorry. That sounded…flippant of me. What I mean is, why does it matter to you so much? I would have thought you're busy enough running Lancaster IT and the charity. What is it that motivates you?'

Wasn't *that* the question? And he understood her curiosity. He longed to peel back *her* layers, to expose her secret yearnings, her belief systems, her philosophies on life. Her reaction to flying had completely thrown him. What had made her so cautious?

'It should be important to all of us.'

At his non-answer, Libby nodded.

Then he completely stunned himself by adding, 'My sister had an intellectual disability.'

His gut twisted, stealing his appetite.

'I wish more people had cared about *her* potential, her future.' Himself especially.

What a time to open this particular can of worms. Why had he brought up his sister? He *never* spoke of Jenny. To *anyone*. Let alone someone he'd just met. What had prompted him to tell this intriguing virtual stranger his motivations? Especially when he barely picked over them himself for fear of what he'd expose.

But, even though their acquaintance was in its infancy, didn't some small part of him already feel closer to her than the hours they'd known each other warranted? She was easy to talk to. She cut through the bullshit. He didn't have to second-guess her every thought and unspoken subtext. And she wasn't constantly flattering him.

Perhaps it was just his dick doing all the thinking. Even so, the most serious of his ex-girlfriends knew nothing about Jenny. Well, nothing *he'd* spoken about. Gossip notwithstanding.

She gave a small nod, her eyes watchful. 'Had?'

It was common knowledge—his professional success and the prominence of his family name had exposed his entire life to public scrutiny. Of course the media had sensationalised the tragedy—the intellectually disabled teenaged daughter of a wealthy family dying from an epileptic seizure had been big news for all of thirty seconds. But they hadn't covered the devastating impact it had had on his parents' marriage, his mother's subsequent nervous breakdown or her intermittent dependence on alcohol.

'She died.'

He swallowed hard, his failure a bitter taste on the back of his tongue.

'I want to offer respite facilities for parents, so they can take a break, recharge, focus on themselves and their relationship. I'm building a purpose-built rural hotel here in the Oxfordshire countryside. Somewhere families can come, where the children can be occupied with the Able-Active programme while the parents get some well-deserved down-time. It's important. Something that gets overlooked.'

Something that could have helped *his* family, perhaps.

She was quiet for so long he was half tempted to fly her back to London, pay her for her time and release her from their deal before she pulled out.

She sipped water, her shrewd eyes flaying him alive.

'So what's on the adrenaline menu tomorrow?'

Thank fuck.

His breath stuttered back to life. 'I'll show you the site of the hotel.'

Her stare held his, bold, astute, daring. 'And…?'

If she kept looking at him like that he'd never make it through one mouthful, let alone a whole meal.

'I thought we'd go hot air ballooning.'

Her composure wobbled, her throat working on a swallow. 'Seriously?'

He nodded. *Quid pro quo, Olivia.* That stunt last night had cost him dearly in the self-denial stakes. Time to return the favour, make her step outside her comfort zone for a good cause, let down that tightly bound hair of hers until her eyes lit up from within.

Her controlled sigh gusted over parted lips, the tip of her tongue darting out. 'Well, that's going to cost you.'

Blood surged to his groin, his limbs twitchy with contained energy. What would that tongue look and feel like on his dick? What would he do to see it there?

'What do you want?' He spoke slowly, his words measured, voice low.

With almost Pavlovian predictability his body responded to the question he'd asked. A question he'd wanted to ask her all day. A question that sounded more like a dare.

For a second her eyelids drooped, her chest rising and falling with shallow breaths that lifted her alluring breasts. Then she composed herself, gave a sexy tilt to her head.

'Well, for starters I'd like a tour of your bedroom.'

He asked her again. 'What do you want, Olivia?'

He was pressed up behind her, his words husking out with his warm breath on the back of her neck.

She practically melted into a puddle on the plush carpet of his palatial master suite. She'd barely registered the opulence and modern elegance of his home as he'd led her here. Every ounce of her focus had been required to keep herself upright and seemingly in control of her own body.

His words—so intoxicating—wrapped themselves around her, a warm cradle. She fought the urge to succumb to them, to blurt out her every wish, every fear, her very soul to him. But she pulled back, forcing herself to stay in command of herself and the heady situation.

If she couldn't have what she wanted, she'd have what she needed right now. And that was Alex.

He'd agreed to play this game by her rules. The fine line of control and concession was a greased tightrope under her feet. But if he intended to push her out of her comfort zone with daredevil pursuits, she'd push back. Force his natural alpha tendencies into submission. See how far she could take him before he snapped.

She turned, and his warmth seared the tips of her breasts mere millimetres from his chest. 'I want you to watch me strip.'

He nodded, face grim, nostrils flared. Euphoria surged inside her, robbing her limbs of structure until she stepped backwards to the bed, pressing her legs against the mattress to keep herself upright.

Just like the night before, Alex stayed where she'd directed him. His limbs twitched as she worked the buttons loose on her blouse, his palms curled into white-knuckled fists.

Libby slid the silk from her shoulders. The slow glide was torturous on her sensitised skin, which prickled under his heated stare until every tiny hair stood on end. She unclasped her bra, releasing aching breasts, and tossed it on top of the blouse.

'*Fuck...*' Alex hissed, eyes almost black, staring blatantly.

Libby felt his gaze slide over her nipples as if he'd touched her with those slightly callused hands of his. Her knees buckled. She could almost *feel* his mouth on her breasts, his bold tongue laving and lashing. In denying him, she denied herself, but the reward would be worth the wait.

She unzipped her skirt with trembling fingers and hooked her thumbs into the waistband, pushing both it and her panties to the floor in one swoop. Every second she tortured him, she tortured herself. The need to see him naked, to touch him, clawed at her, stifling the breath in her lungs until her head buzzed with lack of oxygen.

He teetered towards her, rocking on the balls of his feet.

'Keep the shoes.' Gruff. A command.

Libby raised one brow, a twist to her mouth. 'Is that what you want?'

His command thrilled her. Hers to concede or deny. She'd love to see the excitement flare in his eyes as it had when she'd unclasped her bra. But this was *her* game. *Her* rules.

He nodded, his stare travelling the length of her naked body, stopping to linger on her breasts, the juncture of her thighs and the four-inch heels. When his eyes detoured to the scars on her left hip, she shifted her arm, hiding them from his view. She couldn't go there.

His chest rose and fell, his fingers clenching and unclenching at his sides, and Libby guessed she didn't have long to enjoy the power trip. But it was worth it. Any scrap of command she held over the scorching chemistry between them kept her grounded, reminding her that this was a game. No feelings allowed.

With a small smile she steadied herself on one of the simple posts of his contemporary four-poster bed and removed first one shoe and then another, her challenging glare pinning him to the spot.

The muscles of his jaw bunched as he lost the

battle to meet her eyes and flicked his gaze over her nakedness once more.

'What do you want?' His sexy voice held an almost desperate edge.

Libby exhaled. He was still with her. His reactions matching her own.

'I want you naked.'

She'd barely finished speaking before he'd heeled off his shoes and reached behind him to tug his T-shirt up and over his head. He tossed it away, his other hand tugging at the button fly of his jeans, and with rapid jerky movements pushed his jeans and tight cotton boxers down his muscular thighs, kicking them away.

Libby's mouth had forgotten how to make saliva. She'd been right. His body was a magnificent display of long lean muscles encased in golden skin and scattered with a liberal sprinkling of dark hair, and it stole her ability to think. Her eyes followed the dark scatter of hair covering his pecs, touched on the ink decorating one shoulder and one side of his ribs before dipping to the trail of black hair below his navel that merged with the thatch at the base of his spectacular manhood.

Her brain shut down completely. Alex Lancaster, a specimen of male perfection in his prime, was completely at her disposal.

Awareness returned, and the slight chill of the dimly lit room countered the fire raging inside her. Her nipples pebbled, and moisture gathered between her thighs, She pressed them together to ease the hollow ache inside.

He rolled on the balls of his feet, every muscle tense as if he was forcing himself to stay away from her, at the distance she'd set.

'What do you want?'

More desperation, mimicking the same thing firing along every nerve ending in her body.

'I...' *Him*. She wanted him. 'What do *you* want?'

His stare burned into hers. 'Everything.' His voice a low rumble. 'I want all of you.'

As if slapped, she sobered. His stark declaration brought her back to her senses. She couldn't give him that. She'd done that once. Loved. Planned. Built a future. And she'd lost it all.

The floor solidified under her feet and resolve returned. 'I want you to fuck me.' *That's all.*

In two long strides he reached her. His mouth crashed to hers, guided by her tug to the back of his neck, and she moaned, the relief so overwhelming that if he hadn't banded his arms around her waist, she'd have collapsed to the floor. Her fingers tunnelled through the silky strands of his hair and she parted her lips, welcoming the surge of his powerful tongue with one of her own. Her hands roamed, glorying in the smooth fragrance of skin stretched over hard planes of taut muscle, every inch of him a tactile feast for her fingertips.

He slotted one thick thigh between her legs, the spring of his chest hair grazing her nipples as he pressed closer. Libby rubbed her wet sex on his leg, the friction sublime, but not nearly enough. She tore her mouth from his, her head spinning with an oxygen-deprived head-rush.

'Now, Alex. *Now*.'

She reached between them, her hand circling his hard length, the satiny skin sliding over the steel beneath as she worked him from root to tip.

He stared, his chest working furiously, his mouth swollen and his eyes heavy-lidded.

She wanted him inside her. *Yesterday*.

With a grunt, he lifted her, depositing her in the centre of the bed and following her down. But rather than settling himself between her spread thighs, as she craved, he dipped his head to her breast, his mouth covering her nipple, sucking her inside the moist warmth.

Libby cried out, her flash of disappointment banished by sublime pleasure. Better than she'd imagined…the fantasy a poor relation to the reality. His cheeks hollowed as he drew more of her flesh inside, his tongue flicking the nub erect and then his teeth scraping with just a bite of pain—enough to shoot sensation to her core in a prelude to the spasms she hoped would soon follow.

As if he'd seen this arc of sensation he spread her thighs wider with his knees, his fingers finding her slick centre, homing in on her clit with pinpoint accuracy and the perfect amount of pressure.

She whimpered, her fingers frantic in his hair as

he abandoned one nipple in favour of the second. There was no reprieve from his relentless barrage. His tongue laved, his fingers swirled and plunged, and Libby forgot to breathe as coils of rapture wrapped around her from the inside out.

His dark lashes fluttered open, his stare finding hers as his mouth curled around her breast.

'Alex…' She was close, so close. She wanted him inside her, but she wouldn't make it.

He growled—a feral noise from the back of his cultured throat, as if encouraging her over the edge. Libby latched on to the dark swirls of his irises as his mouth and fingers continued to drag every drop of bliss from her strung-out body.

Her orgasm blindsided her, slamming her back into the mattress with a ragged cry. The spasms rocked her. Alex kept her thighs spread with his, his hand working furiously and his mouth relentless at her breast.

She shoved at him, the pleasure too intense. But he'd drained her of any strength she possessed and her hands flailed uselessly at his shoulders as he abandoned her clit but continued to suckle at her sensitive nipple.

'Stop…please.' She lay boneless, her head swimming.

He pulled back, releasing her from his wicked mouth and pursing his swollen lips to blow a stream of air over her wet, puckered nipple. He smiled. A predatory kind of smile. If she'd had any energy she'd have clawed back command of the situation. But she could only watch as he crawled over her, his lips grazing a path from her ribs across her belly and to the tops of her thighs.

He held her open, kissing first one thigh and then the other before staring at her sex with uninhibited candour and blowing cool air over her wet lips.

'Alex…' He'd completely disarmed her. And he still hadn't given her what she'd asked for. This was *her* game. *Her* rules.

With a lazy smile he kissed one thigh again and then climbed from the bed. His muscular ass flexed as he strode to the nightstand. Amazed that she had any hormones left, Libby licked her lips. The clench of his buttocks and the jut of his thick, proud cock was enough to create an impressive second wind.

What was happening to her? She should leave. Show him she was still in control here. But she craved him inside her as much as she enjoyed her power over their liaison. Shoving away doubts, and the sting of memories, she focussed on him, compelling her breathing into a deep, regular pattern.

He returned to the bedside, his bold gaze on her as he tore open a condom packet with his teeth and rolled the latex down his length with practised, single-handed skill.

'Come here.'

He held out his hand and Libby moved to the edge of the bed before him. He pushed her back until she rested on her elbows and then leaned over her, cupping her face in both hands and kissing her with a passion that stole her sanity and sent fresh spasms through her pelvis. Pulling back, he splayed his large hands on her thighs, slowly easing her open, his gaze darting between her face and her exposed sex.

The way he looked at her... As if he was seconds away from devouring her whole. And that was exactly how she felt. *Consumed.* His stare alone took her there.

'I'm going to fuck you now. That's what you want?'

She nodded, her blood boiling, any snarky retort lost behind her paralysed tongue. If she'd thought businessman, philanthropic, surfer dude Alex was hot, this determined, focussed man scorched the flesh from her bones.

He leaned over her, jaw rigid, and locked his arms either side of her head. Libby lay back, shifting her hips to the edge of the bed. He looked down between their bodies, his bottom lip caught between his teeth. With one hand he gripped the base of his magnificent cock and angled the tip at her entrance. Slowly his gaze locked with hers, and with the scent of sex wafting up between them, carried on a wave of body heat, he pushed inside her.

'Alex—'

His mouth stole her words, his kiss searing as he stretched her, working his way in to the hilt. She whimpered, her nails raking his flanks and her calves pressed to his glorious backside, encouraging him all the way in.

Pulling back from the kiss, he removed her hands from his back, one by one, and his fingers slotted between hers as he pressed their joined hands into the mattress beside her head. Staring down at her, he began to move. Slowly at first, letting her body grow accustomed to him. But then he clenched his jaw and picked up the pace.

Libby closed her eyes—and then slammed them open again, unwilling to miss one second of seeing him stretched above her, his face contorted with pleasure and beads of sweat gathering at his hairline. This time he'd come. She'd *make* him come.

With every pummelling stroke he shunted her on the bed, the edge of the mattress providing a landing place for the force of his thrusts.

'Libby…' His eyes widened, nostrils flaring.

'What do you want?' she asked.

She saw the battle in him, and knew she'd give him anything in that moment. Just for the thrill of witnessing his loss of control. The knowledge that *she* took him there.

He released her hands. 'Touch your nipples.'

Another command. But she complied, too delirious to care about power play. Her fingers plucked at her breasts, twisting and rolling. Alex watched, his jaw hardening, and a strangled groan rumbled up from his chest.

His hips jerked in a relentless pounding that

pushed her closer and closer. When he reached one hand down between them, pressed his thumb down on her clit, she exploded, every muscle in her body rigid as her internal muscles clung to his pistoning cock.

Alex roared, his head thrown back, neck taut, his hips slamming home one last time.

'Fuck… Libby…'

He ground against her as his breathing slowed, forcing the last ripples of pleasure from her core.

After long, delirious seconds, he dropped a chaste kiss on her mouth.

Reality surged.

Libby winced as he gripped the base of the condom and withdrew, the slide of him over sensitised tissue bordering on pain. Allowing herself one last indulgence, she watched him saunter to the en-suite bathroom, his gait a little unsteady.

Despite the tremors and aftershocks jarring her body, Libby flew from the bed, donning her skirt and blouse and stuffing her damp underwear into her bag. She'd never undone her hair, but it had suffered nonetheless. Tucking the wayward strands back into their braid as best she could, she slipped on her jacket just as a still gloriously naked Alex re-entered the room.

He stalled. 'You're leaving?' His sexy, just-fucked features hardened.

'Yes.' Shoulders back, as if she was convincing herself.

He raked at his dishevelled hair. 'And if I wanted you to stay?'

She swallowed, lifting her chin.

She couldn't stay. She'd wanted a fuck. She'd got what she wanted. It had to be enough.

He understood. His jaw bunched and he looked away with a small nod.

Without another word he tugged on his discarded clothes. The atmosphere in the room that still smelled of the intimacies they'd shared chilled Libby to the bone.

Alex grabbed his keys from the dresser, turning to lance her with his black stare. 'Will you at least stay in my hotel?'

He shoved his free hand in his front pocket.

Her face burned as if craving the slide of his warm palm. She missed the warmth in his amber eyes. Missed his smile.

Libby nodded. She couldn't expect him to fly her back to London—not if they had to return here in the morning to put their lives at the mercy of a wicker basket and a giant nylon balloon.

'I'll drive you over.'

'I can live with that.'

CHAPTER SIX

ALEX RAPPED ON the door of one of the hotel's standard rooms, biting back his frustration. He'd instructed the duty manager to give Olivia the best suite—an elegant penthouse with spectacular rural views of Oxfordshire's rolling countryside—but clearly she'd undermined him.

He'd never met such a stubborn, independent woman. The women in his past had been happy to accept his wealth, take his gifts and his generosity, share his affluent lifestyle.

The door opened and his annoyance evaporated. The sight of her sucker-punched him in his gut. She'd pulled her hair into a high ponytail—he'd yet to see her long hair down, wild around her face—and she wore jeans and a long-sleeved shirt. He'd had her belongings delivered to the hotel from London last night, after she'd begrudgingly accepted his offer of accommodation.

Hadn't that been a kick in the balls? He'd wanted her in his bed. He'd fantasised about releasing her hair from its strict braid, waking to find the glossy mass splayed over his pillow or, better, his chest. He'd hoped to spend the night, or this morning, or both, between her shapely thighs, dragging reckless abandon from her with every orgasm. But she'd denied him again, drawing him back to the bargain they'd struck.

It was still dark outside. In the dim glow of her darkened room behind her, he saw her laptop open on the bed. Had she been working? Speaking to someone in America? Booking a flight home?

'Ready to go?'

He clenched his jaw, teeth creaking. He knew nothing personal about her outside of the fact that she was a vegetarian and hated helicopters. Nothing he hadn't gleaned from her company website and her business profile.

Time to change that.

She nodded, her hair swaying. His palms itched to wind that hair round his hand and draw her close for a good morning kiss. The one he'd have given her if she'd awoken in his bed this morning. The one she'd cheated him out of.

He forced his hands to relax.

She glanced down at his side. He held out the puffer jacket embroidered with the Able-Active logo.

'A gift. It gets pretty cold up there.' He pointed skywards.

She blinked, face stony and a little pale, eyeing the jacket as if it was stuffed with snakes, not duck down.

'Thank you. But gifts aren't necessary.'

So prim this morning. Unlike last night, when she'd twisted his hair so hard she'd almost scalped him.

'No?' *Fuck*, it wasn't as if he'd handed her diamonds, or even flowers. 'But here it is anyway.'

It was just a jacket. He doubted she'd packed any serious outdoor gear for a business trip.

'Is there a problem outside of the gift?'

Perhaps she was as cranky at waking alone as he was. Perhaps, like him, she'd woken fully aroused and feeling around the empty bed, the rush of erotic memories making her groan into her pillow. Perhaps he should abandon the hot air balloon trip, suggest they relocate to the palatial suite he'd reserved for her upstairs and christen every surface until he'd made her come so many times she wouldn't be able to help the smile on her face.

She shrugged her bag onto her shoulder and closed the door behind her, reaching for the jacket. 'I'll borrow the jacket—but only because I didn't plan on any wild adventures when I packed.'

Fuck, that smoky voice of hers reverberated through him—another slug of lust. She marched ahead down the corridor, in an excellent move that gave him full access to the view of her denim-clad curves swaying as she walked.

When they were sitting in his Mercedes S-Class side by side, as he navigated the lanes of the Oxfordshire countryside, he glanced over at her striking profile.

'Nervous?'

She stared out of the window, as if formulating her answer, then sighed. 'Yes.'

Her hand rested in her lap. He gripped the wheel to stop himself reaching for it, uncertain of her mood.

'I've been before. You'll love it. And it's perfectly safe.'

She turned on him, eyes blazing. '*Is* it? How do you know that?'

She really was nervous. Perhaps he should have fed her first. Or organised a punt on the river. But he'd wanted to wow her—give her a trip she'd never forget, one she'd embrace when she planned his charity's marketing. But impressing her, it seemed, was no easy feat. And Able-Active wasn't named Able-Relaxing.

'I'd never let you get hurt, if that's what you're worried about.'

She looked away, her pouty lips pursed. 'You can't guarantee that. People get hurt all the time.'

His need to know more about her personally solidified.

'Have *you* been hurt?'

He recalled the irregular silvery scars he'd spotted on her hip last night. Scars she'd tried to hide. He'd interpreted her reaction to the helicopter as first-time nerves. Assumed her caution was just a personality trait not in keeping with the driven and professional businesswoman. But perhaps there was more to her reticence.

'I—I was in a motorbike accident. Three years ago.'

Her gaze returned to the hedgerows and the fields of gold and green beyond, which reflected the first rays of the sunrise lighting the horizon.

His throat thickened. 'I'm sorry about that.'

He should have asked about the scars, but it had been obvious she didn't want to talk about them, didn't want to talk at all, and he'd been overcome with the sight of her naked and her husky command that he fuck her.

'Were you badly hurt?' His ribs pinched, stalling his breath.

She shook her head, shoulders sagging a little. 'Just some superficial cuts and grazes. I was lucky.'

He breathed again, more determined than ever to get to know her while showing her a good time. But perhaps he shouldn't push this. If she'd had a traumatic experience in the past, the last thing he wanted was to force her to relive it.

He pulled off the road, steering the car down a bumpy lane that opened up to a gravel courtyard and some converted stables. Killing the engine, he turned to face her.

'We're here. Look, we don't have to do this. We can get a feel for things, watch a few balloons go up, meet the owner. He's a friend of mine. If you're worried, we don't have to fly. I don't want to make you uncomfortable.'

But I'd love to put a grin of exhilaration on your beautiful face.

Her dark eyes held him hostage. 'I want to do it.' She looked down to her clasped hands in her lap. 'I… I just…'

Vulnerability poured from her in waves. He ached to hold her. To kiss the frown lines from between her brows. To abandon his plans for the week and hole up with her in his Oxfordshire estate, wining and dining her, peeling back her layers, exploring every facet of her fascinating personality.

He held out his hand, palm up, over the centre console between them.

She glanced down and then back up at him, throat moving on a swallow. Slowly, as if she thought his palm might be electrified, she placed her hand in his.

His chest expanded, a surge of oxygen energising him as it always did when he brokered a difficult business deal.

'Let's just have a look around. If you want to go up, we can. If you don't, we'll just watch a few balloons take off and then go and meet Jack early.'

She scrunched her brow. 'Jack?'

'My cousin. He's an architect and property developer. He's visiting the hotel building site I want to show you today.'

She nodded, clearly reaching a decision. 'No. I want to go up.'

He grinned. She was so determined. So possessed. Completely hardcore. However much she downplayed her accident, it must have shaken her up. It would shake anyone. And yet she was still willing to buy into his grandiose scheme to show her a good time and his vision for his outdoor adventure charity.

He squeezed her fingers. 'Let's *do* this.'

'It's amazing!' She clung to him.

He wanted to keep her prisoner in this basket for ever. Her arm was snaked around his waist, her hand under his jacket forcing a fist into his chest to massage his heart until the blood sang through his arteries.

He positioned his body behind her, his arms either side of her, holding the lip of the basket in front of them, his chin on her shoulder, seeing what she saw.

'Having fun?'

Her hair tickled his cheek and he pressed a kiss to the soft skin of her neck. *Fuck*, when she bestowed that rare and beatific smile on him, he felt like a king.

She laughed—a throaty sound that shot straight to his balls.

'I wouldn't go *that* far.'

Her heart pounded so hard and fast, he could feel it thrum through his chest where he was pressed against her back.

'I can't believe how beautiful it is up here.' She rested her head back against his shoulder, a small shudder leaving her.

If he'd orchestrated a huge romantic gesture, he couldn't have anticipated a more perfect reaction from her. She softened against him, her body heavy, pressing back, covering him from thigh to shoulder. Every time the burner fired and the balloon lurched gracefully higher she laughed, or caught her breath and pressed closer—as if she trusted him over the sturdy basket and the balloon's skilled operator.

The only way to improve on this morning would have been for them to have woken side by side, slaking his need to constantly taste her, feel her, be inside her.

What the actual fuck was *happening* to him? He barely knew her, but already he wanted more of her.

'Tell me something…' His lips traced her earlobe, catching the small gold earring dangling there. Would she play the game they'd started over dinner last night? Would her personal admissions soften like her body?

She sighed—a soft escape of air. 'I'm a trained yoga instructor, although I haven't taught for many years.'

He groaned, his imagination running wild. 'Fuck, could you *be* any hotter? I don't suppose there's any chance of a naked demonstration of the Downward-facing Dog?'

'Pervert!'

Her chuckle warmed his blood, lifting him higher than the balloon could ever carry him.

'You tell *me* something.'

Her words echoed his and he grinned. She relaxed deeper into his chest. Her delicious scent tickled his nose.

He took a deep breath. 'I was a game developer in my teens. A real bona fide computer nerd.'

And he'd had the dodgy haircut to prove it—a detail she *didn't* need to know.

'I guessed. The T-shirt yesterday kinda gave you away.'

He loved it that she was so observant—that she *saw* him.

They watched the horizon in strangely comfortable silence, with only the birds for company. He'd just pointed out the spires of Oxford in the distance when his phone vibrated in his pocket.

His stomach dropped. He'd given Molly strict instructions to forward all calls but one to Jeremy in his absence. That meant he couldn't ignore this call—no matter how rude it seemed to answer, or how badly timed.

He stepped back enough to fish the device from his pocket, keeping one arm banded around Libby's waist.

'Mother.'

A pause. Acid surged into the back of his throat.

'Zander? Is that you?'

Hairs prickled on his neck. He knew that wobble in her voice. Dreaded it. Eight in the morning and she'd likely drunk so much she couldn't remember who she was calling. Or she'd suffered one of her 'spells', during which she could barely function, shutting herself away for days on end.

'Where's Clive?'

His mother's second husband protected Alex from the worst of his mother's issues—something he was grateful for and felt guilty about in equal measure.

'Golf. I just wanted to say I'll see you Saturday, at the wedding…' Her voice trailed off but the line stayed connected.

Fuck.

'Mother? Maman?'

He'd have to go to her. What if she'd drunk herself into a coma? What if she'd taken something?

Firing a text to Clive, he swore under his breath.

Releasing Libby, he turned and spoke to the pilot.

'Is something wrong?'

Libby touched his arm, dragging him back to the present, away from a past that refused to lessen its hold on him no matter what he did.

'I need to visit my mother. She's…unwell.'

Still grieving for Jenny, all these years later. Reminding them of their loss with her bouts of depression and her periods of drinking too much. Fanning the flames of his guilt for his own shortcomings.

He could have been a better brother. A better son. It might not have saved Jenny—he wasn't to blame for her death after all—but it might have made all their lives a little easier. Salvaged his parents' marriage. Made Jenny's short life happier.

The balloon began its descent, taking the atmosphere with it. Libby paled, as if her own fears, her own demons, had resurfaced with his ill-timed family interruption.

'It's not serious.' He gripped her cold fingers. 'I just need to make sure she's okay, wait with her until her husband gets home.'

Or organise another stay at the rehab facility where his mother practically had her own room, she'd been there so many times.

Libby nodded, her fingers squeezing his in a display of affection that seemed to shock them both. He gripped them, reluctant to let go of the tenuous trust they'd established.

'I'll arrange a car to take you back to the hotel.'

He'd have to cancel seeing Jack, and Libby's tour of his state-of-the-art respite complex.

His spirits plummeted to the ground with the soft landing of the balloon, his thoughts traversing well-worn pathways of self-doubt. Would he *ever* be good enough to compensate for Jenny's death?

Libby pulled the black velvet ring box from her purse and wrapped her fingers around it, enjoying the familiar comfort of it filling her palm. She still carried it everywhere, even after three years. She didn't need to open the lid. The contents—an exquisite princess-cut diamond solitaire—were a symbol of her life before the motorbike accident that had killed her fiancé a week before their wedding.

The ring itself, whilst precious, represented a happier time of her life. A carefree time when she'd believed anything was possible and life with Callum had stretched before her in an adventure akin to those

Alex planned for his clients. The adventures he insisted on showing her.

Libby placed the box back inside her bag without opening it. Normally she stared at the ring's beauty as if it were a talisman to ward off the image of Callum dying in her arms on the hard, unforgiving asphalt. When she thought of him, the ring helped her to remember him alive and vibrant, with excitement lighting his eyes as he'd proposed. But today her handsome fiancé's face was a little harder to recall, his image blurry, as if photographed out of focus.

She pulled out her phone, firing a text to Alex. She barely knew him outside the physical intimacies they'd shared and their brief working relationship. But the defeated slump to his shoulders as he'd walked away earlier had stirred something in her. Feelings she'd thought long-ago abolished. Dangerous feelings that teetered too close to the edge of caring.

Hope your mother is okay. Thanks for the ride today. I can see why Able-Active clients will love it.

She opened her laptop, picking up on the work she'd begun last night and continued that morning when sleep had had no use for her.

On the surface, the marketing strategy for Able-Active presented little challenge for Libby. Secure corporate sponsorship, launch a national campaign to publicise the charity to a clearly targeted audience and streamline the charity's website and social media presence with an online sign-up form.

But Alex's passion for the work had spilled over, infecting her. It meant so much to him on a personal level. She wanted to do the best job she could. Make it the success he hoped for.

Her phone buzzed. Alex.

Thank you. She's fine. I'm sorry I had to rush out on you.

His answer left her strangely hollow. The ache that had begun when he'd been buried deep inside her last night intensified. The game of getting-to-know-you they'd started was frustratingly incomplete. Game-playing with Alex fed something in her she hadn't known was starving.

Her fingers hovered above the screen of her phone, desire and denial warring for control.

What do you want?

She was playing with fire. But the flames flushed her body with energy. *Irresistible.* Her days here were limited. How much harm could one week do? And she could be called home at any second, their time together cut short, if Sonya's baby decided to put in an early appearance.

He took several minutes before his reply, as if the answer wouldn't come. Minutes in which Libby was certain she'd lost him. That he no longer wanted to play.

I don't want to see you. I don't want to undo your hair and wrap it around my hand. I don't want to make you come. What do you want?

His reply brought a smile to her lips. He'd fully embraced the rules, turning them against her. Clever man.

With trembling fingers and clenched thighs, Libby fired a response that had her breathing fast.

I want you to stay away.

She dropped the phone and rushed to the en-suite bathroom. She had no idea where he was or how long it would take him to get here. But she knew he'd come.

She took a quick shower, taking extra care to fasten her hair securely into a severe French pleat, no strand left free. It seemed he had a penchant for her hair. His hints and requests were glimpses into his desire to see it wild and free, which only intensified her need to push him until he couldn't help but undo her hard work.

She slipped on fresh underwear and her favourite comfortable jeans and sweater. She'd barely had time to slick some gloss onto her lips and wave a mascara wand over her lashes before there was a knock at the door.

He'd aged. Wearing the same charcoal-grey T-shirt and jeans he'd worn that morning, he slouched in her doorway, one muscular arm braced on the doorframe. His intense stare was hooded, his mouth tight, and whilst his hunger electrified the air that separated them, something was different. *He* was different.

She opened the door wider, inviting him in and battling the urge to hold him until the lines around his eyes disappeared. But she couldn't step that close to the edge. This was all she could offer…all she could accept. This game—short-lived, finite and slaking only a mutual physical need.

The door closed behind him and he followed her into the room.

She turned, begging him with her eyes not to break the spell, not to break the rules. 'What do you want?' she said, her voice a whisper.

He stared. Endless seconds in which she felt stripped bare by the intensity in his haunted eyes.

'I want to be buried inside you.'

Stark, honest, hard to deny. But deny she must. For her own sanity.

Without comment, or even acknowledgment, she stripped out of her sweater and jeans, careful not to disrupt her hair. His eyes widened at the lacy underwear she'd donned, but he stood stock-still, waiting and watching.

She approached him as a cat might approach a dog: with slinking bravado, narrowed eyes and muscles coiled tight, ready to flee if he decided to show off his superior strength.

When she was inches away she sank down, catching him by surprise. Her knees hit the carpet at his feet. She unclasped his belt buckle and made quick work of the button fly of his jeans. When she lifted her eyes to his smouldering stare she caught her breath. How had she ever thought she could control this vibrant, fearless, worldly man?

Every muscle in his body seemed to strain, and raw power poured from his dark eyes and clenched jaw. His biceps bulged at the sleeves of his T-shirt as he fisted his hands at his sides.

Uncertain how much time she'd have, she tugged the jeans and underwear down over his hips, her mouth watering at the sight and scent of him.

Leaning forward, she touched her tongue to his steely tip.

'Wait.'

Her gaze flicked up. Would he stop her? Had she imagined the excitement flashing in his dark eyes? Perhaps his brooding mood had left him reluctant to play her game. Obey her rules.

Slowly his hands cradled her face, fingers burrowing into her hair. She pressed her lips together as one by one he tugged the hairgrips free, until her hair spilled down her bare back. He stroked it back from her face, gentle hands fingering the strands with a reverence that made her itch.

Libby looked away. She didn't want to see tenderness on his face. Didn't want to explore his strange mood or the reasons for it. She just wanted *him*. In her mouth, at her mercy, under her control.

She gripped his erection, angling him towards her mouth, and closed her lips around him. He groaned, his teeth snagging his bottom lip. His thighs were steel under her palms and he shifted restlessly on the balls of his feet, his chest rising and falling in rapid pants.

Boldly staring up at him, she took him to the back of her throat, her tongue pressed hard against him to hit all his pleasure points…the ones that made his eyes roll back and his hands fist in her hair. But his stare quickly returned to the action, darting between her eyes and her working mouth while harsh grunts jerked from his panting chest.

'Libby…'

When he tried to back away Libby clung tighter, increasing the suction, her head bobbing with renewed determination. Power surged inside her, flooding her sex with moisture. This big, strong man—intelligent, driven, compassionate—was trembling, frantic, on the verge of shattering. And, although he was legendary for his thrill-seeking and audacious business deals, he'd handed her control like a precious gift. A gift she needed.

With a shout he came, his hands buried in her hair, holding her face as she sucked and swallowed until he was spent and breathless, a wondrous expression softening the hard planes of his face, which seconds before had been twisted in rapture.

She released him from her mouth and he hauled her to her feet, engulfing her in his strong arms and then gripping her face to kiss her with heat.

He pulled back, leaving Libby's head spinning.

'Never go back to America.'

Not bothering to wait for her response, he kissed her again, looped his arms around her waist and flopped them down onto the nearby mattress.

CHAPTER SEVEN

LIBBY'S HEAD ROSE and sank with the movement of Alex's chest as his breaths slowed. His warm fingers traced small circles on her back, his legs entwined with hers, and his heartbeat thumped under her cheek, which was glued to his sweat-damp skin.

It was way too intimate, but her heavy limbs refused to move—as if they'd run a marathon and gone on strike. And in a way they had. This week was a whirlwind of life in the fast lane so far.

'I'm sorry I had to leave so suddenly today.'

His sleepy voice rumbled in his broad chest, his chest hairs tickling her nose.

'I understand. Is your mother okay?'

He drew in a breath that seemed unending, the gust of his prolonged exhalation blowing strands of her now wild hair onto her face. His fingers swooped in, pushing the hair back from her forehead and rectifying the situation.

'She drinks sometimes. Too much. She's never really got over losing Jenny.'

The weight of his confession pressed Libby even

further into the mattress and her breath stalled. Should she pry? He wouldn't have mentioned it if he didn't want to talk, right?

'What happened to your sister?' She held her breath.

His fingers returned to the small of her back, their tips gliding round and round in a hypnotic pattern. 'She had epilepsy.'

Libby waited, still and quiet, so as not to break the confessional spell.

'Around six hundred people per year die of sudden unexpected death in epilepsy. It's called SUDEP for short.' His fingers on her back stilled. 'She was eighteen.'

His matter of fact tone contrasted with the increase in his breathing and the renewed thud of his heart.

'I'm sorry that happened to your family. It must have been a terrible time.'

'For my parents, yes. It essentially destroyed their marriage. The blame game. The what ifs. Although theirs had been a rocky marriage for years prior to my sister's death.'

His hand resumed its stroking.

'Do you like weddings?'

The change of subject was so abrupt Libby lifted her head to stare at him, her neck muscles jarring. What could she say? He'd opened up to her this evening—not that it was part of their deal—but she wasn't ready to do the same. What was the point?

This was temporary. A holiday away from reality. Less than a fling—a business merger, brokered and negotiated. Just sex.

She trained her features to stay neutral, swallowing back the acid in her throat. 'Who doesn't?'

She shifted, untangling herself from his warmth and his long, muscular limbs. She sat on the bed with her back to him, reaching for a robe and shrugging it on. A shield.

'Do you want to go to one? My cousin Isabel is marrying in France this weekend. We should have met her brother, Jack, today. The architect I told you about.'

Libby swallowed. That itchy, impatient feeling was back, making her restless. 'You can't invite a stranger to a family wedding.'

'Why not?'

His fingers continued to work their magic, circling lazily on the curve of her hip. Even through the cotton his touch carried a potency that made her weak.

'You'd be my plus one. Jack and Isabel's grandfather owns a château near Nice. Ever been to the south of France?'

'No. But that's not the point.'

His hand slipped under the robe, locating the lace of her panties at her hip. The glide of his fingertips distracted her racing mind.

'Is it that you don't like my chopper?'

Her lips twitched. The sight of him, relaxed, playful, a self-satisfied grin on his decadent mouth as he sprawled naked on her bed, soaked the panties he was now burrowing inside.

She needed to change the subject. *Fast*.

She forced her features into a stern glare. 'What's on the adrenaline agenda for tomorrow?'

His grin widened, as if he sensed her diversion tactics. 'Jet boating. On the Thames. I need to be back in London.'

His probing fingertips traced the crease of her groin, his knuckles brushing the crotch of her panties.

She rolled her eyes, biting her lip to contain the swell of excitement.

'I have plenty of work to catch up on too. My latest client is super-demanding.'

Why didn't she just push his hand away? Kick him out of her hotel room?

'He is?'

He pressed down on her clit through the damp fabric, stilling her breath. His voice dropped an octave. Was that a hum of satisfaction? At finding her wet?

'I thought he was super-accommodating.'

Her gaze flicked down his ripped chest and abdomen to the thickening cock on his thigh.

'If you want to scrap the thrill-seeking we could *both* get some work done.'

Cool speech had become increasingly difficult, and the words emerged slow and sluggish.

He grinned, one fingertip circling. 'But the adrenaline is the best part. And what about our deal?'

Libby spread her thighs a fraction. She needed more. Wanted more. Mention of the deal had returned her equilibrium. No more talk of weddings.

He sprang up from his slouch, gripping her waist and expertly tumbling her under him. Air slammed from her. His face, an inch above hers, had lost its playfulness.

'Come jet boating tomorrow.'

His thighs slotted between her legs, spreading her open. His teeth caught his bottom lip and he pressed his erection to the damp lace separating them.

Her robe had fallen open. His fingers curved under her bra straps, tugging them over her shoulders as his mouth trailed kisses over the tops of her breasts.

His argument was persuasive. She breathed out an, 'Okay...'

He tugged one bra cup lower, exposing a nipple to his voracious mouth, and then he lifted his head, eyes wicked. 'Good. Because I was about to ask you what you want.'

Although his wandering mouth made speech difficult, she told him—and he complied.

Something tickled Libby's shoulder, her thigh, the back of her neck... Groggy, she stirred aching limbs.

Warm, minty breath brushed her earlobe.

'Wake up, beautiful. It's time to fly.'

Alex.

She cracked open one eye to find her hotel room in darkness. 'Time is it?' She flipped onto her back to see him dressed, his hair damp, presumably from the shower.

'Early. My chopper awaits.'

He pressed a chaste kiss to her mouth, his lips soft and languorous. Despite his chiding, his eyes were playful.

She groaned, her arms looping around his neck and pulling him down. 'Come back to bed.'

He chuckled into her neck. 'I'd love to. But adventure calls.'

His hand slipped under the covers again, fingers sliding up her thigh and zeroing in on her clit so her eyes popped open and she squeezed her thighs together, trapping his hand.

'Thanks for not kicking me out, by the way.'

His lips brushed her ear, her neck, and the sexy rumble of his voice thrummed through her nipples in time with his exploring fingertips.

'My creeping-around-like-a-teenager days are over. Skulking out of my own hotel at three in the morning would have been highly embarrassing.'

She sobered.

She *should* have kicked him out. Shouldn't have invited him back to bed. Snuggling, sleeping together, waking up to his mouth on her—*not* part of the deal.

Batting away his hand, she shot out of bed. 'Do I have time for a shower?'

She ignored his slightly bewildered expression, which heated as it travelled over her naked form. 'Yes. But if you don't want company in there I suggest you hurry. I had hoped to wake you up with my mouth between your legs, but I took pity on you. You were out of it.'

Libby swallowed. Both images—her drooling in her sleep and him waking her with his spectacular oral skills—sent her heart fluttering behind her ribs.

She dived into the bathroom, flicking on the shower and jumping in before he could make good on his word or before she relented and surrendered.

She almost jumped through the glass cubicle when he said, 'So, about this wedding...'

He lounged in the doorway, and Libby was grateful for the frosted glass.

'Do you mind? Some privacy, please.' She poured shampoo into her hair, glaring at his smirking face.

His gaze took one last, lazy tour. 'I've touched most of your body with my tongue, inside and out, and now you want *privacy*?'

'Yes.'

Infuriating man. Bathroom-sharing was definitely *not* part of their relationship.

He shrugged and moved just behind the door, so he could no longer see her but she could still see his reflection in the bathroom mirror.

He raised his voice over the sound of the spray.

'I don't usually have to beg for dates. You're crushing my ego.'

Now he'd mentioned the 'D' word she definitely couldn't go. Even though she'd never been to France. It was on her wish list. Not that she took holidays any more.

'Go away.'

He laughed. 'Aside from the journey there, I promise no daredevil stuff.'

'Weddings are for families.'

Damn, she'd already used that argument.

'I told my mother about you and she thinks you should come too.'

Shampoo ran into her eyes and she winced. 'You told your *mother* about me?'

'Yes.'

'Why?' Without the non-verbal cues, it was difficult to know what he was thinking.

'She needed cheering up. Her second husband is American. She'd *love* to meet you.'

Libby stepped from the shower, shutting off the water and wrapping herself in a fluffy, white towel.

'I'll think about it.'

Her heart wasn't in this argument. She blamed the remnants of jet lag and last night's lack of sleep. But she had no intention of going to his cousin's wedding or meeting his family.

She fastened the towel around her chest and stuck her head through the doorway.

'Aren't you too tired to fly?'

There was no way she'd get in that contraption again if he felt under par.

His gaze gave her the once over. 'Nope. I'm good.'

'Because, strictly speaking, a helicopter ride and jet boating counts as *two* activities.'

He stepped closer, eyes predatory. 'Will it cost me?' His hands found her hips, fingers clenching in the thick towel that scraped her sensitive skin.

She leaned closer, her lips tingling to taste him. 'Yes…' A whisper. This close to him she could barely think, let alone negotiate.

His eyes gleamed. 'I look forward to it.'

He smacked a quick kiss on her lips, leaving her reeling, and headed for the door.

'You have ten minutes to dress that sexy body of yours.'

With a cocky wink, he was gone.

One hour and one hair-raising helicopter trip later, Libby found herself back at Waterloo, on the banks of the Thames, squished into a life jacket. She'd assumed he had a jet boat and that it would be a private ride. He did, of course, own a jet boat—but he'd booked them into a tourist ride. Apparently this added to the 'fun'.

Alex squeezed her hand. 'You okay?'

She nodded, incapable of voicing any of the tart replies queued up on her tongue. Why put herself through this? Why didn't she tell him to stuff his high-profile account up his gloriously muscular behind?

Trouble was, now she'd experienced his sexual prowess the stakes were higher than the deal being simply good for business. And, despite her reservations, the exhilaration and serenity of the balloon ride had been an experience she'd never forget.

He smiled—half-mocking, half-indulgent—and scooped her close with his arm around her rigid shoulders. His lips grazed the top of her head, her forehead, her temple.

'You're perfectly safe. This skipper is the most experienced. Wait until you see their reactions.' He tilted his head in the direction of the other participants, lined up on the dock. 'Feel the sheer thrill of it yourself. I want to make this affordable and accessible for my kids. They'll love it.'

Libby looked at him. Saw him clearly as if for the first time. Excitement glinted in his eyes, transforming their colour from dark chocolate to amber, and his hair lifted in the wind, giving him a boyish air, incongruous with the powerful, urbane man she knew him to be.

And he practically vibrated with energy. He'd called them 'my kids'. This venture fed his soul.

A pang of jealousy rolled in Libby's stomach. It had been a long time since anything had fed her own withered soul. A strict diet of hard work and trigger avoidance had left her seriously malnourished in recent years. She'd pushed aside her own passions, blocking out anything that made her remember Callum, the life she'd planned with him, happier times…

Her reverie came to a halt as she followed Alex to the front of the sleek powerboat. He'd commanded the best seats in the house. The ones with a direct view of the ride ahead and in line with the inevitable faceful of Thames river spray.

Libby pressed frigid lips together. 'You owe me big-time for this,' she muttered as she took her seat, her hands gripping the icy handrail in front.

He laughed, tugging her closer to whisper, 'Why doesn't that feel like *any* kind of hardship at all?'

Before she could formulate a tart reply, the engine fired up and they were off.

It had been a long time since she'd had so much fun.

The boat bumped along, taking her stomach for the ride, and she had a unique view from her vantage point of the iconic landmarks lining the Thames. The infectious screams and laughter of those sharing the journey added to the excitement as he'd predicted. Alex gripped her hand tightly, his face full of laughter every time the boat lurched and she screamed.

By the time she was safely back on dry land she already craved a repeat performance.

Alex kissed her, their wet cheeks sliding, cold lips clinging around their mutual grins. 'Told you.'

'You were right. Must suck, being you.'

He sobered, unclipping the straps on her life jacket and then removing his own.

'Sadly, I have some work to do this afternoon.' He brushed a wet lock of hair from her face, his palm warm and dry against her hot skin. 'I need to play the boss for a few hours.'

His scorching stare told her he'd rather do all the erotic things currently running through her dirty mind, but then he seemed to take command of himself.

She nodded. 'I could work.'

She had stacks to do. For him…for her other accounts. Why did that admission carry less reward than it had a week ago? She *lived* for work. This job in particular would be incredibly lucrative in professional kudos. Why was playing hooky with the charming, contradictory CEO so much fun?

He took her hand, turning them away from the dock. 'Work it is. I'd like you to put together a short presentation, if that's okay—of the ethos behind Able-Active.'

She nodded, her mind racing with ideas.

'I think I've given you enough of a taste to know what we're about.'

'Okay.'

'And, if you're free, I'm hosting a gathering for possible benefactors and investors tomorrow evening. Hopefully my speech and your presentation will help them part with some cash.'

As she followed Alex to the sleek car waiting for them the thrill of sitting at her desk, even working on such a worthwhile project, carried far less weight than it should.

A very worrying turn of events.

CHAPTER EIGHT

THE MARIE ANTOINETTE suite at the Ritz brimmed with elegantly dressed bodies and suited waiting staff. The gilded Louis XVI–style décor and sparkling chandeliers bounced light around the crowded room, which hummed with the chatter of multiple conversations and the tinkle of fine crystal champagne glasses.

Libby focussed on the heat of Alex's hand in the small of her back, which was burning through the simple black silk shift dress she'd packed for any social function that arose while she travelled. Not that it was flashy enough for these surroundings, but she was here to do a job—not parade the latest couture.

Alex had already told her she looked beautiful, despite the simplicity of her outfit. Once in the doorway of her hotel room, when he'd pressed her up against the wall and kissed the freshly applied lip-gloss from her mouth, and again when he'd dug his fingertips into her hip as they'd left his car, whispering to her how he looked forward to repaying his debt for their trip on the river earlier this morning.

Libby shivered. Nerves? But the assembled guests, hand-picked by Alex as possible investors and benefactors to Able-Active, presented a small and hopefully captive audience. Could her jitters have something to do with the way he kept his hand on her at all times? Circulating the room with her, introducing her to too many people to remember, his act of possession as unnerving as it was thrilling.

'Thank you, James. You're doing a great job.' Alex addressed one of the waiters and took two glasses of champagne from the young man's tray.

Libby accepted a glass, noticing that James made no eye contact and rushed away more quickly than perhaps he should have.

'The waiting staff are all kids from the Able-Active programme,' Alex murmured. 'James has autism.'

Libby nodded and glanced around the room. These young, smartly dressed waiters and waitresses weren't, she guessed, typical for the Ritz.

Molly arrived by their side. 'They're ready when you are, Mr Lancaster.'

Alex nodded and handed his PA his glass of champagne. Turning to Libby, he brushed her temple with his and whispered, 'Wish me luck.'

Before she could reply, he made his way to the front of the crowd, where a small podium had been set up.

Libby watched, heat pooling in her belly, as he took his place behind the microphone and commanded the room to silence, his demeanour relaxed and engaging. He didn't need luck. His determination and enthusiasm alone could win over the entire room. No wonder he was so successful. His passion and drive were infectious.

'Ladies and gentlemen—friends.' The dazzle of his confident smile traversed the crowd, landing here and there in recognition and greeting. 'Thank you all for coming tonight to the launch party for Able-Active. Many of you—business associates, mates from uni, partners in crime—know me well.'

His genuine smile made an appearance. Not the reserved, polite one that lent him an air of authority, but the wider, unrestrained version that deepened the grooved dimple in his cheek and showed his playful side.

Libby felt her belly flutter, remembering that smile trained on her this morning in the jet boat.

'You know what this charity means to me, but most of you don't know why.' He indicated a framed photo of a teenage girl on the dais beside him. 'If Jenny, my sister, was alive, she'd be thirty-five years old now.'

The room fell deathly silent. Libby's pulse thrummed in her throat.

Alex sobered, his chin dipping and his voice deepening to a reflective rumble. 'I often wonder what kind of adult life she'd have had. Would she have fallen in love? What kind of job would she have enjoyed?' A pause, his eyes scanning every member of the audience. 'Did she dream of being a mother?

Have aspirations to help others, or want to run the London Marathon?'

Alex glanced again at the photograph, his eyes dimming.

'I was fifteen when eighteen-year-old Jenny died. I don't recall her goals, her passions, her ambitions, aside from the fact that she wanted what the rest of us have. Opportunity, choice, equality.'

He touched the edge of the frame holding his sister's image.

'Jenny's short life was good. She laughed a lot, she smiled all the time and she loved to dance.'

He gave a small smile—intimate, as if he were alone in the room.

'But it could have been better. The only employment opportunity open to her when she left school was a few hours a week volunteer work. She required help and support to do many of the things other teenagers take for granted, and many things, due to lack of trained carers or simply lack of facilities, weren't an option for her and others like her.'

His throat worked, Adam's apple bobbing.

'I could have been a better brother.'

A long silent pause filled the room with skin-crawling discomfort.

'I want a better future for teens like Jenny, and with your help, your support, Able-Active will be a starting block towards a level playing field and opportunities for all. Thank you.'

Libby's gaze, glued to Alex, travelled the room

with him as he became swallowed up into the crowd, accepting handshakes and back-slaps. He'd mesmerised her—mesmerised everyone in the room, no doubt—with his heartfelt and humbling speech.

She wanted to find him. To kiss him just because her mouth missed his and she couldn't think of a single reason not to. But Molly touched her arm, reminding her of her own presentation.

She dragged her eyes away from Alex, handsome in his dark suit, smiling and working the room with practised skill.

Molly spoke first. 'Ladies and gentlemen. Can we please have a round of applause for the waiting staff this evening, who are all participants on the Able-Active programme and have been trained by the staff here at The Ritz?'

Libby's palms stung as she joined the applause, her cheeks aching with the depth of her smile.

'And now I present Libby Noble, from the New York firm Noble and Pullman, to tell us a little more about Able-Active and Mr Lancaster's vision for the future.'

Libby swallowed, flicking the remote to begin her presentation, which would be projected onto the screen behind her. Following Alex's speech was going to be daunting, and she had no hope of matching the impact he'd had on the room. Her goal was to add to it, to complement the picture he'd painted with her own impressions, throwing in a sprinkling of marketing jargon and creating a buzz among the assembled potential supporters.

She glanced down at her notes, stomach churning. The careful, measured words she'd prepared were dancing on the page, as if mocking her with their caution and their detachment.

She cleared her throat. 'Able-Active isn't a unique charity.'

A photo of kids enjoying a kayaking trip that Libby had lifted from the website appeared on the screen.

'Worthwhile? Yes. Rewarding? Yes. Essential? Yes. But what is *exceptional* is the vision, passion and motivation of Alex Lancaster as their CEO.'

The image changed to a photo Libby had taken of herself on the hot air balloon. Her smile shone from her eyes, against a backdrop of the rolling green of Oxfordshire and the distant views of the city spires.

'This is more than outward bound. This is real life opportunity. The chance for meaningful training, employment and recreation for vulnerable members of society who often get overlooked, pigeonholed as having nothing to contribute.'

The picture changed again to a shot of their trip power boating on the Thames. Libby's eyes were scrunched closed as a blast of water sprayed her and Alex in the face, and Alex's delighted grin was firmly on her.

Lifting her eyes, she homed in on his watchful stare across the room. She folded her notes in half, her throat tight but her chest expanding with words that came from her heart, not her head.

'I came to London to work, with recreation the furthest thing from my mind. It's been many years since I participated in anything that carried an element of risk or provided that slam of adrenaline.'

Her insides quivered, her breath stolen by his continued intense focus. The same focus he offered in the bedroom.

'But I haven't felt more alive, or had so much fun since I myself was a teenager.'

She looked away from him, feeling the slow boil of desire now circulating where her blood should be.

'I'm certain that we all know someone who would relish the current Able-Active recreation experiences as much as I have enjoyed sampling some of them this week. And I'm sure we all know someone who would love the chance to have a proper job—one they can take pride in. There are many families who need support—a break from caring for their loved ones with extra needs. Able-Active, with your support, hopes to meet all those challenges. Thank you.'

She moved from the podium to a round of applause, her legs shaky. Molly guided her towards Alex, whose stare still devoured her from across the room.

Halfway there, she found her progress interrupted by Jeremy Wells.

'Great speech.'

He snagged a flute of champagne from a passing waitress, his dismissive and slightly aggressive move surprising the girl so that her whole tray of drinks wobbled.

Libby hadn't liked Jeremy the first time they'd met. She liked him even less now as he derailed the fledgling waitress's carefully woven path through the partygoers.

Libby accepted a glass and thanked the girl. Reluctantly she turned her attention back to Alex's financial director. His suit, whilst clearly expensive, erred on the too-small side, and his paunch obscured the waistband of his trousers and stretched the buttons on his shirt to bursting point.

Tingles—the bad kind—snaked up Libby's spine.

'I'm sure the funds will come rolling in now.' His eyes gleamed, dipping to Libby's chest.

Creep.

'I hope so.' The hairs on the back of her neck prickled to attention. She didn't want to appear rude to one of Alex's valued employees, but this guy made her skin crawl.

Her gaze sought Alex and escape. Sadly he too had been intercepted and was deep in conversation.

Libby stepped aside, making her intention to escape clear.

Jeremy touched her arm, his fingers quickly dropping away at her frosty glare. 'So, I'd love to show you the sights before you leave London. Are you free tomorrow evening?'

He stepped closer, eyes flicking south again. Clearly he had the hide of an elephant—or was simply ignoring her subtle *fuck off* vibe.

Libby fought the urge to cover her cleavage with

her hand. 'I'd have loved to explore London—' *just not with you* '—but every second of my week is committed to my work for Able-Active.'

She stretched her lips into an insincere smile. 'Excuse me.'

She weaved through the bodies, coming to a halt at Alex's side. With their backs to the opulent room's ornate fireplace, he rested his hand at the base of Libby's spine, fingers splayed. She breathed out a sigh.

'Olivia, I'd like you to meet Jack Demont—my cousin, and brother of the bride at this weekend's festivities.'

The handsome Frenchman dropped a kiss to the back of Libby's hand. 'Delighted to meet you, Ms Noble.'

Like Alex, he was tall, his striking eyes partially obscured by a flop of dark blond hair.

'Please, call me Libby. Your English is excellent.' Unlike her French.

Jack laughed. 'Thank you. My father is English and I spend a lot of time here. Plus, I had my accent bullied out of me at school by some notorious thugs.'

He flicked a glare at Alex, who laughed and shrugged, unapologetically.

'You gave as good as you got.' He grinned a lazy smile at Libby. 'I wore braces for much of my schooling.'

So Mr Perfection had once had flaws? A computer geek with braces? She shivered, certain that her fifteen-year-old self—an insecure bookworm dressed from the thrift store—would have found him attractive.

Alex turned back to his cousin. 'I've invited Libby to Henri and Isabel's wedding.'

Jack bowed his head in acknowledgment. 'Yes. You must come. Provence is stunning at this time of year.'

'I'm sure...' Olivia looked away.

'I don't think Olivia is big on romance,' said Alex.

Libby shot him a look she hoped conveyed her contempt. Why would he assume that? He knew nothing about her because she liked it that way.

The sting of his jibe called her a liar. Didn't *some* part of her relish that they were getting to know each other? Not that she'd consciously let him in. She never let *anyone* in. But with his confessions about his mother and sister, his open, raw vulnerability— he'd lured her dangerously close.

Jack slid wary eyes between her and Alex, seeming to sense the tension sparking in the air. 'Well, excuse me. I'm leaving for Nice tonight.' He kissed both of Libby's cheeks. 'It was delightful to meet you. I hope you'll accept my cousin's invitation to the wedding so we can get to know each other better. *Au revoir.*'

Jack departed, talking the room's warmth with him.

Goosebumps raced along Libby's bare arms. She turned to Alex, the take-down she'd planned dying on her lips at his proximity.

He pressed close, leaving the scantest space between his body and hers. 'What did Jeremy say to upset you?'

His breath gusted over her neck, her shoulder, spreading tingles.

She met his hard stare, felt the flickers of heat melting her insides. Was that jealousy? Possession?

'How do you know I'm upset?'

His perusal completed a tour of her face, lazily tracing each feature in turn. 'I've seen you happy, relaxed, excited, replete…' He mouthed each word, his lips and tongue caressing her, as when he'd drawn those emotions from her. 'I'm observant where you're concerned.'

His fingers found the sensitive skin inside her elbow, sliding. The intimacy, for once, was irritating.

She bit her cheek. She shouldn't have let Jeremy get to her. She'd met enough Jeremys professionally to be able to handle them. And, unlike Alex, they were easily forgettable and easy to walk away from.

Libby shuddered, the imprint of Jeremy's fingers still tainting her arm, and his greedy stare still burning her skin.

'Did he come on to you?' A flash turned his eyes molten, burning into hers.

Why lie? She owed Jeremy nothing. And this thing with Alex was temporary. No time for insecurities.

'Yes.'

But didn't she feel his possession in every touch? Crave the spark of it in every look he gave her? What was wrong with her?

His fingers stalled on her arm, the press of the tips a fraction firmer. 'Are you interested?'

'*What?*'

Eyes hard, he thinned his lips. 'Well, we're just fucking—*your* word.'

Libby glanced around to see if anyone was paying them any attention. She had given this thing a crude label, one that clearly outlined the parameters of their contact. Why, then, did hearing her words turned back on her irk so much?

Alex continued, as if unconcerned, but his voice was low. 'I've asked you on a date. A proper date. No games. You haven't answered.'

So he did have an ego—better hidden than most, but there just the same.

'I don't sleep around.' Why tell him that? It made no difference to them. They barely knew each other. Their fuck-fest had a short expiry date. 'Before you, there'd been no one for three years.'

He didn't register her confession. She wasn't even sure why she'd told him herself.

'So why me?'

She lifted her chin, backpedalling. 'Fishing?'

He sighed, his gaze flicking away and then returning, more open. 'Yes.'

At last there was a hint of insecurity in the way he rubbed the knuckles of one hand down his face.

Tempted to tease him, Libby pinched her lips together, hiding a smile. She grasped the chance to lighten the mood, steer them away from the wrong turn this conversation had taken. After all, they weren't a couple, so why bother with disagreements? Their time was limited.

'Temporary lapse of common sense.' She smiled. 'I blame jet lag.'

After a couple of beats he grinned, his hand slipping to her waist and his expensive, heady scent filling her head as he dipped closer.

'Want to be reckless with me tomorrow?' His lips grazed her ear. 'Jet skiing?' He whispered the words as if he'd suggested an illicit sex game.

She shuddered. The thought was not unpleasant. 'Another day freezing on the Thames?'

His mouth twisted, dimples flashing. 'No, I was thinking the Med…' His cocky disarming smile returned.

Irresistible.

'Like to get your own way, don't you?' Her breath gusted, her pulse fluttering in her throat. Any game with Alex was surprisingly addictive.

'Absolutely.' A slow nod.

Clearly sensing victory, he moved closer, his hand sliding to her hip. Seductive.

'And so do you.'

He quirked an eyebrow, fingers gripping tighter, the way they did just before he came, as if he couldn't get close enough, deep enough.

Lust sizzled between her thighs.

This had to stop. She needed to start weaning herself off this exhilarating ride. She wasn't his.

Couldn't be—no matter how right her hand felt against his slightly callused palm.

Time to rein back some control over herself. 'And what do you want right now?'

Hooded eyes held hers. 'I want you to go back to your hotel tonight.' His voice dropped. 'I want you to stay in London tomorrow while I fly to the South of France.' His lips touched her ear, whisper-soft, starting a chain reaction of fine tremors. 'I want you to keep your panties on under that dress so I can't go down on you in the back of my car.'

Libby's knees buckled and she wobbled on her heels.

Bastard. He knew the effect he had on her.

Pulling away, he twitched his decadent lips. 'But, ladies first. What do *you* want, Olivia?'

He'd become so good at her game. *Too* good. But why did breaking the rules with him feel better than getting her own way? And wasn't she still getting what she wanted?

Him.

Still, she tried to discipline herself and her spiralling feelings. 'I'm tired. I want an early night.'

His face fell.

'I'll meet you in the foyer in five minutes if you wouldn't mind giving me a ride.'

She spun on her heel, ignoring the flash of uncertainty in his eyes.

When she emerged from the ladies' room, her panties tucked inside her clutch bag, and rounded the corner to the main hotel foyer, Alex was waiting for her, hands stuffed in the pockets of his pants, an intense, heated stare following her progress.

She couldn't resist. She loved holding him on the brink, disarming him as much as he disarmed her. Redressing the balance so that when she walked away she'd have no regrets.

She made it outside with the minimum of wobble, every step, every second she kept him dangling increasing the throb between her legs.

Alex's driver opened the door of the sleek limo and Libby ducked inside, Alex's hand on her arm, guiding her.

Once inside, the driver said, 'Where to, sir?'

From his seat opposite her Alex raised a questioning brow, a hint of challenge and a large slice of vulnerability in his eyes. How had she missed that before? It was *her* call—as always with him. Aside from pressing the wedding date, he'd always extended her the ultimate control. It was the main reason she was still here. Should she give in one more time? Or should she ration her encounters with him, wean herself from her addiction. He'd never know about the panties.

She licked dry lips. 'Where do you stay when you're in London?' Her throat was scratchy.

Eyes dark, he watched her from the seat opposite. The air crackled with tension, electricity arcing between them when not even their knees brushed. Libby regretted the spaciousness of the luxury vehicle. Right now she'd give anything to be sandwiched next to him in the back of one of those charming Mini Coopers.

He shrugged. 'I have a place in Belgravia.'

Of course he did. She nodded, holding his bold stare with one of her own.

'Eaton Square, please, Roger,' he said.

The car rolled into motion, entering the central London stream of traffic, as constant as the flow in New York.

Alex raised the privacy screen between them and the driver with the touch of a button.

His gaze pinned her. Hot, defiant, demanding.

'Show me.'

The bite of command entranced her—hers to obey or deny. Fire raged inside her, hot enough to melt her clothes away. Placing her clutch on the leather seat with a shaky hand, Libby slowly lifted her dress, millimetre by millimetre, so the fabric bunched at the top of her thighs.

'Wider.' His nostrils flared and he spread his own thighs, as if seeking comfort for the confined bulge at his crotch.

She loved to push him. To see him teeter on the brink of that glorious moment when he shucked his impeccable buttoned-up manners and proper English upbringing and dived for her, eyes glazed with lust.

'Bossy, much?' She pressed her thighs together. This was *her* game.

He nodded. 'I want to give you what you want.

What *I* want.' His tongue touched his bottom lip. 'Let me.'

Yes.

With a sigh she couldn't contain, Libby conceded. Her legs parted, knees spread wide, her heels digging into the luxury carpet. She met his stare, bold, daring, counting the seconds until he snapped.

With a curse, Alex dropped to his knees, his hands gripping her thighs and spreading her open wider to his brazen look.

'Do you understand what you do to me?' His eyes sought hers in the car's gloom, his gruff voice pricking her nerve endings alive. It was a whisper. 'Do you feel the power you wield? Power over *me*?'

Libby stopped breathing. His questions were as close to any true emotions as they'd ever expressed, and they struck close to her own, so close her skin seemed to tighten and shrink.

She gripped the leather beneath her palms to stop herself from pushing him away and jumping from the moving vehicle.

What had started as a game—a risqué diversion of give and take—now erred perilously close to a chasm of emotion she daren't cross.

Sex. This could only be about sex.

She focussed on breathing, her inhalations matching the tempo of his while they waited, watched, warred.

Alex broke first, a sigh gusting from him. 'I can't do this any more.'

Libby's stomach flipped. 'Do what?'

The rumble of the car's engine faded away as the world stuttered to a halt. She only had days left with him. She wasn't ready for this to be over—wasn't ready to think about the end of this wild, hedonistic ride.

With the candour she'd grown to expect from him, he said, 'I want you too much.'

His hand skittered along her inner thigh, his eyes seeking her permission before his fingers probed her entrance, which was slick, ready for him. His thumb circled her clit and her head dropped back, her thighs trembling with the effort of staying open to his avid stare.

He leaned over her, his gravelly voice sin-dipped. 'Come with me.'

She was about to.

'To France.'

The fog cleared and she opened her eyes to his penetrating gaze.

'No games, Olivia.'

His fingers continued their lazy swirling, fogging her mind.

'No jet-skiing. No work.'

He pumped his fingers faster.

'Just two people attracted to each other, enjoying a social gathering in a stunning part of the world.'

Libby fought to make sense of his words while her body sang under his hand. He made it sound so simple. And on the surface, it was. But his idyllic scenario was pitted with potholes—landmines of re-pressed emotion that threatened to blow her carefully constructed and life-saving control apart.

'I...'

He grunted, perhaps interpreting the denial on her face or hearing her unspoken refusal. He shifted, lowering his head between her thighs, his lips kiss-ing her intimately and his tongue flattening against her primed clit.

All thoughts, all arguments fled. Only Alex re-mained, and the pleasure he wreaked expanded to fill her mind with every swirl of his tongue and plunge of his fingers.

'Yes!' she cried out, her hands tangling in his hair, holding him close as she rocked into his mouth.

The sublime glide of his tongue ceased, and the pleasure drained away to a slow simmer.

'Yes, you'll come to France?'

He kept her on the edge, with his thumb where his mouth had been. Not what she wanted, but enough to prolong the haze.

'Yes...yes...' She'd argue later, rescind her ac-ceptance. Any agreement made under sexual duress was null and void.

'Yes, you'll come...on my face?'

The wicked glimmer in his eyes stole the last of her breath and all she could offer was a feeble nod.

When his mouth covered her again a second fin-ger pushed inside her to join the first. She exploded, her thighs gripping his head and her fingers twisting in his hair as she clung on for dear life in the moving vehicle.

The spasms trailed away and she pushed at his shoulders, breaking the divine contact and missing it at the same time. Before her body had in any way recovered from the intense orgasm she pounced on him, kissing his wet mouth and tugging his belt free. He helped, their fingers working simultaneously to free him from his dress pants. She gripped him, her hand fisting his hard length, her tongue tasting him, tasting herself.

He produced a condom from his pocket and Libby jerked him up onto the seat beside her, snatching it from him in her haste to have him inside her. She covered him, feeling that ache back between her thighs. She didn't want to think about games, or weddings, or the past. She craved him more than ever, more than the first time, her need only intensifying with each time they were together like this.

'Hurry.'

She hitched her dress higher, straddling his lap. One hand gripped the leather upholstery behind his shoulder as the other delved between them to align him at her entrance. And then she was sinking onto him, their mutual groans resounding through the confined space, with only the darkened night outside to hear them.

Alex gripped her face in his palms, demanding eye contact as she rocked on his lap. 'Mean it, Libby. Say you want to stop playing.'

He was pushing the boundaries, changing the game plan. But in that moment she'd promise him anything.

She gripped the lapels of his expensive, exquisitely tailored tux, crushing the fabric in her palms.

Part of her *did* want to stop playing. Part of her was desperate to get to know real Alex, the man, flaws and all. Part of her wished she could be the old, unguarded version of herself. But she couldn't give him everything he wanted…everything she longed to give.

Another compromise? She could shore up her dread for one day. Go to this stupid wedding. Act, smile, drink champagne. Just one day. An end to this fairy-tale week that she hadn't planned for but was powerless to stop.

She tensed her internal muscles, forcing another groan from him. Dipping her head to his shoulder, she traced her mouth in a path along the soft skin of the side of his neck, and feathered his ear with her lips.

'I'll come to France. No games.'

And then she'd head home. Try to forget Alex Lancaster and her European adventure.

His hands cupped her buttocks, taking control of the friction with thrusts from beneath. Libby held on tight, knowing this ride, this time, meant something more, that the stakes had been raised to levels she couldn't afford.

They came together—him with a shout the driver

probably heard, and her with the collar of his tux clamped between her teeth. Anything else and she'd have blurted out something suspiciously like feelings. Feelings she had no room for—especially not where a man like Alex Lancaster was concerned.

CHAPTER NINE

LIBBY STARTED AWAKE. The unfamiliar room came into focus and she felt the weight of Alex's arm on her waist, the heat of his naked chest at her back. The dream that had woken her, vaguely familiar in the way recurring dreams were, was still pounding the blood around her body. Always the same. She was searching for something she had no hope of finding, only to jerk awake with the feeling that she'd failed some momentous task and would never be happy again.

She lay still, closing her eyes and slowing her breathing, mindfully scanning her body, willing her tense muscles to relax in the hope of returning to sleep. But, like many nights before, tonight was to be one of mind-racing exhaustion, and after ten minutes she gave up, carefully slid from underneath the slumbering Alex and shuffled to the edge of his enormous bed.

Like the one at his Oxfordshire estate, this bed was a sleek, modern four-poster. He lay sprawled in the middle, his muscular back revealed by the sheets pooled at his waist and his hair a dishevelled mop partly obscuring his handsome, relaxed face.

The tattoo that snaked around one side of his chest was partly visible—a line of script: *Rise by lifting others*. She'd read it fully earlier in the shower, her fingers tracing the ink.

After the limo they'd showered together, soaping and nibbling every inch of each other's bodies until they'd drawn a third orgasm from each other and then collapsed into Alex's very comfortable, too-big bed. Not that he'd let her keep her distance. And Libby had been too tired to object when he'd dragged her by the waist into his spooning.

Finding his dress shirt discarded on a chair, she slipped it on and crept from the room. Her clutch was where she'd dropped it on the hall table. She located her phone and headed for the state-of-the-art kitchen, hoping to find a kettle amongst the seamless cupboards and contemporary appliances.

Within a few minutes she'd brewed tea and was snuggled on an oversized couch, pulling a throw over her legs to ward off the middle-of-the-night chill. A quick calculation of the time difference proved favourable and she dialled Sonya's number. She'd neglected her pregnant friend, sending only daily e-mails. She needed to hear her voice. Reset her equilibrium.

Sonya answered on the second ring. 'What are you doing up? Isn't it the middle of the night over there?'

'Hi, to you too. I couldn't sleep.' Libby sipped

her tea, spotting a well-placed mirrored coaster on the minimalist slab that paraded as a coffee table.

'Still jet-lagged?'

Libby longed to pick apart her insomnia with Sonya, to bounce her unsettled emotions off her friend. She winced. But Sonya was nine months pregnant and solely in charge of their business.

'I guess… How are *you*? I rang to make sure you aren't working too hard.' Libby's throat burned, and she felt inexplicable emotion close to the surface at the sound of her friend's voice.

A long sigh. 'I'm fine. Fit to burst, but fine. I've worked from home these last two days,' said Sonya. 'Vinnie has rescheduled some of my out-of-town appointments for you when you get back next week. Sorry. I guess it's finally catching up with me.'

Libby worried at a cuticle, her shoulders tense. 'Of course. That's absolutely fine. I can come home earlier if you need me.'

She could drop everything and be back in New York in ten hours. No wedding. No more adrenaline. No more Alex.

She barely managed a swallow.

'No need. It's almost the weekend. No one needs you *that* urgently.'

A smile tugged her cheeks. Sonya sounded like her old self. Perhaps she needed *them*. Her friends, her business, her life. That was who she was.

The rush of homesickness tightened her chest, but she suspected the vice would be crossing the Atlantic with her when she returned to New York. The only thing to warm Libby's bed there was Dumbledore, and he hogged the pillow, purred in her ear and had fishy breath.

She scrubbed at her face. Perhaps the idea of a wedding had unsettled her more than she admitted.

'Look, Libbs, I was going to wait until you were back, but I want to give you as much notice as possible. I'm not coming back.'

The silent pause raised the hairs on Libby's arms.

'What? When?'

Libby's tired mind played catch-up.

'After the baby's born.'

'Of course you aren't!'

She should never have left Sonya alone at a time like this. Her friend's voice held a strain.

'No. I mean I want to stay home with the baby. I'm not coming back after my maternity leave. I know it means leaving you in the lurch, but I want to sell my share of the company.'

. Libby reeled. 'I understand. Of course you want to be there for your tiny human.'

But I'll miss you.

Tears threatened, closer than ever to the surface. She swallowed them down, hating the selfishness that had enabled her to leave her heavily pregnant friend in the first place, and now bemoaned her decision to be a stay-at-home mom.

Sonya rushed on. 'I won't pull out straight away.

I'll give you a chance to find someone you can work with. There's no rush.'

'Don't be silly. I'll be fine. You just focus on you and the baby. I'll miss you, though.' The last words were choked out past a constricted throat.

She wasn't fooling anyone—least of all her best friend.

'Libbs, I'm sorry. I just don't want to feel pressured to return to work, or to feel obligated.

'I understand.'

Did she? She'd spent long career-focussed years trying to forget Callum's death and her own misery. Cheated, she'd closed down that aspect of her life, denied herself sex, relationships, even friendships in case they wandered from the friend zone into something too close to what she'd once had with her fiancé. What she couldn't risk feeling again. But could she call it happiness? Living?

Libby clutched her stomach, holding in the emotion that threatened to send her running for Heathrow Airport. What would she do without Sonya? Her dry sense of humour and her shared passion for cute shoes? They were a team. The *best* team. But her friend was moving on…her life was transitioning to the next phase…whereas Libby had purposely withdrawn from the well-travelled path.

Things shifted, became distorted as if being viewed through a cracked mirror. The wedding, her dream—all so trivial.

'Libbs? Are you okay?'

She pressed the heel of her hand to her throbbing eye socket. 'Yes. Just a bit surprised.' She forced the wobble from her voice. 'And missing you, I guess.'

'I miss you too. Look, I'll help you find a new partner, if that's what you want,' said Sonya. 'I've even mocked up an ad. I'll e-mail it through for you to take a look.'

'Don't worry about any of that now. You just concentrate on resting.'

A sigh she was powerless to stop stuttered from Libby. This was real. The end of an era. The end of the only good thing Libby had left in her life.

But Sonya didn't need any extra burden. Libby forced joviality into her voice. 'I found the cutest little outfit for the baby—just wait till you see it.'

She needed to hang up before the floodgates opened and she sobbed down the phone, begging Sonya to stay.

Sonya's relief brightened her tone. 'Send me a picture. So, what's the sexy Englishman got planned for you for the rest of the week?'

Libby spoke without thinking, her mind still fogged with sadness. 'I'm going to France.'

Sonya's gasp brought Libby back to the present. '*Ooh, la-la. So* not fair. I'm a whale, stuck here with the dreadful humidity, and *you'll* be swanning around Paris.'

A feeble laugh. 'Hardly.'

Pressure built behind Libby's eyes. She scrunched

them closed, breathing through her nose. She could no longer hide her true emotions from her friend.

'He's invited me to a wedding.' Her throat shrank, hot and achy, and her voice dropped to a whisper. 'I don't think I can go, Son…'

'Oh, Libbs.' She gave a small sigh. 'Have you told him why?'

'No.' It was too personal for a business associate. And that was the label she felt comfortable with. But weren't they more than that? Their relationship was blurring around the edges… He'd said no more games…

'Well, you don't have to go—come home.'

Home. But without seeing Sonya every day, would her New York life even *feel* like home?

'Look, I know you don't want to hear it, but it's time to focus on *you*,' said Sonya. 'Callum would want you to be happy.'

Libby nodded, although she knew Sonya couldn't see. Her silence spoke of understanding without the need for words.

What *was* happy? And where did she search for it? It had been so long since she'd considered the possibility she'd convinced herself that this—her job, her cat, her friends—were all she'd ever need. But life changed. She knew that better than anyone. Her best friend was moving on. They'd still be there for each other, but it wouldn't be the same. She was truly happy for Sonya. But how could *she* stay the same when everything was shifting under her feet?

'You're right. I just don't know how to do it.'

'Libbs… Don't overthink it. Go to France, drink champagne.' She gave a bitter laugh. 'Have a glass for me.'

Libby sniffed, smiling despite herself. 'Okay.'

'Will you be okay?' Sonya's voice dripped with concern.

Libby injected her tone with a lightness she didn't feel. 'I'll be fine. Thanks for being there.'

'Always.'

'Promise me you'll rest?'

'I will. Promise me you'll try to do what I said?'

'I will. Love you.'

They ended the call.

Libby sat staring at the twinkling lights of the city, her forgotten tea now as cold and unwelcoming as her tumble of thoughts.

Libby opened heavy eyelids, the splash of cold water on her foot startling her from a sun-warmed slumber. Alex stood at the foot of her sun lounger, rivulets of water caressing his tanned, muscular body, which was covered only in a pair of black swim shorts, their wet fabric clinging to his thighs and the bulge of his crotch.

Libby licked dry lips. He was Adonis. Standing on the terrace of this fairy-tale eighteenth-century French château, complete with turrets, he looked as if he'd come from a movie set—or the pages of one of Vinnie's beloved magazines.

She smiled. Her outlandish assistant would pop something if he could see her now.

'Come in. It's warm.'

Libby curled her toes, checking the reality beneath her feet. The whole day had held a surreal quality. A private jet ride from London to the south of France, a waiting car to drive them to this breathtaking château, a delicious brunch on the terrace where she'd met Isabel and Henri, the bride and groom, and now Alex—wet, practically naked—luring her to the pristine blue waters of the estate's swimming pool.

She took his outstretched hand, allowing herself to be pulled from her lounger and into his now familiar embrace. His wet body slid against hers, raising goosebumps, his searing kiss turning her from warm and sun-kissed to hot and achy.

The château, owned by Jack and Isabel's maternal grandfather, had fourteen bedrooms, half of which were occupied by the wedding party. Alex and Libby had sole occupancy of the sumptuous guest wing. She toyed with the notion of dragging him back there now, but perhaps a dip in the pool would cool both her body temperature *and* her libido.

Libby pulled back from the kiss, walked to the edge of the pool and executed a perfect dive into the deep end. When she surfaced Alex was watching her from the side of the pool before diving in himself and surfacing at her side. His arms circled her waist as they trod water together.

'Told you it was good.'

He manoeuvred her to the side of the pool, holding her captive against the tiles while he finished the kiss, stealing her air and plunging her back into tantalising fantasy.

No.

Not again.

She couldn't risk her feelings. The pain wasn't worth the gamble. Fortunately Alex lived on a different continent. Once she arrived back in New York, settled back into her safe, predictable life, these unsettled emotions would fade like her tan. Although without Sonya by her side life would be a little less predictable.

She forced her mind to think about something else. Anything else. But with Alex's lips on her throat and his erection pressed into her thigh beneath the waterline it took every scrap of her resolve.

He provided the distraction. 'Tell me something about yourself.'

His fingers traced patterns at her waist. She almost wished she'd worn a one-piece instead of a bikini.

Libby held his stare, focussing on the amber flecks in his irises until her own eyes burned, infected by the heat spreading from her throat.

Tired of her own games, and the exhausting jumble of her feelings, she blurted out her first thought. 'I grew up in New Jersey, just me and my mom.'

He lifted his chin, encouraging.

'All this...' she glanced around the opulence of

the château's manicured gardens and pristine pool '…is completely alien to me.'

His smile dropped and he pressed his mouth to hers.

She twisted away from the sublime slide of his lips, irritation buzzing beneath her skin. 'I don't need your pity. I've made good for myself.'

His eyes hardened. 'I don't pity you.' Another kiss, harder than the last. 'I *admire* you.'

Warmth spread through her limbs. She didn't need his praise, but it was nice all the same. They kissed again. Libby was uncertain who'd initiated it. It didn't matter. The effect was the same—her mind grew fuzzy, her limbs liquefied and she curled her legs around his hips, deepening their kiss and pressing him between her legs, where she wanted him.

Would she even care if someone saw them? With the warm sun on her back and a wet Alex to explore?

He pulled back, eyes hooded. 'I want to see you again—beyond this week.' He pressed her against the side of the pool, as if he guessed his admission would make her want to flee.

She unlocked her crossed ankles, sliding down his body. 'I…'

An image slammed into her mind, as clear as the crystal blue waters of the Mediterranean—Alex, more dates like this, more adventures, a shared life… Her breath caught, her mind flicking a switch to close down the slug of yearning.

She pushed at his shoulders, trying and failing to create some distance. 'I live in New York.'

He didn't give an inch, his body a wall of solid warmth before her.

'So? My mother is French, my father English.'

He spoke with that sultry drawl, tempting her, as if her reasoning had no effect on his argument, as if the benefits were obvious.

He nuzzled her neck again, his lips seductive. 'You forget I have a plane. New York's not that far away.'

For a second her head lolled back as Alex's kiss found the sensitive skin just beneath her ear. Ignoring the flood of heat to her erogenous zones, she focussed on the prickle under her skin.

'Alex… This is just temporary. Just fucking, remember?' She cringed, the words she'd uttered scalding her vocal cords.

His lips ceased their meandering. Libby wished she'd kept her mouth shut as prickles of unease doused the pleasurable heat.

He leaned away to glare at her, their bodies separating an inch and allowing a rush of cool water between them.

'And if I want more?' Eyes hard, the jut of his chin determined—this was the formidable businessman others saw. The driven man used to making things happen just the way he wanted them.

She shook her head. She couldn't give him more. Sometimes you didn't get what you wanted. Sometimes it was snatched away, no matter how hard you clung.

He clenched his jaw, eyes searing. 'What do you want, Olivia?'

For once she had no answer to the now familiar question that had become a mantra for them—a prelude to their game. Wanting him sexually? Easy. Discovering inconsequential facts about his life? Fun. But more than that…?

She considered herself incapable of more. And not with a man like Alex—wealthy enough to pursue dangerous pastimes, driven to recklessness through never having to accept that something was off-limits, an adrenaline junkie who grasped life with both hands…

Not exactly like Callum, but close enough to amplify the chills set off by this turn in the conversation and the increasing physical distance between them.

Had the moment arrived? Was it time to give it to him straight? She'd always been honest with him.

'I want to do a good job for you. I hope I've done that.'

'You have.'

He sensed the brush-off. That was evident in the minute muscle twitching in his clenched jaw.

Libby covered his mouth with her fingers. She couldn't leave him with any doubt.

'I need to get home, to sort out my business.'

Coward.

'Sonya wants out of the company so she can be

at home with her baby. I need to find someone to replace her—work out if I can afford to buy her out or if I'll need a new partner.'

New shivers came, and the taste of acid, an ache under her ribs.

He shrank against her thigh, easing his body completely away from hers. Her fingers flexed, desperate to pull him back. But she couldn't lead him on. Couldn't let him think there was any future for them beyond this week, no matter how tantalising the prospect.

'That's all I can think about right now.' All she'd allow herself to think about. 'I'm sorry.' She pressed a brief kiss on his mouth, swallowing back a knot of emotion. 'This has been fun. An adventure I didn't expect. Thank you.'

His eyes narrowed, determination sparking in their depths. 'So let me be clear. You're ending this? You have no interest in seeing me beyond this weekend?'

Yes.

No.

I can't.

Alex's phone trilled from the terrace, saving her from answering. She recoiled, shrinking inside. He gave her a hard stare as he moved away, the chill he left behind spreading to the pit of her stomach.

Then he surprised her by returning just as quickly, clasping her chin in his hand and lifting her face so their eyes aligned.

'I need to get that.' His sigh gusted over her fore-head as he pressed a final kiss there. 'But this conversation isn't over.'

Sprinting across the width of the pool, he hauled his body from the water and in two strides reached the table where they'd left their cell phones.

The final look he'd shot her told Libby he meant what he said. Of *course* he wouldn't give in without a fight—he was a cut-throat businessman, used to getting his own way. Something she admired—a massive part of his appeal, despite her little game of power play.

Libby harnessed her restlessness and the dull ache taking residence in her gut, sinking beneath the water and executing a few invigorating lengths of breaststroke. Perhaps the activity would dispel the hollow space where her vital organs should be. Because if her decision was so right, why did unease hound her every stroke?

Why hadn't she kept her mouth shut for once? Glossed over his proposition, laughed it off, side-stepped the debate with the distraction of their pretty constant need to connect physically? No. The sexual game had been fun—a way to control the inferno of their chemistry—but she wouldn't toy with him.

She sank to the bottom of the shallow end, hoping the sun-dappled water would calm her conflicted mind. Why was there even any debate? It shouldn't matter what Alex wanted. If he'd broken the rules, developed feelings, she'd been honest from the start.

Honest with herself?

No.

It was crazy. In a few short days he couldn't be anything more to her than a holiday fling. Clearly Sonya's declaration had upset her equilibrium. Or the sun, the astounding sex and the glamour of Alex's wealthy lifestyle had forced unrealistic fantasies into her head. Back in New York, with real-life issues, she'd find her balance, gain perspective and a firm hold on her emotions. Right?

When she surfaced, her eyes zeroed in on the object of her discord and a sigh escaped her. The itch beneath her skin intensified. He ended his call, striding back towards her with his confident swagger firmly in place. If she'd dented his ego with her less than enthusiastic brush-off, it didn't show.

He reached for her hands, hauling her from the pool when she complied. 'Maman has arrived. Want to say hello?'

No. She wanted to run away, pretend she'd never met him, try to forget the way he made her feel.

'Sure.'

She snagged a towel from the lounger and wrapped it sarong-style around her body. She'd been gifted a reprieve, but the surge of relief failed to materialise.

'Good.'

He reached for his own towel, looping it around his neck and collecting his phone and sunglasses from the table. With his hand clasping hers, he led them back to the pool house.

'And Olivia?' He gripped her around the waist, his arm a steel band. 'Don't for one second think we won't revisit that discussion.'

His mouth covered hers, demanding, hot, so easy to yield to. He pulled back, leaving Libby craving more.

'I won't bend on this particular negotiation. I want you.'

CHAPTER TEN

'OLIVIA, I'D LIKE to introduce Marie—my mother.'

Alex slipped his hand to the small of Libby's back, as powerless to stop touching her as he was to dragging his eyes from the swathe of red silk that sheathed her sun-kissed body.

She'd left her hair down, just how he liked it. How she *knew* he liked it because he'd revealed as much. His fingertips tingled and his balls tightened. Her hair did things to him. Dark things.

Fuck, *all* of her did things to him.

'Maman, Olivia is from New York. This is her first visit to France.'

Olivia shook hands with his mother, who, being a French native, insisted on kissing both her cheeks in that European way. Libby engaged his mother in talk of the sights of the local area and the history of the château while he indulged in his favourite pastime—observing Olivia.

She was holding something back. He felt it. When he'd said he wanted to see her again her pupils had dilated the way they did when he pushed inside her, their gazes locked.

Her hand in his clung, her fingers frequently slipping to entwine between his, squeezing. When she looked at him she flicked her hair over one shoulder, tilting her head to expose the pale column of her neck. Hiding her unconscious reactions from him was as pointless as her affirmation they were *just fucking.*

His ability to read people formed a major part of his success. And he read Olivia like a screen full of computer code. She wanted more too. Now he just had to convince her to admit it to herself.

He stroked the place between her bare shoulder blades, eliciting a thrill of goosebumps he soothed with his thumb. Her careful evasion should have pissed him off. She'd dressed it up for the sake of his ego, but he'd heard the message loud and clear. And yet gut instinct told him her rejection concealed something else.

Part of him didn't blame her for slamming on the brakes. They'd known each other only a matter of days and long-distance relationships were fraught with extra complications. But something visceral had shifted inside him. The thought of never seeing her again after the weekend left his skin crawling with impatience and his fists uncharacteristically punchy. And *damn* if he didn't want every part of her—complete surrender. Her fearlessness and her insecurities. Her sharp mind and her sharper tongue. Her deepest desires and her greatest fears.

His shoulders tensed, impotence like a block of ice in his chest. He'd indulged her. Conceded too much without pushback. Could he make her see? Draw out what she held back until she admitted what he instinctively knew was there?

He knew one thing for sure—one thing he'd promised her at the pool house. He wouldn't stand by and watch her walk away. Not without a fight.

He tuned back in to the conversation.

'…and, of course, if she were alive she'd have loved this family wedding.' Marie clutched her throat, her eyes turning glassy.

Oh, no. Please let that be water in Marie's glass. The last thing he needed was a scene tonight.

'Maman, it's okay.' He touched Marie's arm, hoping to soothe away the demons his cousin's wedding had triggered. At least he'd told Libby about Jenny.

His mother turned on him, her watery stare blazing. '*Is* it, Zander? You never want to talk about her. She was your *sister*.'

Fuck. He'd guessed this weekend might be a flashpoint for Marie's grief—Isabel and Jenny so alike in looks. His eyes scanned the terrace for Clive. He'd need help if he was going to survive this family dinner without a full-blown Gallic scene.

'I know that,' he said.

Fuck, must she always remind him of his sibling shortcomings? As if he didn't relive them every time he thought of his sister. He clenched his jaw and flicked apologetic eyes at Libby, whose own stare had narrowed on him.

Marie seemed to gather herself, and his shoulders relaxed.

'Excuse me, my dear. I'm going to find my husband. It was lovely to meet you.'

Marie touched Libby's arm, shot a hurt look in his direction and turned on her heel, all injured elegance.

Fuck, now he'd upset his mother. He'd hunt her out later. He had a proposition for her—a role at Able-Active that would hopefully give her renewed focus.

'Was that really necessary?' said Libby.

Tension twisted his gut. 'My apologies. Even affluent families have their…dramas.'

Perhaps he could have been a little more sensitive, but his mother had seemed determined to air their dirty laundry.

Libby touched his arm, her eyes softening. 'She's just trying to keep Jenny's memory alive, you know.' She stepped closer, her voice dropping. 'In that way you're very similar.'

Were they? He had his mother's colouring, but that was where he considered the similarities ended. And, yes, in his private moments he catalogued his inadequacies as a brother, but he'd dealt with his grief long ago, channelled it into something positive. Giving back in a way to atone.

'Maybe.' *Fuck*, he was trying to lure this woman into a long-distance relationship—not scare her away. 'I'll apologise. I hope to encourage her to work for Able-Active. Perhaps a rewarding position will make things easier for her.'

Her shrewd stare pinned him. 'Yes. And it will give you some common ground—something you can work on together.'

He shrugged, heat blooming in his chest. She cared—about him, about Able-Active, about his mother. No matter how hard she tried to deny it. Why else would she worry over his relationship with Marie?

She leaned closer, her warm fragrant skin buffeting him, softening the blow of her words. 'It's okay, Alex.' Her voice dropped to a low murmur. 'You both miss Jenny. But it wasn't your fault.'

His mouth filled with ash; his muscles tensed. 'I thought we were just fucking? How do you know what I feel?'

How could she see into him so clearly? Into his darkest places? How could she know him so well?

The jibe hit its intended mark and Libby winced. But she recovered quickly, rounded eyes as dark as night peering into his soul.

'I know you feel somehow you let her down. But, Alex, you were a child. Not responsible for your parents' marriage. Not responsible for your sister. I'm certain you were an awesome brother to her.'

Remembering all the times when as a teen he'd ignored his family, how he'd detested the staring of strangers, how he'd abandoned family outings to hang out with his friends, he swallowed acid.

'How can you know that?' *He* didn't.

Her eyes glowed. 'Because you're an awesome man. Honourable, caring, fun. That came from somewhere.' She placed her palm flat on his chest, its warmth branding him through his shirt. 'In here. It wouldn't be there now if it hadn't been there then.'

She touched his neck, the tip of her index finger finding the hollow at the base of his throat.

'I understand. Your mother is hurting. You're hurting. Don't you see? You both feel like you've let the other down. *Stop*. Embrace the time you had with Jenny. Remember her together.'

'You might be right.'

He mashed his lips together. She claimed she didn't want him as anything beyond a fuck buddy. Didn't want to see him any more. But suddenly she was an expert on his pain?

'And what are *you* hiding from, Olivia?' He had eyes too.

Her hands fell from him, a flash of hurt in her eyes.

Libby looked down at her feet, gave a gentle shake of her head. 'I'm sorry. I'm crossing the line.'

No. She was right about him. Spot-on. He'd charged around throwing time and money at Able-Active, trying to make a difference, to make something he could feel proud of. And he didn't want a line where Libby was concerned.

He cupped her hip, drawing her close. 'I think

you see me pretty clearly.' His lips brushed her earlobe, but the slug of triumph at the flurry of trembles that skittered down her spine was short-lived. 'But I see *you* too.'

She didn't move, her stare eating into him.

At last she nodded. 'I know what it's like to lose someone.' Her huge dark eyes shone in the lights around the terrace. 'I understand the guilt.'

His fingers curled until he forced them to relax in case he hurt her. 'Want to tell me?'

The barest shrug.

He held in a curse, scanning the now deserted terrace. Their timing sucked. Everyone else had moved inside for dinner.

His hollow stomach lurched, his appetite long gone. 'Are you hungry?'

She shook her head, folding her arms across her chest to grip the opposite bicep. Goosebumps decorated her arms. He reached for his blazer from the back of a chair and draped it across her shoulders.

'Me neither.' He gripped her elbows, drawing her close. His hand moved to brush back her hair, which lifted in the cool evening breeze. 'Let's continue this conversation inside.'

Was this the chink he'd hoped for? Was she letting him closer? Opening up that last guarded part of her? Would she retreat? Push him further away?

She nodded, taking his hand. He clasped her fingers, aware that the pressure bordered on being too tight, but unable to stop himself. They skirted the house, cutting across the rose garden, fragrant in the falling dusk, and entered the guest wing via the French doors that led directly into the living room.

The silence crushed him. Libby pulled her hand from his grasp and moved away to the sofa. He poured them both a glass of brandy, gulping back a mouthful before joining her. The spirit warmed his belly, calming him. She was still there, rolling his stomach with her too-big eyes.

She accepted the drink wordlessly, her face pale.

After several beats, during which they stared across the chasm, he leaned close and kissed her, tasting the liquor on her soft lips. He couldn't *not* kiss her.

'You don't have to tell me.'

He could guess. Pain shored up the last part of her heart, holding it hostage. He pulled back a fraction, his finger twirling a thick coil of her glossy hair.

'But I want to know everything about you. I ache to know. All about you—what makes you tick, what pisses you off, what brings out that dazzling smile of yours.'

She smiled, a dimmer smile than he knew she was capable of, and then sobered.

'I had a fiancé. Callum.'

Boom. A blow to the chest.

Her eyes shone bright; her sad smile was apologetic. 'He was a lot like you—driven, adventurous, fun.'

Saliva dried in his throat.

Her smile widened, as if she were remembering. 'I embraced it. We had good years.'

The brandy turned to bile in his throat, and something dark and vicious twisted inside him. She was still in love with someone else. Some guy. *Callum*.

Libby filled her lungs. He braced himself for the blow. An end to his hopes for them.

'A week before our wedding we…'

She took a gulp of brandy, winced, placed the glass on the table and shrugged off his blazer. Her stare clung to his, as if she were daring herself to speak without the emotion swimming in her eyes.

'He died. A motorbike accident.' The last words appeared in a rush. A verbal ripping off of the bandage.

Alex's brain fought to tease her words from the rage of emotions tumbling inside him. He placed his brandy glass on the table. Alcohol wouldn't help.

'The one you were in?'

She nodded, her gaze fixed on her hands in her lap. 'I escaped with scratches. He died almost instantly.' Dry eyes lifted to his. 'He slid under the wheels of an oncoming truck.'

He gripped her tight, needing to feel her in his arms as much as he wanted to offer comfort. 'Olivia. I'm so sorry.'

She felt so *right* there. His chest ached as if the mouthful of brandy had burned through flesh and bone.

She was still for so long he wondered if she was

shedding silent tears, but his shirt under her cheek remained dry and her voice when she spoke was low, but steady.

'I understand how you feel about Jenny. Survivor guilt. Not a day goes by when I don't feel its claws in me. Even three years later.' She lifted her head, spearing him with a sincere, searching stare. 'But it was an accident. One I didn't cause and wasn't responsible for. It could just as easily have been me who died.'

Words shrivelled in his mouth, their sharp edges pricking their way down his throat. How had she seen him so clearly when he'd failed to join all the dots? How could he let her go when for the first time in his life he felt truly connected?

He brushed undemanding lips over hers. 'Tell me what you want. I'll do anything—take you back to London, fly you home to New York. Tell me.'

She pressed her mouth to his, surprising him with the passion lurking just beneath the surface. Twisting her fingers in his hair, she angled his head until he yielded under her assault, welcoming the touch of her tongue to his with a desire that matched that simmering in him.

She broke away. 'Don't ask anything of me.'

Her breath gusted over him, the chips of amber in her eyes masking her vulnerability.

There it was. Her limit. Her ultimate demand.

He'd never wanted to deny her more.

She gave him no time to acquiesce. She straddled

him where he sat, her fingers tunnelling into his hair as she tipped his head back, leaned over him and kissed him with a desperation that begged.

But he was done with games. He'd told her that in London. And he'd meant it. And now she'd shown him the raw, exposed part of her he wouldn't let her retreat. This time he'd control as much as he conceded, show her what he couldn't ask of her, feared telling her in case she skittered out of reach.

She writhed on his lap, pressing her moist heat to his already steely cock. Her whimpers notched up the urgency raging through him—the need to claim her, to convince her they had something worth exploring, something worth fighting for, something beyond a holiday fuck.

But he wouldn't rush this. Wouldn't allow *her* to rush it. Their chemistry, combustive enough to leave them both burnt alive, if harnessed could be ten times as rewarding. And he intended to show her that.

Libby tugged at his shirt, pulling it from his waistband with frantic fingers. He cupped her arse, grinding her onto his erection until she cried out, biting his lip so he tasted blood. *Fuck*, he loved her demanding side. She knew exactly what she wanted and made sure she got it. And he'd make sure he was there to give it to her.

Slipping one hand under her dress, he edged her lace panties aside, finding her soaked. He'd barely touched her. He located her clit, passing a few swipes over the bundle of nerves until she dragged her mouth from his and dropped her head back on a sigh of ecstasy.

He slid his mouth over her exposed neck, finding the sensitive spot beneath her ear and filling his nose with her unique scent as he pushed two fingers inside her and circled her clit with his thumb.

She was close. He could tell by the way her pants stuttered in her throat. Her hips jerked erratically and her eyes, when she opened them and gazed at him, were largely obscured by the dark crescents of her thick lashes. *Beautiful.* What she couldn't give him in words, in declarations, her body gave him in the abandon she couldn't conceal, in the depth of her stare and the way her fingers clung.

His chest ballooned. He was ten feet tall. A king. He did this to her. *Him.*

Her internal muscles gripped his fingers. His other hand loosened its clutch on her hip and he lifted the swathe of dark silk from her nape, twisting her hair around his wrist and tangling the ends between his fingers. He held her captive, his hand cramping with the pressure of his working fingers between her legs and his fist entwined in her glorious, thick tresses.

His. She was his. Possession burned through him with the thrum of his racing blood.

She glowed. A beautiful woman on the brink of intense sexual pleasure. His balls tightened. His own lust was a dull kick in the gut, but he intended to prolong this night, to wring every ounce of rapture from her so that when she left him she'd be in no doubt as to the depth of his rapidly expanding feelings and hard pushed to deny her own.

She could run, but he'd make damn sure she couldn't hide.

Her decadent lips parted on a strangled gasp. Her eyes widened, barely clinging to his, and her hips stilled.

His stare wide, so as not to miss one second of her orgasm, Alex gripped the back of her neck.

'Olivia.'

Crushing her mouth with his, he captured her broken cries with deep kisses, swallowing each one.

Her pleasure became his pleasure. Her pain of moments ago his pain. Somehow, in a few short days, she'd come to mean more to him than any other woman.

She quietened in his arms, the last judders leaving her replete and languorous. He lifted her, scooping one arm under her legs and the other around her back, and carried her to the bedroom they shared.

He saw nothing but her. Didn't give a fuck about his business, the charity or even his family enjoying a meal somewhere else in the château. All that mattered was Olivia, and his need to show her exactly what she meant to him.

CHAPTER ELEVEN

THE SHEETS WERE cool at her back as Alex laid her gently on the bed. She searched his stare, trying to deny what she saw there. After his honest declaration in the pool, meeting his mother and witnessing the pain mirrored in eyes so much like her son's, all his pieces slotted together. And his instincts about her own demons? Alex peered far too closely into her soul for comfort.

She'd tried to stay impassive, to distance herself. But in the end she'd been helpless against opening herself up to him. She understood guilt, knew first-hand how it burned away at you, slowly, like acid. And she didn't want that for Alex—couldn't bear to see it destroy what was left of his relationship with his mother. He gave so much of himself. To people, to his charity, to *her*.

When she'd probed him about Jenny, told him about Callum, she'd feared she'd push him even further away than her attempt to do so in the pool. But he stood over her now, slowly peeling her from her clothes and then shucking his own until there was little between them except the unspoken.

Her mouth filled with all she longed to say. But it was pointless. She was leaving and she wouldn't give him false hope. Wouldn't hurt him even when staying silent left her shredded.

He pulled her up on still shaky legs, her intense climax having robbed her of all but the basic functions of breathing and pumping blood around her body. He caressed her. His eyes and large hands touching on every part of her until she trembled anew with adrenaline. Tenderness seeped from his touch, from his stare. She closed her eyes, struggling to witness the raw emotion spilling out of him. Emotion for *her*. Emotion she longed to accept. Longed to reciprocate.

He pummelled her resolve, pulling her so close that she struggled to breathe. He wrapped his arms around her, tangling one hand in her hair and tilting her head back so he could lavish her throat and upper chest with soft, indulgent kisses.

She swayed, the only thing keeping her upright his strong arms banded around her. She'd never survive this—was already perilously close to the final leap of faith.

'Turn around.'

His words whispered over her neck, skittering down her spine. Helpless, she obeyed, her movements slowed by the easy slide of her hair around his wrist and hand. Not tugging. Never bringing pain, but with enough tension that every hair on her head transmitted pleasure to her strung-out nerve endings. She covered his hand, pressing his palm to her head, feeling what he felt.

He kissed her shoulders, lips gliding, his free hand sliding over her hip as he nudged her feet closer to the bed. Libby's head swam. She scrunched her eyes tightly closed. It was enough to hear the husky command in his voice and to feel the reverence of his touch.

His erection lodged between the cheeks of her ass, the warm, hard length of him shooting tingles up her spine to join with the ones from her stimulated scalp.

'*Fuck*, you're a beautiful woman.' His words tickled her neck, and the brush of his lips at her earlobe buckled her knees.

One hand slid the length of her thigh, gripping behind her knee and encouraging her to climb onto the bed on all fours.

A thrill of excitement fluttered in her belly. She turned her head, her bold stare meeting his over her shoulder. But his eyes skittered away, tracing her back, her hips, and returning.

'Your hair is beautiful.' He twisted his wrist, the thick coil of hair sliding through his fingers only to be captured again. 'I've wanted to do this since the moment I met you.'

His wrist was rolling. Again and again. Her hair tumbling away, then being recaptured. All the while his other hand traced a path of fire from her breast to her hip and returned via her arched back.

Moisture pooled between her legs. Anticipation coiled deep inside. Would he push inside her like this? She felt a bead of moisture in the small of her back, where his hard length rested. This position—the view of her perched on all fours, her hair wrapped in his fist, ready for him, brought the breath gusting from him as sure as her own shallow pants.

She closed her eyes, envisaging him behind her, taking her hard, her hair in his hand, while he grunted out the pleasure he was too far gone to contain. She wanted him wild. Wanted him too impassioned to maintain his gentleman's persona. Wanted him possessive and selfish in his need for her.

'Do you have *any* idea what you do to me, Libby?'

The path of his hand paused at her shoulder, one finger tracing a featherlike trail down the bumps of her spine while he ground the length of his erection into her wet sex. It wasn't enough. She wanted him filling her. Pushing her to the edge again while he shouted her name.

'Alex…'

'I've never wanted anything more.'

His voice was a gruff whisper. He pulled his hips back and she groaned, missing the contact.

'And I can't have you.'

His finger slid between the cheeks of her ass, passing slowly, gliding south.

'Not all of you.'

He found her entrance, fingers probing, a tug on her hair.

'Trouble is…'

His wet finger travelled north again, pleasure dancing under the firm pressure of the tip.

'I want all of you.'

He plunged two fingers inside her, spreading them to open her sensitive walls.

'More than fucking.'

He tugged her hair, tilting her head back.

'More than a few stolen days.'

She twisted, opening her eyes to glance back at him.

His eyes burned with an intensity she'd yet to witness.

'I want it all.'

He latched his stare to hers. The raw hunger she saw in his features, slack with lust, need burning in the depths of his eyes, stole her breath. She had no time to answer or to acknowledge his words. No time to untangle the knotted threads of her own feelings.

Alex released her hair, flipped her onto her back and climbed above her.

His kisses started with her mouth, all too soon departing for her throat and her shoulders. Her restless hands clawed at him, her nails likely leaving marks, but she was helpless, and for the first time in years she was accepting the state instead of trying to outrun it. Completely at his mercy and—for now—*his*.

His mouth lavished her breasts, nipping and sucking until her legs twisted around his in an attempt to bring them closer together.

When he traced her belly with his lips, his hands pushing her thighs apart, she thought she'd die, so great was the need coiled inside her. She cradled his face while he suckled her sex, his grunts of pleasure vibrating through her clit.

His mouth left her abruptly and he kneeled between her thighs, his stare tracing her from top to toe.

'I want all of you. I want you to be mine.'

He reached for the condom he'd tossed on the bed earlier and ripped into it, his eyes holding her captive, bold, daring her as he sheathed himself.

And then he was pushing inside her, and her hands were clasped in his, their fingers interlocked as if they'd never let go, his stare eating her alive and his body rigid above her like a man on the edge.

His head dipped to her breast once more, his hot mouth drawing out her cries and whimpers as his hips ground into hers. Within two or three thrusts she came, clinging to him with everything she had as the slow-rolling spasms rocked her time and time again.

'Yes…' he murmured around her flesh, nibbling at her tortured nipple with firm lips and licks of fire from the gentle scrape of his teeth. 'Give me more, Olivia. Give me everything.'

He kept up the suction, carrying her past the molten liquid phase until the sharp bite of arousal gripped her once more. Sweat gathered at Alex's hairline. He shifted, stretching her hands above her head and raising himself up on his knees to deepen the penetration. His smooth gliding thrusts picked up tempo, jerking to pound her sex with the wildness she'd craved.

His teeth gripped his bottom lip as he fought for his own pleasure. She wanted to push him over, as he'd pushed her. She longed to give him what she knew he wanted. Some promise. Some commitment. Some acknowledgment that what they had between them was as unique for her as he'd hinted it was for him.

She wriggled her hands free of his, reaching between them to cup his face. He twisted his head, his lips kissing the centre of one palm before he sought her eyes once more.

Muscles bulged in his jaw. His face contorted as his hips grew more frantic. 'Come with me, Libby.'

She gripped his face tighter, her stare seeking deep inside his. "Alex… I…'

He roared, his face twisted with rapture as he came, grasping her shoulders and giving her a third orgasm as surely as he'd given her a part of himself.

Libby pressed her toes into the soft sand. The tiny grains reflected the glint of a perfect Mediterranean morning. This early, they practically had the strip of golden beach to themselves, the only sounds the occasional cry of a gull and the constant drone of jet ski engines.

She lifted one hand to shield her eyes, catching a glimpse of Alex streaking ahead of Jack as they traversed the bay, plumes of water in their wakes. Her stomach lurched, and the familiar jolt of adrenaline was one of the reasons she'd opted for sunbathing over skimming the surface of the Med on little more than a bicycle with a propeller.

She flopped back onto her lounger, closing her eyes and forcing herself to think of something other than death or permanent injury. Only one thought emerged—Alex. Opening up to him last night had left her palms damp and her mouth dry. But she couldn't bring herself to regret it for one second. They'd fallen asleep covered in each other, as close as two people could be. Breathing the same air, skin touching from head to toe, sharing soft, sleepy kisses until unconsciousness claimed them.

It changed nothing. This time tomorrow she'd be on a flight back to New York. But something inside her had renewed. A hard kernel had cracked open and the tiny green shoot inside, delicate but brave, was pushing into the sunlight. She'd developed feelings for him. In the space of a few short days. A cliché. A whirlwind. Completely blindsiding her.

Now what? Pining over the changes to her working relationship with Sonya, reeling from her conflicted emotions, living a whole continent away? The obstacles seemed greater than ever. And Alex hadn't verbalised his feelings beyond stating that he wanted to see her again. Perhaps he'd meant once a year, when he travelled to New York on business.

And the reasons for her reluctance still simmered inside her. When he'd winked and suggested she ride pillion with him on the jet ski she'd shrunk away, feigning a desire to work on her tan rather than confess the truth.

She'd been there. Once was enough. If she'd been riding the motorbike that day, been in control, would the outcome have differed? Would she be married to Callum now? About to celebrate their three-year anniversary? Pregnant with his baby?

The daydreams left her skin prickled with goosebumps. She rubbed her arms, trying and failing to rub the unsettling thoughts from her mind. If she'd had all of that she wouldn't be here now, with Alex. She wouldn't know that his eyes sparked when he teased her, that he danced when he was happy and didn't care if anyone saw him, or that on the mornings they awoke together he'd pad to the kitchen dressed only in boxers to make her a 'proper cup of English tea'.

The angry roar of an engine grabbed Libby from her reverie. She sat up in time to see Alex, his jet ski aimed at an oncoming wave, travelling at full throttle.

What the hell?

Libby's stomach lurched into her throat. Her hand covered her mouth as his jet ski hit the wave head-on. The wall of water tossed the small craft into the air, flipping it upside down, and the hollow growl of the airborne engine ricocheted inside Libby's skull until her eardrums threatened to perforate.

Her mind blanked. Her body tensed on the very edge of the lounger while time slowed and Alex seemed suspended in mid-air for what felt like a year. And then, with a slap as it hit the surface, the jet ski righted itself, the somersault complete, and Alex raced over to Jack, hand raised with a fist-pump of victory.

Icy shivers covered Libby's body. Every hair rose to attention. Every muscle twitched. As her stomach settled back inside her abdomen where it belonged, allowing air inside her lungs, the epiphany struck.

She loved him.

She'd fallen in love with an adrenaline junkie. A man not content just to enjoy the thrill, but who wanted to push the boundaries to the limit. A limit that made her hands tremble and her vision darken.

Libby reeled. She had to move. To do something with the restless energy boiling inside her.

She reached for her sarong, slipping it on and gathering up her phone and a set of keys for one of the estate's vehicles.

Before she'd taken two steps she snapped her head round as another guttural roar cut through the warm air. Libby froze. Her feet stuck to the hot sand. Her eyes were glued to the unfolding drama.

This somersault was higher, its angle, even to Libby's untrained eye, more acute, and the wave to which Alex trusted his life bigger. As he disappeared from view over the crest Libby took off running.

Her legs acted independently of her mind, her ears trained for the landing slap. It came, but the wave continued to roll ashore, obscuring her view. Had he made it? Was he unconscious? Bleeding? His lungs full of seawater?

The wave broke and the orange hull of the capsized jet ski flashed. Her eyes scanned the water, her knees almost buckling when Alex surfaced, his arm raised with a wave to let them know he was okay. Within seconds Jack had cruised over to his cousin, the jet ski was righted and Alex had climbed back into the driver's seat.

But Libby was done.

She'd seen enough to last her two lifetimes. The ice in her blood boiled. If he came in now she wouldn't be responsible for the things she said. Changing direction, she hurried up the beach, the heat on her back and under her feet adding to the fury and impotence raging inside her.

She needed time to think. She needed distance.

Everything between them had happened so quickly, and now her feelings for Alex were spiralling out of control. She'd vowed after Callum's funeral never to get this close again. But here she was, in love with a daredevil billionaire with a penchant for fast toys and dangerous sports. *No.* She couldn't do it again. Refused to put herself through it.

She'd loved Callum. She loved Alex. It terrified

her to admit it, but if she didn't she'd make the mistake of being led by her feelings, of succumbing to their insidious allure.

She arrived at one of the vehicles, her hand trembling on the automatic lock. Alex and Jack would have the truck and trailer, so they could get back to the château in time for the wedding. But she had to get away.

If she had to watch Alex do that again... *No.*

She gunned the engine. She didn't know the way back, but the car was top of the range and fitted with GPS. And right now, with all the turmoil pounding through her, getting lost for a few hours wasn't such a bad idea.

She didn't want Alex to worry about her when he discovered her missing, so she plugged her phone into the hands-free and set off. He'd call when he came ashore and she'd text him when she'd calmed down.

She drove, the twisting coastal road that hugged the cliffs a perfect distraction from her riotous thoughts. Halfway back to the château a call came in. But it was Vinnie's voice that startled her.

'Libby? Sonya's been admitted to hospital. I thought you should know.'

Stunned, Libby indicated and pulled off the road, killing the engine. 'What's wrong?'

'All's well, but her blood pressure is high. They'll be inducing labour in the morning.'

She pressed her forefinger to her throbbing temple, her mind flying between thinking of all the necessary arrangements and concern for her friend and her unborn child.

'Change my flight, Vinnie.'

'Sonya said to tell you she's fine. It's just a precaution because she's at term.'

Libby used a tone he'd understand. 'Get me on the next flight home.'

A pause. Then, 'Sure.'

She hung up and pulled back onto the road, breaking a few French traffic laws.

Yes, she probably had time to wait for Alex to return, to explain why she'd left him at the beach and why she was leaving France earlier than she'd planned. But, whether she'd asked or not, Sonya needed her. And would voicing her views on Alex's reckless behaviour change anything? Did she even *want* to change him? The problem was hers.

She swallowed, her throat hot and her eyes stinging. Cowardice won. She chose to run.

CHAPTER TWELVE

ALEX SHIFTED IN the seat as he waited for the call to connect, the creak of leather as irritating as the view of the cumulus through the tiny window of his jet. The brief journey to London crawled, every second drawn out to breaking point. How could he have been so stupid?

When he'd found Libby gone after returning to the beach yesterday he'd feared every scenario but the truth—kidnapping, murder, drowning—as if his mind hadn't wanted to believe the obvious. He'd messed up and she was gone.

He scrubbed his knuckles down the side of his face, the rasp of stubble evidence of his hasty departure from France that morning. He'd have left last night if it hadn't been for his cousin's wedding. He'd missed most of the nuptials anyway, with his mind going over every second of his time with Libby and every word of their conversations.

The call connected.

'Mr Lancaster,' said Molly. 'I'm sorry. I was in the shower.'

Fuck. He had no excuse for behaving like a shitty boss today. He'd make it up to her.

'Can you schedule an appointment for me with Libby Noble at her New York office at her earliest convenience, please, Molly? And send flowers to Sonya Pullman via the Noble and Pullman offices.'

He understood that Libby would be worried for her friend. Of course she'd want to rush to her side. But without saying goodbye? Without any discussion on the state of their relationship?

The final words of her brief explanatory text replayed in his head, over and over, mocking him with their finality.

Sorry to have to say goodbye via text. Thank you for a wonderful week. I'll always remember it. Good luck with the charity, and if you're ever in New York... Libby xx

His fist clenched hard around the phone. 'I'll be on the ground in twenty minutes. Can you have an overnight bag delivered to the airport and make the necessary arrangements? I'll be flying straight to New York after refuelling.'

He'd tried the personal approach, calling and then texting Libby. He didn't blame her for her silence.

He'd enticed her to be his date at a wedding— likely a trigger for her, given that she must have cancelled her own wedding whilst grieving and burying her fiancé.

He'd drawn out her perfect sublime surrender to

him, with their lovemaking opening up new trust, a deeper connection, unspoken endearments.

And then he'd spooked her, no doubt forcing her to relive the worst moment of her life, with his jet ski stunts.

He'd known her reticence as soon as she'd declined to ride behind him. Part of him had wanted to forgo the rush of skimming the bay. But he'd also wanted to demonstrate his competence. Not showing off, but showing Libby that life was for living. The somersault—something he'd perfected from the age of sixteen—had been a step too far.

He pinched the bridge of his nose, answering Molly's brief questions with terse, staccato responses. How had he misjudged things so badly? He'd wanted to give Libby a day that would stay in her memory. One that would remind her of their time together. One that would make it impossible for her to deny her feelings. Feelings he guessed terrified her.

He understood her fear. He felt it too. Their brief encounter had rocked him in its intensity. But to walk away? Never to see her again? Never to explore the burgeoning feelings expanding inside him...

He couldn't do it. What he wanted to know was how could *she*? He'd been away from her less than twenty-four hours, but already he ached to see her again, to touch her, to kiss her.

If there was no future beyond their few stolen days she'd have to tell him face to face, in that frank, forthright manner of hers. Tell him that the connection they shared could be easily discarded. Tell him that she was happy simply returning to her safe life, risking nothing—especially her heart.

His PA drew him back to their conversation.

'One last thing, Molly—send a memo to Human Resources to increase your salary by twenty per cent. That's all for now.'

He ended the call, but not before he heard Molly's gasp.

He sagged back into the seat as the pilot announced their descent. He'd always refused to give up without a fight. He had no intention of conceding now. He'd shown Libby he loved her. Now it was time to tell her.

Libby tapped gently at the door of Sonya's private room in the maternity care unit. She peered through the glass, quietly entering when she saw Sonya was awake.

She placed her gifts on a nearby table and went to her friend, pulling her into an embrace that she never wanted to end.

Sonya's tears seeped into the shoulder of Libby's blouse. Libby clung tighter, her mind racing. 'Shh, it's okay.'

Sonya never cried. Not since her first college boyfriend had broken her heart and they'd commiserated with a tub of Ben & Jerry's and two spoons. Libby pulled back, reached for a tissue from the nightstand and wiped her friend's blotchy cheeks.

Sonya gave a tearful chuckle. 'Sorry. I'm told it's the hormones. It had better stop soon or I'm having my tear ducts removed. Rich doesn't know what to do with me,' she said of her husband.

Libby smiled, smoothing the hair back from Sonya's face. 'I'm not sure myself.'

They laughed, breaking the tension, although Libby was selfishly tempted to add a meltdown of her own. She'd never felt so adrift.

Swallowing back her own tumult of emotions, she focussed on her reason for being here. Her friend.

Libby pointed at the Perspex crib on the far side of the bed, eyes wide. 'Is this her?' she whispered, awe bubbling up in her chest and her smile making her cheeks ache.

Sonya nodded, her watery gaze flicking to where her tiny newborn slept. Libby tiptoed to the crib, her own throat suspiciously choked. Sonya's daughter had a shock of black hair, just like her mom. Her tiny fist was clenched beside her angelic face, which was peaceful in slumber.

It was hard for Libby to breathe. She fought the urge to lift the baby from the crib, bury her face in the soft down of her hair and sob her heart out.

'She's so beautiful, Son…' Libby stroked the blanket covering the baby, so as not to wake her.

She mentally shook herself, sucking in a calming breath. She wasn't prone to ooh-ing and ahh-ing over babies. She always had her shit together and she never cried either. She refused to start now. Sonya needed her.

'Amelia,' said Sonya. 'We named her after Rich's grandmother.

Libby nodded. 'It's beautiful. *She's* beautiful. Well done, you.' Libby squeezed Sonya's fingers and took the seat next to her bed, grinning at her friend.

When their smiles had dropped, Libby said, 'What's with the tube?'

She'd noticed Amelia had a small hollow tube in her mouth, her tiny lips suckling it even in sleep.

Fresh tears gathered on Sonya's lashes. Why had she asked?

'She has a congenital condition.'

Libby hid her shock, passing another tissue to her friend and taking one for herself. Just in case.

'It's called choanal atresia—it means her nasal passages didn't form properly and she can't breathe through her nose.'

Libby scrunched the tissue in her palm. 'Is it serious?'

Her respect for Sonya skyrocketed. Not enough that she'd undergone an emergency C-section to bring her daughter into the world, she now faced further anguish and her tiny newborn might require surgery.

Sonya nodded. 'It's life-threatening. Babies are nose-breathers. She turned blue the first time I tried to nurse her.'

Her sniffs intensified as she tried to continue her

story. Libby could only watch and wait, her own eyes burning.

'Most terrified I've ever been in my entire life.' Sonya gripped Libby's fingers tighter. 'She'll need surgery—probably later today or tomorrow.'

Libby reeled. No wonder her fearless friend couldn't stop crying. 'Where's Rich?'

'I sent him to the cafeteria to get some breakfast. He hasn't eaten anything for twenty-four hours.'

Libby dipped her head. 'I'm so sorry. I should have been here sooner.'

Sonya shook her head, her eyes landing on Amelia and softening. 'You couldn't have done anything. It all happened so quickly in the end.'

Libby nodded, at a loss for words. What could she say to comfort her friend? What did she know about what Sonya and Rich were facing? She'd written off having children after Callum died, but the surge of protective instinct crushing her from the inside out gave her a small insight into what they must be feeling.

The women stared at the sleeping baby, turning to face each other with matching indulgent grins on their faces. It was hard not to smile when such incredible beauty existed.

'I love her so much,' said Sonya. 'I didn't realise it would be so...*instantaneous*.'

Libby nodded, a boulder-sized lump lodged in her chest. 'Of course you do. She's perfect.'

Her gaze returned to Amelia, drawn back to the

tiny human. For the first time in three years she allowed herself to think, to dream of a future. A future that embraced the kind of love Sonya talked about. The kind of love she felt for Alex.

The moment the plane had left French soil—left *him*—she'd realised her mistake. Every mile that had carried her home had pulled her apart. Rather than providing perspective, as she'd hoped, being back in New York, in her apartment, had merely intensified the jumble of conflicted feelings inside her.

She loved him. She had no idea what to do about it, but she accepted it as truth.

Give me everything, Olivia.

Why hadn't she?

Sonya shifted in the bed, pressing her lips together and clutching her stomach.

Libby startled from her reverie, her hand gripping Sonya's arm.

Her friend breathed out on a slow exhalation. 'I'm fine. Afterpains,' she said in explanation.

As if she hadn't been through enough, there were afterpains? What the hell...?

'Tell me about France.'

No... If she thought about France she'd think about Alex and then the gut-churning would return—that fluttery feeling in her chest that told her she'd made the biggest mistake of her life.

She plastered on a fake smile for Sonya's sake. Her friend had enough on her plate without Libby's self-inflicted dramas. 'I didn't see much of it. Just Nice. It was…*nice*.'

Libby's smile turned genuine. She'd managed to entice a giggle from her friend.

'Beautiful countryside.' She clutched her stomach. 'I ate too much. The French people are delightful, although I couldn't understand a word—'

'What about Alex?' Sonya cut straight to the chase.

She'd known it was coming, that the question was inevitable. They'd been friends for many years. But she wasn't prepared for hearing his name, and the blow winded her as much as Sonya's revelation about Amelia.

She swallowed, psyching herself up to talk about him. 'He…he's fine, I guess.'

Please let him be fine. Better than fine. She must have pissed him off, rushing out on him the way she had. He'd understand the emergency, but he was smart enough to fill in the blanks. She'd run rather than face him. Face her fear.

'You don't know? You haven't been in touch? Sonya's brow pinched, her eyes searching.

Libby shrugged. 'I wanted to get back to see you.'

Hot shards pierced Libby's lungs. She'd left him with only a feeble text message in explanation. She'd ignored his calls and texts, telling herself her friend needed her and she could only deal with one life-altering situation at a time.

She looked down at her hands clutched in her lap. 'I was always going to leave.'

Sonya's labour had only sped up Libby's departure. But, oh, how she'd paid the price for her cowardice. Her body was disjointed, her mind flitted aimlessly, unable to settle on one thought, and hateful waves of emotion threatened to break at any second. Would she ever feel normal again? Should she even crave that insipid state? It was so pale in comparison with her wild week with Alex.

She'd never be able to fill her days with enough work, exercise and reading to match the soul-deep contentment she'd found with him. He'd brought her back to life. Not his wealth or his gifts, nor even his enforced adventures. But *him*. The person. The man who gave everything he had to making a difference. The man who'd given her what she needed. The man who'd shown her she could love again.

Sonya had fallen quiet and keenly watchful. Libby brightened and plastered a smile on her face, but clearly she wasn't quick enough.

Sonya's stare was shrewd. 'Are you seeing him again?'

Libby swallowed. Stalled. She wasn't ready to confess her true feelings for Alex. To anyone. She hadn't had enough time to pick them apart and Sonya would think she was mad, falling for a man she'd only known for a week. Who *did* that?

Fortunately she'd prepared a speech for this eventuality. 'Perhaps. But we both work insane hours and

live on different continents, so the chances are slim.'
Acid burned her throat. Chances he'd want to see her
now were less than slim.

'You don't want to make it work?'

It was a question, but it felt like a statement. Sonya
knew her so well. Had been there for her through the
dark times. She should have known she'd see right
through her and her attempts at nonchalance.

Libby looked at her hands in her lap, her throat
tight and her eyes hot. Fatigue made her feel heavy in
the chair, the weight of what she'd done pressing her
down. She'd had long sleepless hours to make sense
of her true feelings—first on the flight from France
and then while she paced her apartment, waiting
for the sun to come up so she could visit her friend.

Without conscious thought she let the confession
tumble out on a whisper, as if the words spoken any
louder would have more power over her. Power to
hurt.

'I fell in love with him, Son.'

She kept her eyes trained on her fingernails, blind
to everything as she forced air into her lungs. Tried
to breathe through a different kind of grief. Not as
acute or violent as past pain, but just as devastating.

'Of course you did.'

Sonya was quiet. Libby swallowed, pushing down
the overwhelming swell of emotion inside. A tidal
wave crashing ashore and destroying every wall
she'd built to protect herself over the years.

'You know…' Sonya stroked her hand, drawing

her back from the abyss. 'Here's the thing about love...'

Libby swallowed, meeting her friend's sincere gaze.

'We have no choice, do we?' Sonya flicked a glance at her sleeping child, her face aglow with maternal love. 'It's the best emotion and the worst, because it has the power to hurt us like nothing else.'

Libby nodded, her throat too constricted for her to respond.

Sonya's sad smile wobbled on her lips. 'But I wouldn't change it. Not for a second. You don't need me to tell you it's worth it.'

Her eyes burned into Libby's, speaking what she hadn't said aloud. Love was worth the pain. Worth the risk.

Alex was worth loving. Not that she had any choice in the matter.

Libby nodded, lips tight, holding on to her panic, which urged her with every passing second to race to JFK and jump on the first flight back to London.

'If he loves you back,' said Sonya, 'it's not too late. Don't wait. Tell him.'

Both women were startled when the door opened and Rich entered, his gaze landing first on Sonya, then on his daughter, and finally on Libby.

As if through a fog, she congratulated him and made conversation for a few more minutes. When Sonya tried to hide a yawn she made her excuses and left the new family to themselves, knowing these moments were precious.

Outside the hospital, she hailed a cab. Sonya was right. Alex *was* worth the risk. And she had little choice. She loved him. She could either live a careful life, nursing that love alone, or she could commit to it. Surmount the obstacles, the distance, and love him with her whole being—the way he deserved to be loved. The way *she* deserved.

By the time she entered her office she'd tried his cell phone and his home phone, with no success. His voicemail mocked her. His deep voice a form of aural torture. She'd had a chance at something rare and extraordinary and she'd let it slip away. No. She'd flung it away, as if it had burned. But the pain of her cowardice hurt so much more than the pain of her bravery—especially as she only had herself to blame.

She slammed through the foyer, startling Vinnie, who was in the middle of a call. He hung up, his grin wide, and then let it fall slightly when he saw the expression she clearly couldn't hide.

He stood, rounding the desk with his arms outstretched for a hug. 'Welcome back, hen. Did you have a good trip? Have you seen the wee one? Och, she's a darling. Made me quite broody myself, she did.'

Vinnie always fired multiple questions, as if he already knew the answers.

Libby laughed into his chest, on the verge of sobbing. She accepted the comfort of his hug for an indulgent, unprofessional second.

'Please don't call me hen. I'm not a chicken.'

Vinnie rolled his eyes, this well-worn argument clearly having no effect on him whatsoever. 'You get settled, I'll make you a brew, and then you can tell Uncle Vinnie all about it.'

Her spirits lifted. She could always rely on her outrageous, thick-skinned assistant to cheer her up. She forced her smile into a semiserious scowl. She couldn't let him get away with everything, or he'd run the show.

'I've told you a thousand times. Libby, Ms Noble or even Boss is preferable.' She handed him the small gift she'd bought in London, her throat hot and achy again. Fuck this day and its crazy mood swings. 'Thanks for caring for Sonya and holding the fort.'

He clutched his mouth, his eyes round. 'It isn't…?' He caressed the square package lovingly. 'Scottish? Och, hen, you shouldn't have.'

She laughed and nodded. 'Would I bring you shortbread that wasn't Scottish?'

He hugged her again, his delight infectious. 'You're the best boss in the world, hen.'

Libby rolled her eyes. 'Speaking of which—work to do. First, can you please get Alex Lancaster on the line for me?'

She checked her watch, calculating the time difference.

'He should be still at the office. Speak to Molly, his PA. He might be at the Able-Active charity. And then you can get me up to speed on everything I've missed—celebrity gossip notwithstanding.'

Vinnie placed his gift in the drawer with reverence. 'I'm on it.'

'And did you send through that list of applicants for Sonya's position?'

He nodded, moving to the coffee machine they kept in the corner, pre-empting her next request.

Her office seemed unfamiliar, disjointed, as if someone had shifted the walls or changed the view through the windows. Had she really only been away a week? So much had changed—her most of all. Now the familiar, the previously comforting, felt like a cage, holding her back.

Distracted, she checked her e-mails, ignoring the fifty or so business-related ones that required her attention before she could leave for the day, her eyes scanning for one from Alex. Nothing. What did that mean? He was over her? He'd accepted her departure without question? He'd moved on?

No. She couldn't allow herself a trip down to that particular mind-trap. Not until she'd spoken to him. Told him how she felt.

With impatient fingers she composed a brief e-mail to him, requesting a phone call. She couldn't put what she had to say in an e-mail. The words were so big she'd break the internet.

Within seconds an automatic response landed in her inbox. Her stomach lurched. Alex Lancaster was out of the office, all requests should be directed to Molly.

What did that mean? Was he still in France? Perhaps he'd moved up that business trip to Japan he'd told her about. Perhaps he'd taken a holiday. Perhaps he wanted nothing to do with her.

Libby straightened her desk, aligning the pens to her left and the pot plant to her right, restless energy bubbling beneath her skin.

Vinnie entered with her coffee. 'No luck with Mr Lancaster, I'm afraid. And I can't get hold of Molly either.' He took one look at her face, placed the coffee on the desk and headed for the door. 'I'll keep trying.'

For the rest of the day she worked in a fog, achieving little, upsetting Vinnie and checking her phone and e-mails every thirty seconds—like a teenager with her first crush. Impotence gripped her, its claws sinking deep until she wanted to climb out of her own skin.

By five, she'd abandoned hope for any constructive work. Her temples throbbed, her eyes were gritty from lack of sleep, and her mind was sluggish with jet lag.

She closed her laptop in disgust, shrugged into her jacket and yelled out to Vinnie, who'd wisely kept a low profile for the last two hours. 'Any news from Sonya? About the surgery?'

'It's scheduled for first thing tomorrow.' His voice boomed back from the outer office through the open adjoining door. He was clearly pissed with her.

Fine. She was pissed with herself. She prided herself on knowing what she wanted professionally.

How had she got it so wrong when it came to her personal life?

She stuffed her tablet into her bag and snatched up her still-silent cell phone, tempted to hurl the useless device through the window.

The time for waiting was over. It was time for action.

She called out to Vinnie again, too impatient to wait the few seconds it would take her to walk to his desk 'Vinnie, book me a flight to London asap.'

What was she thinking? She had work commitments, clients to see, Sonya to support. She couldn't just up and leave again.

But she couldn't sit and do nothing either.

'Ah… Ms Noble,' said Vinnie, his cautious tone carrying through the open door.

Great—now he'd resorted to sarcasm to wind her up. He *never* called her that, despite her constant reprimands.

'I have Alex Lancaster for you.'

Her feet stalled. Her belly flip-flopped. Had she heard him correctly? She reached for the edge of her desk to steady herself.

'Put him through.'

She turned, skirted her desk, dropped into her chair. Her hand hovered over the phone on her desk, her belly rioting. Vinnie mumbled something she didn't catch. Now really wasn't the time for him to have a meltdown. As soon as she'd spoken to Alex she'd apologise to him for her crappy mood today.

Promise to take him for lunch tomorrow at his favourite bistro. Buy him a stack of his beloved magazines.

Why wasn't he putting through the call?

She couldn't wait. With a sigh, she strode to the open door that connected her office to that of her PA. 'Look, I'm sorry. I'll just take the call here.'

She flung open the door.

And came face to face with Alex.

The air left her lungs with a thump. Her stomach recoiled from its temporary location in her throat. Her eyes raked him from head to toe. He was real. He was here. In the flesh.

'Olivia.'

A curt nod. Unreadable eyes. Unsmiling mouth.

But, oh, the scrape of his voice over her strung-out senses was so welcome. Her lungs stuttered back to life, relief pounding through her, quickly followed by thick, syrupy lust. What a sight. Just the way she liked him—nerdy graphic T-shirt, relaxed jeans hugging his hips, his hair an unruly mess that begged for her fingers.

His delicious scent stole all the air from the room. Her mouth dried. Her brain shut down.

'I...'

He's here. Say something.

'How are you?' She flicked her gaze over him. 'What are you doing here?'

Behind Alex, Vinnie was fanning himself, dramatically, his gaze sliding over her man. Libby sheathed her claws. Alex wasn't *her* anything. She'd thrown him away.

'We have unfinished business.' He quirked one brow, his mouth tight, giving nothing away. 'I have a car downstairs. Would you join me so we can discuss it?'

Not frosty, but not friendly either.

He held out his arm, indicating the exit.

Unfinished business? Why was he in New York? For *her*?

She must have performed some jaw-dropping goldfish impersonation, because Vinnie answered for her.

'She's just finished for the day. She'd love to.'

Jet lag, insomnia and stress—a combination disastrous for her usual quick wit and acidic put-downs.

'I...'

She couldn't even string a sentence together to reprimand her heavy-handed assistant. All she could do was stare. Alex's dark eyes were a magnet.

'Please.'

At last she saw a flicker there—one she'd thought she'd never have a chance to see again.

Hope shocked her brain back to life. Vinnie had her bag in his hand now and was shoving it towards her and urging her to the exit.

'I'll finish up here, boss.' He gave her a wink.

She'd absolutely have to fire him. Tomorrow.

She made the short journey outside on seriously

wobbly legs. Alex, at her side, kept his hands to himself and Libby wasn't sure whether to weep or climb over him and remind him how good they were together.

Then she remembered the way she'd left him. Her fingers flexed. She craved the feel of him, but could she face his rejection? Had she broken their connection permanently?

On the street, Alex ushered her inside the waiting car, following her inside and taking the seat opposite. The car pulled away from the kerb, entering the stream of evening traffic.

She looked at him. For the first time free of the shock of seeing him here. The noises of the outside world vanished. Her mind cleared. They stared across the chasm separating them.

Her eyes drank him in, cataloguing every minute detail of his beloved face. The smudged circles beneath his dark eyes, the day's worth of stubble covering his jaw, the muscle ticking there. Perhaps he'd had as little sleep as her over the last twenty-four hours.

His voice, when it came, washed over her, alerting every nerve ending with its low rumble.

'You didn't say goodbye.'

His eyes were piercing, pinning her to the leather. Shame forced her to glance away. 'I… I did.'

He shook his head. 'Not in person.'

Her throat closed. 'No.'

I love you.

Why was this so hard? Would he think her mad? He'd only asked to see her again. Why was her mind, currently struggling to think of *anything*, overthink this?

'Why?'

Good question. She met his stare again, heat blooming in her belly. 'I'm a coward.'

Nothing.

'I'm scared, Alex.' The words fled in a rush.

A single nod and then he stayed silent, giving her the space she needed, time to turn the jumble in her head into words.

'I've been scared for so long I've forgotten how to be anything else.' Libby focussed on his eyes, their unique beauty a lifeline. Perhaps she could say what she had to say. She needed him to understand why she'd messed up so monumentally.

'I held Callum in my arms that day I lost him. I watched the life drain out of him—watched the vibrant man I loved fade away.' She stared harder, willing him to comprehend. Willing him to give her another chance. 'I never want to go through that again.' Her voice broke.

He swallowed, his eyes glittering chips of amber. Still silent.

She reached for his hand, almost sagging to the floor when his fingers squeezed hers. 'I thought I couldn't love again. But I can. Because I love you. And it terrifies me.'

Air gusted out of him, his shoulders sagging. 'Thank fuck.'

He reached for her other hand, tugging her to the edge of the seat. A small smile lifted the corners of his mouth and his gaze wandered her features as he cupped her face between his palms.

'Because I love you, too, Libby. I followed you to tell you.' His thumbs swiped at her cheeks. 'I should have told you in France.'

He stared with so much heat, so much passion, Libby expected her skin to scorch. It had been there all along, this searing connection. She'd just chosen to ignore it. For her sanity. Had taken the coward's way out.

Covering his hand with hers, she pressed his palm to her cheek, turning her head to place a kiss at its centre while her chest inched ever closer to exploding.

'Short of begging you to love me back, I only had one other strategy.'

She pressed her lips together, holding in a smile at the playful twist of his mouth and lifting her eyebrows. 'And that was…?'

He shrugged, a wicked spark flashing in his eyes. 'Fucking you into submission.'

A laugh burst from her, her tension dissipating. She went to him. She'd been away from him for too long. Had missed touching him, kissing him. Holding him. He caught her, strong arms banded around

her back as she pushed him into the seat and straddled his lap.

He cupped her waist with one arm, holding her
close. 'Libby...'

Her mouth touched his and the fire reignited, flaring to life from the smouldering embers they'd left
behind in France.

She kissed him and giggled and spoke at the same
time. 'Well, that sounds fun.'

She tunnelled her fingers into his hair, twisting
them until his head dropped back on the seat behind
him, and then she raised herself over him, deepening the kiss when his lips opened to welcome her.

Then he shook his head, pulling away, his face
serious. 'No. There'll be no more fucking.'

Libby shuffled back. His hand gripped her, pre-
venting her retreating completely.

He gazed up at her, eyes brimming with love.
'From now on we'll be making love.'

He cupped the back of her neck, bringing her
close for another kiss.

She laughed, breaking away to pepper kisses on
his forehead, his cheeks and his closed eyes, loving
the groan she pulled from him.

He joined her, punctuating each frantic kiss with
words. 'Hard...' *kiss* '...greedy...' *kiss* '...fast or
slow...' *kiss*. 'However you want it.'

She smiled, kissing him back, keen to get started
on all that loving. Then she sobered, glancing out
of the window.

'Where are we going?'

She climbed from his lap, settling beside him and holding on tight to his hand in case he disappeared.

He stared at her as if he couldn't believe she was real. She knew the feeling. The comfort of his warm hand in hers was the only thing convincing her he was there.

'Well, as you live here I was hoping you'd invite me to your apartment so we can make a start on that lovemaking.'

He smacked his lips together, eyes glittering as he leaned closer.

'Perhaps we could begin with some good, old-fashioned show and tell?'

His accent grew haughtier, and the disparity between his cultured tone and the searing look in his eyes was enough to make her hot and achy.

'You know how much I enjoy that. And it's a particular skill of yours.' He arched a brow, one finger tracing the top button of her blouse.

She grinned, remembering the torture she'd inflicted on him that first time. 'Good plan.'

Her cheeks twitched, aching with the effort of holding in so much euphoria.

He nodded, a self-satisfied smirk on his face. 'Otherwise we could go to the apartment I've just bought here.'

He flopped back into the luxuriant seat, tugging her onto his lap once more.

'You're joking?'

She tried to think while his lips explored the base of her throat with nibbling kisses. He lived in England. Why purchase an apartment where he'd only spend a few weeks a year?

'I never joke about business, Ms Noble.' He tugged on her earlobe with his lips, his words almost whispered. 'I'll be spending considerable time here in New York. I have a new business venture I'm exploring.'

'You do?'

He pulled back, his stare earnest. He gave a nod. 'And you're the best deal I've ever negotiated.'

* * * * *

LEGAL
SEDUCTION

LISA CHILDS

MILLS & BOON

For my husband, Andrew Ahearne, who dared me to step outside my comfort zone of the area where I grew up and spent most of my life.

Moving with you has been an adventure and a reward.

Love you so much!

CHAPTER ONE

FOUR GLASSES, LIFTED HIGH, clinked against each other. Champagne bubbles foamed over the rims and streaked down the stems of the flutes.

"Cheers to Street Legal," Simon Kramer said, pride for the firm overwhelming him. Sixteen years ago, as a teenage runaway, he'd never thought he would go from living on the streets to owning them.

"Cheers to us," Ronan, one of Simon's law partners, said with a grin as he clinked his glass against theirs again.

"Cheers to you, Trev," Stone said to Trevor, who'd just won the biggest case their practice had ever had. And the four of them had had some damn big cases since graduating law school and starting their practice eight years ago.

After this win, they could close the doors of Street Legal and live off the settlement. But Simon knew that the others were like him: too young and too ambitious to stop achieving. And yet Simon wanted to make sure they took the time to enjoy their victories. So he'd talked his partners into leaving the office to celebrate at the new bar around the corner, The Meet Market.

This victory was especially sweet because Trev had won despite the opposing counsel getting their hands on information from the case files. Simon, as the managing partner, had put a plan in place so that would *not* happen again. If the mole was in their office, he would find it and *crush* it.

Trevor murmured, "I still want to know how the hell Anderson got his hands on that scientist's report."

"Don't worry about it," Simon said. He'd also set up this celebration because they all needed to blow off some steam. Or get blown...

Ronan glanced away from the women he'd been ogling to agree. "Don't give it another thought. It's not like we have a leak in our office, not with Simon doing all the hiring. Nobody can sniff out a con like a con. And our managing partner is the ultimate con."

Instead of being offended, Simon grinned. He wouldn't have survived had he not come up with money-making schemes for himself and for these guys. His friends had once been runaways, too. Simon had been running cons long before he'd met them.

"No, it's more likely Trev brought home some hottie who, after he rolled over and fell asleep, copied the case files he brought home," Ronan said.

Simon laughed. "You guys fall asleep?"

He couldn't sleep with anyone else around. He wouldn't have survived on the streets if he'd trusted just anyone. Only these guys passed his test. They'd survived the streets together. Hell, they'd thrived. They had more money, fancier homes, faster cars and hotter women than any of them could have imagined having.

"I wish that's what happened," Trev said. "But this damn case put a hell of a crimp in my love life."

"That's why I thought we should check out this new bar," Simon admitted. Trying to figure out who was the mole had put a crimp in his sex life, too.

The Meet Market was exactly what it boldly claimed to be: the hookup hub of Midtown Manhattan. All the beautiful people were here: models, actors and actresses, designers…

And them. The most successful and notorious lawyers in the whole damn city.

Simon clinked his glass against Trevor's. "You won the case, so forget about it. Have some fun."

Trevor grinned. "I plan on it. But Ronan's right. We need to be careful about who we bring home or at least around our files."

Stone nodded in agreement. "Yes, because if word gets out that anything got leaked to the opposing counsel, we'll need to hire that damn PR firm to help with our image."

Since the age of social media, most cases were tried before they ever made it to court, which was why they routinely used a PR firm to help sway the public the way they wanted them swayed. To their side, of course.

Ronan chuckled. "Like there's any helping our image…"

They were known for being ruthless—in the courtroom and the bedroom. They all had a reputation for winning, by whatever means necessary. But in Simon's opinion, that was a cause for pride, not damage control.

"We're fine, guys," Simon assured his partners. "I got this." He gestured at the women around them. "Now, let's get one of them…"

"Just one?" Ronan asked with a grin as he watched a blonde walk past him, tossing her long, curly mane over her shoulder. Before heading after her, he slapped Trevor on the back. "Want me to see if she has a friend for you? Si's right. You need to relieve some stress after winning that case."

Trevor glanced across the room at a redhead. "I don't need your help." He blew out a ragged breath. "But I do need to relieve some stress."

Stone bumped Simon's shoulder with his. "Looks like Si here could use some help."

Ronan snorted. "Si needs no one's help when it comes to women. He's the worst womanizer of the four of us."

Simon didn't know whether that was a compliment or insult. Coming from the notorious divorce lawyer, it was probably a compliment. But before he could ask, Ronan hurried after the blonde who'd paused in the doorway, waiting for him to follow her.

"You know, I haven't seen *you* with anyone for a while," Stone said to him.

Simon shrugged. "I've been busy." Setting up trusts,

drawing up contracts, setting his trap. But he was worried those were just excuses, not the real reasons.

He glanced around the bar and recognized some of the models from the billboards in Times Square and some of the actresses from plays. But nobody had his pulse quickening. He knew he could bring any one of them home with him or, as Ronan suggested, two. And maybe that was it. There was no challenge. No thrill of the hunt…

Just easy prey.

Like the redhead waving at Trevor from across the bar.

"Go," Simon urged him.

"Yeah," Stone agreed. "She's a hell of a lot prettier to celebrate your victory with than we are."

"Speak for yourself," Simon said, feigning offense.

With his thick blond hair and bright blue eyes, he'd been told he was better-looking than the hottest male movie stars—which was why he knew he could get anybody in the place to go home with him, even if he were still the broke runaway he'd once been.

Stone laughed, then said, "I may need to have you sit at the table with me for some of my upcoming trial—to sway the jurors like you did for Trev."

"Hey, guys, you're going to have to start working out, so you can be your own jury eye candy," Simon said, his lips tugging up into a teasing grin. "I've got work of my own to do. So damn much money to manage."

Now it wasn't just his clients' but theirs, too. That probably mattered more to Simon than it did the others. But they hadn't grown up like he had—when the only money he'd known had always really belonged to other people.

"Hey, we sway most of the women jurors ourselves," Trevor stated with pride and a trace of defensiveness. "We just need you to sway the ones who like pretty boys."

Simon suppressed a laugh of amusement. He didn't want Trevor to know how funny he was, so he acted offended and replied, "Fuck you."

Trevor shook his head. "Sorry, man, you're not my type. Now, that redhead..." He sauntered off toward the woman.

Stone peered around the bar. "I better find someone, too, or I might wind up going home with you."

"You wouldn't get so lucky," Simon said as Stone headed off. Simon glanced around the bar now, too. It wasn't that he didn't want to be the only one going home alone. Or it wasn't *just* that. He needed a diversion, something to get his mind off the mole in their office.

He couldn't have been conned into hiring someone who would betray them. No. Like Ronan said, there was no conning a con. His trap wasn't going to catch anyone because the leak couldn't be in their office.

So he wouldn't let it get to him. Not anymore. He'd find someone else to focus all his attention on for a little while. He wasn't into blondes like Ronan was. And he'd learned the hard way that redheads were nothing but drama. He needed to find a classy brunette, someone who would actually pose a worthwhile challenge to his charm.

Before he could even look, his cell began to vibrate in his suit pocket. It wasn't a call but the telltale buzz of a 911 text. Did any of the guys need his help? He visually located them all in the crowded bar, but they were totally engaged on the women they'd found. Not one seemed in need of a wingman.

Simon pulled out the cell and cursed when he read the screen. Damn it. His trap had been sprung. Someone was entering the office after hours, and there was probably only one reason for that. Shoving the cell back into his pocket, he hurried toward the exit.

But before he could leave, Trevor blocked his escape. "What is it? Everything okay?"

It sure the hell wasn't, but he forced a grin. "Just got a sext." From the security system. "I have to go."

Trevor chuckled. "Of course you wouldn't even have to work for it." With an envious sigh, he stepped aside to let Simon past.

He hurried out, aware that Trev wasn't the only one watching him. Let the guys think he was anxious to get naked. He would explain later. Right now he hoped to catch their mole in the act of copying active case files. The office was just around the corner.

The person had the security code, so no alarm had gone off, and no warning was sent to building security or the police station. Within moments he stepped off the elevator onto their floor, which was eerily silent and dark. The only light spilled from under the door of an office—*his* office.

He silently crossed the lobby, which had glass interior walls with hardwood floors. The exterior walls were the exposed brick of the old building. The ceilings were open to the ductwork and the rafters, the wood painted black while the copper pipes and steel ductwork gleamed in the dark.

Why the hell was the mole in *his* office? Had they graduated from selling secrets to stealing money? The door was ajar, the crack wide enough that he was able to peer through it.

Someone leaned over his desk, lush curves pressed against the black fabric of a tight skirt. His pulse quickened as he recognized that remarkable ass. He'd been discreetly admiring it for the past two years. He couldn't have afforded to be obvious about it, not with what a sexual harassment case could have cost the firm. And she had certainly never returned his interest. Now he knew why. She hadn't wanted sex. She wanted money.

Anger coursed through him, making his pulse race even faster. In addition to being incredibly sexy, Bette Monroe was cunning. She'd conned the ultimate con.

"What the hell are you doing?"

Bette jumped and the pen she'd been holding

slipped from her grasp, rolled across the oak desktop and dropped onto the hardwood floor. She pressed her hand over her madly pounding heart before turning toward the door. When she saw her boss standing there, her heart beat even faster and not just because he'd startled her.

Seeing Simon Kramer was always a shock to a woman's system. With his golden-blond hair and piercing blue eyes, chiseled features and a muscular body, he was so beyond handsome that it wasn't even fair—to women or to other men. The other lawyers in the Street Legal law practice were good-looking but nowhere near as attractive as Simon. And not one of them wore a suit as well as he did even though they all had them tailor-made. Simon's was a silvery gray with a faint sheen of blue that brought out that startling blue of his eyes.

His voice a deep rumble, Simon asked, "What are you doing here?"

Realizing it was the second time he'd asked, albeit nicer this time, heat rushed to her face. She must have been staring at him like a fool. That was why she always made a point of never looking directly at him. His good looks were like a solar eclipse, staring too closely could cause blindness.

Maybe that was why her eyesight had gotten poorer in the two years she'd worked for Street Legal as Simon Kramer's executive assistant. She'd been standing too close to the sun. Her hand trembling, she shoved her thick frames farther up her nose.

Since she only needed the glasses for reading, her distance vision blurred, and she couldn't see him as clearly now.

Until he stepped away from the door and strode across his expansive office to her. He leaned down so his face was close to hers. His eyes usually sparkled with amusement because he was always teasing his partners, his clients or other office employees. Never her, though. He only talked to her to give her orders. But when he did that, his eyes had never appeared like they did now—cold and hard like shards of blue ice.

She shivered.

"This is the last time I'm going to ask you," he said, "what the hell you're doing in my office."

More heat rushed to her face, and she stammered, "I—I was—"

"Looking for me?" he asked with one golden brow arching with skepticism.

"No," she admitted. She hadn't wanted to see him—not again—not since catching a glimpse of him in that new bar around the corner. Seeing him there—in that meat market—had confirmed she was doing the right thing. Just like her friends had been encouraging her, she needed to leave Street Legal.

It was too hard to work here, and especially too hard to work for *him*. Fortunately, she no longer needed this job.

"I was actually hoping *not* to see you," she said. When she'd noticed him and his partners walk into the bar, she'd been quick to leave, so he wouldn't see her there with her friends. She'd always been very careful to keep her private life private from everyone else at the firm. Most especially from him.

He sucked in a breath as if she'd struck him. "I'm surprised you'd admit that."

"I'm sorry," she said. "I didn't mean that the way it sounded." Which had been rude. Too bad she was such a lightweight that one glass of wine had lowered some of her inhibitions. Like now, when she looked at him again and heat rushed through her body. His eyes were so blue. Why did he have to be so good-looking?

"What do you mean, Bette?" he asked. "Why are you here? You need to give me an answer."

She drew in a shaky breath. "This is why I came when I knew you wouldn't be here," she said. "I didn't want to be caught."

"Damn it," he cursed. "I didn't expect this from you—of all of Street Legal's employees."

She could understand that. Some people, ambitious people, would kill to work at Street Legal. Other people—like her—didn't want to be associated with such an unscrupulous firm. Two years ago she'd had no choice; she'd needed money to be able to live in the city and to pay back her student loans. Now she had a choice. She reached for the note she'd left—unsigned—on his desk. Her name was just a line across the bottom.

"I'm sorry," she said again, and with her hand trembling, she passed the letter to him.

He glanced down at the paper. As he began to read it, his brow furrowed. He must have been confused because he murmured, "What the hell is this?"

Her heart continued to beat fast and hard. "It's— it's my letter of resignation." Which she had hoped to leave on his desk without running into him. Of course he would show up. Over the past two years there had been no escaping Simon Kramer. He even showed up in her dreams—dreams that left her with tight nipples and a pulsing clit. Not that she had a crush on him or anything.

In fact, there was very little she liked about Simon Kramer, except how he looked. But that was more a curse than a blessing—for her and all the weak-willed females he'd seduced. Not that he would seduce her or even try. She'd seen the women he dated: models and actresses—beautiful women. He had no interest in her. Just as she never looked at him, he never looked at her, either.

He shook his head. "I don't understand." And his brow was still furrowed with confusion. "Why are you quitting?"

She'd kept the resignation letter short and sweet. *This is official notice of my resignation. My last day of employment will be...*

Two weeks from now. Or hopefully sooner if he got mad and just fired her, and that was what she was hoping for. She doubted anyone had ever dumped Simon Kramer before—personally or professionally.

Thank you for the opportunity.

Thanks but no, thanks. She wanted no part of Street Legal anymore. No part of their high-profile cases. No part of sending flowers to their jilted lovers. No part of fielding the pleading calls from those same lovers.

She hadn't said any of that, though. She'd given no reason for leaving—because she hadn't had to.

So predictably he asked, "Why?"

Nonconfrontational by nature, Bette could only shrug. She was the one who apologized when someone else bumped into her on the street or jostled her on the subway. And that wasn't just the manners instilled with her Midwestern upbringing.

"You must have a reason." He persisted.

She had several. But she only shook her head. Her hair, which was so heavy, pulled at the knot that had slipped to the back of her head. The pins shifted, sticking into her skull. If she'd been home, she would have pulled them out, let down her hair.

But she couldn't do that around him. The tight bun—the glasses—that was her armor to protect herself around him. Not that he would make untoward advances. She knew even with her hair down and glasses off, she wasn't his type. But she felt more protected in her office camouflage. So that he wouldn't know the real her. Only her most trusted friends knew the real her. And she would never trust Simon Kramer.

"If you had no reason to leave," he said, his deep voice husky with frustration, "you wouldn't be leaving." He crumpled the letter in his fist.

And Bette's pulse leaped with fear. Although she was well aware of Simon Kramer's ruthlessness, she had never been afraid of him before. He'd never been warm and fuzzy with her, but he'd never been mean, either.

"I—I just want to leave," she said. And she wasn't talking only about his employ. She wanted to leave his office, too. But he stood in the path between her and the doorway.

He shook his head. "No."

"But—but you can't refuse my resignation…" Could he? Before deciding to leave the firm, she'd read over the employment contract he'd had her sign when he'd hired her, and she'd seen nothing about not being able to quit. But he was the contracts and trusts lawyer. He was the one who would have come up with the clauses and legal jargon that would make it possible for him to legally enslave someone.

"I can change your mind," he said, and even though his lips curved into a smile, his eyes remained cold and hard. "How much will it take?"

"You think this is about money?" Street Legal paid all their employees very well. That was why she'd come to work for him although she'd really wanted to work in a fashion house. But after interning at fashion houses, she knew how little they paid and how hard she would've worked.

He tilted his head, and his blue eyes narrowed as he studied her face. "Isn't everything about money?"

Maybe it was the wine that made her less censored than she would have ordinarily been but she admitted, "Unfortunately it is—to most people."

"Are you saying you aren't one of those people?" he asked, and one of his golden brows arched in skepticism. But there was more than skepticism in his eyes. He was looking at her a certain way that he never had before, a way that had nerves swimming in her stomach. He was actually *looking* at her, and there seemed to be an appreciation in his gaze as if he liked what he saw.

Damn. She was such a lightweight. She had to be drunk to imagine that Simon Kramer would look at her *that* way, like he wouldn't mind seeing more of her—*naked*.

"I wouldn't have taken the job working here if money didn't matter to me," she admitted. But having him to look at, to fantasize about, had given her the inspiration to succeed at her other job.

"So then more money will get you to stay," he said dismissively, as if he'd closed a case. He tossed her crumpled-up resignation letter into the brass trash can sitting beside his desk.

Frustration—and not just with this conversation—overwhelmed her, overcoming her natural inclination to avoid confrontation, and she blurted out, "No!"

Working for him these past two years had increased her frustration because of all those damn fantasies he'd inspired.

"But you just said—"

"I took the job because I needed money," she said. "I needed money *then*."

His eyes narrowed more as he studied her face. "And you don't need it now?"

"My reason for leaving has nothing to do with money," she said. Had she not found another source of income, she would have been forced to stay, but he didn't need to know that.

"So you do have a reason."

He wasn't the trial lawyer of their partnership, but he could have been. She felt like she was being cross-examined on the witness stand. And she didn't enjoy it one bit. Quitting was not a crime.

"I don't have to give you a reason." At least she didn't think she did.

Maybe she should have had a lawyer look at that employment contract before she'd written her resignation letter. But no matter how much she paid, no lawyer would be as good as Simon Kramer. He was the best.

And, according to his ex-lovers, not just at the law...

"Why don't you want to tell me?" he asked, and he stepped closer now, so close that she could feel the heat of his body through his suit and her cardigan and skirt.

Heat flushed her body, making her skin tingle. She tried to step back but the desk stopped her, the hard wood pressing into the backs of her thighs as he nearly touched the front of her. Her breasts pushed against the front of the gray cardigan as she struggled for breath. She had never been this close to him before. It was more than unsettling. Her knees trembled and her already tripping pulse quickened even more.

"Because it's personal," she murmured. And they had never been anything but businesslike with each other, except in her dreams.

He leaned down, so close that his warm breath whispered across her lips as he asked, "Are you in love with me?"

CHAPTER TWO

HER MOUTH HAD fallen open with the same shock Simon had seen on her face when he'd first caught her in his office. So he repeated his question, like he'd had to repeat his first one. "Are you in love with me?"

Color rushed to her face again. But she wasn't embarrassed. She was amused because she started laughing. Hers was no flirty, girlish giggle, either. Her laugh was deep and husky and had his pulse racing with attraction even as his pride bristled.

Focused on his face, her dark eyes widened. "You're serious? You think I'm in love with you?"

"No," he said, and his face heated a little with embarrassment. But it wouldn't have been the first time someone had fallen for him without any encouragement from him. "I don't."

Not anymore. Not after her reaction.

Apparently, it was a good thing he'd never acted on the attraction he'd felt for her. He had no doubt she might have sued for harassment. But now that she'd already given her notice...

"Then why would you ask…?" She trailed off as her voice cracked with the threat of another giggle. It turned into a hiccup instead.

He caught the faint scent of wine on her breath and asked, "Have you been drinking?"

"What does that have to do with anything?" she countered. "It's after office hours, and I'm not working. It doesn't matter how much I've had to drink."

"It does if it's affecting your judgment," he replied.

Just how affected was her judgment? He wasn't thinking about just tonight or about just the drinking. Other things could affect judgment. Like greed. Or some other kind of coercion. Maybe she had a lover at an opposing law firm. Had something like that affected her judgment enough that she'd sold information from their case files?

Was that why she didn't need money any longer?

He had to find out. Right now was probably his best chance—if she'd had enough alcohol to bring down her defenses. He had never seen Bette like this before. Or maybe he'd just never let himself see her like this—except for a stolen glance or two at her assets.

Simon hadn't been able to stop himself from admiring the lush curves of her hips and ass in her pencil-slim skirts. And the little cardigans she wore did nothing to hide the fullness of her breasts. They strained the buttons at the front, showing little glimpses of the lace camisoles she wore beneath the sweaters.

"So you think the only reasons I could have for wanting to quit are because I'm drunk or in love with you?" she asked, a smile curving her full lips.

Since she didn't usually look at him, he'd never noticed before how full her lips were—so full that she had a slight dimple in the middle of her bottom one.

He wanted to tug at that lip—with his lips and with his teeth. He wanted to nibble on it until she gasped for breath. Then he wanted those lips to touch him, to close around his cock as she sucked him deep into her throat.

His heart slammed against his ribs as desire sneaked up on him. This was Bette, his boring assistant. Except that she didn't want to be his assistant anymore.

So what did that make her? The spy who'd betrayed their practice? Simon needed to know for certain if she was the office mole. But how the hell was he going to get her to talk?

She wouldn't even give him the reason she was resigning. Why didn't she want him to know? What was she hiding?

In order to get her talking, he needed to talk first. The best way for a con to gain the confidence of his mark was to share a confidence of his own.

"I've always had a problem keeping assistants," he admitted to her. It wasn't exactly a deep, dark confession, but it was the truth. "You've lasted much longer than anyone else has." About a year and a half longer than her longest-working predecessor.

"I know people who would love to work for you."

He sighed. "For the wrong reasons. Professionally, they want to get ahead." They wanted to use the position as his assistant to launch their own legal careers.

Or they wanted to give him head. He wouldn't mind if Bette had wanted to do that, but that obviously wasn't why she'd taken the position as his assistant. She had never once showed any interest in him. Until now. "Or, personally, they want me."

Her eyes widened again, and so did her pupils, dilating as she stared up at him through the lenses of her black-framed glasses. The glasses were too big for her delicately featured face, which was probably why they kept sliding down her small nose.

"I—I don't want you…" she murmured, but there was no amusement in her voice now. Not even a hint of laughter. But her voice had grown more husky, and her pulse quivered visibly, erratically, in her long, slender neck.

He leaned even closer, so his lips just brushed over hers as he whispered, "Liar…"

She gasped, which moved her lips against his. He took advantage of her open mouth and deepened the kiss. First, he nibbled on her lips, like he'd wanted. Then he slid his tongue between them, into the sweet heat of her mouth. Would her body feel the same?

Hot and wet? He wanted to find out.

He clutched the back of her head in one hand, his

fingers closing over that knot of soft, thick hair. It tickled his palm, making his skin tingle. The sensation surprised him. This was Bette, his assistant. She wasn't supposed to make his skin tingle or his cock swell and throb behind the fly of his dress pants.

But she was…

And it was…

His body pulsed and ached. He wanted her aching for him, too. So he moved his other hand, the one not in her hair. He slid it over the curve of her hip down her thigh to the hem of her skirt. He wanted to lift it, wanted to skim his fingers up the inside of her thigh to the heat of her core. But how drunk was she?

He didn't want to take advantage if she'd had too much to drink. And he suspected that she had because she was kissing him back, her tongue chasing his into his mouth. He tasted the wine on her tongue, crisp and slightly sweet. He wasn't surprised that she would drink a sweet and fruity white. She wasn't sophisticated like the women he usually dated.

Not that he wanted to date her. All he wanted was the truth. Why was she leaving? And was she the one who'd sold their secrets to opposing counsel?

At least that was all his mind wanted. His body was making demands of its own. And he found himself giving in to temptation. He moved his hand beneath her skirt, stroking his fingertips up the inside of her thigh.

She wore stockings, but they stopped halfway between her knees and her core. His finger touched lace and silk. She was wearing a garter?

He never would have thought Bette was the type to wear sexy underwear, let alone lingerie. His breath caught as he touched bare skin, which was even silkier than the stockings and the garter.

But the stockings and garter excited the hell out of him, too. Was she hiding something else—something super sexy—beneath that cardigan?

He moved his hand from her hair down the nape of her slender neck, then around her throat. Her pulse beat madly beneath his fingertip. She was as excited as he was.

He traced his finger lower, over her collarbone to the first button of that sweater. He flicked it open and then moved down to the next and the next, revealing the deep valley of her cleavage. She wasn't wearing a camisole, like he'd thought. She wore a red lace bustier adorned with tiny bows.

A garter and bustier?

His breath escaped in a ragged groan. Who knew Bette Monroe was so damn sexy and sensual? He'd had no idea.

Did someone else? Had she worn this lingerie because she was meeting someone? At the moment he didn't care. He didn't care about anything but the desire burning him up. His cock pulsed with excitement and the need for release. A release only Bette could give him…

She gasped and trembled against him. Then she

tensed. And her hands pressed against his chest, pushing him back.

"I—I…" she stammered. Her face was flushed with color, and her eyes glittered behind the lenses of her glasses.

"You want me," he finished for her.

She shook her head and her hair tumbled down around her shoulders. He'd loosened the pins, which fell onto the hardwood floor. Her hair was long, so much longer than he'd realized. It reached nearly to her waist. And it was thick and wavy. How had he never noticed how damn sexy it was? How damn sexy she was?

"I want to leave," she said, her voice steadier now as if she'd forced herself to stop stammering.

He stepped back and swept his arm toward the door. "Go ahead." He'd never had to hold a woman against her will. Usually he was the one who had to fight to escape.

Bette moved forward but swayed slightly. Maybe she'd had more to drink than he'd thought, which was another good reason to stop. Because despite what she claimed, she wanted him. He could easily change her mind about staying with just another kiss, another caress…

And he was tempted to do just that because he wanted her, so much that it surprised him. She could have betrayed his and his partners' practice. She could be a con, like him, like his father. Maybe the cardigan sweater and black-framed glasses were just part of the act and the lingerie was the real her.

Was that why he was suddenly attracted to her, because he hadn't had a challenge in so long? Bette Monroe might pose his greatest challenge yet. He watched as she walked toward the door, watched her hips rock back and forth beneath that tight, sexy skirt. And he swallowed a groan of desire.

Then she stopped, halfway to the door, and turned back to him and said, "I won't be coming back."

He arched a brow. "Really?"

"I am not working out a two-week notice," she said, and her voice wasn't just steady. It was dead calm with determination.

He grinned at the challenge she was going to pose. Then he told her, with equal determination, "Yes, you are."

She shook her head, tumbling all that glorious dark hair around her shoulders and over the cardigan. The thick tresses hid some of the red bustier he'd revealed. He'd always been a sucker for brunettes.

Had she known that? Was that why she'd interviewed to be his assistant two years ago? Had she been working him all this time?

"No," she said. "I can't work with you *now*."

He shrugged. "Why not? Because I kissed you?" He intended to do a hell of a lot more than that to her. Over and over again. Now he wanted to see what was beneath that lingerie. He wanted to touch and taste every inch of her silky skin.

She nodded. "That's sexual harassment."

"You already turned in your resignation," he reminded her. It was probably a fine line, but he was a damn good lawyer. His employment agreements were indisputable. "And you will serve out your notice, just as stipulated in your contract."

"But—but…" Her mouth fell open on a gasp. "You can't want me to work here still."

Knowing that she was probably the mole, no, he shouldn't want her to work at Street Legal a second longer. But he would be careful to keep her away from all the case files.

He had other plans for keeping her busy. His body throbbed as some of the images he intended to act out flashed through his mind. Her on her knees, sucking on his cock.

Her sexy bare ass bent over his desk as he drove himself inside her…

Sweat broke out on his lip as tension gripped his body. He intended to sensually torment and seduce her into revealing her betrayal. But all of the thoughts of how he would do that were torturing him.

"Oh, I intend to work you," he warned her as he stepped closer to her. His chest bumped against her breasts, which rose with her pants for breath so much that they nearly spilled over the top of the bustier. "Long and hard…"

And that was just him.

She gasped again, and her dark eyes widened even more with shock. And that desire she kept denying.

"You can't make me do anything but work," she insisted, her voice husky and breathless.

He nodded but a grin tugged at his lips. "We'll see…"

She had no idea how persuasive he could be. He had never turned his charm on her before. But he fully intended to do that now.

He was going to seduce the office mole. He was going to con the con until she revealed all her secrets and begged to stay with him—in the office and in bed.

It was just a dream. That was all it had been. It couldn't have actually happened last Friday night. Simon Kramer couldn't have really hit on her.

On Bette Monroe.

He hadn't kissed her, hadn't touched her…hadn't hinted at wanting to do even more to her.

No. It was just a dream. And convincing herself of that was the only way she'd managed to come in to the office on Monday morning. That and that damn contract she'd signed. She had no doubt that he would enforce it had she decided to not work out her two-week notice.

The elevator bell dinged as the car reached the top floor. When the doors slid open, she sucked in a deep breath—bracing herself before she stepped out onto the floor for the Street Legal law practice. It was just two weeks. She'd lasted two years working

for Simon Kramer, which—by his own admission—
was longer than most of his previous assistants had.

Two weeks was nothing.

She lifted her chin and forced a smile for the receptionist as she walked past him on her way to her
office. Miguel nodded in return. The former gang
member looked more like a bouncer than a receptionist, which was appropriate since he often had to
act more like a bouncer than a receptionist. His voice
was like deep velvet, though, when he answered the
phone. "Street Legal, how may I help you?"

Would he help her if she asked? Not if she needed
help with Simon Kramer. Miguel was fiercely loyal
to the managing partner of Street Legal. But she
wouldn't need help. Simon wasn't going to attack
her. Even if what had happened Friday night hadn't
been a dream, he hadn't attacked.

He had seduced, which was far more dangerous.
An attack she could have fought off. Even before
moving to New York City six years ago, she had
taken self-defense classes. She also carried Mace in
her purse. She was prepared for an attack. She was
not prepared for Simon Kramer's charm.

She couldn't believe she'd managed to walk away
from him Friday night, that she hadn't been tempted
to stay and find out if he was as good as all his ex-
lovers had claimed. If he was the best…

She shivered and shook her head. No. He didn't
tempt her. Not at all.

Liar, she called herself like he had called her that night.

The minute she stepped into her office, he turned that charm on her, grinning at her from where he reclined in her chair, his feet up on her desk. That grin stole away the breath she'd drawn. He was so damn good-looking. The grin didn't just curve his sensual lips and show his perfectly straight white teeth; it made his blue eyes sparkle, highlighting the glint of mischief in them.

As if she'd looked directly at the sun, she squeezed her eyes shut for a moment. But when she opened them again, he was still there. Ignoring her pounding pulse and heart, she narrowed her eyes and focused on him. Sure, his masculine beauty would probably burn her retinas, but she risked it to study him. Despite the grin and the relaxed posture, he had tension in his broad shoulders and the rigid line of his jaw.

Something was bothering him. She doubted he was that upset about her resignation. Sure, hiring a new assistant would be an inconvenience, but he'd barely noticed let alone appreciated her these past two years.

His grin widened, and he greeted her with a "Good morning, sunshine."

The greeting was more apt for him. With his golden-blond hair and sparkling smile, he was the sun. With her dark hair and eyes, she felt more like a dark cloud, especially after her sleepless nights since Friday. How could she have just dreamed that kiss when she hadn't slept at all?

And from the way he was looking at her, his gaze moving like a caress up and down her body, she knew it had happened. He hadn't just kissed her, though. He'd touched her.

Even though he hadn't moved from her chair, she felt his touch again. Felt his fingertips gliding over her skin...

And another shiver chased down her spine, making her skin tingle.

His grin widened.

She glared at him. "Apparently, you've already filled my position," she said. "So it's not necessary for me to work out my notice."

He laughed now, a deep chuckle that affected her nearly as much as his kiss and his touch had. It was so damn sexy. Just like he was.

She turned on the pointy heel of her pump and headed toward the door of her office. Her space was so much smaller than his, with just a few feet between her desk and the door. But she didn't make it before a strong hand closed around her arm and jerked her to a halt.

"You're not going anywhere," he told her.

She tugged, but his fingers were locked around her arm, his grasp too strong for her to break. Even though she wore one of her long-sleeved cardigans, she could feel the warmth of his skin through the fabric, and goose bumps of awareness rose on her skin.

"I am leaving," she said.

"Not for two weeks." Using his hand on her arm, he spun her around as if they were on a dance floor.

But Bette was not graceful, especially in heels. She stumbled and fell against him. Her breath escaped her lungs in a gasp as her breasts pressed against his chest. Her hips pressed against his, and she felt his reaction to her closeness.

Instead of being embarrassed or apologetic, he chuckled. "I fully intend to enjoy every minute of these two weeks," he told her as he pushed his hips more firmly against hers. "And I'll make sure you enjoy them, too."

Heat rushed through her from her nipples, which had tightened against the silk cups of her bra, down to her clit, which pulsed with desire for him. *Damn him...*

"If I'd enjoyed working for you, I wouldn't have given my notice," she said as she stepped back. She needed space between them. But with his hand on her arm, she could only get inches and couldn't escape the heat of his body.

She needed feet. No, she needed miles. Miles between them would be good. Then she might not feel him, might not want him.

He lifted his free hand toward her face and ran his fingertips along her cheek. "That was because I wasn't making sure you enjoyed it," he said. He stepped closer and lowered his head. His lips were just a breath away from hers when he added, "You will enjoy working for me now, Bette. You'll enjoy it so much that you will never want to stop."

With the heat of his breath against her lips, she could smell a trace of mint and coffee and could almost taste him. Not the mint and coffee but him...

How he'd tasted Friday night. Dark and rich and hot.

That desire pulsing in her core had Bette leaning toward him. She wanted his lips against hers again. She wanted to make sure that the kiss—*his kiss*—hadn't been a dream or, worse yet, just a manifestation of two years of longing. Longing for his kiss, his touch.

When her lips touched his, a jolt of sexual awareness shot so violently through her that she jerked back, fast and strongly enough that she pulled free of him. But it didn't matter that he was no longer touching her. He still had a hold on her—with his charm, with his aura.

And he knew it. The knowledge was in his grin and the sparkle in his blue eyes. She had no doubt he would use the power of that attraction over her.

For what? To convince her to stay?

She was not going to change her mind. Street Legal was never where she'd wanted to be. Law was not her passion. And Simon Kramer would not sway her with his charm and his good looks.

"Oh, Bette," he murmured with an ever-widening grin, "you and I are finally going to have some fun."

Fun? That she doubted, just like she'd doubted her earlier pep talk to herself.

Two weeks wasn't nothing. If he kept turning on the charm like this, it would be a lifetime. And because of that damn employment contract he'd had her sign, she wouldn't be able to cut that time. But he could. He was the only one who could waive the requirement for her to work out the two-week notice.

What would it take for him to get rid of her right away? Then she remembered what he'd asked her Friday night when he'd caught her leaving the resignation letter on his desk—the reason he'd thought she was leaving. That she was in love with him...

What if she hadn't laughed? What if she'd answered yes? Would he have shown her the door right then and taken away her key? Was that why she'd sent flowers to so many women for him over the past two years?

Because they'd fallen in love with him and had gotten clingy and desperate and he'd wanted nothing to do with them? From their calls pleading with her to let them talk to him, to see him...just one more time.

Yes. She knew what it would take to make him want to get rid of her right away. She would have to convince him that she'd fallen for him.

CHAPTER THREE

SIMON DID NOT miss the sudden sparkle in her eyes and the slight curve of her lips. Bette Monroe was up to something. And he had a feeling he wasn't going to like it. It wouldn't be the first thing she'd done that he didn't like. He didn't like her giving notice. If she was the mole, he sure as hell didn't like that she'd sold secrets from their case files. And if she was the mole, he would make damn certain she paid dearly for her betrayal.

As if she'd read his mind, her smile slid away, the brightness of her dark eyes dimmed and she shivered. She couldn't be cold, not with another damn sweater buttoned up to her neck like it was. What was she wearing beneath that? More lace and silk like on Friday night? Or had she only worn that because she'd been meeting someone after she'd left him?

He wanted to find out what she was wearing beneath her conservative skirt and sweater. He fully intended to find out. But he'd have to be patient for now as the phone on her desk began to ring.

A shaky sigh slipped through her lips as if she was

relieved for the interruption, and she reached for the phone. But before she could pick it up, he caught her wrist in his hand.

"Before you answer that," he said, "we need to go over our schedule for the day." He stroked his thumb over the silky skin of her delicate wrist, and her pulse leaped beneath his touch. "And the night."

Her throat moved as if she had to swallow before asking, "Night?"

He grinned. "Yes, we're going to be working late."

"H-how late?" she stammered.

"Quite late," he warned her. "Tonight and every night for the next two weeks. At least…"

She drew in a shaky breath now. "Two weeks," she said. "Just two weeks." And she reached for the phone with her other hand, lifting it to her flushed face.

"Bette Monroe, assistant to Simon Kramer, how may I help you?" she asked the caller.

She could tell Simon the damn truth. But he didn't expect her to freely divulge her secrets. Few people were honest about everything, and some, like his old man, were never honest about anything. He wasn't certain into which category Bette Monroe would fall. But just like he intended to find out what lingerie— if any—she was wearing, he fully intended to find that out, too.

He would execute the plan he'd concocted Friday night and seduce the truth out of his sexy executive assistant. He just hadn't realized how damn much he was going to enjoy the seduction. For the first time in a long time, he might actually have found a challenge. Ironically enough, it—*she*—had been right under his nose for the past two years.

While he had noticed Bette's ass and hips and the swell of her breasts beneath those sweaters, he'd never thought she could possibly be nearly as big a con as he was. He'd have to be careful that she didn't get access to any more case files and that she didn't get to him any more than she had already started to.

Just that faint brush of her lips across his had his pulse leaping like hers did beneath the pressure of his thumb. Just seeing her had his dick swelling behind the fly of his suit pants.

Damn. He wanted her. Seducing the truth out of her wouldn't be a hardship for him. Well, especially once he got a release from the tension building inside him.

He watched her lips move as she spoke to whoever had called. The dimple in the full bottom one seemed to wink at him, tempting him to take her mouth again—to kiss her like he had Friday night. It had been one damn long weekend waiting for Monday, waiting to see her again, to touch her again, to kiss her…

But she had work to do. And so did he. He had to plan his next move in the seduction of his sexy little office mole.

Just one week and four days left…

That was what Bette told herself as lights began

to shut off on the floor for the Street Legal law practice. Miguel had left for the night along with most of the rest of the office staff. Actually, she wasn't certain if there was anyone else on the floor but her.

Simon hadn't lied about working late. Fortunately, working was pretty much all he'd been doing—meeting with clients in and out of the office throughout the day. Of course every time he'd had a free minute, he had either stopped by her desk or called her into his office. And every time, he had treated her to another strong dose of his sexiness until she'd gotten drunk on it.

Maybe that was why she felt so light-headed now. Or maybe it was because she'd been so busy herself that she'd had to skip lunch. She would not survive nine more days like today, not with her sanity intact. She had to make him cut the two weeks short.

Very short.

Like she wished this day would have been. Would it ever end? Simon had left a while ago for his last appointment, but he'd given her orders—with a wink and a grin—for her to stay until he returned. And the way he'd looked at her…like he was already undressing her.

Her face had flushed and her body had heated and she'd tried to stammer out a protest. But he'd only laughed and claimed he would have notes for her that wouldn't wait until morning. He was enjoying this…enjoying how rattled she got when he turned his notorious charm on her.

She could not let it affect her anymore. In order to get him to cut short the two weeks, she would have to rattle him instead. And she knew just how to do that—act like she was in love with him.

She didn't have any experience in the theater, though. Unlike so many other women, she hadn't come to New York to be an actress. She had come to be a fashion designer. But apparently, she had acted her ass off the past two years as an executive assistant in a law firm.

She could do this. She *had* to do this.

The elevator dinged. Here was her curtain call.

She drew in a deep breath and forced a bright smile. But she didn't hear the quick taps of Simon's shoes against the hardwood floor. Instead, she heard the creak and whine of metal wheels rolling over the wood.

"What the hell…?" she murmured. And she stood to peer into the reception area just as a chef, complete with tall hat, white uniform and apron, rolled in the metal cart she'd heard.

He paused in her doorway. "You—Miss Monroe?" he asked, his accent thick and impossible to place—at least for Bette.

Despite six years of living in the melting pot of New York City, the only accents she could readily place were ones like her own: Midwestern. This man could have been French, Belgian, Swiss, Austrian or faking it. There were a lot of people in this city who pretended to be from someplace they were not. Who pretended to be what they were not.

So she should be able to pretend with Simon.

This man she answered honestly, "Yes, I'm Bette Monroe."

The chef's beady-eyed gaze traveled from her hair, drawn into that tight bun, down to the closed toes of her pumps and back. His brow furrowed as if he doubted her. Would she have to show her license?

She hoped not because whatever he had on that cart, simmering in chafing dishes with burners beneath them, smelled like heaven—if heaven smelled like savory spices and beef and potatoes.

Her stomach growled, and her mouth began to water.

The guy made a noise, too, in his throat. It was either a groan of disgust or exasperation. "Mr. Kramer said you would be expecting me."

She glanced at her computer, which was open to her email, then down at her phone, which had no new texts. "Mr. Kramer didn't mention you to me yet."

What was this? Along with the chafing dishes were two plates, cloth napkins and a couple of candles ready to light. A romantic dinner for two? Who was Simon meeting here?

The elevator dinged again and she realized she was about to find out. But the taps were Simon's quick footsteps, not the clicks of a woman's heels. At least he had arrived before his date.

"Bruno!" Simon exclaimed as he strode through

the reception area and saw the chef standing just outside the open door to Bette's office. "Excellent timing."

"She did not know I was coming," Bruno remarked as if disparaging Bette for not being psychic. He was definitely not criticizing Simon for not telling her. From the way he stared at Simon, it was clear he found nothing wrong with the blond lawyer and everything right.

Simon grinned. "Of course not. It's a surprise."

"For me?" Bette asked as her heart began to thump faster and harder.

"There is no one else," Simon said with a wink.

She bit her bottom lip to hold in the laugh at the blatant lie. She'd never known him to date only one woman at a time—if what he did could actually be called dating.

More like heart breaking…

Her heart rate quickened with the reminder. But now, with his gaze turned on her, she understood how he'd broken so many hearts. He wasn't just outrageously good-looking, as if that wasn't enough.

"Bruno, please set up in my office." Simon directed him, gesturing with his briefcase toward his closed door.

Bruno nodded and wheeled his cart away. And Bette's stomach growled in protest.

Simon raised a golden-blond brow. "Sounds like Bruno arrived just in time."

Heat rushed toward her face. "I skipped lunch," she explained.

"I know," Simon said. "Miguel told me. That's why I asked Bruno to prepare dinner for us."

She shook her head. "That's not necessary. I can eat when I get home." And work. She had so much to do for her new job. She really needed to cut short these two weeks—as short as she possibly could.

"That won't be for a while yet," he told her.

"But—but it's already so late…" From last Friday night, she knew that it was not a good idea to be alone in the office with him.

"We will work over dinner," he said, "and finish up so you can get home to your…" He raised an eyebrow again as he waited for her reply.

"Apartment."

It wasn't any of his business why she was quitting; it wasn't any of his business if she lived with someone or had a boyfriend. The less Simon Kramer knew about her the better off she would be.

He was undeterred and asked, "Is anyone waiting for you in that apartment?"

She let a smile slip out as she shook her head. "No. I don't have a cat. And the building doesn't allow dogs."

"Good," he said. "I'm allergic."

She wanted to tell him that there was no way in hell he was ever coming to her apartment. But before the words slipped out like her smile had, she remembered her plan. So she smiled wider and murmured, "Then it's good I don't have one."

His blue eyes momentarily widened with surprise at her remark before narrowing with obvious suspicion. He studied her face. "So you're going to invite me to your place?"

Her pulse kicked into overdrive, racing away. She was nervous about her plan. She wasn't imagining him in her apartment, although he would look damn good in her new place. That wasn't going to happen. Ever.

"That wouldn't be appropriate while I'm still working for you," she said. Then, summoning all the acting ability she possessed, she batted her lashes at him. "Guess you'll have to wait two weeks for that invitation."

He laughed and shook his head. "I've never been a patient man, Bette."

Bette had more ability to be patient than act. She'd had to wait to move away from her small hometown in Michigan to attend fashion school and move to New York. She'd also had to wait six years for the career she'd wanted, for which she'd worked so hard, to finally take off. But now that it had, her patience had worn thin. There was no way she was waiting two weeks to end her relationship with Simon Kramer, such that it was.

"I can leave now," she offered. "A temp service could send over someone until you hire my replacement."

He laughed again and reached for her arm, tugging her toward him. "Oh, Bette, think of all the fun you'd miss if you left so soon."

"Fun?" she parroted. "I thought we were working over dinner."

He stepped closer, so that his body brushed against hers, his thigh touching hers, his chest bumping hers as he breathed deeply. Then he leaned down and murmured, "Work is very fun for me."

She knew that was true. He obviously loved being a lawyer, probably loved being the managing partner of Street Legal even more. What she couldn't understand was his sudden interest in her. Was it only because she was leaving?

Something about wanting what you couldn't have?

She hoped that was the case, so that when she made it clear he could have her, he wouldn't want her. Instead of stepping back as she had every time before, she stepped closer to him, pressing her body even tighter against his. She felt his erection pushing against her hip. And she parted her lips with a gasp. He felt big—really big—rubbing against her.

His gaze dropped to her mouth. His pupils dilated until they swallowed the bright blue. And he lowered his head even closer to hers.

"Dinner is served," Bruno called out, his accent not nearly as thick now, from Simon's office.

Her boss groaned and released a shuddery sigh. "We'll eat first," he said.

First?

What else did he have planned besides work and dinner? Bette's knees trembled a bit as she walked with him the short distance to his office. As if she didn't know where it was, he moved his hand to the small of her back, guiding her. Or branding her?

She felt the heat of his palm through her sweater and the lace camisole she wore beneath it over her bra. His hand was big, so big that his fingers reached over the top curve of her butt. Could he feel the bow at the top of the G-string she wore beneath her pencil-slim skirt? A matching bow held together the cups of her bra.

She always wore lingerie—for a few reasons. He was not one of them. But would he think she'd worn it for him—if she dared show it to him?

The heat already flushing her body increased, burning her up. The lack of food and all the doses of his charm must have addled her brain. She wasn't thinking clearly at all, not like she'd been when she'd turned in her resignation. Then she'd been thinking more clearly than she had in the two years she'd worked for him.

His fingers moved, sliding over that bow, as if he was trying to figure out what it was. He glanced down at her, and again his eyes had widened with a look of surprise. "How is it, Bette, that we've worked together for two years but yet I don't feel as if I know you at all?"

She could have told him that she'd just been lucky all these years to have escaped his notice. She had been just an office fixture to him, like a computer or the coffeepot. But she only smiled and shook her head. "I have no idea."

"Well, let's fix that," he said. And finally, albeit reluctantly, he removed his hand from her ass and held out a chair for her. His office was so large that in addition to his desk and chair, he had a couch and a small conference room table and chairs.

Bruno had set up their feast, complete with lit candles, on that table. The tall windows looking out over Midtown reflected back the flickering flames. She smiled at the chef as she took her seat, but his only interest was in Simon. She was surprised that he wasn't holding out his chair.

"Is everything to your satisfaction?" the chef asked as he poured glasses of wine.

Simon took the chair right next to her and picked up the wineglass. He swirled the red liquid, studied the glass as the wine slid down the sides of it, then he sniffed it, all before taking a sip.

Bette usually went out with guys who drank beer or mixed cocktails. The few wine drinkers she'd dated had performed the same ritual Simon had but with them it had seemed pretentious and unnecessary. Simon seemed to know what he was doing and why.

She had no doubts—from the calls of all those desperate women—that he was the same with sex. That he knew what he was doing and why.

She drew in a shaky breath.

Finally, he took a sip. But he held it in his mouth for several moments before swallowing. "Excellent," he said. Then he held out a glass to her.

She usually drank white wine. Reds were too bitter for her taste. But she was too intrigued to find out what he considered excellent to refuse the glass. Like him, she took only a sip and held it in her mouth for several seconds. Flavor burst on her tongue. She could taste berries and spices; it was as rich and full of nuances as his kiss had been, as he was.

She let it slide down her throat, enjoying the sensation and the taste. "Excellent," she agreed.

Bruno lifted the lids from their plates. "And the meal, Mr. Kramer?"

Beef Wellington with steamed vegetables and parsnips and red-skin potatoes. Bette's mouth watered, reminding her of how hungry she was—for food. Ever since Simon had come back to the office, she'd been hungry for something else.

For more of his kisses, more of his touch.

More of his lethal charm.

As Simon cut through the flaky pastry and the meat, juices oozed onto the plate, swirling around the potatoes and vegetables. Like with the wine, he took just a small bite and held it in his mouth for a long moment before chewing and swallowing. Then he sighed and pronounced it excellent, as well.

Bette's heart pounded in anticipation and not just of the meal. Would sex be the same way with Simon? Would he savor every moment of it?

He cut another bite and held it out to her. Again she copied him, closing her lips around it before holding it on her tongue. The spices and flavor of the meat overwhelmed her with pleasure. She chewed and swallowed, and a moan of that pleasure slipped through her lips.

Simon groaned. Then he glanced up at Bruno, as if just realizing the chef was still in the room with them. "You can go," he said. "I'll have Miguel return everything to you in the morning."

Bruno hesitated, but then, obviously realizing arguing with a lawyer would not be smart, he nodded and left, closing the door behind him.

Once again, Bette was alone with Simon Kramer. Her fingers trembled as she reached for her glass of wine. She was afraid and not just of what he would do. She was afraid of what she would have to do in order to carry out her plan. How the hell could she convince him that she was falling for him and that if she did, she would get clingy and crazy?

She'd been so focused on her designs and her career that she'd never really fallen for anyone before. Unlike her mom and sister, she hadn't been about to let any man mess with her plans. So she had no idea how to act in love, especially with someone like Simon Kramer for whom she would never be stupid enough to fall.

For the past two years she'd seen exactly how he treated women—like they were disposable. And to him, they were. Even before he'd dumped one, another had come along. But that was a good thing for her.

He always dumped them.

So if she could pretend to fall for him, he would dump her, as well. But how far would she have to go to convince him she was falling?

Just being alone with him was a risk. Not that he would ever physically hurt her. He didn't have to physically coerce anyone to do his bidding. He used his sex appeal instead.

And even though she knew exactly what he was doing and that it was just a game to him, she was not immune.

She doubted she would escape this time with just a kiss. But she wasn't entirely sure that she would mind. For two years she'd dreamed of what it would be like to have his attention turned on her. For two years she'd imagined how his kiss would taste, how his touch would feel.

Now she knew. And she wanted more.

CHAPTER FOUR

FOR THE PAST two years Simon had surreptitiously ogled his assistant, but he'd had no idea that she might wear lingerie beneath those tight skirts and buttoned-up cardigans of hers even though he had seen lace peek out between those buttons. Friday night he'd seen that lace when he'd undone a few of those buttons and discovered that sexy bustier. He wanted to undo all the buttons tonight, and he wanted to unzip that skirt and peel it off her luscious ass.

He wanted Bette Monroe.

His hand shaking a little, he set his wineglass back on the table. He hadn't had much to drink but he made a point to never overindulge. At least not on alcohol...

He wanted nothing affecting his mind or his control. But Bette, sitting close to him, was affecting the hell out of him. What was wrong with him? When he was focused on something—like he was now on finding the office mole—he was never distracted from his task.

But she distracted him. He watched her lips part

as she forked in a bite of steamed broccoli, and he wished her lips were parting for his tongue. While Bruno's food was as incredible as it always was, Simon wanted to taste her more than the meal.

And not just her lips or her mouth.

"What?" she asked as she lifted her hand to her face. "Do I have broccoli in my teeth?"

He shook his head.

"Why are you staring at me?" she asked.

She really didn't seem to know. He wasn't used to that, not when he usually dated models and actresses whose egos rivaled his.

"Are you completely unaware of how beautiful you are?" he asked.

Her lips curved into a smile but it was a little mocking and she murmured, "For the past two years, you were *completely* unaware of me."

He grinned. "That's what you thought?"

"It's what I know," she said. "I might as well have been a copy machine for all the attention you paid me the past two years."

He narrowed his eyes and studied her face. Was that why she'd done it, why she'd given information to the opposition? Because she'd been resentful that he had never seemed to notice her?

"Did you want my attention?" he asked.

Her gaze slipped away from his, and her teeth nipped into her bottom lip. Maybe she was too embarrassed to admit that she'd wanted him to notice her, so he assured her, "You had my attention."

Her teeth still nibbling on that full, sexy lower lip, she shook her head. "I find that very hard to believe."

His seduction wouldn't work if she didn't believe that he found her attractive. So he leaned closer, pressing his thigh against hers, and he murmured, "I have spent countless hours admiring your ass...ets."

Her lips curved into a smile. "If only that were true." She gave a wistful sigh then.

"You really did want me to notice you?" he asked as a warning bell began to sound inside his head. She was acting very differently than she had Friday night when she'd left her resignation on his desk.

Her brown eyes widened behind the lenses of her glasses, and her lashes fluttered. "Yes..." Then she leaned against him, and her fingertips skimmed over his thigh.

His body tensed, with her touch and with the thought that just dawned on him. Maybe he wasn't the only one turning on the charm. He had a feeling he was definitely getting played.

For what? More case file secrets?

But he was curious as to how far she would carry her charade. So he covered her hand with his and guided her fingers to stroke up and down his thigh.

She glanced sideways at him, and her lips curved into a smile while her already-dark eyes darkened more with desire. Or was that wishful thinking on his part? Then she moved her hand farther up his leg, toward his groin.

And he sucked in a sharp breath. "Bette..."

She tugged her hand from beneath his and brought it back to the stem of her wineglass. Then she stroked her fingers up and down it, like he wanted them stroking up and down his cock. Mischief sparkled in her dark eyes; she was completely aware of what he wanted, what he needed.

The need startled him. Sure, he'd felt desire before. Often. As a teen runaway, he'd wanted so much stuff—stuff he hadn't had. Like a safe place to sleep, food, clothes.

He'd wanted those things so badly that he'd used some questionable methods to get them. But he'd succeeded then, just as he would now. He would succeed in getting the truth out of Bette.

The truth wasn't all he wanted from her. He wanted release from the tension gripping his body. He was so damn tense that when she leaned against him, he jumped a little, making his chair squeak and nearly tip.

Her smile widened. And he knew for certain he was being played. While he hadn't been as unaware of her as she'd thought these past two years, he'd had no idea what she was really like—or who she really was.

But he intended to find out. He had to regain control in order to do that, though—over himself and over her. So he reached around her and poured some more wine in her glass.

She giggled and asked, "Are you trying to get me drunk to have your way with me?"

"Would it work?" he wondered aloud.

"I'm a lightweight," she said. "Just a few more sips and I'll either be stripping off my clothes or passing out." She brought the rim to her lips and tipped up the glass for a long, deep sip.

"If I have a vote in this, I'd prefer the stripping," he teased.

She arched a dark brow above the top frame of her glasses and murmured, "I'm sure you would."

Was she mocking him? The arched-brow gesture was one he'd been doing since he was a kid. While he wasn't as aware of her as he obviously should have been the past two years, she seemed to have been aware of him.

"Do you play cards?" he asked.

"Why are you asking?"

"I was thinking we could play a hand or two of poker—strip poker." He was really good at cards but most especially at poker.

She giggled again. "We're supposed to be working," she reminded him. "Not playing. You said this was a working dinner, something about taking notes."

He chuckled now. "Oh, I'm taking notes."

But he hadn't learned much about her yet.

"I'm supposed to be taking notes," she said.

He touched the stem of her glass as she took another sip. "You're too drunk." Was she? He wanted her, but he didn't want to take advantage of her.

"Nope," she said. "I'm just drunk enough." And she rose from the chair.

Maybe she meant that she was sober enough, to know to leave before he seduced her, like he'd intended. Disappointment gripped him. He wouldn't try too hard to persuade her to stay, not if she'd truly had too much to drink.

He narrowed his eyes. "Just drunk enough for what?"

She pulled her glasses off her nose and dropped them onto the table next to her barely touched meal. Bruno would be so disappointed that they hadn't eaten much.

But Simon wasn't hungry for food. And despite her stomach growling earlier, Bette hadn't eaten very much. That was probably why the wine had hit her so hard—hard enough—that she reached up and tugged the pins from her hair. The sable-brown tresses tumbled down, falling in thick waves nearly to her waist.

He groaned. She was so damn sexy.

Then she reached for the buttons on her cardigan. She flicked open the first one and the second one. And Simon jumped to his feet and stepped close to her. Like he had when she'd touched his leg, he covered her hand with his. But now he stopped her fingers from moving.

"You're not drunk enough," he corrected her. "You're too drunk."

She tilted her head and stared up at him as if surprised. "You really want me to stop?"

"Hell, no," he admitted. "I want you to undo every one of those damn buttons. I want you to unzip your skirt and take off your clothes, so I can see what the hell you're wearing underneath them." Because it was driving him crazy imagining her in lace and nothing else.

She stepped back and pulled her hand free of his. Then she continued undoing her buttons until the cardigan parted and slid down her arms. She wore a lace camisole that was so thin he could see the bra beneath it.

"Bette," he murmured, but he couldn't summon the protest he knew he should be making.

She touched her hip, pulling down the tab of the zipper until her wool skirt dropped to her feet.

His breath escaped in a gasp.

Her underwear was lace, too—black like the camisole and the bra beneath it. Then she tugged the camisole up and over her head until it fell to the floor atop the skirt.

"Damn," he cursed her. She tested his control in a way it had never been tested before. He closed his eyes, but he couldn't shut out the image of her standing before him in that sexy black underwear. Her breasts nearly overflowed the cups of that black bra, and those cups were held together with only a bow.

He had to know. So he opened his eyes again, and he spun her around. Just as he'd suspected, there was a bow at the top of her luscious ass holding together the lace panel at the front of her panties to the tiny panel in the back.

And the control he'd fought so hard to regain

snapped completely. He'd intended to seduce her, but she was the one seducing him. "Bette, what the hell are you doing?"

Bette couldn't answer his question because she had no idea what the hell she was doing, either. Despite what she'd said, that she was just drunk enough, she would be able to remember with perfect clarity what she'd just done, how she'd just undressed for him...

And worse yet, he wasn't drunk at all, so he would remember, as well. He stepped closer to her, and his hands gripped her shoulders. "What the hell are you doing?" he asked again, his voice gruff while his eyes were completely black. The pupils had swallowed his blue irises whole.

"I'm a horrible poker player," she said. "So I just saved myself the trouble."

"I didn't think you wanted to play."

She was playing a very dangerous game. She wanted Simon Kramer to think she was in love with him, so that he'd cut short her two-week notice. She didn't want to actually fall for him.

Of course she was in no danger of that. She knew him far better than he knew her. No woman ever held his interest for very long. Since he hadn't even noticed her the past two years, she was surprised she had his interest right now.

Maybe that was because of the underwear...

He stared at the bow between the cups of her bra. And she smiled as pride surged through her. The pride was in the design, though. And maybe in the fact that she knew she had his attention now.

His full attention.

"I never said I didn't want to play," she reminded him. "I just thought we were supposed to be working."

"It's working," he said, his hands sliding from her shoulders down her bare arms. "Whatever game you're playing is working."

She widened her eyes and feigned innocence. "What game? I told you I'm no good at poker."

He narrowed his eyes and studied her face. "Oh, I think you're a damn good poker player, Bette Monroe."

She reached for his tie and tugged the knot loose. "Then you better take off your clothes, too..." She moved her fingers to the buttons on his shirt, undoing them like she'd undone her cardigan. "Since you're losing."

"I am losing," Simon said, his chest rising and falling with his erratic breathing. "You've completely taken control."

She smiled again at the frustration and desire she heard in his voice. Her fingers skimmed down his washboard abs to the buckle of his belt.

"No," he said, and his hand caught hers. "You don't understand."

"What?" she asked. "What don't I understand?"

"*I* don't lose control," he told her.

She smiled but assured him, "You haven't." He

hadn't even touched her. Maybe the underwear wasn't as sexy as she'd thought it was, as it made her feel.

"If you're just playing some game with me, you better stop," he told her. "Because I really—genuinely—want you." For two years she'd wondered what it would feel like to have him look at her the way she looked at him, with appreciation and attraction. He was so damn handsome that he was actually beautiful. Beautifully masculine. Muscles rippled beneath her touch as she tugged her hands from his and skimmed her palms up his chest to push his shirt and suitcoat from his broad shoulders. Muscles rippled in his arms, too, when he shrugged it off.

For two years she'd dreamed about him turning his attention to her, about him seducing her as he'd seduced so many other women into losing their minds and hearts to him. She knew he didn't want either her mind or her heart, though. So they would be quite safe from him. He wanted only her body. And she wanted his.

She had been so busy lately that she hadn't had any time to date. It had been a while for her since she'd had sex with anything not battery-operated. And it had never been Simon. She wanted to experience his notorious sexual prowess while she had the opportunity. And she didn't have to worry about losing her job afterward. She actually hoped that she did.

"I don't want you to stop," she assured him.

"Good," he said. That control he'd sounded so worried about must have snapped because he dragged her against his hard, tense body and lowered his mouth to hers.

He kissed her as if he was starving, nibbling and nipping at her lips. She gasped as his teeth tugged on her lower lip. Then his tongue slid inside her mouth, mating with hers.

Her pulse pounded while heat rushed through her body. She didn't feel the least bit of chill, standing in his loftlike office in only her thin lace lingerie, especially as his hands began to move over her body. His touch spread fire through her.

Tension wound tightly inside her core. She needed the release that she instinctively knew he could give her. But he seemed to be in no hurry to do anything but kiss her.

And a kiss had never turned her on as much. He stroked his tongue in and out of her mouth like she wanted his cock sliding in and out of her body. She moaned.

And he groaned in response. "You taste so damn good..." he murmured against her lips.

"It's the wine..."

"It's you..." Finally, he lifted his head from hers. But he stepped back.

She thought maybe he'd changed his mind; maybe he didn't really want her. But his chest rose and fell with pants for breath, and she understood that he was just fighting again, fighting hard to regain control of himself.

She wanted him out of control. So she lifted her fingers to the bow between her breasts.

But he caught her hand and pulled it away. Then he shook his head. "No…"

She stared up at him through her lashes and asked, "You don't want me?"

He groaned again. "I want you too damn much." And he didn't sound happy about it. "So let me do this…" He tugged on the bow until it slipped free of its knot, and the cups of the bra parted, falling away from her breasts. The bra dropped to the hardwood floor atop her clothes.

He cursed. And his skin flushed like hers, with passion. "Damn, Bette…"

She wasn't cold, so that wasn't why her nipples tightened. It was desire. For him.

He touched her. His fingers sliding from where he'd untied the bow between her breasts up to her collarbone and her neck. He found her pulse and traced his fingertip over it. It leaped like her desire for him.

And he must have known it. He smiled, just slightly, as if it was all he could manage with his lips parted as he panted for breath. His chest—his glorious naked chest—rose and fell, muscles rippling.

She had to touch, too. So she slid her hands over his skin. Soft, golden hair tickled her palms. How could he look like an angel but be such a devil—in business and pleasure?

She didn't care, though. She wouldn't be working for him much longer. And she was never really going to fall for him. But she had to convince him that she might. So she said, "I've wanted you for so long."

His eyes narrowed slightly as if he doubted her. But then he must have remembered how handsome he was because he nodded in acceptance.

And she smiled.

"You're not drunk enough," he murmured. But he didn't reach for the wine to pour her any more. Instead he reached for her. "You're too in control," he said, as if it was a complaint.

Then he proceeded to drive her out of her mind with his touch. His hands moved over her breasts, gently kneading and stroking while his palms brushed over and over her already tight nipples.

She moaned and leaned toward him, needing more.

He gave more. His hands moved down to her hips, and he tugged at the bows holding her panties in place. They fell onto her bra and clothes. Bette might have fallen, too, as her knees began to shake, but he lifted her into his arms. Her breasts rubbed against his naked chest as he carried her across the office to his couch.

The leather was cold against her back and butt and thighs, but it did nothing to cool the heat of her passion-flushed skin. She locked her arms around his neck, trying to pull him down with her. But he held back and knelt beside the couch. Then he feasted on her body as if she were a banquet Bruno had laid out for his pleasure.

But the pleasure was all hers.

He kissed her lips—just briefly, nibbling gently at them. Then her chin before he moved his mouth to her breasts. As he kissed them, his hands moved lower, over the curve of her hip and down the length of her thighs.

She shivered as sensations raced through her.

He pulled back. "Are you cold?"

Too choked with desire to speak, she shook her head.

He smiled now. He was back in control. Not just of himself but of her. And he knew it.

Before she could protest, though, he moved his mouth back to her breast and closed his lips over a nipple. As he tugged at it, she felt heat and moisture rush straight to her core. Then his hand was there, his fingers moving inside her. She arched against his hand, and he rubbed his palm against her mound.

"Simon..." His name slipped out on a gasp of pleasure.

"Bette," he murmured. "You're so damn hot!" And whatever control he'd regained snapped. "I have to taste you." And his mouth replaced his hand between her legs. He dipped his tongue inside her, teasing her and building the tension. Then he withdrew it and flicked it over her clit.

She rose up and cried out as an orgasm shot through her.

He groaned. "You are so damn responsive…" But he stood up and moved away from her.

She reached out in protest. The orgasm had been good, better than she achieved on her own. But she knew there was more. She held out her arms to him.

But he stepped back and stared down at her. And disappointment filled her that he might stop. He unclasped his belt and pushed down his pants and briefs. He was so damn beautiful—his dick so long and hard as it jutted from a bed of curls even more golden than the hair on his head.

Somehow, as if he was a magician, a condom appeared in his hand. He tore the packet and rolled it over his cock. Then he joined her on the couch, connecting their bodies.

He stretched, then filled her. Bette arched and adjusted, making room for his impressive length and girth. She was so hot and wet that it was easy. And it felt right, like he fitted perfectly inside her.

He lifted her legs so that he sank even deeper and began to thrust in and out. Bette came again—that quickly—just from his movements. He was that damn good…

But then he got better. He leaned down and arched his back until his mouth could close over the point of one of her breasts. He sucked on the nipple as he moved.

Tension spiraled inside her again, and Bette

arched and shifted, seeking to release it. She bucked beneath him, losing all control. They moved in a frenzy, like they were convulsing and then she did— as the orgasm slammed through her. Her muscles quivered and sensations gripped her. She had never felt anything as intense for as long. She just kept coming, the pleasure overwhelming in intensity and duration. She screamed his name.

Then he tensed and cried out as he found his release. Panting for breath, he leaned his forehead against hers. Staring into her eyes, he asked, "What the hell was that?"

She had no idea, either, beyond the most passionate sexual experience she'd ever had. And because it was, she was too stunned to remember her act. She said nothing as he slipped away from her, into the bathroom off his office. But she moved, dressing more quickly than they'd had sex.

She didn't care if he wanted her to stay any longer. She had to get away. She had to regroup. So she left his office and stopped in hers only long enough to grab her phone and purse. Then she ran for the elevator, jabbing her finger against the button.

While she waited for the car to arrive, she heard him call her name. But before he found her, the elevator dinged and the doors opened. She jumped inside and jabbed at the button to close the doors. When they finally closed, she leaned against the wall and began to shake.

What the hell had she done?

CHAPTER FIVE

EVEN THOUGH HE'D SHOWERED, Simon could smell her on his skin. Or maybe her scent was in his office. Or, worse yet, in his head, just like the image of her standing before him in nothing but that scandalous lingerie—the lacy bra and panties with those strategically placed little bows. Bows that his fingers twitched to untie yet again.

"Simon!" a deep voice yelled as fingers snapped in his face. "What the hell's going on?"

He blinked but the image of Bette lingered yet in his mind. He forced himself to focus on the men sitting around the conference table in his office. The partners met every Tuesday morning, their slow day, to discuss Street Legal. He should have told them to meet him somewhere else, though, because he couldn't focus in here.

It smelled like Bette, and it smelled like the vestiges of their dinner the night before, even though the metal cart with the dishes and wine bottle had been returned to Bruno's restaurant. Another cart sat next to the table, this one with a carafe of coffee and an assortment of fruit, Danish and croissants.

"Yeah," Stone said, his brow furrowed with concern. Then he echoed Ronan's question, "What the hell's going on with you? You're completely out of it."

Simon shrugged. "Nothing's going on." Except that he'd lost control last night. And that was something that never happened to him. He was supposed to have seduced Bette Monroe but she'd seduced him instead.

"Who is this woman that had you tearing out of the bar last Friday?" Trevor asked. "The one who sexted you?"

"Ah, that's why he left in such a damn hurry," Ronan said. Then he snorted derisively at himself. "I should've known it was because of a woman. Is that why you're so distracted right now?"

Simon snorted this time. "Like a woman has ever distracted me before…"

The others laughed, like he'd wanted them to, but he was unable to join in. He'd just misled his friends, and he'd never done that before. A woman had distracted him last night. He'd completely forgotten why he'd wanted to seduce her—for information, for evidence—not for pleasure. At least not just for pleasure.

But hell, what he'd felt last night with Bette had gone beyond pleasure. He'd never felt anything like that.

He'd wanted her so badly that he'd acted like a teenager—with no finesse. He'd just had to have her.

Especially after he'd tasted her. She was sweeter than any pastry on that cart. And hotter than the coffee steaming in the mugs on the table. So damn hot…

She'd nearly burned him as he'd plunged his cock into her. The sensation had been incredible. She was so tight, so wet. She'd fitted him perfectly. Then when she'd come, her inner muscles had rippled and squeezed him. And he'd completely lost it. He couldn't remember the last time he'd come that long or that hard.

"So if it's not a woman," Trevor said, "what's bothering you?"

He shrugged, but the tension remained in his shoulders and neck and lower in his body, where his groin swelled with the need to experience that beyond-pleasure release again. "Just had a busy day yesterday. Back-to-back meetings with clients or potential clients all day." And at night…

He had Bette. Or did she have him?

"Yeah," Stone said. "You worked really late last night."

Simon glanced up, and across the table he met his friend's intense gaze. The knowledge was in Stone's dark gray eyes. He knew…

"You were here?" Simon asked uneasily. He'd thought everyone was gone and that he and Bette had been alone in the office last night. Obviously, he'd thought wrong.

"I have to make sure my defense is ready before the trial begins," Stone said. His gaze increased in intensity. "And I have to make sure none of my defense plan leaks to the prosecution."

"Hillary Bellows," Trevor murmured with a lustful sigh. "I wouldn't mind going toe-to-toe with her."

Stone glared at him. "Yeah, you're an idiot, then. She's a pain in the ass."

"Because she's good," Trev goaded him.

"I'm better," Stone said. And it wasn't just his ego talking. All his past victories against her proved it true. "I will win this case as long as there are no surprises like there were in Trev's trial." He was staring at Simon again.

He nodded. "There will not be any surprises. Nobody's going to get into our files again." He would keep Bette too busy with work and sex to sell any more secrets.

"So you got it handled?" Trev asked. "You found out who got their hands on that report from my case files?"

He wasn't ready yet to share his suspicions about Bette. First, he had no proof. Second, if his partners knew he suspected her, they would want him to toss her out of the office immediately. And he wasn't ready to let her go just yet.

At least not until he had proof…

Then he would.

She hadn't given him much of a choice last night. She'd run off before he'd finished cleaning up. He'd come so much—because of her.

"I'm working on it," he said. His voice sounded

gruff, so he had to clear it before continuing. "But now that we're aware of what happened, we're all more vigilant. Nobody's going to pull anything on us again."

Least of all Bette Monroe. She would not seduce him again. That was not going to happen.

He slapped his palms onto the tabletop so forcefully that he had coffee spilling over the rim of his mug. "Anything else we need to discuss this morning?" And he gave Stone a pointed look, so that he wouldn't bring up what he knew about the night before—about Simon's late night with Bette.

Ronan, who was always full of energy, jumped up from his chair. "No. We're good. I trust that you've got everything handled. It's not like we could actually have a mole in our office anyway, not with you doing all the hiring."

Heat rushed to his face now from where it had pooled in his groin with thoughts of Bette. How had she fooled him so completely? She was nothing like what he'd thought she was the past two years.

If he'd only known how damn hot she was...

How responsive. She'd come so easily and so many times. He was good. But he wasn't that good. He hadn't even given her his best effort because he'd lost control. That damn tension had wound up so tightly inside him that he'd snapped completely.

Trev stood up, as well. "I'm the one with back-to-back appointments with potential clients all day today," he said and sighed. "The burden of being a winner. Everybody wants you."

Simon wriggled his eyebrows and grinned. "Everybody's always wanted me."

Apparently, even Bette...

But she'd never given him that impression before. Did she know that he was onto her? The thought of her distracted him again, so that he barely noticed that Ronan and Trevor had left his office.

Stone had remained, though, sitting across from him, his eyes narrowed as he studied Simon's face. "What the hell are you thinking?"

"Right now?" Simon asked. "I'm not sure you'd want to know." Unless Stone had a thing for Bette Monroe, too, because Simon couldn't stop thinking about her and that damn lacy lingerie she'd been wearing the night before. What would she be wearing today? He couldn't wait to find out.

"Last night," Stone said. "What the hell were you thinking?"

"What are you talking about?" Simon asked. He could probably guess, but he'd learned it was smarter not to make any assumptions. Maybe Stone didn't know who'd been in the office with Simon.

"I was here," Stone reminded him. "I heard Bruno wheel in the cart for your romantic dinner." His brow furrowed with either confusion or concern. "With your assistant."

Simon chuckled. "So—we were working late."

"You weren't working," Stone said. "Your office

isn't soundproof and that wasn't dictation I overheard as I was leaving."

Heat rushed to Simon's face, but he chuckled again and teased, "Jealous?"

Stone shook his head. "Concerned that you're exposing Street Legal to a potential lawsuit. She's an employee."

"Not for much longer," Simon admitted.

Stone groaned. "You're firing her? That makes it even worse."

"No," Simon said. "She already gave her notice."

"Oh…" Stone nodded as if he suddenly understood.

But what could he understand? Simon hadn't told him that Bette could potentially be the mole. Again, he hesitated about revealing that information. It was smarter to keep his suspicions to himself until he had proof.

And yet he was compelled to ask his friend, "What does that mean?"

"I've seen the way you looked at her the past couple of years," Stone said. "So I get you going all out since she's no longer off-limits."

Hell, if she was the mole, she'd be more off-limits than she was as an active employee.

"All out?"

"The fancy dinner, the seduction…"

He was responsible for the fancy dinner, but the seduction had been more her than him. He shrugged. "What can I say?"

Stone sighed. "I just hope you know what you're doing," he murmured as he stood up and headed toward the door.

Simon got up and followed him out. He hoped he knew what the hell he was doing, too. The first thing he did was head to Bette's office. But it was dark and empty. As he turned around in the doorway, Miguel waved him over to the reception desk in the lobby and informed him. "She called in sick."

Yeah, right…

She wasn't sick. She was scared, scared that he was going to find out what she was up to. And she was damn right to be scared because he was more determined than ever to get the truth out of Bette Monroe.

Unfortunately—after last night—that wasn't all he wanted from her.

Bette twirled in front of the oval mirror in her walk-in closet. She admired the flow of the green silk negligee against her body, but she couldn't look at her face. She was too disgusted with herself.

About last night…

About sleeping with Simon Kramer. What had she been thinking? Sure, she'd spent the past two years wondering what it would be like. But it would have been safer to just keep wondering.

Because being with him…

That had been a lot more powerful than she'd ever imagined it could be. The man was incredible. His body, the way he'd touched her, the way he'd moved inside her.

She shivered. But she wasn't really cold. Heat suffused her body, as it had every time she'd thought of the night before, of what she and Simon Kramer had done in his office, on his couch.

How many other women had he taken against the supple black leather? She hadn't thought about that in the incredible heat of the moment. But she'd been thinking about it ever since...

Not that she wanted to be anything special to him. She didn't want to be *anything* to him. She didn't even want to see him again.

That was partially why she'd called in sick, which was another reason she couldn't look at her face in the mirror. She was disgusted with herself for lying and for being a coward. She was tougher than that; if she wasn't, she wouldn't have made it on her own all these years in New York.

Maybe it was better that she didn't go into the office because then she wouldn't have to endure the humiliation of being walked out with her box of belongings. And she had no doubt that Simon would walk her to the door. He had no use for her anymore, not after last night.

Her doorbell rang, and she tensed. Who could that be? Hardly anyone had her new address yet. She still hadn't unpacked all her boxes, which was another reason she'd decided not to go into the office today. She had too much to do. But the box of

lingerie samples had distracted her, and she'd found
herself trying on some of the things. She'd wanted
inspiration for more designs but all she could think
about was Simon and last night.

The doorbell rang again, insistently, as if someone
had her or his finger pressed against it. How had the
visitor even gotten past the doorman? This wasn't
like her old building in Queens that had a broken lock
on the door to the lobby, so there had been absolutely
no security but for her overprotective neighbors and
the two roommates with whom she'd shared the two-
bedroom apartment.

Thank goodness for them.

Maybe she hadn't survived entirely on her own in
the city. But this building, in the Garment District,
was supposed to have high security, at least that was
what the property manager had claimed. So maybe
it was a new neighbor introducing her or himself,
which would be nice since no one had been particularly friendly or warm yet.

At least she had one friend in the building, the
one who'd recommended the place to her. But Muriel was out of town on a photo shoot. If Bette hadn't
had to work out these two weeks, she could have
gone with her.

Damn Simon Kramer and his employment contract. No matter that Bette was doing better finan-
cially than she ever had, she still couldn't afford a
lawsuit that she was certain to lose.

She grabbed a long fleece robe from a hook on

the closet wall before heading through her bedroom, with the sheets tangled on the unmade bed, to the living room. The sun shone through the tall windows in the brick walls, casting a warm glow on the dark-stained hardwood floor. She loved this place. But she wasn't entirely convinced it was as safe as the property manager and Muriel had claimed.

How had someone found out where she lived? Unless Muriel had sent congratulatory flowers for Bette quitting Street Legal. Or had Simon sent the kiss-off flowers he'd sent to every other lover he'd tired of?

But Simon didn't know where she lived.

To be safe, Bette paused before opening the door. She rose up on tiptoe and peered through the peep-hole. And her breath caught in her lungs as fear filled her.

No…

How the hell had he found out where she lived? And how had he gotten inside the building? But then she knew. He had somehow charmed his way inside, just like he'd charmed his way inside her the night before.

Abandoning the button for the bell, he pounded on the door instead. "Bette, I know you're inside, and I'm not leaving until you let me in."

She didn't doubt that he would keep ringing her bell and pounding on the door until she did. And if she ever wanted the neighbors to warm up to her, she shouldn't risk alienating any of them with a noise disturbance.

With a sigh, she turned the dead bolt and opened the door. "What are you doing here?" she asked as she leaned against the jamb, blocking his way inside.

But she didn't deter him. He put his hands on her shoulders and moved her aside so he could enter. "Simon!" She gasped. But she closed the door behind him.

"Don't you mean how?" he asked. "You didn't change your address with HR."

HR was a couple of women who handled payroll and benefits. He was really Human Resources, the one who personally interviewed and hired all applicants. Her face flushed at the thought of him asking those gossipy women where she lived.

"Then how?" she asked.

"One of your former roommates gave me your good news."

She tensed. What roommate? And what exactly had he told him? She was afraid to ask so she returned to her original question. "Why?"

He grinned. "John Paul couldn't resist my charm."

John Paul. He had probably fallen in love with Simon at first sight. But JP loved her, too, so he wouldn't have revealed too much information. He'd probably only told Simon where she was because the guy was a hopeless romantic.

Bette was too practical for romance. Or at least that was what she'd always thought until last night and that romantic candlelit dinner Simon had catered for them.

"Why are you here?" she asked. That was the question she really wanted him to answer. Did he want more the way she did?

"I should have tracked you down last night," he said, "after you ran out the way you did."

Her face heated with embarrassment. She had acted like a fool, thinking she could act. That had been stupid. "It was late," she said. "And I was too drunk to work." Maybe he would think that was why she'd done what she had, undressing for him.

"I'm here to bring you to work," he said. "You still have nine days to go on your two-week notice—if you still want to leave."

Her already racing pulse quickened even more with surprise. "You still want me there?"

He stared down at her, and his blue eyes darkened. Then his gaze skimmed down her body, over her fleece robe, as if he could see right through it.

Her nipples tightened in reaction, and heat rushed to her core. She'd never wanted anyone the way she wanted him. And that had been before she'd even known how he felt inside her and how much pleasure he could give her.

"I definitely still want you," he said, and there was no mistaking the intent in his deep, sensual voice.

"But—but that's not your usual MO," she protested.

"Usual MO?" he asked as he arched a dark blond brow. "What is my usual MO?"

Maybe she was still a little buzzed from the wine

the night before or the sex, because her filter was off again. She answered him honestly, "You're notorious for being the king of one-night stands."

He didn't deny it; he just chuckled. "Is that why you ran out the way you did last night?"

She nodded. "And since we had one night…"

"You thought that was all I would want?"

Realizing she should have used more tact, she sank her teeth into her bottom lip and just nodded her head.

He stepped closer, until his body pressed against hers. And dropping his voice to a low, sexy whisper, he murmured, "One night with you would never be enough."

She gasped as her core began to throb with desire for him. And he took her mouth, kissing her deeply. His tongue slid between her lips, like his cock had slid inside her last night. His hands moved to her shoulders again, but he didn't move her aside this time. He pulled her closer.

Her breasts crushed against his chest; her heart pounded madly—in perfect rhythm with his. Just like they'd been last night…

That rhythm had been fast and frantic, though, as they'd both lost control. She couldn't lose control again the way she had before. She had to remember who and what he was: Simon Kramer, heartbreaking charmer and ruthless attorney.

CHAPTER SIX

S<small>IMON LIFTED HIS</small> head from hers and tried to clear it. He needed to focus on anything other than her beautiful face. She wasn't wearing her glasses today. She probably wore no makeup, either, but her pale skin was flawless, her lashes long and thick and as deep a brown as her hair. She didn't need makeup, not with her natural beauty.

Apparently, she didn't need her glasses, either. At least not all the time. But until last night he'd never seen her without them. Were they necessary? Or just part of her disguise?

He felt like she'd been wearing one the past two years. Like she'd deliberately been trying to mislead him about who she really was.

Because he'd had no idea how hot she was, how wet and responsive...

He suppressed a groan that burned the back of his throat, like she'd burned him up the night before with her passion. Who the hell was Bette Monroe really?

Her hair was down, too, falling in long, rich, brown waves around her slender shoulders. Even with the long fleece robe covering up her substantial curves, she was damn sexy. Then the sash of that robe slipped out of its loose knot, and the fleece parted to reveal dark green silk and lace.

His breath escaped in a gasp, like he'd been sucker punched. Not that he knew what that felt like. Nobody had ever sucker punched him before. He was always too aware, too prepared, to get suckered.

Until now.

Until Bette Monroe.

"What the hell are you wearing?" he asked, his voice gruff with desire.

Her face flushed with embarrassment, and her fingers trembled as she fumbled with the sash, trying to retie the fleece robe.

He caught her fingers in his and tugged the sash free of the loops. Then he pushed the robe from her shoulders. Her bare shoulders…

He wasn't certain how the hell the negligee wasn't slipping right off her body. Then he noticed another bow on her back, tied between her shoulder blades. If he undid that bow, the negligee would drop to her feet. His fingers twitched. He wanted to untie that bow so badly.

But that was probably her plan, keep him so sexually charged that he couldn't think straight, so that he wouldn't catch her in the act of stealing case files. Why else was she wearing lingerie around the house?

Unless…

He glanced around the apartment. "Are you

alone?" Or had she stayed home because she was
entertaining a lover?

Her brow furrowed slightly. "Yes, I live here
alone. I don't have a roommate."

"Then how can you afford this place?" There were
doors off the main living room, so it had at least
one bedroom. Street Legal paid their employees well
enough that she should have been able to afford more
than that tiny two-bedroom in Queens that John Paul
had admitted they'd shared with another roommate,
apparently his boyfriend.

So maybe she'd saved up some of that money but
she couldn't have saved enough to be able to pay
the rent for a one-bedroom in the Garment District
with a full kitchen. She actually had full-size appliances, not just a two-burner stove top and half-size
fridge like she'd shared with John Paul and his partner. There was also a big bay window where a table
would fit if she had one. She didn't. But then she'd
obviously just moved in. Boxes sat on the hardwood
floor. Maybe that was why she'd called in to work—
so she could unpack.

He looked back at her and arched a brow as he
waited for her answer.

She narrowed her eyes and glared at him. "That's
really not any of your business."

He nearly growled in frustration. "That's what
you said about your reason for resigning."

"I don't have to give you one," she reminded him.
"Your own contract says that." She gestured to where

the document was laid out on her reclaimed-wood coffee table. While the place wasn't totally furnished, he liked the pieces she had. He liked her taste but not just in furniture.

He could taste her on his lips yet. She tasted like some kind of citrusy tea and dark chocolate. A cup and a piece of foil with chocolate crumbs on it sat atop the coffee table, as well.

"Why don't you want to give me one?" he asked. Usually people told him why they were quitting. *I'm in love with you and I know you'll never love me back.*

It's too hard to work with you.

You expect too much.

Bette had claimed none of those reasons. In fact, she'd never complained about the workload or about him. So why did she want to leave?

"Like I told you before," she replied, "it's my business. Not yours."

"You didn't mind my being in your business last night," he reminded her as he stepped closer again. "I was all up in your business..."

And he wanted to be all up inside her again.

Her lips parted on a gasp as she stared up at him. She wanted him to; she had to after last night, after how incredible it had been.

Or hadn't she felt it?

He'd never lost control like that before, had never come so quickly. Usually he made sure his partner had many, many orgasms before he found his own release.

He wanted her to be as out of control and crazy as she'd made him the night before. So he reached for that bow between her shoulder blades. The bodice of the long negligee loosened and released her full breasts before it pooled like a green silk puddle around her bare feet.

She was bare all over. She didn't even wear panties beneath that gown. And he was damn glad of that. His hand was shaking so badly he wasn't certain that he could have untied another bow. Not that he figured all her panties were made that way. But he wanted to find out.

"Why are you so damn sexy?"

Her mouth curved into a smile. "It's the lingerie."

He reached out and traced his fingertips over the curve of her breast, then over her flat stomach to the curve of her hip and ass. "You're not wearing anything right now." But that sexy smile. "And you're gorgeous."

She sighed. "When you turn on the charm like that…"

"What?" he asked. Did he tempt her to reveal all her secrets? To admit that she'd betrayed him?

"You make me crazy," she murmured. And she reached for him. After pushing his suit jacket from his shoulders, she attacked the buttons on his shirt, frantically freeing them. And each inch of his chest she revealed, she pressed her lips against in silky kisses. Then her tongue flicked over his nipple.

And he groaned. She was the one making him crazy, making him lose control. But he couldn't risk that again. He was the one who was supposed to be seducing her.

Besides the coffee table, she had a couch—thankfully—or he would have taken her on the table. The couch was big and deep, nearly the size of a bed with soft cushions and pillows. He pushed her onto it and followed her down.

And he went down on her. He didn't just taste her like he had the night before. He feasted on her. While he used one hand to massage her breast and tease the nipple, he used the other on her pussy. As he slid his fingers inside her wet core, he nibbled and sucked on her clit.

She screamed as she came. And he lapped up her sweet release.

He groaned. And damn it, his control snapped again. He had to be inside her, had to be in all that wet heat. He shucked his pants and briefs and fumbled with the condom. She took the packet from him and tore it open. Then she rolled it over his pulsating cock. He nearly came as she pumped him through the latex. But he wasn't having it…

He was having her. So he dragged off her hand and spun her around. Then with her clutching the back of the couch cushions, he moved his dick between her legs. As he stroked her ass, he found her core and slid inside her. Then he cupped her breasts, rolling her nipples between his fingers and thumbs while he thrust inside her.

She arched her luscious hips and took him deeper, grinding against his groin as she sought her orgasm. She came again with a scream of pleasure. His balls ached, stretching as they filled. Then he found his release.

She came again before he pulled out. Her inner muscles clutched him as she whimpered with pleasure. He hated to separate. But he had to clean up. He found the bathroom through the first doorway off the living room. After disposing of the condom and washing up, he came back to find her lying limply against her couch cushions.

Her glorious breasts rose and fell and shimmied as she panted for breath.

"Are you trying to make me fall in love with you?" she asked breathlessly as she stared up at him with those big dark eyes of hers.

He waited for the panic he usually felt when someone professed feelings for him he knew he'd never return. And when he noticed how closely she watched him, he wondered if she was looking for that panic, too.

He grinned and replied, "Just trying to get you to work."

Instead of looking hurt or even disappointed, she laughed and sat up. "All right. I'll shower and come into the office." She gestured toward the door. "I'm sure you can show yourself out."

He had no intention of leaving.

Yet.

Bette should have gone into the office that morning. But then she had never imagined that Simon Kramer would track her down at home. Not that she would ever feel entirely at home in her new place, especially now that he'd been inside it with her. That he'd been inside her.

She'd showered but she could still smell him on her skin. Just like he'd been in her body, he was inside her head, as well. But she wouldn't let him into her heart. Despite what she'd said to him, she knew better than to fall for a man like Simon Kramer.

He would break her heart for certain. But hell, that would probably be better than falling for some man who wanted to keep her heart. Or her...

Like the men for whom her mom and sister had fallen. Dad had forced Mom to give up all her dreams and live his as the preacher of a small-town church. Her mother had once been wild and full of fun. But Bette had never seen that except in the old photo albums her mother had hidden where she hadn't thought anyone would look.

Her sister should have known better, but she'd fallen for a man just like their self-righteous father. A youth minister—and she lived the same quiet, boring life their mother lived.

Bette shook her head in disgust of their choices. Of course they acted like they were disgusted with hers, especially her father. He'd disowned her years ago. At least Mom and Sissy still sent her cards on her birthday.

Carrying her heels, she hurried out of her bedroom. She needed to get to the office quickly or Simon might return for her. But apparently, he hadn't left because she found him standing over her coffee table. She dropped her shoes and pressed a hand against her madly pounding heart. "You scared me!" she said.

He glanced up as if he'd been caught unawares, too. And he almost looked guilty. What had he been doing while she'd been showering? She'd left the employment contract lying out on the coffee table. But he wouldn't have to read that over; he'd written it.

That wasn't all she'd left out in the living room, though. Her purse was lying beside the table. But he wouldn't have been going through that. Would he? It wasn't as if Simon Kramer needed to steal any cash from her wallet. She didn't carry much else in it but some makeup and her checkbook.

She hadn't shaken all of her damn old-fashioned, small-town upbringing because she was too cautious to do everything online. Or maybe she needed the checkbook because she needed the peace of mind of keeping track of everything she spent and earned. And finally, after years of barely getting by in the city, she was getting those things in the right order. She was finally earning more than she spent.

"I thought you left," she said. "I told you I would meet you at the office."

"And I thought I better wait for you," he said.

For what? Another romp on her couch? Her heart flipped at the thought but then she noticed his face. There was no disarming grin. No teasing twinkle in his blue eyes. He didn't trust her for some reason and she felt that it was more than her calling in sick.

"You didn't need to do that," she said. "I know you're busy."

He was so busy that she was surprised he'd taken the time to track down where she was, let alone wait for her after he'd done that—after he'd done her.

"I am busy," he said. "That's why I needed to make sure you didn't have a sudden relapse of whatever illness you claimed was keeping you from coming into the office today."

She faked a cough, then laughed as he glared at her. Unintimidated, she pressed the back of her hand to her forehead. "I am feeling a little warm still…" But that was because of him, because even though he'd dressed, she could still see him gloriously naked. He was so damn good-looking. It wasn't fair. It really wasn't.

"Don't try to con a con," he warned her, and his eyes were as cold and hard as they'd been the day he'd found her leaving the resignation letter in his office.

"Con?" she uneasily repeated as a chill chased down her spine. "Are you admitting that you're a con artist?"

Was he not even really a lawyer? She'd seen his college degree and law license framed on his office wall. But that didn't mean they hadn't been forged. As infamous as Street Legal was, someone would have discovered if the managing partner was a con artist. Wouldn't they?

He shook his head. "I wouldn't call myself a con artist," he said. "Not anymore. But I still recognize a con."

She smiled and assured him, "I'm not trying to con you." But could he say the same?

What exactly would he have to con out of her, though? Sex? She'd given that freely enough. No con required. He hadn't even had to pile on the charm very much, except for the compliments he'd given her.

"When were you a con artist?" she asked. "And why would you tell me that?" Obviously, he was onto her little game of pretending to fall for him. But now he'd made it a challenge for her to be able to convince him.

He shrugged. "It's not exactly a secret that my partners and I were teenage runaways. To survive on the streets, I had to run a con or two."

Shock gripped her. "You really did grow up on the streets?"

He nodded.

"I thought that was just a story that PR firm concocted to make you guys sound glamorous."

Over the past two years, she'd personally witnessed how fast and loose McCann Public Relations, and Allison McCann in particular, played with the truth.

Simon laughed now. "Glamorous? There was nothing glamorous about that life. But we weren't going to lie about where we came from, so Allison decided it would be smarter to make the most of it."

Allison.

Resentment churned in Bette's stomach. She wasn't a fan of the owner of McCann Public Relations. The woman was cold and ruthless. And so beautiful that there was no way any man would have gone two years without noticing her. Not that Bette was jealous or anything.

She would have rather had Simon never notice her at all. Now she was the liar. She knew that wasn't the case or she would have never experienced the most mind-blowing sex of her life. What they'd done...

How he'd made her feel...

He'd made her crazy with desire and then with pleasure.

"I'm not conning you," she said. At least not about calling in sick. "I didn't come into the office today because I really didn't think you'd want to see me again after last night."

"Is that why you ran out while I was in the bathroom?" he asked.

She nodded. Despite his warning, she had to try to con him in order to get him to release her from that contract. "I also didn't want to risk seeing you again."

He narrowed his eyes—those gorgeous blue eyes— and his brow furrowed with suspicion. "What's the risk, Bette?"

"My heart," she told him and forced a shaky sigh. "I'm worried I'm going to fall for you." As she uttered the words, they didn't ring as hollowly as she'd thought they would. And she actually felt a twinge of fear.

But she couldn't—she wouldn't—fall for Simon Kramer. There really was no risk at all.

Was there?

CHAPTER SEVEN

Who the hell was Bette Monroe? The shy woman with the glasses and her hair in a bun? Or the sexy siren in naughty lingerie?

He studied her across the small space between their seats in the back of the town car. She was wearing the glasses again, and her hair was all bound up. He suspected that was just a disguise—an act, like her worry that she was going to fall for him.

Just a few nights ago she had laughed when he'd asked if she loved him. So what had changed since then?

They'd had sex a couple of times. He was good. But he wasn't that good, not good enough to make her fall for him just because he'd given her some pleasure. While other women had professed as much, Bette was different. Those women had already been half in love with him because of who he was and what he had: a hell of a reputation and bank account.

Bette had never seemed very impressed with either. But then she claimed money didn't matter to her. That even if he gave her a raise, she wouldn't stay working for Street Legal. He knew why now that he'd gotten a look at her checkbook. She'd made some recent deposits. Some pretty damn good ones.

She had to be the mole.

A pressure settled heavily on his chest with disappointment—which was weird. He should be relieved that he'd found the mole. Now he would be able to stop any more information leaks. He would be able to stop her.

All he had to do was fire her and block her access to Street Legal. Delete her passwords, change the locks.

She wouldn't be able to sell any more of their information. But somehow it didn't feel right. Maybe she'd received that money another way.

An inheritance…

"What?" she asked as she lifted her hand to her mouth like she had the night before. "Do I have something on my teeth? Lipstick smeared?"

"Not yet," he said. But he wanted to smear it. Hell, he wanted it smeared on his cock as she sucked him off.

Her lips curved slightly. "Then what is it?" she asked. "Why are you staring at me?"

She really had no idea how beautiful she was. "I'm trying to figure you out," he admitted.

She tilted her head and studied him as intently as he'd been studying her. "You wonder how I could fall for you when I laughed the other night when you asked if I was in love with you?"

He laughed now. "That's the least of my questions about you, Bette."

She sighed. "Are you still wondering why I'm quitting?"

"Wondering…" He laughed again. "That's putting it a little mildly." He was more than curious. He was desperate to know her reason.

"I don't know why you care," she said.

"I want to know what your better offer is," he said. "To see if I can match it."

"I already told you it's not about money."

"Why?" he asked. "Do you have family money? A trust fund or inheritance you just got access to?"

She laughed. "My father is the minister of a very small church in a very small town in Michigan. If he and my mom didn't have housing provided by the parish, they wouldn't be able to afford groceries."

"Your mom doesn't work?" he asked.

She shook her head, and her lips curled slightly with disgust. "Being his wife is her full-time job."

So those deposits in her bank account hadn't come from her parents. Bette Monroe was no trust fund baby. Where the hell had she gotten that money?

He could think of one place. Their opposition in court.

"She's a loyal wife," he murmured. As far as he knew, his parents hadn't been married. He didn't even remember his mother. According to his father, she'd abandoned them. But that didn't mean it was true. His father hadn't had any idea how to be honest. It had always been easier for him to lie than tell the truth. "That's commendable."

Bette sighed. "It's sad."

"So you're not looking to get married anytime soon?"

She opened her mouth. And he expected an adamant *no* to come out of her lips. But then it was as if she caught herself and forced out a wistful sigh instead. "I would have said no," she admitted, "a few days ago…"

"What's changed?" he asked.

"You." She slid forward and dropped to her knees on the floor between their seats, and she was between his legs. "You've changed. You notice me now."

"You're kind of hard to miss," he murmured. And he wondered again what the hell she was up to…even as he was up again, his dick hardening and pushing against the fly of his pants.

Even though he couldn't trust her, he wanted her. But then he couldn't trust anyone. So it didn't matter much. He just knew that he would never be able to trust her.

Bette glanced at the dark glass separating the front seat from the back seats. There was no way the driver could see back there. Was there?

Did she care?

As a preacher's daughter, she should. But hell, Daddy had consigned her to hell long ago when she'd professed her love of fashion over bible studies. And she didn't consider pleasure the sin that Daddy did.

She'd never felt as much pleasure as she had with Simon Kramer. And she knew it was going to end soon like all of his liaisons did. She was unsettling him with her actions and her words. While he was off balance, Bette wanted to push him over the edge, to the madness that he'd driven her to just a short time ago on her couch.

So she stayed on her knees between his legs, and she reached for the zipper on his pants. His breath hissed out with the sound of the metal sliding down as she lowered his zipper. She pushed aside the fine cotton material of his briefs and freed his penis. It pulsated and vibrated in her touch, veins bulging on it like the veins bulging on his neck as he arched his head back.

"Bette…" Her name was just a groan on his lips. "What are you doing?"

She peeked up at him through her lashes. "You don't know? And here I thought you were the experienced one."

He narrowed his eyes and stared down at her. "You're really a preacher's daughter?" he asked, and there was skepticism in his deep voice.

"I'm the black sheep," she admitted. "The one who left for the big city and a life of sex and drugs." Even though it was what her family believed, she laughed like it was all a joke. "Since I'm not into drugs, I guess I will have to settle for the sex."

"You should never settle," he told her.

She felt the same way, that her mom and sister had settled for security. But in that security, they were insecure because they had no idea who they were anymore. Because they had had to change so much for their partners.

If Bette ever really fell for anyone, he would have to love and respect her for who she was and not try to change her to fit into his life. Not that she wanted to fall for anyone.

So she didn't risk settling for a person, she'd rather just settle for sex. But sex with Simon wasn't a consolation prize. It was the grand prize.

Like most lottery winners who couldn't make the money last, she knew the pleasure would eventually end, as well. So she had to make the most of it. The most of her time with him…

She lowered her mouth and closed it over the tip of his penis. It moved against her tongue, which she swirled around the girth of him.

He groaned and reached out, tangling his fingers in her hair. She'd have to redo the pins later because she felt some slip free. But she didn't care.

She didn't care about anything but driving him crazy.

He was too big for her to take all of him in her mouth. So she used her hands, too, sliding them up and down the length of him while she sucked on the head. Then she'd draw in a deep breath and take him as deep as she could manage in her throat.

Teasing him…

His hands moved from her hair to her shoulders and gripped them as if trying to pull her up from her knees. "Bette, you're killing me…"

With his cock in her mouth, she looked up at him. Then she swirled her tongue around the tip.

And that control he seemed so reluctant to let go of must have snapped again. He arched his hips with the need to thrust. So she took him deeper in her throat.

Then she slid her mouth up and down him.

His hands gripped her shoulders as his body tensed, and a deep growl sounded as if it was torn from his throat. Then he came, hot and sweet on her tongue.

She licked him from her lips and smiled up at him.

He stared down at her, his eyes still dark with the dilated pupils swallowing the blue like she'd swallowed him. He shook his head.

"What?" she asked.

"How could I work so closely with you for two years and know nothing about you?"

"You didn't ask," she reminded him.

"Would it have mattered if I did? You're not inclined to answer the other questions I ask you." He tucked himself back into his briefs and pulled up his zipper and shook his head again as if he was unable to believe what had just happened.

And she was unable to believe that it hadn't happened before. Women probably gave him blow jobs in back seats all the time. He was that damn gorgeous…

And irresistible.

She licked her lips again, loving the taste of him. Loving that she gave him that pleasure. And maybe that was what had taken him aback, that mousy Bette Monroe would do something like that. That was what kids had called her in school. She'd even been dubbed that in fashion college because she hadn't had the piercings and tattoos, or worn the wild clothes her classmates had.

But what she designed wasn't meant to be seen by everyone. Just the women who wore them and the men those women cared about enough to show.

She'd showed Simon more of her designs than she had other men. But it wasn't because she cared about him. That wasn't why.

"You remind me of the *Mona Lisa*," he said.

She laughed. "What?"

"It's obvious in that painting that she has some salacious secret," he said. "And it's obvious that you do, too."

"I guess we share a salacious secret now," she murmured as she stroked her finger across her bottom lip.

He groaned. "Damn it…"

"What?"

"You just made me hard again," he admitted. "And I wouldn't have thought that would be possible yet…"

Neither had she. But she was kind of glad that he was—because her pulse was pounding in her core, demanding release from the tension pleasing him had given her. She wanted to feel what he had, wanted the pleasure they gave each other.

And now he was the one sliding off his seat onto his knees on the floor between them. But even on his knees, he was taller than she was sitting. So he had to lean down to kiss her. His mouth sliding back and forth across hers. He groaned, probably because he could taste himself on her lips.

She touched him, moving her hand from his chest to his groin. And sure enough his cock was pressing against his fly again—long and hard and hot. She smiled against his lips.

"Siren," he murmured.

She lifted her head and listened. "I don't hear anything."

His mouth curved into a slight grin. "You," he said. "You're the siren."

"The mermaid who lures sailors to their deaths?" she asked. "I'm not sure that's a compliment."

He laughed. "Oh, it's not a good thing," he agreed. "At least not for me." His fingers shook a little as he moved them to the buttons of her cardigan. "Ever since you walked out of your bedroom all dressed up like this, I've been dying to know what you're wearing underneath."

But he took his time with each button, undoing them slowly as if he was building up the anticipation. That was probably how he unwrapped presents, as well—slowly to savor them.

But as a runaway growing up on the streets, had he had presents? How had he survived let alone thrived like he had?

She didn't know him as well as she'd thought she had. There was much more to him than his charm and his ruthlessness—because now she understood why he had both.

For survival…

She wasn't sure she would survive his slow, sweet torture of her. At last, he parted her sweater and pushed it from her shoulders. Then his breath hissed out between his teeth.

"Damn, Bette…"

She'd put on another bustier instead of a camisole. This one was leather, with cups, and of course her signature bow. It was tied at the bottom of the leather strap that bound the bustier together.

"Where the hell do you find this stuff?" he asked. "I've never seen anything as sexy."

Pride suffused her. She could have told him he'd never seen it before because she'd designed it. But he would be seeing it soon since she would have her own line at the fashion house for the premier retailer of lingerie in the country.

He was already so surprised that she wore lingerie that she didn't know if she was flattered or offended. If he laughed, like so many other people had, when she said she designed it, she would definitely be offended. So offended that it would be impossible to work out the rest of her notice for him.

Unless she could get him to cut that notice short…

But then he untied that bustier and released her breasts so he could play with them, and she wasn't so certain she wanted to cut that notice short anymore. Because that would mean cutting short the pleasure he gave her…

And he gave her pleasure now.

While he suckled on one of her nipples, he moved his hand beneath her skirt. He pushed aside her panties and slid his fingers inside her. She was already wet and ready for him. When he moved his thumb over her clit, she came, crying out his name.

And he cursed.

Blinking away the desire, she stared up at him.

"We're at the office," he told her, his voice gruff with desire and disappointment. "We'll have to finish this later."

Her hands were shaking so badly that he had to bind her back into the bustier and button her sweater back up. But he did it, even as a muscle twitched in his cheek—just above his tightly clenched jaw.

"Definitely a siren," he murmured.

She wasn't one. But she heard one, a warning that she was getting in too deep with him. So she was almost honest when she said, "I really think I could care for you."

But she wouldn't let that happen. She wouldn't let herself fall for anyone, least of all someone as ruthless and charming as Simon Kramer.

CHAPTER EIGHT

DESPITE HAVING THE partner meeting every Tuesday morning, Simon had nearly forgotten about it. But a lot had happened in the past week.

A lot of sex with Bette. A hell of a lot of crazy, mind-blowing sex. That was the reason he'd nearly forgotten the meeting. Losing his memory was probably a side effect of having his mind blown so often and so completely that he'd nearly forgotten the reason he'd begun the seduction of Bette Monroe. He'd nearly forgotten that she was the office mole.

Probably.

He still had no proof. Sure, he'd gotten a look at her checkbook. But those deposits could have come from something else. Maybe she'd sold something other than that information from their case files.

Like her body...

He would certainly pay if she started charging him. She was so damn passionate and sexy and generous.

And distracting.

He needed to focus on finding evidence. Real evidence. Because right now he had nothing but his suspicions.

Apparently, he wasn't the only one with suspicions. Ronan and Trevor studied him through narrowed eyes. And Stone wouldn't even look at him as if he was too disgusted.

"What?" he asked them.

"We heard about you and your assistant," Ronan said.

Now he knew why Stone wouldn't look at him. "Thanks a hell of a lot," he told his friend.

Stone shook his head. "I didn't tell them."

"You knew?" Trevor asked.

"Yeah…"

"And you didn't stop him from risking the whole damn practice getting sued?" Trevor asked.

"She's not going to sue me," Simon assured them, although maybe he should have been worried about that. If she would steal secrets from them, why wouldn't she sue?

Stone sighed. "I'm not as sure as you are about that. Just because she's given her notice—"

"She's given her notice?" Ronan asked. Then he groaned. "Damn it, we're certain to get sued if she's quitting over sexual harassment."

"I'm not harassing her," Simon said.

"But you are sleeping with her," Ronan said.

They had never actually slept together. But they'd had a hell of a lot of sex.

"Everybody's talking about it," Trevor said.

So much for him and Bette sharing a secret, their salacious one. He glared at Stone. "What—you've been gossiping like a little old lady?"

"I've got a hell of a lot more important things to worry about than your love life," Stone said.

Simon's heart slammed against his ribs. Love life? Hardly.

"You're not in love, are you?" Ronan asked.

Simon's heart slammed against his ribs and he exclaimed, "Of course not!"

"Then what the hell are you up to?" Trevor asked.

"I'm trying to find out if she's the mole," Simon admitted.

The color drained from Stone's face. "You didn't tell me that."

He sighed. "Because I don't know for sure if she is. I need proof."

"Why do you even suspect her?" Ronan asked.

"Because she's leaving," he said. And because of some of things he'd seen in her purse, specifically in her checkbook, like the ATM receipt for the deposit of a big check. The slip had also shown that she carried a very healthy balance. No wonder she'd been able to afford her new place. And she'd admitted she hadn't inherited any money or come into a trust.

"So?" Ronan said. "That doesn't prove her guilt."

"I got close to her so I could find proof," Simon admitted. But he felt a pang of guilt over that. What if she wasn't the mole? And what if she was starting to care for him like she'd been warning him she was?

Then he'd been seducing and using her for no reason. No. There was pleasure. More than pleasure.

"Have you found any proof?" Trevor asked skeptically.

Maybe he knew that Simon had gotten sidetracked—with her beauty, with the sex...

The incredible, mind-blowing sex. She was the most responsive and generous lover he'd ever had. And the way they moved together, the way they fitted...

She matched him in a way he'd never been matched before, but he was worried that it wasn't just with sex. Not that he was falling for her or anything. These unsettling feelings he had for her weren't anything more than desire and attraction and suspicion. Maybe she didn't just match him as a lover but as a con, too.

"Nothing that would hold up in court," he said. And because these were his friends, he was honest with them and admitted, "But she's come into some money. She's moved. She's bought stuff."

Her lingerie collection alone probably cost a fortune. The materials were decadent and the designs were works of art. But to him, the outfits were just like a light bulb showing off the work of art that was her perfect body.

"Maybe she inherited some money," Trevor said.

He shook his head. "I checked around." He hadn't just taken her word for it. "She's not been anyone's heir."

"Mistress?" Ronan asked.

Anger surged through Simon. "Of course you'd think that." He had, too. But when would she have time for a man—even a married one—with as much time as she'd been spending with Simon?

Ronan snorted. "I'm a divorce lawyer. Of course I'd think that. And you, being the con, would think she's the mole. But it doesn't track."

"Why not?"

"I agree that it makes no sense," Stone said. "If she's making money off us, why would she leave?"

The others nodded in agreement. They didn't understand a con the way Simon did.

The trick was to get out before getting caught. He figured that had been her intention. But it was too late for her now. He'd caught her. He just needed the evidence to prove it. To his partners and to the police and to himself. He didn't want to believe that it was her. Still, it was the only thing that made sense— for her leaving and for her coming into that money.

As much as he'd wished it wasn't true, he had to face the fact that she'd conned him. He wasn't buying that she was falling for him—no matter how many times she'd claimed that she was.

He wasn't sure which con he was more pissed about: her selling information from their case files or trying to make him believe she might genuinely care about him.

A sudden chill raced down Bette's spine and raised goose bumps on her skin. She shivered and glanced up from the computer monitor she'd been studying and discovered three men standing in her small office.

Why were all of Simon's partners paying her a visit? Like Simon, they had barely paid her any attention the two years she'd worked for Street Legal.

"Can I help you?" she asked.

Unlike Simon, they were all dark haired. Ronan Hall's hair was black. Stone Michaelsen's was dark brown like hers and Trevor Sinclair's was more of an auburn. They were also all bigger than Simon. The three of them barely fitted into her office, their broad shoulders rubbing against each other's.

How had they entered so quietly?

They'd lived on the streets. Maybe they'd learned to be quiet there. Or maybe she'd just been too distracted with thoughts of their managing partner to notice if an entire circus had entered her office, riding elephants while juggling rings of fire.

"You can stay," Trevor Sinclair suggested.

"Simon told you that I gave my notice," she said and leaned back in her chair.

Maybe one of them could convince him to let her go early. She only had four days—including today—left on her notice. She could last four days.

Couldn't she?

But she was already boneless from all the pleasure he'd given her. She didn't want to lose her backbone completely the way her mom and her sister had. She didn't want to get addicted to him and desperate and clingy like all of his other ex-lovers. No. The less time she spent with Simon Kramer the better. At least, the safer...for her.

"Why are you leaving?" Ronan Hall asked.

She hadn't told Simon; she damn well was not going to tell him, either. She just shook her head. "This just isn't a good fit."

Stone Michaelsen studied her like she was one of the criminals he represented. As she'd told Simon, quitting was not a crime.

"Street Legal or Simon?" he asked.

Heat rushed to her face. She and Simon fitted together perfectly, like her body had been made for his. But then his body was so perfect that she couldn't imagine him not fitting with every woman he seduced.

Had he actually seduced her? Or had she seduced him?

"I don't have a background in law," she said. "I am really not a good fit as a legal assistant." So why had Simon hired her two years ago?

The three men exchanged a glance as if they were all wondering the same thing. From the way Ronan glanced down her body, it was clear he had his suspicions. He wasn't wrong about them—now.

But she knew that wasn't why Simon had hired her since he hadn't even noticed her until she'd given him her notice.

"You must have done a fine job the past two

years," Stone said, "or Simon wouldn't have kept you."

Now her embarrassment gave way to annoyance. Simon did not own her. He never had and he never would. No man owned Bette Monroe. Instead of telling his partners those thoughts, she just offered them a tight smile.

"We hate to have you leave," Trevor said. But he didn't sound particularly sincere. In fact, he sounded suspicious, and he studied her with a strange look on his face, kind of like the look that had been on Simon's when she'd caught him in her apartment.

Actually, Simon had looked both suspicious and guilty that day, like she'd caught him doing something. Rummaging through her things? Her purse?

Had he seen any of her designs?

She doubted it. Those were on the desk in her bedroom, and she didn't think he'd gone in there while she'd been showering. And he hadn't been back to her apartment since that day—except for in her thoughts.

She kept imagining him there.

She kept imagining him everywhere but most especially inside her. It was almost as if she could feel him in there, filling her completely.

Heat rushed to her face again and pooled lower in her body, between her legs. She crossed them and clenched her thighs together, but that only intensified the sensation. She needed Simon again.

No. Four more days was too many. She was too

close to getting addicted to him, to becoming desperate and needy for him like all those other women he'd dumped.

"If you all feel like I should leave now, I understand," Bette told them. "If you're worried about the confidentiality with your clients."

"Should we be worried?" Stone asked.

"Yeah," Ronan said, "it's not like you're going to work for the opposition or anything, is it?"

She shook her head. "No. Like I told you, I'm not suited at all for a job in law." Her passion was fashion. For years that was the only real passion she'd had.

Now there was Simon. But he wasn't just a passion. He was becoming an obsession, as well. She needed to get away from him as soon as possible.

But his partners were no help. "You're welcome to stay," Stone told her. "As long as you'd like."

She'd like to leave now. For some reason she hesitated to admit it. And they were gone before she could form the words. It was only four more days. Four more days of Simon Kramer...

She wasn't really falling for him, though. She couldn't. She knew him too well.

Didn't she?

CHAPTER NINE

How could Bette have worked for him for two years and Simon still know so little about her? When he'd hired her, he'd checked her references and résumé. But now he had to pull up her employment file again to refresh his memory. She'd worked in fashion houses before she'd worked for Street Legal. Her degree was in fashion.

He'd dated a couple of design assistants. They didn't make much. That was the reason he'd figured she'd quit the fashion house and applied for the job as his executive assistant. She could have worked as a model if she hadn't been able to break in as a designer. She looked amazing in all the lingerie she wore.

The image of her standing in his office in just that black bra and G-string held together with bows flashed through his mind again. Hell, that image had never really left his mind. She was so damn sexy. And much too distracting...

He needed to find out if she really was the mole,

especially now with the guys putting pressure on him over getting involved with her. What if she wasn't?

Would she—could she—sue him for seducing her? Of course she'd seduced him first, though. Why?

Had she realized that he was onto her?

He pressed the intercom button on his phone.

"Yes?" Her voice filled his office, just like her scent and her image did.

"I'd like to see you…" In the flesh and not just in his mind. Due to the meeting with his partners, he hadn't seen her yet this morning. And there was a strange tightness in his chest.

She hesitated a long moment before replying with, "I have to finish a couple of things first."

"Are you stalling?" Maybe she didn't want to see him as badly as he wanted—as he needed—to see her.

She sighed. "No. I was distracted this morning with a visit."

Who had come to see her?

"Who was your visitor?" he asked. In the two years she'd worked for him, he couldn't remember anyone ever coming by to see her.

From what she'd said, her family didn't approve of her moving to the city. So they probably never visited. What about friends? He'd never met any of them. But then it wasn't as if they were dating or anything.

After another long pause, she replied, "Your partners."

He suppressed a groan. Why hadn't they trusted him to handle this—to handle her—on his own? After all, he was the managing partner. And that was because Street Legal had been his idea. He'd come up with the plan back when they'd all been living on the streets:

Go to college.

Get their law degrees.

Start their own practice.

They should have trusted that he would do whatever necessary to protect that practice. Of course doing Bette Monroe was no hardship.

"Bette, I need you in here right now." As he said it, a chill chased down his spine. He really did need her.

She sighed again, a sigh of frustration, and murmured, "I'm coming."

"Not yet," he said, then promised, "but you will be."

"Simon!" She admonished him, but there was amusement in her voice. And it certainly wasn't long before his door opened and she hurried inside.

Did she need him as much as he needed her?

He damn well hoped so—because he didn't like this feeling, as if the balance of power had shifted in her favor. As if he needed her more...

That wasn't the case, he assured himself. He needed the truth. He needed to know if she was, indeed, the mole.

"What did you want?" she asked as she strode over to his desk, her heels clicking against the hardwood floor. She wore another of her pencil-slim skirts with another cardigan. The skirt was gray, the sweater a deep purple. He wondered more what she wore beneath them.

"You," he said. "I want you."

Her lips curved into a smile. "Simon…"

But she didn't protest. Instead, she walked around his desk and pushed back his chair. And he knew she wanted him just as badly as he wanted her.

Instead of unbuttoning her cardigan or wriggling out of her skirt, she reached for the zipper on his pants as she dropped to her knees in front of him.

His cock swelled and pulsated, begging for the release he knew she could—and would—give him. But he couldn't let her seduce him again. He had to be the seducer.

This time he wanted more than sex from her. He wanted the truth. He didn't believe she was really falling for him. If he demanded it, would she tell him everything? Would she finally answer his questions and be completely honest with him?

Was she capable of complete honesty, though?

So few people really were.

He caught her hand before she could tug down his zipper and held it in his for a long moment. She stared up at him, her dark eyes wide with surprise.

"I thought that's why you called me in here."

"Then why didn't you come running?" he asked. "If you're really falling for me?"

She smiled her siren's smile at him. "Sometimes it's more satisfying when we have to wait."

Like the day they arrived at the office and had to get out of the car. That had been one long damn day.

He shook his head. "I'm not a patient man, Bette."

"I'm patient," she said. "I waited two years for you to notice me."

Had she really, though?

He pulled off the glasses she wore and dropped them onto his desk. Then he reached for the pins in her thick, luxurious hair, letting the silken tresses fall down around her shoulders.

"Or did you spend two years trying to make certain I wouldn't notice you?" he asked.

And that smile curved her lips even more.

She was the most challenging woman he'd ever met. How hadn't he noticed that about her? He'd seen her beauty despite her attempts to disguise it. But he'd never realized how clever and conniving she could be.

"Some men like the librarian look," she said.

He nodded in agreement. "I am some men," he admitted. Then he reached for the buttons on her cardigan, flicking them open to reveal the lacy camisole she wore beneath. It must have been designed by the same maddening person who designed her lingerie because there were little bows on the pink lace. "I also am the some men who love lingerie."

Her smile widened even more. "You love my lingerie?"

His breath shuddered out in appreciation. "Oh, yeah." But after pushing the cardigan from her shoulders, he reached for the bow that held up her camisole in the back. After he tugged it loose, it slipped down and revealed her naked breasts. "But I love your body even more."

Love. The word felt strange on his tongue. But in this case it wasn't a con. He really did love her body. It wouldn't betray him like her clever mind or her greedy heart might.

He flicked a fingertip over her nipple and it tightened in reaction. Her body could keep no secrets from him. He knew exactly what pleased it.

What pleased *her*...

He spent a long time on her breasts. Massaging the fullness of them, teasing the tight nipples. She moaned and wriggled and arched and finally she gasped as she came—just from his playing with her breasts.

He'd never known a woman as responsive as she was, as passionate. Or as generous.

She kept trying to undress him, reaching for the buttons on his shirt or the tab of his zipper. But he caught her wrists and locked them together in one of his hands, holding her back.

Then he moved his other hand between her legs. He stroked over the lace covering her mound. That was all he did, stroke his fingers over and over across the mound and over her clit. And she came again, nearly sobbing his name.

"What are you doing to me?" she asked. "Why?"

"You act like I'm punishing you," he said with a slight grin.

"Are you?" she asked.

If she was the mole, he would punish her. But this wasn't punishment. "This is pleasure, Bette. Don't you know the difference?"

"Pleasure is better if it's shared," she told him. And she tugged her wrists free of his grasp. Then she attacked the buttons of his shirt and the zipper on his pants.

After stripping off his clothes, she rolled a condom onto him. He wasn't sure if she'd found the condom in his pants or if she'd brought it with her. But he didn't care. He didn't care about anything but feeling the pleasure she'd promised him—that he knew she could deliver.

His body was wound so tight that he didn't move. He stayed in his office chair, his bare ass against the supple leather. And she straddled him.

As she guided his cock inside her, she settled onto his lap and released a shaky breath. He sank so deeply into her this way, was joined more completely with her than he had ever been. She must have felt it, too.

Her brown eyes widened in shock and pleasure. "You feel so damn good…"

He shook his head. "Are preachers' daughters supposed to swear?"

"I do a lot of things preachers' daughters aren't supposed to do," she told him. "Like you…" Then she kissed him, her tongue sliding between his lips like he slid into her body.

He arched his hips, thrusting up as she moved with him. Their mouths mated like their bodies—in a frantic rhythm. The chair creaked and rocked and threatened to break beneath the weight of their bodies and the crazy motion of them. But Simon only bought the best, so it held up.

And he tried to hold on…to his control. He tried to wait. But she kept rocking and bouncing and driving him out of his mind.

The tension wound so tightly in his body he felt that he might break before the chair. Like he might just snap…

She cried out and tensed as her inner muscles convulsed and clutched at his cock. Then heat rushed over him. She was coming. He tried to hold off, tried to give her more orgasms. But then his body stilled as his control exploded. And he came, her name on his lips.

He'd tried to seduce her. But just like every time before, she wound up seducing him. She was so damn hot. So damn sexy…

"Oh, Simon," she murmured as she settled her head against his shoulder. "You really are trying to make me love you."

That had been the new twist in his plan. But just like the seduction, he had to make sure it went according to plan. That she was the one who actually fell for him. Not the other way around...

Bette could have used Simon's private bathroom. But after the encounter she'd just had with him, she needed some space. Some perspective and some cold water splashed on her face. When she'd said what she had to him...

It hadn't been premeditated. It had just slipped out. Like she'd meant it.

But she couldn't mean it.

No. She'd just spent too much time too close to the sun, to the heat and passion that was Simon. So she needed to cool off. She rushed into the staff bathroom and headed toward the sink.

The doors of two of the stalls were closed, and the occupants spoke to each other. She shuddered in disgust. Apparently, she was in some ways still the repressed preacher's daughter.

"So how long do you think it's been going on?" the occupant of one stall asked the other. "The entire two years she's worked for him?"

The other woman laughed. "I don't think so. How could she have stayed when he was dating all those other women, too?"

"Maybe she has no pride."

Oh, my God. They were talking about her. She

stiffened with the very pride they didn't think she possessed.

"He's Simon Kramer," the first woman said with a lustful sigh. "For him I would have no pride, either."

"She's so damn lucky," the other agreed with a lustful sigh of her own. "I would love to work for and under him."

Bette had no idea who the women were, but if they were so eager to work for Simon, why hadn't they applied for her job?

"Well, you know he'll be done with her someday, just like he's been with all his other women. Maybe she'll summon some pride and quit then, and her job will open up."

"I can only hope."

A toilet flushed. Then another.

Bette could have turned on her heel and hurried out of the room. But despite what they thought, she had too much pride to run from the gossipy women. As the stall doors swung open and they stepped out, she stared at both of them.

One gave a nervous laugh and remarked, "We didn't realize you'd come in."

And she wondered about that. Even growing up in a small town in the generally friendly Midwest, she'd known mean girls. While these women hadn't been girls for a while—they were easily ten years older than her twenty-eight—they could still be mean. And they were obviously gossipy.

She shrugged. "I'm sure it wouldn't have stopped you if you had."

The woman's eyes widened at her boldness. "Well, of course we wouldn't—"

"What do you expect?" the other interrupted. "You're screwing your boss."

"He won't be my boss much longer." Just a little over four days. It didn't matter to her that Simon hadn't posted her position. She wasn't staying beyond the two weeks even if he hadn't replaced her.

One of the women tilted her head and gave Bette a fake sympathetic smile. "Oh, he's already dumped you."

Bette laughed. "I gave my notice before we even started…"

What?

They weren't dating. They had only shared that one meal together. They'd never attended a show or a movie together. No. They weren't dating.

They were just having sex and lots of it.

But she was fine with that. Dating would make it real. And it wasn't real. It was just a dream, a very real dream. But that dream needed to end soon or it was bound to become a nightmare.

She was afraid—very afraid—that she wasn't conning him anymore with her warnings that she was going to fall in love with him.

She was conning herself to think that she wasn't.

CHAPTER TEN

THE DOOR TO Simon's office opened with such force that it slammed against the wall. He glanced up from his desk in surprise and was even more surprised when he saw Bette standing in the doorway. Her face was flushed, and her eyes were bright with anger.

He'd never seen her like this. But as he did with everything about her, he found it incredibly sexy. He was also concerned. "What's wrong?"

Just as she'd slammed the door open, she slammed it closed and strode over to his desk. "I wondered why you hadn't been interviewing replacements for me."

Because he didn't think anyone could replace her. He'd never known anyone like Bette Monroe before. Not that he knew her even now. She was an enigma to him. A puzzle he had yet to find all the pieces to, like the proof of whether or not she was the mole.

But even if she was, he wasn't in any hurry to replace her. He would take his time screening applicants from now on and make sure he knew everything about them before he hired them. Because he'd had no idea when he'd hired Bette how passionate she was or what she wore beneath her conservative clothes.

If he'd known, he certainly wouldn't have waited two years to seduce her.

"But I didn't realize that you hadn't even posted my job yet," she continued.

He leaned back in his chair, the chair on which they'd just had sex. "For some reason I don't think you're really going to leave."

"Yes, I am!" she exclaimed. "I will only be here four more days."

A pang struck his heart. Was it possible? Would she really be gone that soon? That pang, that felt almost like panic, was only because he hadn't discovered the evidence against her. That had to be what it was. It couldn't be that he was upset that his time with her was coming to an end.

Two weeks was about the longest any of his relationships ever lasted anyway. Usually, he grew bored before then, or the woman started making demands that he wouldn't ever be prepared to meet. Like a commitment...

And he always got too bored to commit to anyone. He'd always be looking for the next challenge, just like he had his entire life.

Maybe that was why he hadn't grown bored with Bette yet. She challenged him like no one else ever had.

"You should already be interviewing candidates for your new assistant," she told him.

"I thought you'd be devastated if I tried to replace you," he said, "what with you falling in love with me and all."

She'd never actually said that she loved him, but she'd claimed that she was falling for him. But every time she'd told him that, she'd issued the statement like it was a threat.

And she'd had that little glimmer of mischief in her eyes that had told him she was up to something. Except for that last time, just moments ago when she laid her head on his chest…

Then she had seemed almost sincere. But maybe she'd just gotten better at the lie. Like his father used to say, a lie well told and stuck to was just as good as the truth.

Her face flushed now with embarrassment. And he knew that, just as he'd suspected, she'd been lying to him.

"What?" He arched a brow. "You're not in love with me?"

She didn't say anything. She just sighed. "I guess I might as well come clean with you now."

"What?" he repeated, and this time he was astounded. "You're going to tell me the truth?"

Would it be this easy? While she hadn't fallen in love with him, maybe she'd enjoyed their time together enough that she was feeling guilty over her betrayal.

"Please, Bette," he implored her. "Be honest with me."

Her face flushed a darker shade of red and she

wouldn't meet his gaze. "You're going to get mad at me."

And his heart plummeted in his chest. She was the mole. While he should be relieved to know his suspicions were right, he was disappointed. Hell, he was more than disappointed.

He was devastated. For the first time in his life, he had actually wanted to be wrong.

Not that he'd gotten attached to her or anything. But at least he wouldn't have been conned when he'd hired her, when he'd trusted her.

Apparently, that was not the case.

Apparently, he never should have trusted her.

Bette studied his face, waiting for him to assure her that he wouldn't get mad at her. But he didn't. Instead, he just looked very tense, his jaw tightly clenched.

But she shouldn't care if he got mad. In fact, maybe that would be the best way to get him to release her four days early from serving out the rest of her two weeks. Or maybe it would at least get him to post her job.

She drew in a deep breath and admitted, "I've been playing you."

He released a sharp breath as if she'd punched him. But he nodded and said, "That's what I thought." He cursed and admitted, "I'd just hoped I was wrong."

"That night I undressed in the office." Heat rushed from her face throughout the rest of her body as she thought of that night, of how she'd taken off her glasses and taken down her hair...

She should have stopped there. But then she never would have known what sex with Simon Kramer was like and why all those other women had been so desperate for it to never stop. She didn't want to become that desperate, though.

So she had to make sure there was an end in sight for them. For the sex and the job.

"I was playing you," she said.

His brow furrowed. "You didn't really want to have sex?"

"I—I had always wondered what it would be like to be with you," she admitted. "I just didn't have this undying attraction to you that I'd said I had."

He stood up now and walked around his desk. He didn't reach for her, though. In fact, he leaned back against the front of his desk and crossed his arms over his chest. "You're not attracted to me?"

She snorted with self-derision. "I'm not a liar. Of course I'm attracted, but I'm not in love with you." At least she didn't think she was.

Of course she wasn't...

"I just wanted you to think that I was falling for you," she said.

"But why?"

"So you wouldn't make me work out the two-week notice," she said.

He shook his head as if he was having trouble fol-lowing her—which was strange since she'd figured he was onto her this entire time. "How would that make me release you from the terms of your employment contract?"

She snorted again but this time in derision of him. "I've worked for you for two years," she reminded him. "I see how you treat women."

His face flushed now, his skin getting a little ruddy. "What do you mean?"

"As soon as they profess any feelings for you, you dump them," she said.

"You think that makes me heartless?" he asked.

She'd thought once that it had but now she understood. "It's probably the nicest thing you can do," she said. "If you're not able to return their feelings, it's better to break it off before they fall any harder."

"You sound as if you're speaking from experience," he mused.

She shrugged and admitted, "I've never been in love." She'd been too focused on fashion—on her designs.

"But you've had men fall for you?"

She shrugged again. There had been boys in school who'd professed love. She figured they'd just been trying to get her to have sex with them. She hadn't really believed they'd loved her—not when they hadn't really known her. But then they hadn't cared about her goals and aspirations. They'd cared only about their own. And if she'd fallen for them, she would have gotten sucked into their lives instead of living her own. Just like her mom and sister had and countless other women she'd known.

"I don't know," she said, willing to give those old boyfriends the benefit of the doubt. "Who knows if another person's feelings are real?"

He chuckled. "Apparently, I don't."

"You didn't really think I was falling for you," she said. "Or you would have cut me loose last week."

He grinned. "Why would I have done that again?"

"You can't stand clingy women," she said. "So I was trying to act clingy."

"Hmm, I guess I didn't see the clinginess."

"We've been spending so much time together," she reminded him. "More time than you've spent with any other woman."

"That's because we work together," he said.

"We haven't been working the whole time," she reminded him. And she gestured around his office at the couch and the chair and the desk and the conference table.

They'd had sex on every surface in his office. And on every surface in hers.

"You've been working me," he said. "Why didn't you want to work out the two weeks? Did you tell your new employer you'd start sooner?"

She shook her head. She was already working for them. She'd been working for them for years as a freelance design assistant. Between Street Legal and fashion, all she'd done was work. Maybe that was why sex with Simon was so amazing.

Because she'd denied herself too long.

"Maybe I felt like you with all those women you refused to see again after you broke up with them," she told him. "Once I gave my notice, I didn't want to have to keep coming back here for two more weeks."

"Why not?" he asked.

"I didn't want to keep seeing you." And she knew that was probably as much her reason as wanting to start working only on her new line. Despite everything, she knew that she would miss working with Simon. He had the same passion for his job that she had for fashion.

But it wasn't just her designs that she had a passion for anymore. It was Simon, too.

He pressed a hand over his heart and said, "Ouch. Guess that's karma for me."

"You've broken a lot of hearts," she reminded him. And she'd mopped up some of those tears for him. She hoped she wouldn't wind up mopping up her own before the week was out. "That's why I know better than to fall for you, because I know you too well."

He arched a brow. "That sounds like a challenge."

She shook her head. "No, not at all."

But he was already reaching for her. "I'll make you clingy," he warned her as he lowered his head to hers. Despite the grin curving his lips, he kissed her deeply. And as he kissed her, sliding his tongue in and out of her mouth, he touched her.

He ran his hands over her breasts, but he didn't

undress her. He didn't need to. She could feel the heat of his touch through her clothes, and her nipples tightened. She moaned. Then he moved his hands lower, over her hips and ass.

She arched her hips against him, feeling his erection through her clothes and his. But it wasn't enough. She wanted him inside her.

Then he lifted her, and just as he'd promised, she was clinging to him. He shoved up her skirt and pulled her panties aside, and somehow his zipper was down and he'd rolled on a condom. Then he was inside her, thrusting deep. And she clung to him, her arms and legs wrapped tightly around him. She clung as he drove her up and out of her mind with pleasure.

He felt so good. His cock so long and hard. As he continued to thrust, the tension wound tightly inside her. She ached for release, and finally, an orgasm slammed through her, making her body shudder with the explosive power of the release. He caught her cry of pleasure in his mouth as he continued to kiss her. And he didn't stop thrusting his hips, didn't stop driving as deeply as only he could, until she came again and again.

Her muscles quivered and she could barely hold on, her body was so limp with pleasure. Then finally, a deep groan ripped from his throat and he came, too. His legs shook slightly beneath their combined weights, and he leaned his forehead, damp with perspiration, against hers.

Staring deeply into her eyes, he said, "For some reason I don't mind when you're clingy, Bette Monroe."

She minded. And she was scared to death that she really might fall for him.

CHAPTER ELEVEN

SHE WAS GONE. Simon knew it the moment he stepped out of the elevator. Of course he shouldn't have been surprised; it was well after five. Everyone else was gone, too, except maybe for Stone.

His office was far enough down the hall that Simon couldn't see if a light was burning under his door. But his own office was dark. He headed toward it anyway. Since he was just returning from a dinner meeting with a client, he had some notes to drop off on his desk.

He pushed open the door and uttered a sigh of disappointment when he confirmed it was empty. It would have been nice had Bette been waiting for him wearing only her naughty lingerie. But just as he'd suspected when he'd stepped off the elevator, she was gone for the night.

If she'd been there, he would have felt her presence in the tingling of his skin and quickening of his pulse. When she was around, he was always aware of her and the attraction that sizzled between them.

But attraction was all it was. She'd confirmed that

this afternoon when she'd confessed that she wasn't falling for him, that it had all just been a con.

Was that the only one she'd run on him? Or was there another one—a far more dangerous one—at least to the practice and to his pride?

The guys didn't understand how a con worked. That she would leave even though she was making money off them. She'd do that if she was as smart as he'd known she was. Quit before you get caught—that was what had kept him out of prison while he'd been growing up.

His father hadn't been able to say the same.

The other part of a good con was to disarm the mark's suspicions with a confession—but only to confess something innocuous, like her pretending to fall for him. That way the mark wouldn't suspect there were any more secrets.

He suspected Bette Monroe had many, many more secrets than what she'd confessed. And he intended to learn them all. But when he set his briefcase onto his desk, he found an envelope sitting on his keyboard addressed to him. He immediately recognized the artistic handwriting as Bette's. She'd already turned in her letter of resignation. What was this?

After today he knew it wasn't a love letter. She didn't love him, had laughed at the possibility of ever falling for him.

Because she had someone else? Someone who was willing to support her? He could. Hell, he would if she asked. He doubted that was what this letter was about, either.

His hand shaking slightly, he tore open the envelope and pulled out the piece of paper. It wasn't a letter at all. It was a job description—her job description. And at the bottom of the list of her duties was another, but it was his.

You need to post my position ASAP.

And he knew she wasn't staying. What the hell had happened to him? He used to be such a good con artist. He hadn't met a woman who he hadn't been able to seduce into doing what he wanted. But while Bette had sex with him, she wasn't malleable. She wasn't staying.

And she wasn't revealing any of her secrets.

He needed to turn up the seduction. Despite her claim of knowing him too well to fall for him, he had to make her love him. That was the only way he suspected he would get the truth out of her.

But he was beginning to worry that wasn't what he really wanted from Bette Monroe. He wanted even more than the truth.

Did he want her love?

Despite all the women who'd claimed to feel that way about him, he'd never really believed it, just as Bette had seemed to doubt the profession of love she'd had. Was it because—like him—he'd felt like none of those women had known him well enough to love him?

Only his friends knew him well enough to love him.

But if he wanted Bette's love, he would have to let her know him. Really know him. Not just what she thought she knew about him. After working for him for two years, she probably already knew him better than most. And then he'd told her more than he had anyone else.

Damn.

Who was conning whom?

Bette Monroe was far more dangerous than he'd thought. Even if she was the mole, she was only a danger to the firm. Now she had become a danger to him…

Bette flinched as she felt a twinge of guilt. Maybe she should have waited for Simon to return to the office before she left. But he hadn't asked her to stay. Maybe he had assumed that she would.

But she'd finished her work. Most important, she'd listed the duties for her job description. He needed to know that no matter how much charm he turned on her, she wasn't staying. These two weeks were already cutting in to valuable time that she needed to come up with more designs.

Pride coursed through her. She'd accomplished what she'd always dreamed of doing. She had her own line and for the premier retailer of lingerie worldwide. They loved her creativity and innovation.

She could not disappoint them or herself. She couldn't sacrifice her dream for a man. She had too many friends who had. Her mother and sister had done that and now lived dull lives of quiet resent-ment. She had no intention of ever winding up like them.

She didn't need a man.

But she wanted one...

An emptiness stretched inside her, an emptiness she was never aware of until she had started having sex with Simon, until he'd filled her.

Completed her.

She shook her head and laughed at herself. While she loved designing lingerie, she was not some hope-less romantic. She didn't need a man to complete her. She didn't need Simon.

She needed to focus on her designs. So she re-turned her attention to the sketch pad lying across her bed. Tightening her fingers around her pen, she swept it across the page as she designed a corset with, of course, her signature bow. Bette's Beguil-ing Bows—that was the name of her line. She put the bow at the bottom, though, so it would sit atop her ass, where Simon loved her bows. Even when she had her clothes on, he skimmed his fingers over her skirt until he found it.

What would he think of this design?

She couldn't wait to sew up a prototype to get his opinion. But that would take a couple of days and... she only had four before she left Street Legal. That didn't necessarily mean that their relationship would have to end. But then it wasn't really a relationship.

She wasn't sure what the hell it was.

And she didn't think he knew, either.

Her doorbell rang, and her pen shot across the page as her heart leaped. It could have been a friend. She'd shared her new address, with the ones who hadn't already known it, when they'd called to complain about being MIA the past week. She'd explained that she needed to finish up things at work before she could leave. But what she needed to finish the most at work was whatever this thing with Simon was.

No. They could not continue seeing each other once she left. She would be too busy. And he was too…Simon. He would grow bored soon, if he hadn't already.

The doorbell rang again, as if someone was leaning against the button. And she knew that he hadn't grown bored yet. Smiling, she headed toward the door. A quick glance out the peephole confirmed her suspicions regarding the identity of her visitor.

It wasn't one of her girlfriends.

Her pulse quickened, and her skin tingled. As she opened the door, she asked the question she'd wondered the last time he'd shown up at her apartment, "How do you keep getting past security?"

"I know the doorman," he said, his face flushing slightly as he looked away.

"You dated someone in the building," she guessed.

He nodded.

"A model?"

A model had recommended the building to her. Her friend Muriel also had an apartment in it.

He nodded again. And his face grew a little redder. But she realized he wasn't embarrassed when he held out a crumpled-up piece of paper to her. He was mad.

She sighed and stepped back as he strode into her apartment. "I already know you crumpled up my resignation," she reminded him. "It still doesn't change the fact that I'm leaving."

"You made that clear when you left this on my desk," he said.

And she saw what the paper was. "Ah, my job description," she said. "I figured that would help you when you post the job, which you should have done last week."

"Bette…"

"Unless you intend to just hire someone through a temp agency," she continued. "That's your prerogative."

"Yes, it is," he said. "It's my business. Isn't that what you keep saying to me?"

She smiled at his grumpiness.

"This isn't funny," he said.

"You really aren't used to it, are you?" she asked. "Your charm not getting you your way."

He tensed and stared down at her as if he'd just realized that was the case. "It's not exactly like you're immune to me," he said as he stepped closer to her. And as if he'd once again taken her words as a challenge, he touched her, sliding his thumb across the fullness of her bottom lip.

Her breath escaped in a gasp as desire raced through her. But he sighed wistfully, as well.

"I'm not immune to you, either," he said. "You make me forget..."

"What?" she asked.

But he just shook his head.

"To post my job?" she teased.

"How can I forget that?" he asked. "When you keep nagging me about it?"

She took the crumpled-up piece of paper from his hand. "You didn't like my job description?"

"I think some things are missing," he said.

"Like what?"

He slid his hands over her ass. "Like 'must look good in a tight skirt.'"

She'd been so eager to start working on her designs that she hadn't changed yet. She'd only taken off her cardigan. The camisole she wore beneath it was silk and so thin that it was evident that her nipples had tightened. They pushed against the fabric as his fingers traced the bow on her underwear.

"And 'must wear lingerie under those tight skirts.'"

She was on board with that. She needed to sell out her line to impress the retailer and extend her contract with them. "Might be kind of hard for a man to find skirts and corsets big enough."

He chuckled and lowered his head to hers, pressing a quick kiss against her lips. "I never knew how funny you are, Bette Monroe," he said.

"Yeah, I'm quitting Street Legal to devote myself full-time to my stand-up act," she said.

He chuckled again but then sighed. "Hell, maybe you are."

It would probably be more believable to most than finding out she was a lingerie designer.

"I feel like I barely know you at all."

It was true. He barely did. But she'd done that to protect herself. She didn't want to get too close to him. She didn't want to really fall for him.

"What are you going to do once you quit?"

She tensed.

And his grumpiness returned as, his voice gruff with irritation, he asked, "How can that still be none of my business?"

"What do you think has changed?" she asked.

"I've seen you naked."

She smiled and shook her head.

"I haven't?" he asked with an arched brow. "Do you have a body double I've been having sex with, then?"

She laughed and said, "You've definitely seen me without my clothes. But you haven't really seen me naked." Telling him about the hopes and dreams she had worked so hard to pursue would have truly been the way she would have lain herself bare to him. And she wasn't ready to do that with someone she couldn't trust.

His brow furrowed as if he was confused.

So she added, "I haven't seen you naked, either. Not really. I don't know much more about you than Allison McCann has put out in the press releases for Street Legal."

He cocked his head and studied her face, skepticism on his handsome one. "Really? After working for me for two years…"

"I know how you've been the past two years," she said. "About how hard you work…" She smiled to soften her next words. "How hard you play…"

Because the conversation was getting so serious between them, she wanted to play now. She was far more comfortable with that than with the conversation heading where it was—into very personal and private matters of hearts and souls.

She wasn't ready to let him see either her heart or her soul. Not now—not when they had so little time left to be together and not when she was beginning to feel so damn vulnerable with him.

She stepped closer to him until her body pressed against his. Arching her hips into his, into the erection straining against the fly of his suit pants, she teased, "I love how *hard* you play…"

He narrowed his eyes as if he was completely aware that she was trying to distract him and he wondered why. But he couldn't resist her any easier than she could resist him. Those narrowed eyes darkened as his pupils dilated, and his chest began to rise and fall as his breathing grew faster and shallower.

Her pulse quickened even more than it had when he rang the bell. He excited her so damn much with his touch and his kiss.

But he didn't touch or kiss her. He just continued to stare at her. And she knew she wasn't the only one who was afraid of being seen naked—truly naked. Simon wasn't any more comfortable about laying himself bare to her.

She'd once thought that he didn't have a heart or a soul. But now she knew he had them. He just hid them to protect them, like she did.

And knowing that about him, knowing that they had something in common, scared her even more. She could not fall in love with Simon Kramer.

CHAPTER TWELVE

WHAT THE HELL did she do to him? With her, he had no control. He couldn't resist her; he couldn't do anything but want her.

He swung her up in his arms and carried her toward the room that had to be her bedroom. But she caught the jamb before he could carry her over the threshold.

"Put me down," she told him.

"What—why?" Had she changed her mind? That wasn't like her. She didn't have much more control than he did once they started kissing.

Touching…

"I—I have to put something away first," she said. She wriggled down from his arms and rushed into the bedroom.

Before he could follow her inside, she closed the door on his face. As if that wasn't bad enough, he heard a lock click, as well.

She really did not want him inside her bedroom. The last time he'd been in her apartment, he hadn't gotten beyond the couch in the living room where they'd had sex. Tonight he'd wanted to be in her bed nearly as badly as he wanted to be inside her.

But now he wondered if he would be allowed in either? Had she locked herself inside for the night? Did she want him to leave?

Stunned, he could only stand there for several long moments. What the hell was going on in there? What was she doing? He lifted his hand to knock, but before his fist could strike the white-painted wood, the door opened.

She reached for his hand and tugged him inside the room with her. Looking over her head, he peered around the space. Like the living room, the floors were dark hardwood—the plaster ceilings high. The exterior wall was brick with a tall window while the other walls were painted a dreamy blue. The bed, a fluffy-looking queen-size one, shared the space with a library table that had been converted to a desk. If she'd taken any records from the office, they were probably stashed in that desk.

"Should I check the closet?" he asked. "Did you push a lover in there?"

She laughed. "No. I was getting this out of the closet." She stepped back and twirled around to show off the negligee she wore. It wasn't as long as the one she'd had on the first day he'd come to her apartment. This one barely covered her luscious ass.

Like all her other outfits, it had a bow on it— this one on the front—at the top of the satin ribbon that crisscrossed the bodice, binding it together. The pale blue fabric was a wispy lace through which her nipples showed.

He groaned. "Damn, woman, how much of this stuff do you own?"

And who had bought it for her? Had she bought it for herself? Or had a lover picked out the lingerie for her to wear for him?

Something flashed through him—something he hadn't felt since he was a kid—envying kids who'd had a mom and a dad and a house, who hadn't had to con people for money for food and clothes.

How he'd hated those kids, hated that they'd taken for granted what he'd always wished he had.

Her brow puckered as she stared up at him; she must have caught the expression on his face. "Don't you like it?"

He automatically reached for the bow, running his fingers over the satin ribbon. "I love it," he said. "I love it all…" Most of all, he loved her body, the sweet curves of it, the soft skin.

The heat and the passion that burned him when he slid inside her, when he slid home. Desperate for her, he tugged the bow loose so the negligee dropped from her body. Then he pushed her back onto the bed.

He'd never felt this way, never felt so desperate to claim someone as his. Hell, he'd never wanted to claim anyone as his—until Bette.

He moved his hands and lips over her body, spreading his kiss and caress as if he were branding her as his. He had never felt possessive of another human being before. Had never felt this madness in his blood and his fiercely pounding heart.

Her heart pounded just as fast and furiously beneath his palm that cupped her breast. She was just as excited as he was, her chest heaving as she panted for breath.

He'd never had anyone match his passion the way Bette did. He didn't have to make sure she was ready for him. He knew she already was. And of course when he stroked his fingers over her mound, he found her hot and ready. And a pulse beat there for him, in her clit.

Her breath shuddered out as she arched off the bed. "Simon…"

She needed him just as badly as he needed her. But with her, he wanted to make sure she got as much pleasure as he did. So he moved down her body. And he slid his tongue over her clit, back and forth.

She whimpered and shifted against the bed. Her hands clutched his shoulder and then his hair. "Simon!"

He thrust his fingers inside her. And she came.

His vision blurred as his desire intensified to insanity. He undressed in such a frenzy that a button popped off. Then he tore open a condom packet and sheathed himself before sliding inside her.

She was so hot. So wet. So ready…

She moved beneath him and around him. They rolled across the sheets, tangling them, tearing them from the bed. Passion burned between them. They clutched at each other. Despite her release, she was desperate again, desperate for more pleasure. He made sure she got it, making her come again and again before he finally let himself come.

Then he dropped limply onto her body, struggling to breathe again as his heart finally began to slow its frantic beating. He raised his head from her breast and stared up at her in wonder. "What the hell do you do to me?"

She just shook her head. She either didn't know or couldn't speak. So he didn't think she'd be able to move, either. But after cleaning up in the bathroom, he strode back into her bedroom, and she wasn't there.

Where the hell had she gone?

"Bette?"

She stepped out of the other door, the one to the walk-in closet. But she was wearing only the robe that had been lying across the foot of the bed. So why had she gone back inside there?

Was she hiding something in there? Or in the desk? She glanced at that, too, as if checking to make sure she'd left nothing out. But then she grabbed up his shirt from the bedroom floor and held it out to him.

"Trying to get rid of me?" he asked.

"Uh, no," she stammered, but her eyes widened in surprise. "You don't want to stay, though."

She must have heard that rule of his, how he never

spent the night with anyone. If he wanted a chance to search her closet and that desk, he was going to need to make an exception to that rule. So she wouldn't catch him snooping again, like she nearly had last time, he had to wait until after she fell asleep.

"You are trying to get rid of me," he said, and the hurt he allowed in his voice wasn't entirely feigned. "I really should check to see who you have stashed in that closet."

"Nobody," she replied quickly, almost too quickly.

He doubted any man could have hidden in there while they'd had sex. Even if he was married, Simon damn well wouldn't have done it. He would have taken apart the guy who dared to touch her while he was seeing her.

"You really aren't seeing anyone else?" he asked.

"No," she said. "I told you I don't have time for dating right now."

"What are we doing, then?" he asked.

"We're not dating," she said. "That's why it would be weird for you to stay."

He'd had women beg him to spend the night in their beds. But this one—the one with whom he actually wanted to spend the night—seemed almost on the verge of begging him to leave. He reached for her, closing his arms around her shoulders to draw her close to his chest. "How 'bout I just stay until I recover enough for us to do that again?"

She rubbed her hips against his. "I think you're recovered enough."

He chuckled. He was. Just being close to her made him hard as hell. "Not quite yet." He tugged her toward the bed, pulled back the tangled blankets and pulled her down onto the mattress with him.

"You really want to stay?" she asked.

"Just for a little while," he lied. He didn't know how long he'd have to stay for her to fall asleep.

She settled her head against his shoulder. "What do you want to do until you recover?" she asked.

"Talk."

She tensed.

"Don't worry," he told her. "I'll talk. You can just listen."

She must have been intrigued enough that she moved her hand to his chest, and her fingers began to stroke the skin over his heart. Did she feel how hard it was beating yet for her?

"I will post your job," he promised her.

She released a shaky sigh but he didn't know if it was of relief or disappointment.

"Do you want me to add the tight skirts and lingerie into the job description?" she asked.

He shook his head. "No. It would be hard for a guy to find and I probably would be better off with a male assistant. I'd be less distracted—" he moved his hand down her back to the curve of her hip and ass "—because you sure as hell distracted me the past two years."

She snorted in disbelief.

"You did," he insisted. "I couldn't stop staring at your ass…"

A giggle slipped through her lips. Then she suggested, "Maybe Miguel has a friend. Another reformed gang member."

"Too damn few of his friends are even alive yet, let alone reformed like he is," he said.

"How long have you known Miguel?" she asked.

"A hell of a lot longer than two years," he said. "I knew him from when I lived on the streets."

"Why were you living on the streets? Did you run away from home?" she asked.

And he was glad that she had, that she actually wanted to know something about him. Other women had pried for information about his life, about his past. Until now, Bette hadn't seemed to care. She hadn't wanted to get to know him.

But maybe if she did, she would open up to him, too. So he told her everything: about never knowing his mom, about his dad training him to con people before he'd hardly known how to walk or talk, about how the only way he'd been able to escape that life was to run away from his father.

"Didn't he try to find you?" she asked.

He shook his head.

She stroked her hand over his heart as if she was trying to soothe away the hurt. Miraculously, her touch seemed to do just that. It didn't bother him like it usually did when he talked about his father.

"It would have been hard for him to look for me,"

he said, "since shortly after I ran away, he got arrested."

She gasped, her breath brushing warmly across his skin.

He chuckled but without any humor. "Fortunately for me, he is still serving that sentence." If he wasn't, Simon would have suspected his father of somehow being the mole. Hell, even with him being in jail, it made more sense for him to be the mole than it did for Bette. But she had access; he didn't.

"Why is that fortunate?" she asked, her voice soft.

"Because he blamed me for his getting arrested," he said, then shrugged as if it didn't matter to him. But it did, and she must have known because she pressed her lips to his chest in a gentle kiss.

"Were you responsible?" she asked.

He'd never told anyone else this, but he felt compelled to tell her. "Yes. I turned him in, had some evidence."

"Did you do that just to get away from him?"

"He had to be stopped," Simon admitted. "He was conning people who couldn't afford it. I had to do some things…when I was living on the streets. But I made sure nobody got hurt. He didn't care."

Least of all about his son.

She must have heard what he left unsaid because she reached up and pressed a kiss to his lips and nuzzled her hair against his cheek. "Sounds like both our fathers disowned us."

He had never realized how much he had in common with Bette. She was an amazing woman, even if she was the damn mole. He hoped like hell that she wasn't, though.

He moved her hand from his chest to his groin. "Look, I'm recovered."

Her fingers closed around him, and she began to stroke him up and down. While she teased him with her touch, he reached for his pants and fished a condom from the pocket. Before he could sheathe himself, her mouth slid over his shaft—up and down. He nearly came then. But he wanted more.

He pushed her onto her back and feasted on her body, on her full breasts with the ultrasensitive nipples, on the curve of her hip, on her dimpled knee… then he moved between her legs. And he made certain she had recovered, as well.

Her fingers clutched his shoulders, and she dragged him up. Then she guided his cock inside her. They moved with less urgency this time. Taking their time with slow strokes and long kisses…

And when they came, they came together—shouting each other's names. Simon had never felt as connected to another person. Or as scared…

Bette felt connected to Simon in a way that had nothing to do with the physical. She felt connected to Simon emotionally. She'd seen him naked, truly naked. And she knew she should return the favor.

What he'd shared with her was far more personal

than her career goals and dreams. What he'd shared with her...

Scared the hell out of her, not because of what he'd done or who he was. But because she was really beginning to fall for him. Panic coursed through her, like moments ago passion had, and she tensed.

She should tell him to leave, show him to the door. He'd already been here too long, too vividly. Now she would always imagine him here. It hadn't been bad when he'd been in just the living room. But now he'd been in the bedroom, in her bed. And like Goldilocks, he was still there. He must have fallen asleep, for his body—his beautiful body—was relaxed.

Instead of pounding on his chest to wake him up, she rested her head on it and curled up against his side. Sure, she had work to do. But she was tired. And she only had a few more days with him.

She would take a moment to enjoy just being with him. It wasn't as if he would actually spend the night. She was certain he would wake up and slip out before morning. If not much sooner.

The thought of him leaving relaxed her enough that she began to drift off to sleep. While her mind told her she wanted him gone, her body wrapped around his, holding him close. And she had to admit the truth.

She didn't want him to leave. Not just tonight but maybe ever.

That thought filled her with such terror that she jerked fully awake. She must have been asleep longer than she realized because he was gone. Her arms clutched nothing but the pillow that smelled yet like him. She should have been relieved that he'd left.

But a chill chased over her bare skin, raising goose bumps. She wasn't just cold, though. She was scared for a couple of reasons.

One—the disappointment that filled her over his slipping out. Sure, she'd suspected that he would. She'd even thought that would be a good thing. But she hadn't realized how good it would feel to actually sleep with him.

The second reason she was scared was because she heard a strange noise. The creak of floorboards and a weird scraping noise. It wasn't coming from the living room. So it wasn't Simon walking to the door. The noise emanated from her walk-in closet. She reached for her nightstand where she'd stashed her purse in the cabinet beneath the drawer, and she pulled out the canister of Mace she always carried.

With it clutched tightly, reassuringly, in her hand, she slipped into her robe, tied up the sash with her other hand and headed toward her closet door. She jerked it open and prepared to spray her intruder in the face…until she recognized him. Then she demanded to know, "What the hell are you doing?"

CHAPTER THIRTEEN

"WHAT THE HELL are you doing?" Bette demanded to know, and like he'd done the day he'd caught her in his office after hours, she had to ask him twice.

But he still didn't know how to answer her. Heat rushed to his face with embarrassment that he'd been caught snooping. He'd wanted to know what the hell she'd hidden in her closet. He'd noticed the clothes knocked askew on the bottom rack, and he'd reached behind to find what she'd stashed there.

It wasn't a man but a sketch pad. She had a portfolio full of them. Then he'd found the box of lingerie, which he was on his knees leaning over at the moment. And he understood that all those sexy outfits weren't gifts from a married lover or from any lover at all. Next to the box, he'd found a sewing machine and some reams of lace and silk. And he'd figured out what her big secret was and it wasn't selling any of Street Legal's secrets.

"Why didn't you just tell me?" he asked.

Her face flushed a bright red that nearly matched the color of the corset he held in his hands. "I don't have to tell you why I'm quitting," she said. "Even your employment contract states that."

"I know," he said. "You didn't have to tell me. But why wouldn't you?" Was she ashamed of what she did, because of her upbringing?

Her face flushed an even deeper shade of red. "You would have laughed."

That wasn't the reply he'd expected. "What? Why would you think that?"

"Boring Bette Monroe designing lingerie?" She uttered a short chuckle of her own, but it was full of bitterness. "Even I think that's funny."

He was more confused now than when he'd discovered her secret. "Why in the hell do you think you're boring?"

She snorted. "Come on, you thought that, too— the past two years."

His face heated a bit, and he had to admit that he had. But in his defense, he explained, "I was going off the way you pull your hair into such a tight bun and how you dress. I had no idea what you've been wearing under your clothes this entire time." He held up a handful of the lingerie. But even then he'd still been attracted to her; he'd seen her beauty no matter how hard she'd tried to hide it.

"Why do you dress that way?" he asked. "Why do you wear your hair that way? And the glasses, I don't even think you need them." He stepped closer to her. "What are you hiding from, Bette?"

She took the lingerie from his hand, but she wouldn't answer his question.

"Are you hiding from me?" he asked.

"Given your reputation, I thought it was a good idea to dress a little more conservatively than I used to," she said.

He flinched as a twinge of pain struck his heart. "You were afraid of me? Afraid that I'd force myself on you?"

Then he glanced down and saw that, in her hand not full of lingerie, she clutched a canister of Mace. He sighed. "I guess you are afraid of me."

"I thought you left," she said. "I didn't know who was in my closet. I can't believe you've been snooping through my stuff."

"I knew you were hiding something," he said. He'd thought she'd been hiding the evidence that she was the mole. But she wasn't. And he was so relieved that he laughed.

Anger flashed in her eyes. "See, I told you that you'd laugh at me!" She threw the lingerie at him and stomped back into the bedroom.

He rushed after her so quickly that he was still knocking G-strings off his shoulders as he joined her near the bed. "Guess I should be glad you didn't mace me."

"I almost did," she said. "You scared me."

"I'm sorry," he said.

"For scaring me or for snooping?" she challenged him.

"For scaring you," he admitted.

He'd hoped she would sleep through his search. And that he would be able to slip back into bed with her before she'd even noticed he'd left it. He hadn't wanted to. She'd felt so warm and soft and somehow comforting sleeping in his arms, her head against his chest.

"You're not sorry for snooping," she said with disgust.

He was unapologetic. "I had to find out the truth."

Her brow furrowed. "The truth about what?"

He couldn't tell her—not now. She was already mad at him. If he told her that he'd suspected her of selling secrets from Street Legal's case files, she would be furious, so furious that she would throw him out of her place and out of her life.

And he couldn't have that because then he couldn't have her. Now that he'd learned her secret, he wanted her even more.

"I already told you," he said. "I knew you were hiding something." He just hadn't realized that something was herself. "And you never answered me. You never told me why you were hiding from me. Are you afraid of me?"

Bette had never been as afraid of Simon as she was now. She was afraid that she was beginning to have feelings for him. She nearly laughed now over the irony of that. For days she'd wanted him to believe she was in love with him, so that he would cut her notice short. But now that she was actually falling, there was no way she wanted him to know.

She'd pretended to have feelings for him because she'd known it would horrify him. She didn't want to horrify him. But she did want to be honest with him just as he'd been honest with her.

"I'm afraid of becoming my mother or my sister," she said. "I don't want to get so into some guy that I forget who I am and what I want out of life."

He laughed again. But this time she didn't mind that he was laughing at her. "I think you know exactly who you are, Bette Monroe," he said. "It's the rest of the world you don't want to know you."

"My friends know me," she said.

"You don't dress in the cardigans and skirts around them?" he asked.

He probably hadn't seen much else in her closet.

"That's as much a habit from how I was raised as a way to hide," she said. "I had to dress conservatively when I was growing up."

"But you're all grown-up now," he said, and his blue eyes darkened with desire.

"I'm still mousy Bette in so many ways," she said.

And he laughed as if she'd told him the funniest joke he'd ever heard. Then he focused on her face and stopped. "You've got to be kidding," he said. "You can't really see yourself that way."

"That's how I saw myself for a lot of years," she admitted. "So it's a hard habit to break. Designing and wearing my lingerie makes me feel sexy, though."

"And beautiful," he added.

She smiled but shook her head. "And you told me you stopped conning people."

"I'm telling you the truth," he said. "You know the women I've dated."

She nodded. "Models. Actresses. That's why I know you're lying."

Anger flashed in his eyes now. He jerked her into his arms and tipped up her chin so she had to look into his face—his gorgeous face. "You, Bette Monroe, are a beautiful, sexy woman."

Maybe he was a hypnotist as well as a con artist because she was beginning to believe him, especially since he kept repeating those words between kisses.

His mouth nibbled at her lips. "Women pay to have lips like these," he said. "Full, silky, sexy…"

He tangled his fingers in her hair. "And this… It's real, no extensions." He pushed the robe from her body and skimmed his hand over her breasts. "Like these. You're real, Bette."

"I never knew that was sexy."

"The sexiest," he said.

And with the way he looked at her, she felt sexy, even without her lingerie. She felt sexy naked.

"And beautiful," he added.

He pushed her back onto the bed. And he touched and kissed her with an almost reverence, as if she was a work of art. She believed him.

She was no longer mousy Bette Monroe.

She was the siren he'd called her.

And she wanted him to feel what she was feeling. She wanted him to have feelings for her, too. So she pulled him down on top of her and pressed kisses to his chest and his shoulders and onto his washboard abs that rippled beneath her touch.

"Bette…"

"You're the beautiful one," she said.

Of course he didn't deny it. He couldn't not know how handsome he was. He'd undoubtedly used his looks when he'd conned those people with his father and with his friends when they'd all been struggling to survive on the streets.

And even though he'd claimed he'd stopped conning people, she worried that he was conning her now. Not into believing she was beautiful and sexy; she felt he was sincere about that. But she couldn't help but think he'd been trying to make her fall for him.

He joined their bodies again, driving his shaft inside her. She clung to him, riding him as he drove them both to insanity. The orgasm shuddered through her body, more powerful than any even he had given her before.

And she knew she was in trouble, that she was getting in deep…

CHAPTER FOURTEEN

"THIS ISN'T TUESDAY," Simon said as his partners stormed his office.

"Her last day is today," Trevor said. "So this can't wait until Tuesday."

He sucked in a breath, feeling like his friend had punched him. It was true. Today was her last day. He'd been trying not to think about it. But Miguel had kept asking him questions about the going-away party that Bruno was catering at the end of the day.

The last thing he wanted to do was celebrate her leaving. Throwing her a party was the right thing to do now that he knew the truth. She had landed her dream job. While he didn't want her to leave, he wanted her to be happy. That was why he hadn't told her about his suspicions.

He knew she would be hurt. That she would feel used that he'd seduced her to find evidence against her. So he couldn't tell her.

"I hope like hell you found something to prove she's the damn mole, something we can bring to the police," Ronan said. His face was flushed and his dark eyes glittered with anger.

Simon narrowed his eyes. Usually Ronan was the most laid-back of all of them. "There is no evidence," he assured them.

"There has to be!" Ronan exclaimed.

He shook his head, and he stood because he felt vulnerable sitting with the others standing over his desk. Growing up on the streets, he'd always made certain never to be in a vulnerable position.

Never to sleep with anyone else around…

He'd broken his own rule the other night when he'd slept over at Bette's. He was surprised she hadn't thrown him out after catching his snooping. But she hadn't.

"If there was any evidence against her, I would have found it," Simon assured the others. "She's not the mole."

"Then why is she leaving?" Ronan asked.

"Because she got a better job," he said. "I don't understand why you're all so uptight about this. You're the ones who didn't believe it was her, that she wouldn't be leaving if she'd been making money off us. What's changed?"

Ronan pushed his hand, which was shaking slightly, through his dark hair. "I got reported to the bar for misconduct."

Simon snorted. "So? You've been reported before." With the exception of him, they all had. "What's the big deal?"

"I have a friend at the bar association who looked into it for me," Stone said. "The evidence came from our case files, on our letterhead."

"Damn it!" Simon slammed his fist onto his desk. He was furious that there was a mole in their office. And he was furious that his friends hadn't come to him right away with this latest threat to Street Legal. "Why didn't you guys tell me about this?"

"You've been preoccupied," Trevor said. "With her."

His blood heated as he thought of how preoccupied he'd been—with her crazy, sexy body and their crazy, hot sex. But then it had gotten even crazier than that when they'd shared so much of themselves with each other.

"I was trying to find evidence," he reminded him.

"In her panties?" Ronan crudely asked.

And Simon surged forward, his fists raised. Before he could swing, Trevor caught him, wrapping both arms around him as he pulled him back from Ronan. He wasn't quite as tall or broad as the other guys. But they knew how strong he was.

"You son of a bitch!" he cursed his friend. "Don't talk about her like that!"

Ronan had little respect for women—with good reason, given how his mother had treated his father and how he'd seen other wives treat their husbands. But Bette was different. She wasn't like Ronan's cheating mother.

"Oh, my God," Stone exclaimed, his gray eyes wide with shock. "You're in love with her."

It was a good thing Trevor hadn't let go of him yet. Or he would have swung at Stone, too. "You're fucking nuts!" he said instead. "All of you are. The mole is not Bette."

"Just because you didn't find evidence doesn't mean there isn't any," Stone said, and his voice was lower now, as if he was talking to a child.

Simon glared at him. "I understand that. But she's leaving for a new job."

"With another law firm?" Trevor asked.

"With a fashion house," Simon said. "She's going to have her own line with a major retailer." He would have told him which retailer, but Bette hadn't wanted him to know she designed lingerie so she probably didn't want his partners to know, either.

But Ronan named the retailer.

"How the hell do you know that?" Simon asked. It had taken him nearly two weeks to find out.

"Because Muriel Sanz will be exclusively modeling Bette's Beguiling Bows," Ronan replied, his voice gruff with bitterness.

"Muriel Sanz?" Simon recognized the name of the model and not just because she was famous. "You obliterated her in her divorce."

"She did that to herself," Ronan insisted. "She's a lying, cheating bitch, and I had the witnesses to prove it."

"So what does that have to do with anything?"

"She's the one who reported him to the bar," Stone said, "for the subornation of perjury."

Simon sucked in a breath.

"She and Bette must have cooked up the evidence together," Ronan said, "using our letterhead."

"Anyone in this office could get ahold of our letterhead," Simon pointed out. "Hell, anyone we mailed anything to would have a copy of our letterhead, like Muriel's lawyer. You have nothing connecting Bette to that report to the bar."

"They're friends," Ronan insisted.

With the exception of her former roommate John Paul, and she hadn't introduced them, Simon hadn't met any of Bette's friends. They hadn't had that kind of relationship. It had only been sex.

Would that end today with her last day of work?

Or would she continue to see him if he asked? Or begged? He'd never begged. And he wasn't about to start now. Not even for Bette.

"Just because Muriel is modeling her line doesn't mean they're friends," Simon said. "Not everyone who works together is friends." He wasn't certain how much longer he would be friends with Ronan if the guy continued to bash Bette.

Trevor pulled Simon back a little farther as if he sensed that Simon still wanted to swing.

And Stone cautioned Ronan, "Simon's right. You have no proof that Bette has anything to do with you being reported."

Ronan uttered a ragged sigh.

And Simon felt a twinge of pity for his friend.

"The bar will dismiss the report," Simon assured him. "They'll figure out the evidence is fake."

"Then Muriel Sanz will be the one in trouble," Trevor added.

Ronan nodded. But then he stepped closer to Simon and warned him, "Just because we haven't found any proof that Bette's involved doesn't mean that she isn't. You need to be careful."

Simon was afraid that it was already too late for that. But he reminded his friend, "Today is her last day. She won't have anything more to do with Street Legal."

"What about you?" Ronan asked. "Will she have anything more to do with you?"

He shook his head and yet he didn't know. Would she want anything to do with him once she was gone? Or would she be too focused on her new career?

He should have been relieved that she wasn't like all the other women with whom he'd hooked up. She wasn't looking for roses and a ring. She didn't want a future with him or with any other man.

And maybe that was what made her so damn sexy. But hell, he found everything about her sexy. While he couldn't force her to keep working for him, he wasn't ready to let her go completely. Not yet. Maybe not ever...

And that scared him far more than he'd ever been scared in his life.

Simon had given her a heads-up about the going-away party. He'd told her that morning, as they lay in bed together. Since that first night he'd stayed, he'd spent every subsequent night. She should have been freaking out because she felt smothered or over-whelmed. But those weren't the reasons she was freaking out. She was freaking out because she was beginning to expect him to stay.

And she knew that was stupid. No woman held Simon Kramer's interest for very long. She wasn't sure how she'd had him for two weeks. In the two years she'd known him, that was probably the lon-gest he'd dated anyone.

Not that what they were doing was really dating. She wasn't sure what the hell it was, but that she wasn't ready yet for it to end. Would it—once she left Street Legal?

Should she stay?

Not forever. Not even full-time...

But she could help out for a while, make the tran-sition easier for her replacement. Even while she'd been working for Simon full-time, she'd had the time—and maybe the inspiration—to come up with the designs that had become her own line.

But staying, after her going-away party, would be awkward and anticlimactic. No. She had no choice now but to leave Street Legal.

What about Simon?

Should she just end that—whatever it was—too?

Her heart ached at the thought of no longer seeing him, of being with him. Was she in love with him? No. That wasn't possible. She wasn't that stupid.

She drew in a deep, bracing breath and stepped out of her office. Someone called out, "There she is!" Music began to play and confetti rained down on her from some kind of gun Miguel blasted at her.

She blinked against the bits of paper and wished now that she'd worn her glasses. But since Simon had accused her of using them to hide, she only wore them when she was sketching now. Otherwise, she really didn't need them. She also left her hair down, too, which meant it would probably be full of those bits of paper.

But she forced a smile since she was the guest of honor. At least for some. The gossips from the bathroom glared at her with resentment. To them, she was probably the guest of dishonor.

No. Leaving was a smart move. Working with Simon and sleeping with him was stupid. She'd known that when she'd started and couldn't believe it had lasted two weeks. But she was glad now that it had.

She only wished it would last longer.

Sleeping with him...

Not the work.

The gossipy women weren't the only ones glaring at her. A couple of Simon's partners were, as well. Where was Simon? She peered around the crowd of faces but couldn't find him.

With his good looks and charm, he always stood out in any crowd. So he hadn't arrived yet.

Was he coming? Had he authorized the party and

warned her about it only to not attend himself? It made no sense.

"Here's a drink," Miguel said as he pressed a flute of champagne into her hand. "Not that I care to celebrate. I'm really going to miss you."

Warmth flooded her heart. "I'm really going to miss you, too," she said. Despite his past, she'd always felt safe with Miguel—like he had her back and wasn't going to stab it like some of their coworkers. She hugged him.

As he pulled back, he peered over her head. "Guess I'm not the only one who doesn't feel like celebrating," he said. "Simon's not here."

She'd already known that, but a twinge of pain struck her heart with Miguel's confirmation.

"He hasn't even interviewed replacements for you yet," he said. "Of course quite a few current employees have been jockeying for your position."

"I'm sure they have," she said with a sigh.

Miguel squeezed her again before releasing her. "They don't understand you're special to Simon. They will never have the relationship with him that you do."

She wasn't sure what they had could be called a relationship. Yet it was deeper and more meaningful than anything she'd had before.

"You should take the job," she told him. "He can hire someone else for your position."

Miguel tilted his head as if considering it. "I love Simon. But I kind of like being the guy at the door."

That was kind of what he was—the bouncer, allowing people into an exclusive club or throwing them out.

Would he throw her out after today? Would Simon?

"Speaking of which," he murmured as the elevator dinged. He walked off to find out who'd arrived after hours.

Other coworkers replaced him, offering hugs and well-wishes—some sincere, some obviously not. She smiled over how most workplaces were similar to high school. How there were cliques and outcasts in both.

She had never cared to be in the cliques, so she'd been an outcast. But she hadn't minded. She'd used the free time to design. And it had paid off.

"Congratulations," a deep voice murmured.

And she turned to face one of Simon's partners. It was clear from the coldness in Ronan Hall's dark eyes that he wasn't any more sincere in his well-wishes as some of her catty coworkers had been.

"Thank you," she murmured back.

"You've accomplished what no one else ever has," he told her.

Her head began to pound with confusion. "I'm not sure what you're talking about," she admitted. "Plenty of other designers have established their own lines."

She knew Simon was close to his partners, close enough that he would have shared what he'd learned about her with them. Her face warmed, but it wasn't with embarrassment over designing lingerie. As Simon had pointed out, she should be proud of her accomplishment. No. She was embarrassed over what else he'd probably told them about her, about having sex with her. Had he told them how wild, how wanton, he made her with his kisses—with his touch?

They were grown men. Not boys bragging in the locker room. But then she reminded herself that like so many other places, Street Legal was like high school. Of course he might have bragged about banging her.

"I'm not congratulating you about that, and I think you know it," Ronan said as his voice dropped to a low, gruff whisper.

She sucked in a breath of surprise. Even if Simon had talked about their sex life, it was crass of his friend to bring it up.

"I don't know what you're talking about," she said. "Or why."

She glanced down at the glass in his hand. It was empty. Maybe he was drunk. That might explain why he was making no sense.

"Simon," he said. "He's the ultimate con, you know." But he said it like he didn't expect her to know.

"He told me about his past," she said. "About his father."

"Wow!" Ronan exclaimed. "You really are good, lady."

She didn't miss his ironic emphasis on *lady*. Obviously, he didn't consider her to be one at all.

"You've conned the ultimate con," he continued.

And she laughed. "That's ridiculous."

She'd had enough of his drunken rambling. Even if he wasn't drunk, Ronan was her least favorite of the four partners. He took too much pleasure in his work as a divorce lawyer. And he was so determined to win the best settlement for his client, that he didn't care what means he used or how mean he got or who got hurt. Recently he'd hurt someone she'd come to care about so badly that he'd nearly destroyed her.

She started away from him, but he grasped her arm—not painfully, just hard enough that she wasn't going to go anywhere.

"Somehow you managed to convince Simon that you're not the office mole," Ronan said. "But I know he's wrong. And I'm going to prove it."

Wishing she'd worn her glasses, she squinted and stared up at him, trying to see if there was amusement in his eyes. He had to be kidding. "Office mole?"

"Someone's been selling secrets from our case files," Ronan said. "But you know that. And you've taken it a step further when you and Muriel Sanz fabricated evidence to report me to the bar."

She gasped. She'd missed a few calls from Muriel but hadn't had the time to return them—with how busy she'd been with Simon. What had Muriel done? Not that Ronan didn't have it coming. He'd done far worse to her.

"I don't know what you're talking about," she said as she tugged at her arm.

"Ask Simon," Ronan said. "Ask him why he seduced you. It was to find the evidence that you're the mole."

She'd wondered why he'd suddenly found her attractive after two years of ignoring her. Was this the reason? He'd suspected her of something. Then she remembered all those times he—and his partners—had acted suspicious of her. Her stomach churned, and she felt sick.

That was why he'd searched her apartment. For evidence.

"I am not a mole," she assured him, although she had been called mousy so many times that it had affected her self-esteem. Simon had tried to fix that, though. Or had that only been a con, as well?

Ronan shook his head, refusing to accept her word. "I don't believe you. And I can't believe you convinced Simon that you aren't. You must be damn good."

If he hadn't been holding her wrist, she would have swung at his face. "You son of a bitch!"

"Yeah, I am," he agreed. "That's why a woman like Muriel Sanz or you would never con me the way you've conned Simon."

"Ronan..." It was Stone Michaelsen who spoke to him. She hadn't even noticed him approach, but he must have been near this entire time. He put his hand over Ronan's on her arm. "You're out of line here."

Ronan shook his head. "I might be out of the bar association because of her and her friend."

Bette looked at Stone and assured him, "I have nothing to do with anything he's been accusing me of."

Ronan snorted in derision. "Yeah, right. Simon was supposed to seduce the truth out of you. And instead you seduced him into believing your lies." He shook his head in disgust.

Simon was supposed to seduce the truth out of you...

Suddenly it all made sense. And she knew Ronan wasn't lying. He was wrong about her being the mole. But he was right about what Simon had done, about why he'd done her.

Pain squeezed her heart so hard that she could barely breathe. Tears burned her eyes so she could barely see. She rushed off, but she wasn't entirely blind. She knew exactly where she was going.

CHAPTER FIFTEEN

SIMON WAS NO HYPOCRITE. He couldn't go out there—
to the party in the lobby—and celebrate her leaving.
Not when he selfishly wanted her to stay. It would
be selfish to expect her to stay here, in a position for
which she was overqualified, just so that he would get
to see her every day just as he had the past two years.

He'd wasted those two years. Of course he hadn't
wanted to risk a harassment charge. But Bette was
obviously attracted to him, as well.

Wasn't she?

Or had she been conning him like Ronan believed? No. He could not accept that—and not just
because of his ego but because of Bette. She was
not a con.

The door to his office opened and he glanced up
from his desk. His heart flipped in his chest at the
sight of her. She was so damn beautiful, never more
so than now with her hair flowing down her back
and around her shoulders. Bits of colored paper pep-
pered the sleek, sable-colored strands. She closed and
locked the door behind her.

And another part of his body leaped to attention, his dick hardening. "Bette…"

He was so damn happy to see her. He stood up and rushed around his desk to her. But as he leaned his head down for her kiss, her hand connected instead of her lips. And his head snapped back with the force of her slap. His skin stung from the blow. "What the hell?"

"What the hell?" she echoed. "How could you think I would betray Street Legal? That I would betray you?"

"What?" he asked. But he knew and he took a step back to sit on the edge of his desk as his legs began to shake slightly beneath him.

"I know why you seduced me," she told him. "That it was just part of your sick plan to get evidence that I'm the office mole."

His phone began to buzz on his desk. He didn't need to read the text to know what had happened but he glanced down at the warning from Stone. "Ronan talked to you."

"Talked?" She made a noise and blinked as if tears were about to sting her eyes. "He accused me of being a con artist, of tricking you and selling out the practice."

"He shouldn't have done that," Simon said.

"Why not? It's what you thought," she said. "I wish you would have just told me that instead of playing games with me, instead of having sex with me." Her face flushed and her eyes gleamed with anger. "That must have been quite a sacrifice for you, sleeping with me in order to get the information you were looking for."

"Sacrifice?" He snorted now. "It was never a sacrifice."

"I know you," she said. "I know you would do anything for this practice. I guess even me."

"Bette..." He'd thought he'd convinced her that she was beautiful and desirable, that he wanted her for her. But that wasn't why he'd started showing an interest in her. And now she knew that. "You know I want you. Even now." He stood up and reached for her, pulling her soft body tightly against his hard, tense one.

Her lips parted on a soft gasp. "Simon..."

"You make me crazy," he told her. And he proceeded to show her just how crazy she made him as he leaned down and covered her mouth with his. He kissed her deeply, sliding his tongue in and out of her open lips. He pushed her back onto the desk, atop his papers and pushed up her skirt.

She didn't fight him. Instead, she locked her legs around his waist and ground her hips against him. She wanted him, too.

He kept kissing her, his mouth making love to hers. But he pulled out a condom as he did it, fumbled with the packet and rolled it over the cock he barely managed to release before it shoved right through his zipper. Then he was inside her—and she was already wet and ready for him, already half coming as her muscles clutched him.

She convulsed around him, squeezing him until he came, too.

"See how crazy you make me?" he asked.

"According to your friend, I've conned you," she said. "Do you believe that?"

"No!" Maybe he'd said it too quickly or maybe he'd hesitated too long. Either way he hadn't answered it correctly because she jerked out of his arms. He reached for her again, but she stepped farther away and jerked down her skirt.

"You don't trust me," she said.

"I don't trust anyone," he told her. "And you know why."

"You trust your friends," she said.

"I grew up with them. I wouldn't have survived if they hadn't been worthy of my trust."

"So you must believe Ronan—about Muriel."

He tensed now. "Is she your friend?"

She nodded.

"Why didn't you tell me that?" And now he was suspicious. Could he have been wrong about her? Had she conned him after all?

"Do I know all your friends?" she asked.

He chuckled. "Yeah, you probably do."

Her face flushed.

"Why didn't you introduce me to any of your friends?" he wondered. "Were you embarrassed to be dating me?"

He hadn't considered it until now. But it made sense that she might be, considering their practice had hurt one of her friends.

"I didn't know what we were doing," she said. "And I didn't expect it to last as long as it has."

"No," he agreed. "That was why you started it so I would release you early from your two-week notice." So she had conned him. "Was your contract with the fashion house your only reason for leaving Street Legal?"

"No," she admitted. "I don't respect the way you do business. The way you and that PR company obliterated Muriel."

He sighed. It hadn't been pretty. He couldn't deny that. "Ronan had witnesses. He had proof. It was the truth."

She didn't argue that, just replied, "It wasn't fair."

"If you want to win, you can't always fight fair," he said.

"Winning shouldn't be that important," she said. "It shouldn't be at the expense of other people."

"When we win, someone else loses," he said. "That's life, Bette."

"That's your life," she said. "And I don't want any part of it anymore."

He didn't think she was talking about just her job now. "Bette…"

But she wouldn't look at him. Instead she was looking down at her wrist and the thin gold watch on it. "My two weeks are up," she said. "I never have to see you again."

She didn't have to. But did she want to?

"And Ronan can threaten as much as he wants," she continued, "but he's never going to find any evidence that I'm the mole. I haven't done anything wrong."

He knew he was wrong to have doubted her again, even for a moment. Hell, he'd been wrong to ever doubt her. She was no con artist.

"Except get involved with you," she continued. "That was stupid. I should have known it would bring me nothing but pain."

He had hurt her with his doubts and suspicions. "I'm sorry," he said.

"Why?" she asked. "You won. So it doesn't matter if the other person gets hurt, right?" She must not have cared what he really thought, though, because she didn't wait for his reply. She ran to the door, unlocked and dragged it open, then she ran out of his office.

And out of his life…

So Simon couldn't tell her what he'd just realized. He hadn't won. In fact, for the first time in his life, he'd lost. He'd lost her…forever.

Bette stared down at her sketch pad, but the page was blank. She hadn't felt very inspired the past couple of days, not since she'd run out of Simon Kramer's office and out of Street Legal.

She'd thought maybe coming here—to the fashion house—would inspire her. She was around all the beautiful people since models, photographers and other designers overflowed the old warehouse. But none of those people were as beautiful as Simon. He was really beyond handsome, beyond gorgeous.

And the way he touched her, the way he kissed her...

Heat rushed through her body as tension wound inside her, tension only Simon could fully release. Her vibrator had no effect on her the past couple of nights. She wanted Simon instead.

"Hey, Bette Bow!" a husky, feminine voice called out before slender arms wrapped around her from behind. A head settled onto her shoulder as Muriel Sanz peered down at the sketch pad. "What gorgeous confections are you creating for me to advertise next?"

She tensed in her friend's embrace. And Muriel pulled back. "What's wrong?"

"You should have given me a heads-up," she said, "before you went to the bar association." Then she wouldn't have been so blindsided. But then Simon should have been honest with her about his suspicions, as well.

"I left you some messages to call me back," Muriel reminded her. "You've been MIA since you gave your notice at Street Legal."

She couldn't deny that, but she didn't want to admit why she'd been. "In one of those voice mails, you could have told me what you'd done."

"You had to know I would go straight to the bar association," Muriel replied, her usually smooth brow furrowed with confusion, "when you gave me those notes."

Bette shook her head, and the pins holding up her hair pulled at her scalp. She wore her glasses, too. But she wasn't hiding anymore, not like she'd done at Street Legal. Her hair was up to get it out of her way. And her glasses were so she could see her sketches...if she ever again summoned the inspiration for a design.

"I did not give you any notes," Bette said. "I don't know what you're talking about—just like I had no idea what Ronan Hall was talking about when he accused me of betraying the firm for my *friend*." Now she wasn't sure how good a friend Muriel really was.

Bette had thought the supermodel was sweet and down-to-earth. But maybe that was just an act. Maybe everything Ronan and that PR firm had said about her was true. She couldn't be trusted.

"Ronan..." Muriel's wide mouth twisted into a grimace of distaste as if just the sound of his name on her lips made her sick. "Of course he would be furious at having his lies exposed."

He was mad. But he'd also been self-righteous. If he'd been lying, would he have felt that way?

Bette didn't know what or whom to believe. She only knew one thing. "I didn't give you anything," she said. "I had no idea what he was talking about."

Muriel's pale green eyes widened in shock. The

light color of her eyes was such a startling contrast to her naturally tanned-looking skin. Her hair was a mass of different-colored streaks of blond, red, brown, gold and black. But it was too random to have been salon styled. The woman had inherited only the best trait of each of the many nationalities making up her heritage. "Those notes really didn't come from you?"

Bette shook her head. "Why did you think they did? Was there a note or anything?" Had someone forged her name? Now she wanted to know who the hell this mole was, too.

"No," Muriel said. "The envelope was just shoved in my box. It wasn't even postmarked. I don't think it had been mailed."

"So someone personally dropped it off?" Bette asked. "What was in it?"

"Notes on Street Legal stationery. Notes about the witnesses and what Ronan had told them to say about me on the stand." She looked sick again, sick of the lies that had been uttered and then spread to ruin her reputation.

But Muriel had risen from the ashes. No matter that it was a lie, she'd started making the most of her bad-girl reputation. And modeling Bette's Beguiling Bows was one of the ways she'd come back into the limelight.

"I can't believe he would do that," Bette murmured.

Muriel gasped. "Do you think those people told the truth about me?"

"No," Bette assured her. Despite her brief moment of doubt, she believed Muriel was a good person. She wasn't the monster her ex-husband and Ronan had made her out to be. "But I can't believe Hall would commit the subornation of perjury and risk his law license."

He, like his partners, had had to overcome so much to become lawyers and build their practice. There was no way that Simon could have known the truth. He cared too much about Street Legal to risk its future.

"He's a bastard," Muriel said. "They all are."

But Bette could not agree with her. She'd seen Simon do good things. He was so patient with his older clients, so supportive of former street kids like Miguel. He was not the bad guy Muriel thought he was. He was not the guy Bette had once thought he was.

She felt a flash of regret over slapping him. But she'd had a good reason. He had seduced her. Too bad she wished that he would do it again.

And again.

But he'd only been doing it—doing her—to find out if she was the mole. He didn't really want her. Like she wanted him.

She had to forget about him and focus on the future she'd fought so hard and for so long to realize. But her pen didn't move across the page. She'd lost her inspiration.

She'd lost Simon.

CHAPTER SIXTEEN

"So what did you think of that one?" Miguel asked from where he leaned against the jamb of Simon's open door.

He glanced up from his desk and focused on his employee, his favorite one now that Bette was gone. He just shook his head.

"She's not Bette?" Miguel wasn't the one who asked this question. Trevor had replaced their male receptionist in the doorway. The two of them were too big to share the space. And Simon could hear the phone ringing at the front desk.

Simon sighed and admitted, "Nobody will be."

"So go get her back," Trevor advised him.

"She has a new job," Simon reminded him. "In the field she always wanted to work in. Hell, she has her own damn line. She's not coming back."

"I didn't mean to the office," Trevor said. "Get her back to you."

Simon shook his head again. "She's damn well not coming back to me, either. Not after Ronan told her I was only sleeping with her to get evidence against her."

"Ronan was upset," Trevor defended their friend. "He ran his mouth when he shouldn't have."

"He doesn't regret what he said," Simon reminded Trevor. "He still thinks Bette was the mole." Which left them vulnerable to the real mole. But Simon already had some other potential suspects—the women who'd been trying to take Bette's place—in his bed more than her office. He had no intention of seducing the truth out of them, though.

"You don't think she is?" Trevor said.

"I did for a little while," Simon said. "That's why I got close to her in the first place." Why he'd seduced her. He hadn't been able to defend himself against those accusations because they'd been right. Then Bette had defended herself. "But no, she's not the mole."

Trevor nodded. "I trust your judgment."

"Bette will never trust me again," he said. She thought everything had been a con. And they could never build a relationship—a real one—without trust.

For the first time in his life, Simon wanted a real relationship. And for the first time in his life, Simon knew that his charm and his drive wouldn't get him what he wanted.

No matter what he did or said, he wouldn't get Bette back.

Bette jumped as her doorbell rang. But she shouldn't have been surprised. It was probably Muriel. She lived in the same building and was the one who recommended Bette find an apartment in it. And since she'd learned Bette had nothing to do with those notes from Street Legal, she'd felt so bad over using them that she kept apologizing.

Bette had forgiven her friend. It was Simon whom she couldn't forgive. Sure, he hadn't known her very well when he'd suspected her of betraying the firm. But once he'd gotten to know her, he should have been honest with her. He should have made sure she wasn't blindsided at her own going-away party the way Ronan Hall had blindsided her.

At least she never had to see the sleazy divorce lawyer again.

But then she wouldn't ever see Simon again, either.

Her heart dropped at the thought, hanging low in her chest. She missed him so much, even though she saw him everywhere in the apartment: in the closet, in her bed, in her living room.

She passed through it on her way to the front door. And as she reached for the knob, she allowed herself to hope that when she opened the door, it would be to him. But when she opened the door, Ronan Hall was the man she saw first. He wasn't alone, though. The other two partners from Street Legal stood on either side of him.

Only Simon was missing.

God, she missed him.

"What do you want?" she asked the men. Were

they serving her with papers? Suing her for breach of something or other? Not that she'd done anything wrong...

Ronan Hall had been scary mad when he'd confronted her at the party, though. Maybe he'd pressed charges against her or filed a lawsuit.

"We'd like to talk to you." Trevor spoke for the three of them. Usually Simon spoke for the four of them. He was more than the managing partner of Street Legal. He was the gorgeous face of the law practice.

"Talk?" she asked, allowing her skepticism to creep out. "I already told you that I had nothing to do with those notes Muriel sent to the bar association."

At just the mention of the model's name, Ronan's mouth twisted into a grimace of distaste. Hopefully, he wouldn't run into the model on his way out of the building.

She held tightly to the door, prepared to swing it closed in their faces, as she added, "So we have nothing to talk about."

But Stone pressed his palm against the door, holding it open. "Simon. We're here about Simon."

He didn't have to push his way inside then. She hurriedly stepped back to allow them to enter her apartment.

"Simon!" she exclaimed as her pulse quickened with fear. "Is he all right? Has something happened to him?"

He dealt with trusts and wills and such, not the

kind of clients or cases the rest of them handled. So she doubted a client had hurt him. But a jealous ex-lover might have. Or some random criminal. He could have been mugged. Or run over on the street.

Her heart pounded fast and fiercely with panic at the thought of all the horrible things that could have happened to him.

The three of them stared at her. So she prodded them, "What is it? What's wrong?"

Ronan sighed. "Damn it."

And more panic clutched her heart. If something had happened to him… "What?" she asked. "What is it?"

"Simon was right," Ronan said, his voice gruff with disappointment. "You're not the mole."

"No, of course not," she said. "While I didn't often agree with how you tried your cases—in the media—I wouldn't interfere. And I wouldn't betray the practice." But most especially, she wouldn't have betrayed Simon. "Now, tell me what's wrong with Simon!"

"You," Ronan replied, but his voice was softer now, his dark eyes warmer. "You're what's wrong with him."

Her head began to pound with confusion. "I don't understand."

"We didn't at first, either," Stone said.

"Speak for yourself," Trevor remarked. "I got it."

Ronan snorted. "Well, I sure as hell didn't. None of us has ever seen him like this."

"Is he hurt?" she asked as concern overwhelmed her. "Is he sick?"

"If I had to guess," Stone began, "and I would have to because I've never felt that way myself, I would have to say that he's heartbroken."

"What?" They were not making any sense. "This is Simon you're talking about? Simon Kramer?"

Ronan nodded as a grin curved up the corner of his mouth. "Yup."

"You broke his heart when you left," Trevor said.

Even as her own heart ached, she laughed. "That's ridiculous. Did you guys come here just to make fun of me?"

"There's nothing funny about it," Ronan said. "He's miserable. And we love him too much to let him continue like this."

"Like what?" she asked.

She couldn't imagine Simon Kramer being miserable. He thrived on adversity and had his entire life. There was nothing and nobody that would or could ever keep him down. Not his own father and not life on the streets.

"He's not eating or sleeping," Trevor said.

Stone added, "He looks like hell."

She narrowed her eyes, skeptical again of their claims. It wasn't possible for Simon Kramer to look like hell. "I doubt that."

"It's true," Trevor agreed.

"And I can't have him looking like that," Stone said, "not when I have a jury trial coming up."

She wasn't certain why or how Simon looked would affect Stone's case, but she didn't ask that. Instead, she asked, "What makes you think his not eating or sleeping has anything to do with me?"

Ronan stepped closer to her and studied her face. "Are you eating or sleeping?"

The dark circles beneath her eyes and thinness of her face provided the evidence he was looking for. She didn't have to answer his question.

But then he asked another. "Do you miss him as much as he's missing you?"

She snorted. "I doubt he's missing me."

"Why do you doubt that?" Stone asked.

"Because Simon Kramer goes after what he wants," she reminded them. "And if he wanted me, he'd be here instead of the three of you."

"That's what makes you different than everyone else," Ronan said as if he'd come to a sudden realization of his own. "You know him. You know him probably as well as we do, and we grew up with him."

Again she wasn't following the lawyer. These guys were brilliant of course, like Simon, but she wasn't stupid. "Yes, I know him, so I know if he was missing me, he'd be here—charming me back into his bed."

Trevor laughed. "It's almost eerie how well she knows him."

"Yes," Stone agreed. "That's why she's scared the hell out of him like no one else ever has."

Ronan nodded. "And we came up against some scary guys on the street. But Simon never flinched until now—until you."

"I don't understand," she admitted.

"When I met Simon, he'd been living on the streets for a while already," Stone said. "He's a little younger than us. Back then he was a lot smaller than us."

"And a hell of a lot prettier," Trevor added.

"Which put him in great danger living on the streets," Stone said. "From other street kids and from adults looking to take sick advantage of runaways like him."

She shuddered, thinking of what could have happened to the man she...

She what?

Before she could answer herself, Ronan was picking up the story. "But Simon wasn't the least bit scared," he said. "He owned those streets and could outsmart everyone else on them."

"Including you," Stone added the verbal jab.

"You, too," Ronan said.

"And he, younger and smaller than us, took care of us," Trevor said.

And she had her answer. She loved him.

"Now we're trying to take care of him," Stone said.

"But I don't understand why he won't come to me himself," she said, "if he's really missing me." He obviously didn't return her feelings.

"He's scared," Ronan said.

"First time I've ever seen him like this," Stone said. "Maybe it's because he cares more about you than he ever has anyone else. I don't know what it is, but he's scared."

"I hate seeing him like this," Ronan said and all his frustration was back in the gruffness of his voice. It was obviously killing him that he couldn't help his friend. Was he really the monster Muriel thought he was? "And I think you're the only one who can give us back the old Simon."

That was why he was here. She doubted he was convinced that she'd had nothing to do with the information Muriel had received. But for his friend, he was willing to put aside his anger and animosity toward her.

She had always wondered how four alpha dogs worked together without killing each other. It was because they all loved and respected each other. And because Simon was the alpha in charge. His being scared seemed to be scaring them, as well.

But they had no idea what true fear was. She did; it filled her now. It filled her because she knew she loved Simon Kramer. And she wasn't sure what the hell to do about her feelings or about him.

CHAPTER SEVENTEEN

SIMON BLINKED AND tried to focus on his computer monitor. It was late. Or early. He didn't even know. Since Bette's two-week notice had ended, he'd been working around the clock—doing his work and hers. He'd finally brought in a temp, but it was easier to do most of the work than try to teach the new guy, especially when it was so hard for Simon to see anyone else at Bette's desk.

That was why he'd begun doing most of his work before and after the office opened for business. Then he didn't have to see the temp or anyone else for that matter because there was only one person he really wanted to see. But she hated him.

And he could hardly blame her. She undoubtedly felt used and betrayed. That was the part he'd hated most about being a con artist. It was why he'd run away from his father. And when he'd been forced to con people in order to survive on the streets, he'd made certain they never realized he'd conned them, so they wouldn't feel that way.

The way Bette felt…

He wanted to make it up to her, but he didn't know how. Anything he did would just come across as another con to her, as his trying to seduce her again.

Oh, how he wanted to seduce her. His body ached for hers, for the release only she could give him. He could have called any other old girlfriend. Hell, he could have taken up half the office staff on the blatant invitations they'd been issuing since Bette left. But he wanted no one but her. She was the one.

He rubbed his hands over his face. God, he was losing it. He didn't believe in that bullshit soul mate stuff. Hell, he didn't believe in love. But then he'd never felt the way he felt about Bette...

It was new. It was different. Hell, it was love.

He needed a drink. The guys had been trying to get him back to The Meet Market for weeks. Maybe he would call them up and see if they were available. He'd been spending too much time alone, and it was making him lonely, which was something he never was, even when he was alone. Before he could reach for the cell phone sitting on his desk, he heard the ding of the elevator doors opening onto the floor for Street Legal.

Someone was here.

Probably Stone. Or Trevor. Or all three of them. Ronan wouldn't dare come see him alone, not unless one of the other two was available to pull Simon off him. He still wanted to pound the shit out of him for going after Bette, for accusing her of betraying the firm and most of all for telling her that Simon had just been conning her the entire time.

She must have been devastated if she cared about him at all. Did she care?

His heart began to pound fast at the sound of heels tapping across the hardwood floor. The guys didn't wear heels. Half the time they didn't even wear dress shoes. Stone wore boots and Trevor and Ronan wore tennis shoes. It wasn't one of his partners who'd gotten off the elevator. And it certainly wasn't Miguel, who sounded like a train coming when he approached.

But just because whoever had arrived was probably female didn't mean it was Bette. It was probably one of the employees who'd blatantly offered to take her spot in the office and out of it.

Or maybe it was someone else…

He remembered what he'd thought the last time he'd caught someone coming into the office after hours. That he'd caught the mole. He'd been wrong that time. But perhaps this time he would find out who was really betraying Street Legal.

Because while Ronan was wrong about Bette providing that material to Muriel Sanz, someone else from the office definitely might have. He needed to get focused on that again, on discovering who the mole might really be. And he needed to focus on his work. But she was all he could think about at the moment. She was all he could think about every moment of every day.

The tapping stopped right outside his door. But

there was a long silence before the knob turned and the hinges creaked as the door opened.

He wasn't armed. Even on the streets he'd never needed a weapon beyond his mind and his mouth. But now he was beginning to wonder if he should carry one. How desperate would the mole be if he or she got caught?

As desperate as Simon was to see Bette again?

Because he imagined she was the one standing in the open doorway. Even though the person's face was in shadow, the silhouette looked like her curvy one. But if she was wearing a skirt and cardigan, it was covered by an overcoat with the belt bound tightly around her small waist.

His pulse quickened. And while he was more afraid than he'd ever been, he knew he didn't need a weapon.

If this was Bette, he had no way of protecting himself from her. The visitor stepped forward into the light cast by the lamp on his desk. And his heart slammed against his ribs.

It was Bette. Her hair was piled on top of her head. But it wasn't tightly bound. And she wasn't wearing her glasses, either. Her long, thick lashes fluttered freely as she blinked and looked at him as if she couldn't believe her eyes.

He ran his hand over his face again and felt the stubble. He'd forgotten to shave today. Maybe yesterday, too.

Damn, he probably looked like hell.

She continued to stare at him as if she barely recognized him. He couldn't stop looking at her, either, but because she was so damn beautiful. The most beautiful woman he'd ever seen...

"Where are they?" she asked.

He cocked his head. "Who? It's after hours. Everybody's gone for the night."

"The flowers," she said. "The past two years I sent flowers to every single one of your flings when you ended it with them. But I didn't get any flowers."

"I didn't end it," he reminded her. "I wouldn't have ended it."

Ever.

The thought shocked him, but it didn't scare him now, like it had when he'd first acknowledged that he had real feelings for her and they weren't going away even though she had.

"I still would have liked some flowers," she said.

He gestured at the paperwork on his desk. "I don't have any."

She sighed. "Then I guess you'll have to make it up to me another way."

He sucked in a breath. "Any way you'd like." *In the chair, on the desk.*

But he wasn't pushing his luck, so he didn't suggest any of those things. "What would you like?" he asked her.

"An opinion."

He hadn't expected that, so he arched a brow in

question. She walked closer and ran a fingertip over his brow.

"I've missed that," she murmured and her lips curved into a small, wistful smile.

"I've missed you," he admitted, his voice deep and gruff with the emotion rushing over him. "I've missed you so damn much."

Her smile widened, and her breath shuddered out as if she was relieved. And happy…

"So you're glad that I've been miserable without you?" he asked. "That I've missed you so much that I haven't been eating or sleeping?"

"Yes," she answered.

"And the only reason you've come to see me to-night is for an opinion?" he asked, hoping to prod her into making the same admission he just had.

That she missed *him*, that she needed *him*.

But she just nodded and reached for the belt of her overcoat. She undid the belt, then shrugged off the jacket so that it dropped onto the floor around her feet. She wore one of her designs beneath the coat. It had to be hers because it was adorned with those damn beguiling bows.

It was a braless corset that was more satin ribbon than material. The ribbon zigzagged through a thin piece of blue silk which must have had enough starch to it to boost her breasts up so they were even higher and fuller than usual.

His breath escaped in a hiss while his cock hard-ened and pulsed. "Damn…" he murmured.

She twirled around, showing off the back, which was all ribbon and bows, as well. "You don't like it?"

He stood up so quickly and abruptly that his chair toppled over. Then he reached for her, jerking her up against his body. "No," he told her.

Her bottom lip, with that little crease in the middle of the fullness, poofed out in a pout. "You don't? I was thinking about using this for the line…"

"I don't like it," he said. "I love it."

But that wasn't all he loved. With his hands on her bare, silky shoulders, he eased her away from him. Then he reached for one of the bows, his fingers trembling slightly as he tugged on it. The ribbon stayed in place. And he narrowed his eyes in frustration.

She laughed. "You didn't think I was going to make it easy for you, did you?"

He shook his head. "Not you…"

She would always be a challenge to him. She would never bore him.

"You're going to have to keep trying until you find the right bow," she said, "before you'll see me naked."

"Will I see you naked?" he wondered. "Even if I get this thing off you? Will I see you really naked?" Because that was what he wanted. He wanted to know Bette in the way that she'd gotten to know him. Completely.

He was asking for more than her body. For more than sex…

And for the first time in her life, Bette was ready

to give herself completely to someone else. She wasn't worried anymore that she would wind up like her mom or sister. She knew she wasn't like them. And Simon was definitely not her father or brother-in-law. He wouldn't expect her to give up anything for him.

"I missed you," she said, her breath escaping in a ragged sigh. "So damn much."

"I'm sorry," he said. "I should have told you about my suspicions."

She smiled. "But what if I had been the mole? You would have tipped me off."

"You're not the mole. I figured that out pretty damn fast," he admitted. "But I wanted to keep seeing you, keep being with you."

"I wanted to keep seeing you," she said. "Keep being with you. I even considered offering to stay on part-time as your assistant."

He shook his head. "As much as I hated you leaving, I wouldn't want you to stay. This isn't the job for you. Being a fashion designer, that's what you love."

And he was whom she loved. More than she'd thought it possible to love anyone.

"Before I could offer," she reminded him, "Ronan confronted me about Muriel."

He lifted his hand from the satin ribbon to her face, his palm gently cupping her cheek. "You should be the model," he murmured. "These designs aren't just made *by* you, they're made *for* you."

She shook her head. "You are the only one I want

seeing *me* in them." She drew in a deep breath, bracing herself, before admitting, "You're the only one I want to see me naked." She tugged on the right bow, the one that had the corset dropping away from her body. "Really naked."

He tensed and stared at her face, his blue eyes wide with hope. "Bette."

"I have really fallen in love with you."

He laughed and wrapped his arms around her. "It's about damn time!" he said. "I have loved you for so long!"

She snorted at his claim. "Not very damn long," she said. "You ignored me for two years."

He shook his head. "I tried to ignore you," he said. "But I never should have hired you in the first place. You have no experience or education to work in a law firm."

She eased back and studied his face. "That's true. So why did you hire me?"

"Because I wanted to see you every day," he said. "Even if I couldn't touch you, I wanted to see you."

"You can touch me now," she said.

Now he stepped back and looked at more than her face. He looked at her body. And his breath hissed out between his clenched teeth.

"You are so damn beautiful."

She didn't argue with him or doubt him. She knew it was true. And she felt beautiful. "Thank you."

He grinned. "Thank *you*."

"I haven't done anything yet." But she reached for the zipper of his pants.

He caught her hand in his and held it still in his gentle grasp. "You came here," he said. "I was afraid to come to you."

"If your friends hadn't told me that, I probably wouldn't have found the courage to come," she admitted.

"My friends? The guys came to you?"

She nodded.

"Assholes," he murmured. But he was grinning as he said it. "Now I'm going to have to thank them, too."

"Hopefully, not like you're going to thank me," she said.

He laughed as he reached for her. Swinging her up in his arms, he carried her to the couch. After he laid her on the supple leather, he stood up. And again he just stared at her, his blue eyes dark with passion and something else.

Something she recognized now as love. She'd wondered before how she would be able to know for certain what someone else was feeling. She would never have to wonder with Simon. She could see the love in his eyes.

She lifted her arms, holding them out for him. But before he joined her, he shrugged off his suit jacket and unbuttoned his shirt. Then he finished lowering his zipper and kicked off his shoes and the pants and his briefs. Finally, he was naked, too.

As naked as she was.

But he didn't join her on the couch. He knelt on the floor beside her, like he was worshipping her body. And he made her feel that way, with his gentle touch. He glided his fingertips along her shoulder, down her arm to the curve of her hip. He traced her entire silhouette as if he was trying to memorize the shape of her.

"You are perfect," he said.

She would have teased him for laying it on a little thick. But she saw in his eyes that he was sincere. To him, she was perfect.

Love for him overwhelming her, she reached out. She traced the line of his broad shoulders and the muscles in his arms and chest. Then she tried to move lower, to slide her mouth over his pulsating shaft and take him deep in her throat.

She was pulsating, too, her body quivering as the tension he'd built inside her became overwhelming. "Please, Simon," she implored him. "I need you."

"I need you, too," he assured her.

But he didn't hurry. He took his time. Lowering his head to hers, he kissed her gently, his lips just whispering across hers.

She gasped at the sensation, and he dipped his tongue inside her mouth. She suckled on it like she wanted to suck on him. And he groaned. Then his hands moved to her breasts, molding the flesh, teasing the nipples.

She whimpered as that need became unbearable.

Tears of frustration stung her eyes. Then finally he touched her core, and she came apart.

It wasn't enough, though. She needed him inside her.

Plastic crinkled as he tore open a condom packet. His hand shook as he rolled it on, then he lifted her onto his lap where he knelt on the floor beside the couch.

She locked her legs around his back as she bounced and rocked, sliding up and down his shaft. He teased her nipples, then he reached between them and rubbed his thumb over her mound, finding the most sensitive part of her.

She cried out as she came again.

And he stood, with her locked yet around his waist, with him buried deep inside her. And he arched his hips up, making love to her standing up. Until his legs began to shake.

Then finally he yelled her name and his body shuddered as he came, too. They collapsed onto the couch where they'd had sex for the first time. This time it hadn't been just sex, though. They'd made love—because they had really fallen for each other.

She smiled, and he must have felt her cheek move against his chest from where she'd settled in his arms. He smiled, too.

"This feels so damn right," he murmured.

"Yes, it does," she agreed.

"You and me," he said. "The fashion designer and the lawyer."

They might not have been the likeliest combination. But she was certain they would make it work because they respected each other, respected how hard each other had worked to accomplish what they had. But what Simon had worked so hard to achieve was in jeopardy now.

"Do you have any idea who the mole really is?" she asked him.

The smile slid away from his mouth. "No."

"You'll figure it out," she assured him. He was the smartest man she'd ever met. "And I'll do whatever I can to help you."

He tightened his arm around her shoulders, holding her more snugly against his chest. "This helps," he assured her. "Just having you here."

"In your office?" He didn't actually expect her to come back, did he? She'd liked that he hadn't wanted her to sacrifice her dreams for his.

As if he felt her tension, he stroked his hand down her back and assured her, "I told you that I want you to focus on your passion."

She smiled.

"And you're mine. That's what I meant about having you here—in my arms." He chuckled. "In my heart, too, Bette Monroe."

"You're in my heart, too," she assured him because she knew how hard it was to be so vulnerable, how scary it was.

But Simon didn't seem scared anymore. He seemed happy. "Loving you has put things in perspective for me," he continued. "The practice isn't everything to me anymore. You are."

She sucked in a breath, surprised by just how vulnerable he'd made himself to her. He was so damn brave.

"It's okay if you don't feel the same way," he assured her. "I know your designs—working as hard as you have to get your own line—mean everything. And they should—"

"They mean more because of you," she said. "They mean more because you understand and support me. While I haven't always agreed with the way Street Legal has handled cases, I understand and support you, too."

He grinned now. "And that's everything."

She had to agree that it was—whatever they had, it was so special, so unique. "And you're everything to me," she assured him.

He released a breath she hadn't realized he'd been holding. As if he'd needed that assurance from her.

He needed her as much as she needed him. They were equals—in their lives and in each other's hearts. Bette knew now that she'd achieved the goals she'd always had, the ones she'd admitted to herself and the one she hadn't even realized she'd had until she'd applied for the job as Simon Kramer's assistant. She'd wanted him to fall in love with her.

And she was glad that she'd fallen for him, too.

* * * * *

LET'S TALK
Romance

For exclusive extracts, competitions
and special offers, find us online:

f facebook.com/millsandboon

⊙ @millsandboonuk

𝕏 @millsandboon

Or get in touch on 0844 844 1351*

For all the latest titles coming soon, visit
millsandboon.co.uk/nextmonth